FORWARD, THE BAGGAGE!

ARTHUR EAGLESTONE

OVERDALE PUBLICATIONS

First published in 2004 by
Overdale Publications,
17 Overdale, 60 Hollins Lane, Marple, Cheshire, SK6 6AW, UK.
5 River Parade, Mildura, Victoria 3500, Australia.

Copyright © The Estate of Arthur Eaglestone 2004
Designed and set by Ketchup
Cover Illustration: *The Rearguard*, J. P. Beadle (© The Royal Green Jackets Museum, Winchester.)

British Library Cataloguing-in-Publication Data
A catalogue record for this book is available from the British Library

ISBN 0-9579426-1-3 (pbk)

FOREWORD

With the exception of Sir John Moore and his senior officers, characters in the following narrative are creatures of fiction. But while the regiment has no place in military annals, the experiences of Colonel Foulkes and his men reflect similar happenings in the autobiographical records of the Corunna campaign.

Drink, and sullen reaction to retreat, were the twin problems with which Moore had to grapple. Until this phase, the army conducted itself well in Spain; there was little or no trouble with the women who accompanied the force; the excesses of Badajoz and San Sebastian in later years form a different story.

A.A. Eaglestone

PUBLISHER'S PREFACE

Arthur A. Eaglestone was born in Parkgate, South Yorkshire in 1892. Leaving school at the age of twelve, he worked successively in the family's mineral water manufactory, in a steel mill and as a clerk in a coal pit.

From an early age he was an avid reader of the classics of English literature, and as a teenager was writing articles and short stories. Writing under his pen name, Roger Dataller, his account of life in the mines From a Pitman's Notebook was published in 1925 to widespread critical acclaim. Subsequently, he was granted a Miner's welfare scholarship to New College, Oxford where he wrote A Pitman Looks at Oxford. For his thesis on the Radical Major Cartwright, he was awarded a B. Litt. degree by the University.

From Oxford he returned to the Coalfields (the subject of his third autobiographical work) as a Tutor in Literature for the Worker's Educational Association in South Yorkshire. Later he was appointed a Staff Tutor in Literature at Sheffield University. This position he held until his retirement.

Well-known in the Rawmarsh and Rotherham area, he served on several local committees and was for many years the President of the Yorkshire Association of Bookman. He held the same post in the Rotherham Antiques Society, the outcome of a strong interest in Rockingham porcelain, the subject of a further book, published in 1964, which he co-authored.

During his long retirement he worked on two projects: another work of autobiography, *A Yorkshire Lad*, and the present book, *Forward the Baggage* which occupied him for many years. It was completed, but unpublished, at the time of his death in December 1980. It is in many ways Arthur Eaglestone's finest work of historical and imaginative fiction. It has been edited for publication by his grandson Andrew Lockett.

Nov 2003

CHAPTER I

"The list, Harriet, is damnably long," observed Major Foulkes, chewing the tip of his pen as he glanced across at his wife. They were seated in the drawing room of Bellaby Chase, their South Yorkshire home; and as her brown darting eyes met his she drew the Paisley shawl about her shoulders, for though the long July day had been one of sunshine, a cool wind had arisen. He took the hint, closed the open window and returned to his seat.

His brow furrowed. Lithe, a little more than medium height, with a lean clean-shaven face and chestnut hair extremely thin at the temples, one might have guessed his age at just under forty. His movements were so ordered and precise that but for the well-tailored scarlet and gold tunic, he might have passed for a respectable country attorney. He paused to take a pinch of snuff, carefully dusting the front of his tunic with a cambric handkerchief. He would be vastly relieved when the field equipment that he was to take into Spain was complete.

"Read what you have written," said Harriet, studying her rings intently. She was all concentration – very still.

"For the canteen," he began, "one dozen soup plates – "

"The cheapest Wedgwood," she interposed. And after his pen had scratched dutifully. "Continue."

"One dozen soup plates," he repeated, "the same number of meat plates, four medium sized dishes for joints, five side dishes, a dozen good sized tea cups and saucers, a tea-pot, milk jug and slop basin – all to be placed in a strong wicker basket protected by oil-cloth."

"You can leave out the side-dishes," she said, "but insist that the plates and saucers be packed with the edges upwards, or you will have half of them broken."

"I hadn't thought of that." He made a note.

"Now, as to the matter of clothes – " He lifted his head for a moment to consider the gathering dusk. "Spanish nights, I suspect, can be very cold, so I thought a camlet with proof cloak, a plain blue single-breasted greatcoat, and say, a couple of white kerseymore waistcoats. Then, of course, flannel drawers; a pair of worsted elastic pantaloons. And ankle stockings. All these from Windeler. Oh, and a hat from that shop in Bond Street."

"Towels? Soap?" she prompted.

"Of course." He scratched on. "Nor must we forget pens, paper, and an almanac."

She smiled faintly.

"Why do you smile?" he asked.

"At nothing in particular."

"In the field," he said, "one day tends to be very like another. Hence the record. So then—" He turned to his notes. "The whole to be dispatched to the Hythe depot – draft for payment on Greenwood and Cox."

"Yes," she murmured as he threw down his pen. She looked up suddenly. "Percy, will it be a long campaign?"

He pretended not to hear, allowing his eyes to stray around the room, with its delicately sprigged wallpaper, the clear pale yellow of the damask curtains, the olive grounded chintz, the miniatures flanking the fireplace. "A supply of preserved tongues," he remarked, "with soup powder would help out the rations."

"No doubt," she said dryly. "I inquired however, if you thought the campaign would be a long one."

Foulkes pursed his lips and shrugged. "Who can say? Spain is a great country, four hundred miles across. We shall be well-equipped militarily, you may be sure of that. But a great deal will depend upon the Spaniards themselves; Baylen and Saragossa are much to their credit. On the other hand their armies have been, and are being, badly knocked about by the French." He paused, eyeing her grimly. "We must wait on the event."

"Who will take command?"

"You mean of our people?" He rubbed his chin doubtfully. "Arthur Wellesley has sailed, but as he is the youngest lieutenant-general, likely enough some senior fellow will be set over him." He muttered vaguely, "Horse Guards," and grunted contempt. "Of course there is only one general officer of reputation."

"Moore?"

"Yes, indeed." The note of finality in his voice was impressive.

"But is not Sir John off in Sweden?"

He looked up startled. "How do you know?"

"I read the newspapers."

Foulkes nodded. "He has been sent on a wild goose chase, though the Almighty and the Government alone know why. In the meantime we must look to this Spanish business and do the best we can."

He gathered up his papers, tied them neatly and set the sheaf aside. Silence fell between husband and wife – a certain inquietude. He waited uneasily for Harriet to speak, wondering if he ought to comment further upon the impending campaign, and his own place in it, but she seemed to have lost interest in the subject. When she did speak it was in a tone almost of whimsy. "What am I to do while you are away?"

The question startled him, but he was glad that it had been posed. "Better hammer it out now," he thought, "sooner than later." He smiled tightly as he tapped the lid of his snuff box. "Do, my dear Harriet? When have you ever been at a loss for anything to do? Goodness knows there is enough about house which, remember, will run on full establishment. There is your father in the Dales whom you can visit, your brother in town, and your sister within a stone's throw of this place. Look up your friends. If you feel inclined, travel south with me and see me off ... After that you shall write me long letters for which you have certainly a gift. They will brighten up camp life. Indeed, you may have much more to say than I."

He looked away, retaining as he did so an impression not only of neatly parted raven hair, her fresh colour and of eyes glinting derisively. And he shifted, sensing mischief afoot. He was not afraid of tears, of undue emotion; but his wife he knew, was capable at times of impulsive, unpredictable action, so that when she rose slowly from her seat and moved to the occasional table where his sword lay, took it up and drew the blade from the scabbard, he watched her intently. What was she up to?

For a moment she studied the weapon with a slightly amused curl of her lip, the highly tempered steel, and then with a flourish brought it to arm's length, until it formed a glinting barrier between them. He waited. For some reason, which he would have found it difficult to explain, he was relieved when with a cushioned click, she returned the sword to its sheath. "Pray what was the meaning of that?" he inquired as she assumed her seat. "I thought I would like the feel of it," she replied simply, whereat Foulkes grunted. "Duelling is out," he said.

He took another pinch of snuff and turned once again to the matter of equipment. "Speaking of horseflesh," he said, "I intend to take the bay, Felix."

She shook her head decisively. "That you cannot do."

"Why not?"

"I shall need Felix for my own use. He is the only mount upon which I feel at ease."

"Very well," he assented, though he did not attempt to conceal his disappointment, "You shall have Felix, but for heaven's sake give him plenty of exercise."

"He will find all he needs in Spain."

The Major gazed blankly. "In Spain?" he repeated.

"In Spain," she said smoothly.

"But you – the animal – the house?" The Major's eyes narrowed. "I don't understand."

"In a word, Percy, I intend to go with you."

Foulkes stiffened. A blow across the face could not have brought him to smarter attention. He stared fixedly ahead, his hands clenched upon the papers. The plangent ticking of the clock upon the mantelpiece became the loudest sound in the room. It was as though both man and wife suspended breathing. At least he said, "Did I hear aright, that you wish to accompany me to Spain?"

"You did indeed, Major Foulkes." The formal mode of address served to emphasise her words.

"What is this, a joke?"

"On the contrary, I am completely serious."

He turned his eyes slowly upon her; but she met his gaze boldly.

"No!" he said.

Gently, she nodded her head.

"My dear Harriet – " His tone became one of pained, but patient forbearance. "What absurd notion is this: Never at any time or in any circumstances have you mentioned the possibility of accompanying me to Spain. And now – out of the blue – this!"

"Because," she explained, "I had not decided in my own mind."

"And now you have?"

"Absolutely."

Foulkes sat limply, his mouth drooping almost in the lines of a tragic mask. He tried to speak, but could find no words to match the situation. He searched for some hint of raillery, of teasing in her voice, but could find none. Suddenly he recalled how earlier that day he had surprised her in the library poring over three works on Spain – Swinburne's *Travels*, *Don Quixote*, and *Gil Blas* – but this he had laid merely to a wifely interest in his future activity; when all the time she had been nursing a secret purpose of her own! *Don Quixote* indeed! He muttered helplessly.

"All arrant nonsense!"

"You will grow accustomed to it."

"Never!"

"Please, Major Foulkes, oblige me with pen and paper."

She left the chaise-longue upon which she had been sitting, and took a chair at the other side of the table. As he handed over the writing material – he became less tense. Taking the pen she cast her eyes to the ceiling.

"Unthinkable!" he persisted.

He might as well have held his peace. Serenely she dipped her pen and inscribed the heading – "Mrs Foulkes – her equipment" – drawing a firm line beneath. The Major took more snuff. "Let the play-acting go forward," he thought, "she cannot possibly persist. Soon she will relent, dissolve in laughter."

But Harriet showed no sign of dissolving in laughter. "I shall require," she murmured, "an excellent water-proof – an oilskin for preference; I gather it rains heavily in Spain."

"How do you know?" he asked.

"Swinburne is quite emphatic."

"Swinburne!" he snorted.

"Two riding costumes," she continued, "one of black and the other of grey; two hat boxes ... or it may be three – we will consider that later ... valises for dresses, a toilet case, and a *garde de liquer*."

"A *garde de liquer?*"

"For restoratives in the field."

"A regimental *vivandiere!*" He smiled sarcastically. "On no account omit your jewel case!"

"You think of everything," she said gratefully. "One jewel case ..."

"And a poke bonnet."

She pondered, her pen upheld. "Let me think."

"The heat also is difficult in Spain."

"As you say."

Foulkes could restrain himself no longer. He had so far displayed commendable patience, but now the farce was about played out. "Harriet," he said firmly, "the thing is altogether out of question."

"One must be mindful of one's complexion," she said lightly.

"I mean the whole stupid proposal."

Her smile vanished as her lips tightened. "You found no difficulty in taking me to Dublin."

"Dublin!" he said with a despairing gesture. "Assembly Rooms, soirees, musicales, card-parties, picnics – and you compare that to a campaign in the Peninsular. God damn my soul!"

"You needn't blaspheme."

"Snow, rain, hunger, thirst, vermin, camp-fires – off at the crack of dawn; at the day's end without a pillow for your head, and you refer me to Dublin! Where is the common sense, the logic of it all? I would do anything at any time to satisfy you Harriet; but you ask the impossible."

His face went marble white as it always did under strain; he beat a brisk tattoo with his finger tips upon the polished surface of the table. Colour began to mount in her cheeks. "Do you mean to inform me," she rejoined tartly, "that women are no longer admitted to the army?"

"Soldier's wives," he jerked.

"And what am I?"

"I referred to the rank and file."

Her eyes smouldered ominously. "You know too well, Major Foulkes, that if you wish to do so, you can take me with you; you have only to inform the Transport Department – three lines of a letter. Or would my presence tend to compromise you with the ladies of Spain?" The accusation was unjust, but she had been carried beyond the bounds of discretion.

"I refuse to comment upon your last observation," he said coldly. "Returning to more sensible matters, allow me to point out that you are acquainted only with the social side of military life – field days at Shorncliffe, reviews at Brighton; pavilions and picnic tents. We shall go with our guns shotted."

"I am not afraid of that."

He drew a long and quivering breath. "Now for the last time hear me," he pleaded. "In other circumstances I would assent quite gladly, but not in the matter of active service."

"I might even be able to assist." Her voice pleaded, though her lips retained the firm outline he knew so well.

"Assist?" he repeated incredulously. He could see her in a hundred situations, horrifically involved, mangled by round-shot, hemmed in by enemy sabres, desperately alone …

"You would have someone in whom to confide."

She had touched him there. A markedly reserved man, few fellow officers could claim that they really knew Foulkes. "Confide?" He shook his head.

"I do not see," she insisted, "why I should not take up what many women are doing and have done in the past."

He placed his hand on hers – was there in response a faint hesitation, a tremor of submission? "Ah, Harriet," he pleaded, "I am anxious only for your wellbeing. I implore you – think again."

"I have thought a great deal, and am still of a mind."

She withdrew her hand, and taking up the memorandum, moved towards the door.

"At least, sleep on it."

She shook her head, and left the room …

Sighing impatiently, Foulkes watched the door close, and turning to a newspaper scanned the closely printed columns without attempting to read. The devil was, in actual practice, she was right! Women always had followed the armies; in the old days troops of females, wives and shameless trollops alike trailed with the baggage. In the German wars a special officer, termed ironically, "The Captain of the Queens," had been appointed to look after them. The British, more circumspect, allowed six married women only to the rank and file of each company. Officers might take their own wives if they choose, though the practice was not encouraged. The Colonel, pishing and poohing enough in private, would not, could not, refuse. Foulkes drew in a pettish breath. What daemon had moved his wife to this embarrassment? She had complained little in the past. Why now, at the moment of departure?

He turned to the newspaper, glanced at the date – July 19th, 1809 – noting that it was two days old. More alarms and excursions! Bounaparte – no end to the fellow's impudence! – had annexed the Papal States. And to crown all, Joseph, his brother, had been appointed King of Spain and the Indies. "Hope it keeps fine for both of 'em," muttered Foulkes. Thank heaven the Spaniards were beginning to show their mettle; if the Councils or Juntas were to match words with deeds then the whole Peninsular would be alive. But what high-falutin' lingo they used! "You must either clank your chains in infamous slavery, or fight bravely for liberty!" A man of rational mind, Foulkes distrusted rhetoric – a screen too often for muddled thought and ineffective action. Still, the Spanish were as God had made them, and would doubtless improve on closer acquaintance ...

His eyes wandered to the social columns, where he noted that HRH the Prince of Wales had returned to Carlton House. Humph! ... Lord Castlereagh was back from Ireland, but Mr Canning had gone into the country. One dodging t'other, Foulkes assumed ... Names less public caught his eye. A Colonel Fitzclumber had arrived in Portsmouth – the illegitimate son of a duke, whom the Major recalled as a porcine, pimply ensign, but who in next-to-no-time – he could not be more than twenty-two – had been promoted to the command of a regiment. "Thus," thought Foulkes acidly, "is virtue rewarded!" ...A certain Captain, the Honourable Anthony Harte, had joined a brigade dispatched to the Peninsular. He remembered Harte as something of a fop who in the Brighton season had so captivated Harriet. "A man of engaging wit," she declared, "an unimaginably graceful dancer." "We will see what tune he dances to in Spain," thought Foulkes as he tossed the sheet aside, at the same time wondering if his wife had noticed the reference. Not that it signified ... "Give her but a day," he reflected, his mind reverting to the immediate problem, "a couple of days perhaps, and the notion will die of its own inherent absurdity. It cannot, must not, be sustained ..."

There might, he reflected, be an official loophole. In order to assure himself on this point he turned to his valise, and extracting papers issued by Sir John Moore at Shorncliffe, turned up the regulations concerning women. These directives, however, were much to the point. "The number of women allowed by Government to embark on service are six for every hundred men, inclusive of all non-commissioned officer's wives... It should never be exceeded on any pretext whatever, because the doing so is inhumanity of the falsest kind. Women who have more than two children can also never be of the number to embark except in extraordinary cases, because that is a still greater act of inhumanity."

Foulkes pondered for a moment on the phrase, "It should never be exceeded on any pretext whatever ..." but could make nothing more of that, for obviously the condition was one which applied only to the rank and file ... He read on. "All women of immoral or drunken character, or who refuse to work for the men, are warned that they will not be permitted to remain ever to disgrace the Corps ... To help the married women all regimental needlework and washing is to be done by them." Followed a further outline of chores. "The officers will distribute their linen nearly equally among the sergeant's wives ... The number of shirts and socks to be washed for each soldier per week is two of each and at least two turnovers. For this the laundress will be paid 5d by the pay sergeant ..."

Foulkes continued to the end, and dropped the paper. There was no regulation forbidding a serving officer either at home or abroad to be accompanied by his wife ...

CHAPTER II

Night sounds around Bellaby were many and varied, and through the long hours that followed, Foulkes fancied he heard them all. The eerie long-drawn hoot of an owl as it flitted over the keeper's lodge, the occasional baying of a hound in the kennels, the hoof-beats of some wayfarer – a farmer probably returning home late from Rotherham market – the soughing of wind in the elms, the constant tapping of a shutter, all tended to emphasise the intervals of profound silence through which the Major unsleeping, wrestled with his problem. Was it possible that in roundly opposing his wife he had employed the wrong tactic? Yet what alternative was there? He tossed and turned upon the feather bed, and finally transferred himself to a plain palliasse – a requisite of campaigning – which he always brought with him.

More at ease there, he considered a line of counter-action. If on the morrow his wife still remained obdurate, he would be compelled to sap and mime, enlist auxiliaries, the friendly intervention of those whose opinion carried weight – her sister, Jane, for example. She lived reasonably close at hand. Nor could one neglect the Vicar of the parish, the Reverend Granby Selman, for whom Harriet had the greatest respect. Assured of their support – for what rational person could for a moment condone her mad proposal to gallivant through Spain? – he felt he would be able to face the coming day.

At last he fell asleep; but if he had assumed that a beautiful sunshine day, and a sky of unflecked blue were hopeful omens to readjustment, he was soon disappointed. Harriet and he exchanged commonplaces until noon, but when she inquired almost casually if "he was by now getting used to the idea," his heart sank. "By no means!" he replied firmly. "You will," she smiled, in a voice no less decided. "Bend your mind to it, Percy, and you will see how little you have to fear."

"Bend my mind!" he breathed ironically. But he managed to remain smooth and smiling, preserving amenity.

The day passed and Wednesday morning came. Harriet had not appeared downstairs, when, after a brief session with his bailiff, Foulkes called for his horse and set out for Hickersley Manor where Jane lived. The two sisters had always held closely together. Daughters of a North Riding clergyman, living near Richmond, they had fluttered the male hearts of their native parish to some purpose; but fate awaited both at York where at the Assembly Rooms they were introduced to Major Foulkes and his friend Sidney Welsh, who were both up for the County Meeting. Harriet, whose lively impulsive nature was in startling contrast with her younger sister's composed affability, had been attracted by Foulkes' peculiar restraint; the impression he conveyed of inner strength and resolution. It was not improbable that information of a newly inherited estate ("Two thousand pounds a year, my dear!" whispered the Archdeacon's wife) had something to do with her decision, to say nothing of the trim scarlet and gold uniform which the owner wore. Foulkes for his part was affected not only by her handsome appearance, but also by the necessity of providing a mistress for Bellaby – a chatelaine, he told himself, who would control it effectively in his absence. To Harriet's intense relief the Foulkes citadel capitulated with surprising ease. And – what could have been more Providential? – the Major's sturdy gentleman-farmer friend had proposed to her sister Jane. Sad at the domestic disruption, but at the same time intensely relieved that his daughters were to be comfortably settled, the lonely father waved them off to their respective homes in the West Riding. Jane, now a blooming young matron with two children of her own, lived in a renovated Elizabethan house, which on a clear day was within signalling distance of Bellaby Hall. Foulkes was glad of this. If ever Harriet needed a restraining hand, it was now.

He took his time. It had rained a little during the night, and beneath an almost cloudless sky the surrounding fields were fresh and green. The neat little gardens of the hamlet flaunted lilac and laburnum, and raindrops still sparkled in the sunshine; but Foulkes dwelt little upon this beauty as he cantered by. He had no aesthetic sense, and while at times he wished he could apply himself to rural pursuits and pastimes with the whole-hearted enthusiasm of his brother-in-law, farming he left to his own bailiff. By habit he surveyed the landscape with a military eye; patterns of tactics and strategy shaping in his mind. The ridge of Robinson's ten-acre field, would amply conceal a battalion from hostile eyes, the broad stream flowing silently to the east ensuring the flank. The ford through which he would shortly splash, made for complication, but riflemen (he judged) posted in the adjoining coppice could make themselves damned awkward for a time … He acknowledged with a perfunctory salute the greeting of a passing labourer. Though Foulkes had changed that morning into plain clothes of bottle green with buff waistcoat, he rode stiffly upright, one arm pendant as though on parade.

As he cantered between the hedgerows he reflected for the thousandth time upon his own undistinguished career. Of middle-age, dogged by an impecunious past, he was still knocking at the door of promotion. His father, a provincial attorney, had died early in life, leaving his mother with nothing more than a hundred pounds of income, and a spirit much too independent for comfort. After scheming and scraping to procure Percy's commission she had followed her husband to the grave. Three years an ensign, nine years a lieutenant, eleven years a captain – that was the sum of it all. Twenty-three years of devoted service! Had it not been for the sum of five hundred pound advanced by two maiden aunts (bless them!) he would not have secured his majority. Now that he was modestly affluent – three relatives in line had died to bring Bellaby – the colonelcy still eluded him. Patrons failed at the sticking point; too often he had heard the apologetic, but none the less damning, "I should have been happy to serve you, sir, but my interest has been promised elsewhere." Always that! He had served in Holland, Ireland, Sicily; had been wounded three times. But what did wounds amount to? Others had fared no better. Many were called, few were chosen …

The supreme irony was that no man had applied himself more closely to his profession; followed more ardently the directives of Shorncliffe; memorised manuals and texts without number, delved more deeply into military history. At Bellaby there was a portrait which he never looked upon without a pang of disappointment: that of a youthful ingenuous ensign, complete with cockaded hat, side-curls stiff with powder and pomade, four inches of leathern stock, and ruffles foaming at the wrist. And of course a dropping queue … He remembered the heavily thumping heart with which he had first walked across the square to meet his commanding officer. There had been many changes since then – the queue and the ruffles had gone – but what of the cherished dream of promotion? …

The entrance hall at Hickleby was shadowed, cool, still. He gazed indifferently at Sidney's hunting trophies. The chase had never appealed to him, and he contracted out whenever he could … Now he could hear Jane's voice, and presently discovered her in the parlour. As it happened she was alone, her husband having taken the gig to Rotherham cattle-market. How like, yet unlike, Harriet she was! – her hair chestnut, where by contrast Harriet's was jet black; but with both, the same frank challenging gaze. He wished sometimes that he did not fall into the habit of averting his eyes. An open stare made him self-conscious.

Jane at once served her visitor with wine of her own distillation, the elements of which she refused to divulge, since (she said) she wished for a completely unbiased opinion. Foulkes simulated interest to please her; but his thoughts were concentrated upon matters other than the amber liquid in the glass. After the usual family inquiries, he introduced the subject of Harriet and Spain.

He cleared his throat heavily at a loss how to begin. At last, "Jane," he said, "I have always held the highest opinion of your judgement."

She looked askance. "What a tease you are, Percy," she said. "Believe me," he continued, "I am in no teasing mood. I need your assistance."

"In that case—" Jane hesitated for a moment. He brother-in-law she knew, would not consult her on army matters, or on general aspects of the estate. "This," she thought, "almost certainly concerns Harriet." Aloud she remarked, "First I must know what the problem is." She raised questioning eyebrows.

"Of all the improbable, impossible situations," he blurted out, "Harriet wishes to accompany me to Spain!"

He paused to note the effect of the announcement upon his sister-in-law. To his profound annoyance, dismay even, she laughed aloud.

"It is no laughing matter," he protested.

"What do you expect me to do – shed tears?" she rejoined. "You should be delighted, Percy, that Harriet is so much in love with you."

He tapped his hessians impatiently with the switch. "There is a time and a place for everything, and her place is not with the armed forces in Spain."

"Nonsense!" cried Jane. "What do you take her for? A piece of furniture to be swaddled in a dust sheet? Consider her position when once you have gone—"

"She has been talking to you?" he said darkly.

"Indeed no, but one needs only the slightest imagination to consider Harriet's position. I have Welsh and the children – what has she to bind her to England? Can you see her stitching at altar clothes, making gooseberry wine, curing marigolds and such? She would be very welcome to stay with me, but how long would that last – a week at most."

"She could visit her father."

"Who would be delighted to have her, but a fortnight in the Dales though would bore Harriet to extinction."

"There is still your brother in London," he said stubbornly.

"London?" repeated Jane doubtfully. "Tom and she get on well enough, but there is always Fredrika in the background, and you know what that means – at each other's hair in the first five minutes. And it would be unthinkable for her not to stay with them if she went to town."

Foulkes sat staring despondently ahead. Jane was right. Their London sister-in-law was a vixen to say the least. Nor could he see Harriet sequestered in the Dales. At last he said severely, "Your sister married a soldier."

"Well," said Jane, "why should she not follow the drum?"

"A thoroughly romantic notion," he rapped.

"What of that?" Jane extracted a spool of silk from her work basket. "Have you never had a romantic notion?"

At the point of dissenting, he refrained. And as he intercepted her eyes he was glad that he had done so; his own past had not been entirely free from tender complications – twice he had been drawn into commitments with the other sex from which he had withdrawn only with difficulty. He wondered how much of this Jane knew. Had Welsh been talking? "My wife," he muttered, "dwells too much with fiction-of-the-wrong-kind."

"Great heavens!" Jane protested, "How can she refrain from reading and remain civilised? Come! – Major Foulkes!" Words failed her.

As he watched his sister-in-law's nimble fingers disentangling the vari-coloured threads and weaving these into a pattern, he wished that he could

relieve his own feelings with movement so deft and automatic. She drew out
a single thread.

"There is bound to be danger," he gloomed.

"On picket duty, I suppose?" Jane's eyes glinted sceptically.

"Be reasonable. Spain is a country where she would find much entertainment. Take her with you to Cadiz, or wherever you hope to land, and after
that see how you both feel about the matter. She may wish to return sooner
than you expect." Jane looked up. "Of one thing I am assured – that if Harriet
elects to go abroad, I for one will not attempt to persuade her to remain at
home." Conclusively, Jane snipped a thread. "Indeed, I wish that I was going
with her."

Mortified by this turn of conversation Foulkes rose to his feet. "I had
expected something very different from you," he said reproachfully.

"I know Harriet."

"And so do I."

"Do you?"

Their eyes met, challenged, and as Jane's did not falter, he knew that further argument would be useless ...

He made his farewell and rode away. As he cantered through the gateway,
the flavour of the wine that he had sipped still lingered in his mouth. He curled
up his tongue. He had forgotten to praise it. On the tart side, he reflected ...

* * *

He had hoped for much – perhaps too much – from Jane ... now this! He
would turn to Selman. Harriet held the personable, urbane cleric in great
esteem. For the most part they met on a common ground of literature. They
discussed together authors of whom Foulkes had never heard, exchanged
slim volumes of ballad poetry, sometimes practised a little conversation in
French. Selman was that oddity, an Anglican Whig; but what could you
expect from one who had been chaplain for a time to Earl Fitzwilliam?
Selman played up to Harriet – who did not? Charming, she invited response.

Foulkes turned his horse's head in the direction of the vicarage, and on
arriving found the clergyman in the garden. Selman, whose wig surmounted
a face lean as a hawk, waved his hand in the direction of the summer house
which stood half-way down the lilac walk. Giving instructions for refreshment to be brought out, the Vicar led Foulkes to a shadowed seat, and soon
the two men were taking Madeira. ("Don't know how he affords it," thought
Foulkes, "must be from the Wentworth cellars.") The wine, the Major noted,
washed down the bitter taste of Jane's.

With a nonchalance he was far from feeling, the visitor crossed his legs
and listened to a dissertation on parish affairs – the repair of the church
tower, two pinnacles of which had lately fallen; the carting of stone from a

distance, the wretched condition of the main road and the necessity of a vestry meeting to deal with it. At length Foulkes mentioned marching orders for the Peninsular, whereupon the Vicar sighed. "I wish my dear Major," he said, "you were something less of a bird of passage, but I suppose there is no complaining. Happily we shall have Mrs Foulkes."

"One would hope so," said Foulkes.

The Vicar looked up, surprised. "Are you in doubt?"

"She wishes to accompany me to the Peninsular," said Foulkes bluntly.

"Dear me," murmured the other, "dear, dear me!"

The mild rejoinder irritated Foulkes. The Vicar could not have been more composed than if he had heard simply that Mrs Foulkes intended to buy a set of new ribbons in Rotherham. The clergyman was too shrewd however not to note the undertone of anxiety in the Major's voice. "I gather you don't like the idea?" he ventured.

"Most emphatically not! The unspeakable hazards of the field, of transport, the rude contacts and associations impels me – " Foulkes threw out his hands. "But it is all common knowledge."

"This you have pointed out?"

"Naturally."

"The fearful war," said Selman reflectively, "tends to rob the parish of its very best. Wilson, the blacksmith's son – his father's mainstay – and young Turner, the wheelwright, enlisted yesterday morning. Two fine upstanding young men. I have often reflected in the quiet of my own study – "

"Gad! not a sermon!" thought the Major impatiently. He was in no mood to listen to a disquisition on the horrors of conflict, on wounds and death, still less to the wisdom or otherwise of expeditions abroad. The Whigs had never taken kindly to the war; and the Major, whose party affiliations were, if anything, Tory, began to beat impatiently on the rough-hewn arm of his chair.

"In the quiet of my own study," repeated Selman, "I have often pondered how by universal philanthropy a permanent peace might be established. An idea, I fully admit, demanding philosophy in statesmen, but which in the present constitution of government—"

"Yes, indeed," the Major interrupted, "but reverting to my own appearance here, I felt I must call upon you in order—" His voice faltered as it struck him how furious Harriet would be if by some means she were to learn that her decision had been made the subject for discussion. The Vicar completed the sentence for his visitor. "In order," he smiled faintly, "that I may intercede and prevail upon her to change her mind?"

The Major nodded. "That's the hang of it." He took out his snuff box, while the Vicar, consulting as it were, a crystal ball, raised his wine glass to eye level.

"I acknowledge the compliment," said Selman, "but I have always held the axiom never to intervene between husband and wife. If it were a question of morals, but that most decidedly it is not."

"A priest is a privileged person," returned the Major stubbornly, "to whom we look for sound practical advice."

Selman shook his head gravely. "The question is not one of simple right and wrong; but of equal interest. You are bound by a valid military concept; your wife by her feminine impulse. You have your sanctions, but she has hers."

"That is the devil of the matter," said Foulkes.

"Ah," said the Vicar raising his forefinger, "we must tread delicately here. Your wife has also a romantic temperament – a being of fire and air. You follow me?"

Frankly, the Major did not. He shifted impatiently. What was the fellow driving at? A perfectly clear-cut issue was being metaphysically clouded. Unperturbed, the Vicar charged both glasses. "The truth is, things are not what they were. Old ideas, old customs are being challenged at all points. Time was when we should have deprecated this. Not now." The Vicar nodded gravely. "We are, my dear Major, confronting the spirit of the age."

Foulkes was quite lost for an answer. Harriet – and the spirit of the age?

"If the great world does not stand still, neither do individuals in a truly liberal sense Mrs Foulkes – "

"You feel," said Foulkes cutting through the tangle of words, "that she should be humoured?"

"Your wife," replied Selman smoothly, "should not become an object of frustration. I think on the whole she might be allowed to accompany you." His eyes twinkled. "Though always under discipline."

"I am very doubtful." said Foulkes slowly. It seemed that the crows overhead cawed derisively.

Selman leaned forward. "One thought does occur to me – are you afraid that your wife's presence with the regiment would impair you in the performance of your duties?"

The question annoyed Foulkes, yet he could not complain for the Vicar's tone was completely inoffensive. "On no account, and in no circumstance," he replied firmly.

"I should have known that." Selman eyed a frond of sun-drenched laburnum thoughtfully. "It burns," he reflected, "and is not consumed," though whether the image pertained to Mrs Foulkes' ardent temperament or to the Major's sense of duty, it was difficult to say. He made a commonplace observation, and his visitor who was in no mood for small-talk, reached for his switch. "I won't trouble you further," said Foulkes rising.

"No trouble at all," smiled the Vicar. "Convey to your wife my kindest regards, and intimate that I shall do myself the honour of calling upon her tomorrow."

Foulkes mounted, and was about to ride away when the clergyman raised his arm, calling, "Just a moment. I have a correspondent, an Anglican chaplain in Lisbon, who might possibly be of use if you were to disembark there – the language difficulty you know, and all that. I will bring up particulars. An excellent fellow. He was with me at Christ Church."

"You are very kind," said Foulkes saluting. He was moved more than he cared to admit by the Vicar's reference to his military duties. What did the old fool, who at best had only watched the militia shambling, know of military matters? Or being a confirmed bachelor, of marriage either! The visit had been so much wasted time. The "spirit of the age" indeed! Words – words... words...

Soon, he came in sight of the trim, bright-brick, cream-pillared façade of the hall. An attractive Queen Anne mansion, he was not moved by any deeply seated affection for it. The late owner had spent his childhood here, had grown almost with the walls; but since Bellaby had become his (Foulkes) parcel of land, here he supposed he would end his days. All the more reason then that the house should be kept as a going concern, tended, lived-in. "Harriet's occupation," he told himself firmly, "is here."

It certainly was. He had stabled his horse, and turned the corner of the rear premises when he heard a shot from the direction of the kitchen garden. "The devil!" he ejaculated, at a loss to understand why a firearm should be exploded in a place so remote and peaceful. He increased his pace, and rushed through the gate to behold his wife, pistol in hand, confronting a row of empty wine flasks, with Dagg, the gardener loading a second weapon. At once Dagg desisted, and dutifully touched his hat. Harriet cried, "Good morning, Major Foulkes! Congratulate me!" and pointed triumphantly to a litter of broken glass about the bench. As she raised her weapon to take aim again, Dagg who was taking no chances, dodged behind her. "Don't wave the thing around so, Ma'm," he pleaded, "It ain't a fan, you know." The gardener's hand being bound in a bloodstained rag, it was obvious to Foulkes that his wife had been somewhat liberal in her choice of targets. Harriet squinting along a double-barrelled pocket pistol, was further cautioned by Dagg. "Don't sight wi' a leetle weapon like that. Aim a bit lower than you'd think. Wait a bit though." He dropped on his haunches. When however, Harriet pulled the trigger the flasks remained intact, but a few leaves fluttered from an apple tree in the middle distance, and crows protested in the elms. She was not abashed. "Practice," she observed tritely, "makes perfect."

"One would hope so," said her husband dryly. "What is the meaning of this?"

"Self defence."

"Against whom?"

"The French, of course."

He smiled, sardonically eyeing the gardener's hand. He was annoyed to note that they had brought with them – but discarded as being too awkward to handle – his case of duelling pistols, weapons he could not bear to look upon without a twinge of regret. In his younger days, using one of these, he had shot a fellow subaltern through the chest. It had been touch and go with his victim for days, and recalling that anxious time, Foulkes turned sharply to Dagg. "Collect the weapons and return them at once to the gun-room." As between master and mistress, the gardener hovered doubtfully. "Don't be a tease," drawled Harriet, "and on no account blame Dagg who simply acted on my orders."

"Very like." All the same he would talk to Dagg later. The man should never have loaded the weapons in the first place. Grimly Foulkes turned towards the house. So much for "the spirit of the age!" …

But clipped speech and dark disapproval were of no avail. She became so endearingly persuasive that by late afternoon Foulkes was visibly weakening, hum'ing and haw'ing in a most unusual fashion. After all, he conceded, she was uniquely herself, intelligent, lively, capable of holding her own in almost any company. She might even temper Colonel Pomeroy's brashness. Indeed, he began to speculate with some amusement upon his colonel's possible reception of the news – the grizzled eyebrows would twitch, the port-wine cheeks blow out; Pomeroy would roll and grunt like a porpoise. Let him! Harriet would turn him around her little finger. Foulkes, it will be noted, had no sympathy for his commanding officer …

* * *

Jane – the smiling traitress! – tossing bonnet plumes, and flaunting a new silver embroidered gown of taffeta, came later in the day. He managed to intercept her at the door where he enjoined a word of caution concerning their earlier conversation. She tapped his shoulder, laughing. "I will be a model of discretion, but not to the extent of changing Harriet's mind!"

So he left the two sisters conferring deeply on clothes, packing, and other matters of consequence. Later, though still feeling that he had been shabbily treated, he contrived to be indulgent when the Reverend Granby Selman called. After that he wandered restlessly from one room to another dwelling upon the future. Very well, Harriet should go, and – as Jane had suggested – maybe tiring of Spain (he could think of many reasons why she should do so: excessive alternations of heat and cold, fever, mosquitoes) she would be more than happy to return. He recalled with a smile that Jane had mentioned Lisbon, which was of course, still in the hands of the French. How ill-informed women were! but Lisbon or Cadiz, it mattered not …

He shrugged, replenished his snuff box, and went to look at the horses. In the stables a thought struck him and he returned immediately to the house. Jane had gone, and he found his wife alone kneeling beside an open chest.

"Harriet," he said abruptly, "there can be no entourage."

"Entourage?"

"In the matter of servants. You will be allowed one only."

"I have already provided for that," she said calmly. "It is to be Betty." (Betty Aspinall was Harriet's personal maid.) "She can both plain sew and cook."

"That's your affair," he replied curtly, "but remember, no more than Betty."

"Very well, sir," she murmured, with a hint of mock submission.

"I shall write to the Colonel directly," he said.

"Then please lose nothing in attaching my own compliments," she observed.

* * *

The next day brought unlooked for complication. A loose board in the back stairs sent Betty Aspinall crashing to the bottom where she lay piteously calling for help. The Major was the first to hear her, and after placing Betty in the charge of others hastened upstairs to find his wife surrounded by what must have been pretty nearly the whole of her wardrobe. She was so engrossed in the business of final selection that she did not notice her husband's entry. "Lay everything aside," he said abruptly, "your maid has broken her ankle."

"Impossible!" exclaimed Harriet, "she only left a moment or two ago and was quite well."

"Very like," he commented, not without a certain relish, "but now your Betty is decidedly ill. In a word she has fallen down the steps leading to the kitchen."

"Where is she now?"

"In the housekeeper's room. The surgeon has been sent for."

"I must go and see."

Harriet darted out …

Betty Aspinall, pale and much shaken by the fall, but faintly pleasured at being for the first time in years the centre of so much anxious attention, was sipping a cordial, her leg propped on a chair. It had all happened (she explained) at a dark bend in the stairs; were she able she could lead them to the defective step, the cause of all the trouble. She had noticed the same step more than once during the past few weeks.

"If you knew of the wretched board," wailed Harriet, "why did you not take proper care?"

"You was in such a hurry Ma'm for needles," said Betty weakly. She began to weep. But there was no point in scolding. The stairs could be mended, but the condition of the girl's ankle was such that she would be out of action for many weeks.

Presently Harriet joined her husband upstairs. "What am I to do now?"

she inquired desperately, "I was absolutely dependent on Betty."

"Await a report from the surgeon," he said smoothly.

"To what end. He cannot perform miracles."

Foulkes, who for a wild moment had hoped that the mishap might deflect Harriet from her purpose, remarked slyly, "Could you manage with an orderly?"

She reacted sharply. "A man? In personal attendance!"

"He would fetch and carry."

"No thank you. I must have a female among all those savages."

"Savages?"

"Foreigners then. Let's not quibble. What – what on earth shall I do?"

"That," he responded with annoying composure, "is a question which I cannot answer."

Indiscreetly, he smiled. "You appear to find the situation amusing," she said darkly. "I suppose you are thoroughly pleased that this has happened!"

"Oh, come now," he protested. "I shall be accused next of tripping up Betty on purpose."

"You might show a little more concern!" But she realised that she was being unjust. She held a muslin dress up to the light, allowed it to fall, and with tightly compressed lips gazed through the window at a bright vista of greensward shadowed by yews. The admirable Betty, so deft of touch, so accomplished a needlewoman – Betty who anticipated every requirement, laid low! Travel would be intolerable without her. What more cruel stroke could fate have devised?

"Take her with you in the barouche," suggested Foulkes.

"And crutches, I suppose, in addition?"

Harriet's scorn was complete. She stood by the window wondering who conceivably might take Betty's place; certainly not the housemaid, a stupid wench whose every movement would need watching. There were two kitchen maids, but these at best were frumpish, tongue-tied. She continued to move restlessly about the room. Was it possible to enlist the services of some person in the village? The Reverend Selman had a competent servant; but could she (Harriet) deprive the old man of so essential a helpmeet? There was young Mrs Gibbs, who had been in service, but she would hardly leave her husband. Gradually, the field thinned. Perhaps Jane might be in a position to assist. Harriet decided to ride over and consult her sister.

It was at this point, still confused and irritated, that glancing through the window she saw something which at once attracted her attention. Susan Thompson, one of the kitchen maids had appeared round the corner of the house carrying a basket of garden-produce, carrots, onions, and the like, for use in her ordinary line of duty. The stable-boy, an oaf whose breeches sagged half way down his calves, slouched immediately behind; and from the wide grin which split his features made some remark to which the girl responded with a disdainful toss of the head; but before she could move out of arm's reach he lurched forward, snatched at her apron strings from behind and untied them. From her point of vantage Harriet could hear faintly the youth's gangling laugh, and the girl's irritated comment. She watched the maid set down her basket in order to retie the apron, but not content with the first stroke of annoyance the youth set his foot under the basket rim and calmly tilted the contents on the gravel path. This accomplished, he set one foot on the riding stone, and viewed his handiwork with a grimace of mock horror.

Harriet watched …

Flushed with anger, Susan Thompson looked once, and only once at the grinning face before her, and then with a buffet which caught her tormentor completely off-balance, sent him head over heels across the border. After that, calmly disregarding the oaf, she began to replace the scattered garden produce. In other circumstances Harriet would have paid little attention to such by-play – now she did not take away her eyes. She saw the lout pick himself up and mouthing threats begin to dust his clothes with his hands. But there was no further violence. The maid with arms akimbo advanced upon the youth with so resolute a bearing, that bully and coward combined, he began to edge slowly away. He made a few silly gestures, but plainly he had had enough, and turning tail, left her master of the field. At once the girl set her apron to rights, and went her way.

As the maid disappeared, Harriet gave an exultant cry. "I have it!" she exclaimed.

"What indeed?" inquired Foulkes.

"If Betty cannot go, Susan Thompson shall."

Susan Thompson?" he asked, "who the devil is she?" Foulkes paid little attention to members of the household staff.

"The kitchen maid, of course."

"And what has she especially to recommend her?"

"Courage – enterprise – resolution."

"Is that all?" He shrugged.

"As to other things," Harriet continued, "She can learn."

"Have it your own way," he concluded, not without a tinge of disappointment that a substitute should have been found so soon. "It is completely your own affair."

"You may safely leave her to me."

A kitchen maid – why not? Percy had spoken of rough living, of strange halting places, of barren bivouacs. Yes, an ability to peel onions, to shred vegetables, in fine to stir the pot, would not be unacceptable in the country of Don Quixote, for Harriet's thoughts reverted to the grasping innkeepers, the hardy muleteers and the roving gypsies of La Mancha. The strong hand she had observed chastising the garden boy, would be of much greater use in Spain, than the tender, fluttering fingers of Betty. The more this concept flowered in her mind, the more Harriet liked it. She laughed softly. Dona Quixote, of course, presupposed a robust female adherent, a faithful Sancho Panza.

"I feel that I am altogether right," she said.

But her husband had gone ...

CHAPTER III

Susan Thompson, into whose menial round Mrs Foulkes had incidentally peered, was – apart from bickering with the garden boy – nursing her own peck of trouble. Aged twenty, her step quick and buoyant, a wealth of auburn hair crowning her fresh but slightly freckled cheeks, you might have supposed her without a single anxiety in the world. But the truth was very different. A letter received from home that morning had thrown her into a state of intense gloom and confusion. It was not often that her father wrote, for James Thompson being a miner, was more at ease with a pick than a pen.

The letter in question brought shattering news. Robin, her only brother, arrested on a poaching charge, had been brought before the Justices, and committed for trial at York. "We held off from telling you as long as we could," her father wrote, "but now you must know the worst. We are overwhelmed that this calamity should have come upon us, not knowing which way to turn for comfort, or where to look for means of defence. For your poor mother's sake, I wish you was at home." Reading the script so painfully indicted, Sue wished profoundly that she was there too. Here, she felt completely, desperately, alone. The letter mocked the cheerful bustle of the kitchens, the golden sunshine, the fragrance of the garden, and had so disturbed her habitual good nature that she had reacted violently to the garden-boy.

Preoccupied, she carried out her duties, trying the while to comprehend a situation in which her brother, a young man habitually industrious and studious, had become involved. Although a miner, his interests when not at work, were bookish, indeed (as she knew) his secret ambition was to become a schoolmaster. Of all the persons within her knowledge, he was the least likely to be found poaching or in the company of poachers. If her father had been charged with high treason, or her mother of witchcraft, Sue could not have been more shocked. She could only conclude that a terrible mistake had been made, and that after a thorough investigation, her brother would be released. In the meantime she was anxious not only for the hapless Robin, but for her parents also. What could she do? The twenty miles which lay between her present place of employment and her native village of Tollgate, might well have been a hundred. The only course, she felt, would be to write immediately asking for further information, though even that would be difficult. Paper and pens were not easily come by. She had little time on her own. It was Sue here, and Sue there. She was in constant demand …

She had no sooner returned to the kitchen and set down her basket, when Mrs Foulkes' bell rang, though it was Falder the housemaid who answered the summons. In a very short time that young lady returned, and with a shrewish look and a significant nod in Sue's direction, remarked, "You're the one she wants."

The girl started in surprise. "What for?"

"I didn't ask," said Falder pertly.

Adjusting her apron and hastily tidying her hair, Sue ran upstairs. As she sped along the corridors, sins of omission flitted through her mind. Was it possible that the garden-boy had complained? In the event of the Foulkes' dispensing with her services, breathless though she was, she wondered where she would find elsewhere a situation so good. At the head of the stairs she slackened to a walking pace, and as the boudoir door stood slightly ajar, she coughed gently to announce her presence. Harriet heard. "Come forward," said her mistress indulgently. "I wish to talk to you, Susan. You may sit."

With a sigh of relief at the amiable reception, but still apprehensive, Sue sat on the edge of a chair, and hands in lap, composed herself to listen. Mrs Foulkes sat also. When she had sufficiently arranged her skirts, she began. "Have you ever been abroad, Susan?" she asked, "I mean to foreign parts. Of course you have not," she continued without waiting for an answer, "so that it is now in my power to afford you a splendid opportunity to see the world. Major Foulkes wishes me to accompany him to Spain with the regiment. I cannot go well without attendance. I am in need of a maid – a good one – and my choice has fallen upon you. What do you say?"

Sue gaped surprise. "I have hardly words to speak, Ma'm," she stammered.

"I can understand that," said Mrs Foulkes. "Few girls in your position would be so fortunate as to travel in such favourable circumstances. We shall I take it, be away for some considerable time, but rest assured you will be well-cared for."

"Yes, Ma'm."

"And you would be with me constantly."

"Yes, Ma'm."

"I felt certain that you would agree," said Mrs Foulkes smoothly. It did not strike Sue as in any sense peculiar that her own consent should be largely taken for granted. Ladies like her mistress were accustomed to their own way; it was not for those in humble station to oppose their wishes. "Now, there are certain duties that I shall ask you to perform. Answer truthfully. You can sew?"

"Yes, Ma'm – plain."

"And cook?"

"I was taught at home, Ma'm."

"Have you learnt nothing here? … Never mind. Now concerning the arrangement of hair—" Harriet frowned as she considered Sue's curls. "You may have been favoured by nature, but that, you know, is not *à la mode.*"

"I am willing to learn, Ma'm."

Harried sighed. "I see I must take you in hand. You will, of course, require an appropriate dress, and a cloak. These, however, I can provide."

"As you please, Ma'm."

After one or two further observations, Harriet concluded, "It occurs to me that since we shall be absent for some months you may wish to see your parents before you leave. You have my permission."

At this uncovenanted privilege Sue swallowed hard; it was more than she dared to hope.

"The matter can be contrived," said Harriet, after learning where Sue lived. "You may go first thing in the morning. Hallows will run you to Bawtry where you can catch the stage to Doncaster; but return for certain within the twenty four hours." Consulting a road-book, she jotted down coach arrivals at Bawtry and departures for Doncaster, handed over five shillings for fares, smiled, and nodded dismissal. The whole interview had not occupied more than ten minutes.

Sue descended to the lower regions hardly conscious how she got there. In other circumstances she would have been highly elated, dazzled even by the prospect held out by Mrs Foulkes. For the time being, however, her chief anxiety was to meet her own people; to learn first-hand how Robin fared. In the kitchen after imparting the news – Falder alone, who felt that she had been overlooked commenting acidly – Sue fell into profound silence until her companions began to inquire if she were indeed 'ailing'. She made no answer, and the day wore leadenly on …

Next morning early, sitting beside Hallows in the trap, she watched the countryside wheel by with unresponsive eyes. The stableman's crude pleasantries jarred, so that she answered only in monosyllables. When an arm slyly inserted around her waist failed to evoke response, he too became silent and fell to flicking with his whip, leaves from occasional overhanging branches. Sue was relieved when they ran into Bawtry, where, after waiting three quarters of an hour, the Doncaster coach rolled in. She climbed aboard, and they set off at a spanking pace throwing up a rolling wake of dust from the parched road. Soon, skirting the racecourse, they entered the busy town. In the market place she found a carrier who plied between Doncaster and Rotherham, returning during the day, so that he would be able to pick her up in the late afternoon. When she settled into the seat beside him she had still another nine miles to go.

The carrier, glad of a companion, was talkative. He pointed to the crumbling stones of Conisbro' Castle, devastated by Cromwell, a wicked man if ever there was one. But Sue who knew nothing at all about the Protector, turned with greater interest to the wayside pits, some in full working order, others backed by discard heaps and rotting timber, long abandoned. The mine where her father was employed lay well off the Rotherham road. She would see the village first.

Entering Tollgate at last, not a stone seemed altered. It was quiet now, most of the men being underground, but soon the colliers would troop across the fields. By early evening the taverns would be full. A chestnut-shaded Anglican church stood at the west end of the main thoroughfare, and a set of weathered stocks were placed on a broad green verge before it. Somewhat recessed from the main road, its austere façade half hidden by the angle of a large cottage, stood the Wesleyan Methodist Chapel, of interest to Sue since it was attended by her parents. Three miles across country, the parklands ringed by a substantial stone wall, was Wentworth House, the seat of the second Earl Fitzwilliam, inheritor of the broad estate of his uncle, the late Marquis of Rockingham. This was the Strafford country, where remote from courts and camps, the ill-fated 17th century statesman had once walked in his garden.

The cart rumbled down a street quite empty save for a bull terrier asleep in the doorway of the "Miners Rest". Mrs Thompson, as her daughter expected, was at home. Extremely neat, in a pink-sprigged bed-gown and white mob-cap, she threw up both hands at the sudden appearance of one whom she considered inaccessible miles away. "Oh, Sue – Sue!" she murmured tragically drawing her daughter into the parlour before she embraced; being Yorkshire, she would make no public display of emotion.

Red-rimmed of eyes and pallid of cheeks told of harassed days and sleepless nights. The poor woman wept. "We don't know what in God's mercy to do!" she exclaimed, at once reverting to their great trouble. York was so terribly remote, their information sparse, their resources few. "Yes, but first I must know what really happened," said Sue as she took off her things. From her mother's somewhat disjoined account, she gathered only that Robin had been caught red-handed with a poached hare in his possession. "Don't ask me how," said Mrs Thompson hopelessly, "it was all mixed up with another chap – a reg'lar good for nowt. Wait till your father comes home from t'pit; he'll tell you. I'm downright moithered – sick to death with it all."

She brewed tea as she talked. When Sue mentioned the ostensible purpose of her visit, attendance upon her mistress in Spain, the only observation her distracted mother could make, was, "I expect Mrs Foulkes an' all will take great care of you. Don't fall into mischief. I am sure you will be faithful and honest." To Mrs Thompson the assignment was another extension of domestic service. Her thoughts were centred upon "the poor lad" in York Castle prison ...

About three in the afternoon James Thompson came in from work, his grizzled hair matted with coal dust, the whites of his eyes rolling weirdly in the streaked grime of his face. He stood stock still beholding Sue, no less surprised than his wife had been. "What's her doing here?" he cried. "Have they finished you?" Returning home earlier than usual, he explained that there had been a "fall" in his part of the workings, stopping work for the rest of the day. He listened to his daughter's explanation almost without comment, except to remark that "Spain was an awful long way off." He washed and ate, talking as he did so. His speech interlarded with dialect, would have seemed peculiar to a stranger; not so to his daughter.

"We're bound lass," he announced gloomily, "hand and foot as I see it, though the lad's got a lawyer working for him. I went into Rotherham and seed Mester Badger me'self. It was the best that I could do."

"Did you manage to see Robin?"

"Aye, they let me in, but they watched like ferrets – thought I'd pass him a file, a key, or something. I've often looked on that gaol door, but I never thought to see one o'mine inside." He shook his head sadly, and ran his hand through his hair. His lips moved silently.

"How did it all come about?"

James Thompson sighed profoundly. "A bit of a tangle, if you ask me. As near as I could make out the lad had been walking across country, Elsecar way, and was coming back through Hoober Coppice – you know the path 'at runs atween the trees?"

Sue nodded. In season she had gathered bluebells and primroses among the silver birch. "Was it by night?"

"Just after half past ten," said her father, "about dark. A bit afore that he had been joined by Jacob Harker – old Harker's son, you know – who was walking home t'same way. Robin had never been partial to Harker's company, but they had lighted on each other by chance, and set off towards home. Well, they were a'most through the coppice when this Harker stops dead in his tracks, and says, 'By gow, I've gone and dropped me knife – I thowt I heard summat fall when we got over t'stile. I'll slip back and look for it. Don't thee come. Just hold this bit o' belly pork. It'll free me hands.'"

"Belly pork?" questioned Sue.

"That's what he said. But it was a hare, in a sack. Robin thinking nothing, takes it while Harker goes back to look for his knife, which if you ask me, he'd never lost at all. The lad had no sooner took the sack and leaned up against a tree waiting for Harker to come back, when up pops two keepers and pounces on him. Robin, not knowing what the game was, lands out. The head keeper, Bates, well nigh got his nose broke, and that didn't help Robin any."

"What became of Harker?"

James Thompson snorted. "You may well ask. He'd gone as clean as a whistle. The keepers swear they had followed the culprit, not knowing who it was for a good mile, and as he was making tracks for Tollgate, cut across the fields to take him at the coppice. It's my belief 'at Harker saw 'em, or at least heard 'em, and so pretends to go back for his knife."

"Didn't Robin explain this to the magistrates?"

"Aye, and much difference it made! The head keeper swore 'at they'd collared the right man."

"What was Robin doing that way?"

"Taking a walk. Enjoying the rustic scene. When he told the Justices that, they laughed."

"A rare laughing matter, I must say!" she cried indignantly.

Her father made a resigned gesture. "The plain fact is they caught him with the hare on his person – snickle an' all, which was in the sack. That's good enow for the law."

"Where is this Harker now?"

"Gone."

"But if he lives here?"

"I tell you he's gone – cleared out – nobody knows where."

"He must be found," said Sue resolutely.

"Aye," muttered her father ruefully, "but tell us where to look. He hasn't been near t'pit since that night, nor seen anywhere else."

"They're all good-for-nowts, t'Harkers," interposed Mrs Thompson.

"It's my belief he's 'listed," Thompson continued. "But what if we do track him down, what then?" He beat his knee gently with his fist. "Would he come forward like a true, honest man and admit his guilt? He would not. I saw t'owd un yesterday morning sniffing and sniggering behind his hand. He knows where his son is I'll warrant, but he'll none tell." Sue's father turned his head aside with a gesture of despair. "I will laugh when thy calamity cometh," he said, quoting Scripture.

"Can't you go see the Earl himself?" asked Sue.

"I would," said Thompson, "but he's over the water in Ireland – as well be in America so far as we are concerned. Well, lass," he concluded, "now you've got it all."

For a little time Sue sat quite still. No one spoke. Then, impulsively, she rose to her feet, and put on her bonnet, tying the strings with quick deliberate fingers.

"Where ter goin'," inquired her mother, surprised. "'Tisn't time to be getting; back, surely."

"I intend," said Sue firmly, "to find Harker's dad."

"What good will it do?"

Sue evaded the question. "Does he still live by the brook?"

"He'll o'ny insult thee," said her father.

"I can stand that."

"He's as sly as a fox."

"Do be careful," pleaded her mother.

"Leave him to me," said Sue.

Mrs Thompson shook her head dubiously. "No good ever came out o' that family, and you'll get none now."

"I'd go with thee," said Thompson, frowning, "but the Lord forgive me for saying so, I should be provoked to violence."

"I am certain," said Sue finally," that I had better go alone." She had no precise idea of how to approach the old man, but with so much at stake, she felt she could not be idle.

Leaving the shadowed parlour, she stepped into the sunlit street, and hurrying towards the church turned the angle of the graveyard wall. Fifty yards further on she entered a rough cart-road at the end of which, half hidden by elder bushes, stood a couple of tumble-down cottages, hovels which had fallen into such disrepair that they had long been written off as ruins. None the less, both buildings were occupied. Clarice Bray, the village drab, occupied the first, and Harker senior, the second. A widower, once employed as horse-keeper at the mine, he had for many years eked out a living by carting small coals, and collecting rags, bottles and bones. On the side was business less reputable. Items filched from the great house often passed through his hands. He knew how to dispose of the odd silver spoon, the loose pair of buckles, the occasional candlestick. He managed also a limited amount of poaching, and some part of this craft he had taught his son Jacob. A creature of shifts and stratagems, he would not be easy to question.

As Sue approached the two cottages, a slatternly woman in a stained black bodice and sacking skirt, appeared in the doorway of the first, staring brashly. The girl effected not to notice wondering if Mrs Bray would recognise her after so long an absence from the village. She passed without a word. Harker's place, a garden span further on, flanked a stream which gurgled lazily through a litter of stones, broken earthenware and glass. A few scraggy hens pecked among docks and nettles. A pony, its matted hair untouched by curry-comb, stood tethered to the upturned shafts of a light cart. Harker's cottage looked what it indeed was, a hideout, a mere convenience for eating and sleeping. One of the windows sported a ragged quilt for a curtain; the other, fully boarded up, made it as difficult for the tenant to look out as is was for the passer-by to look in.

She knocked at the door and waited. Though complete silence followed, she was quite certain that some person or indeed persons, lurked behind the shabby exterior. she knocked again, this time more loudly, and after a lengthy pause a bronchial voice cried, "Who is it 'at's theer? What do yer want?" She decided not to speak until the door actually opened, and after a few seconds knocked a third time. From inside came a crash as though a stool had been overturned, and a muffled curse. At last the door, which was suspended on only one hinge, scraped open, and Harker's leathery brown cheeks and whiskers of dirty white, appeared. A pair of weazel eyes flittered to her face, to the lane beyond, and rested finally on the flags at her feet. In one hand he held a half-fashioned cudgel, and in the other a large clasp knife the blade of which had been worn thin with grinding. He made a cut at the knob he was shaping.

"Are you Mr Harker?" she inquired.

He gave a slow smile. "I've bin that some time." It was evident that he did not recognise her – she had left the village at the age of fourteen.

"You do not know me?"

"I don't want to know thee. What is it thou art after, a nice little brooch? I got just the thing to suit ye."

"Nothing like that," she replied, "I want some information."

Suddenly his eyes narrowed. "Who is it ye're after – my son?" Sue, who had expected to introduce the subject more obliquely, was somewhat taken aback. The question came head-on. Harker senior however, did not wait for an answer. Rolling his smoky grey eyes in mock concern, he continued, "That's the third lass i' the past fortneet 'at's come askin' about him – 'Wheer has he gone? Wheer can we put us fingers on him?' Well, all I know is that he's left his poor old dad i' the lurch." The man dropped his voice and leered. "Now ye know as much as I do."

So that was it – a closed door! Harker sniggered as the chips flew from beneath his knife.

"Why did he run away?"

Harker hacked at the cudgel. "Run away?" he repeated.

"You heard me." Even as she spoke, she realised that she would get nothing here. Her father had been right. The man was artful. For a second his eyes transfixed hers. "Hey," he said, slyly, "what may you be called?"

Sue hesitated. Ought she to withhold her name? She decided to make it known. "I am Susan Thompson."

"Not Jim Thompson's daughter?"

"Yes," she said defiantly.

"That's torn it!" he cried stepping backwards. "I might ha' known ye were out o' that stable."

"Where is your son?"

"Wouldn't you like to know?" he grinned, opposing a set of yellow fangs, "well, I'll tell you, but promise to let it go no further. He's in the horse marines, them as wears their spurs back to front."

Advancing his knife, he began to weave a pattern in the air until the point came to within a few inches of her nose. She did not flinch, and the knife point fell. Frontal attack was not in Harker's nature.

"So he is in the army?" she persisted.

"I didn't say that!" He paused irresolute, wondering if by his crude raillery he had given too much away, then with a cry of, "Interfering young bitch!" he backed into the cottage and slammed the door in her face. She could hear muffled cursing, the shuffling of feet; the tattered curtain stirred slightly and his rheumy eye appeared at a peephole. After that, she felt, it was no use waiting. She turned away. But other eyes had been watching. As she retrieved her steps, the slattern whom she had noticed on her approach, took a few paces forward from the first doorway, beckoning. The woman wiped a slack, slobbering mouth with the back of her hand, and with the other swept a wisp of greasy hair from her eyes. "Birds of a feather", thought the girl; a fitting neighbour for the man whom she had just left. She would have passed without a word, but the woman crooked an ogling finger, "Missy," the drab croaked, "you be interested in young Harker?"

Sue did not answer.

"It'll not be t'owd 'un, I reckon," smirked Mrs Bray. "Now cross me 'and wi' silver, and' I'll tell yer wheer t'young un's gone."

Looking into the elder woman's crafty eyes, Sue hesitated. The ingratiating smile did not invite confidence; the move, of course, a gypsy trick to make a little easy money.

"Do you really know?" the girl asked.

Mrs Bray hawked and spat. "I beg your parding," she wheezed, "it's me poor owd chest. Now is it worth a sixpence for your future 'appiness?"

Eager as she was for any kind of information, Sue's hand stole towards her pocket. "Come on," said Mrs Bray, "you'll none regret."

Sue took sixpence from her purse and handed it over. Mrs Bray seized the coin, fastened her teeth on it, and being assured that it was genuine, bent over and slipped it in her shoe. "Tell me, and don't lie," said Sue, "where is Jacob Harker?"

In response, the woman raised the forefinger of her right hand, spread fingers and thumb out fully, and after that described a circle in air.

"Pray what," inquired the mystical Sue, "is the meaning of that?"

"One-five-nowt," said Mrs Bray.

"A number?"

Her mentor nodded emphatically. "Soldier reg'ment – one huner and fifty that is."

"Yes – go on."

"'Listed – off to Doncaster – recruitin' serjeant."

"That's where he's gone?"

"For sartin'. I 'eeard 'em talkin'. So t'owd man put's the pony in t'shafts, an' off they goo i' the night. Next mornin' t'owd vill'an comes back by hissen. Do yer see?"

"I understand. What else?"

Mrs Bray screwed up her face in a grotesque wink. "If yer want moor, it'll cost moor."

"Tell me."

"Nay, nowt for nowt!"

"Very well," said the girl reluctantly. She had dipped into her purse again, when Mrs Bray cast a startled glance in the direction of Harker's door. With a surprising change of front she began to strut to and fro, pausing only to shake her fist in Sue's face. "Away, ye brazen hussy!" she shouted. "I ain't a dealin' with the likes o' you. You get nothink outer me – the downright impertinence!" At the same time she contrived an expressive wink. At once Sue understood. Old Harker had reappeared in his own doorway and was regarding his neighbour with a basilisk state. The tattered dame who concluded the exchange by shouting, "I tell you nothink!" whisked about, and almost scampered into her own den. Sue walked away. She did not look behind.

"One – five – nought," she repeated, "a regiment." The number had a familiar ring. Where had she seen or heard of this number before? One hundred and fifty? Then in a flash she recalled that it was painted upon the Major's trunks and valises at Bellaby – the number of his regiment. Harker had apparently joined the Hundred and Fiftieth Foot. A surge of elation filled her. The visit after all had not been in vain.

But when she reached home and conveyed the information to her parents, they were not impressed. "Tha's thrown good money away," said her father bluntly, "that woman 'ud sell her soul for a farthing." Assuming that Mrs Bray had spoken the truth to what use could her revelation be put? "Given time," Thompson concluded, "we might trace the scamp, but what of that? We've no handle on him. He warn't caught red-handed like our lad …"

The remaining hours at home passed all too quickly, and after a meal when all ate sparingly, Sue, cloaked and bonneted, sat awaiting the return of the carrier. During the last quarter of an hour her father fell upon his knees and prayed with simple but profound fervour. "O Lord God of Israel," he said, "look with compassion on this little family. Preserve to us them that shall pass through the valley of tribulation. Place Thy loving arms around him that is in chains. Watch tenderly over the lass that will sail across the great waters. Restrain the hand of the evil-doer …" The sonorous voice faltered. "And unite us at last in Thine eternal peace …"

The girl opened her eyes upon the two kneeling figures, the willow-patterned plates and shining brass, the rich blue and orange of the equestrian pottery flanking the clock on the mantelpiece, as though by so doing she would retain through the months to come, an impression of the well-loved place. Her eyes lingered on the shelf containing her brother's books – slim volumes of poetry: Milton, Collins, Gray. The slut's "One – five – nowt" still lingered in her mind. One hundred and fifty. She would make certain of this once back at Bellaby. When her father arose and dusted his knees as he was wont to do in chapel, she said, "I hardly remember Jacob Harker. What is he now like?"

"Lean enow," replied her father, "a bit taller than t'owd one, and smarter in appearance – slick, you might say. He was in the Earl's service for a bit, but blotted his copybook before he finished. So back he came to the pit. Ah – and that reminds me – a scar he has across his right hand, jagged like a flash o' lightning. Said he got it underground, but I don't know. I reckon it was a from a keeper's gun. If you've seen the old man, you've seen Jacob."

Sue nodded. "I've seen the old man," she said.

"You might come across him in your travels," ruminated her father, "but the army's a big body and the world is wide, my lass."

"Tell me about Harker again," said Sue. "It may lead to something."

"I wish I could think so." He shook his head sorrowfully.

The carrier came, and she left her parents standing pathetically in the doorway. She had reminded them that letters directed to Bellaby, care of Mrs Foulkes, could always be forwarded. "I must know everything," she insisted, "no matter where I am. It's so much worse – being away." As the cart moved off she turned her head to conceal tears. Since the last time she had seen them her parents seemed to have grown so old ...

* * *

A full moon silvered the Don as Sue rode into Doncaster. She met the south-ward bound coach without difficulty, but approaching Bawtry became anxious lest Hallows and the trap would not be waiting. She need not have worried. The stableman having passed a convivial hour at the inn, was in a spacious, genial mood. As they rattled at a spanking pace along the moonlit roads, she questioned him concerning the Major's regiment. "Aye, the Hundred and Fiftieth Foot it is," said Fellows, "and that's all I want to know bout it. Soldierin' means nowt to me; if you don't finish up in a cosy grave, you comes back with the screws and a wooden leg. Who wants you then? I never seed the Major with his mob, and I don't want to. They tell me you are going with him."

"With Mrs Foulkes," she replied primly.

"Same thing," said Hallows. "Mark my words, before he's finished with you, he'll have you too marching up and down the barrack square. Damme! he'd drill the stable brooms if he could!"

"The Major may take you," she suggested.

Hallows laughed. "They on'y want militia men. Mind you at one time I did think of handling a musket, but I thowt again ..."

Sue was not listening ... Lean, her father had said, very like the old man ... hand marked with a scar ...

They entered a bank of fleecy ground-mist, and more than once between spectral hedgerows, lumbered over the grass verge. At last they drew clear and saw the gables and chimneys of Bellaby clearly outlined in the moonlight ...

CHAPTER IV

The journey south bore every appearance of a holiday. The weather remained fine; they clattered down the Great North Road throwing up clouds of dust, but this being the commonplace of summer travel, no one complained. They assuaged thirst with milk and ale at wayside farmhouses. The inns where they sought lodging for the night, were haunts of such creature comfort, that they were reluctant to leave.

At Bellaby no furniture had been stored and sheeted, nor indeed the staff reduced, since Foulkes held stubbornly to the belief that his wife would return ere many weeks had passed. "The house," he contended, "is a living thing, a going concern." With a secret, enigmatical smile, Harriet concurred. "I am in full agreement," she said, "that we must return – some time... ."

At last the Foulkes barouche came to a halt in the yard of the *White Hart* at Hythe, where they put up for several days until the Major engaged rooms in one of the smart red-brick houses facing the sea.

Harriet well nigh purred with pleasure in her new surroundings, as well she might, for Hythe was as gay as a garden. Mid-day the shopping centre became an herbaceous border of colour; the scarlet and gold tunics of the offices flecking the flowered muslins, the chip bonnets and flowing ribbons of the ladies. The social round offered every attraction. For the inclusive charge of three and sixpence you were entitled to dance or game at the Guildhall; or through the sunshot hours meet your friends at the Circulating Library, where you gossiped and drank coffee. Then there were the salt-water baths; outings to Shorncliffe, Sandgate and Folkestone. The long day seemed too brief for it all, and though Harriet complained that after the invigorating air of the Pennines the atmosphere of the south made her intolerably lazy, she missed little by way of public entertainment.

When for the first time in her life, Susan Thompson glimpsed the sea she confessed to acute disappointment. She had expected a close resemblance to the engravings, which embellished her brother's volumes of poetry vistas of billows tipped with foam. At Hythe the waves ran gently up a shelving beach, while away offshore, shimmering blues and greens melted in a surface smooth as glass. A slight undertow ground the pebbles. That was all. The level front was broken only by the late Mr Pitt's Martello Towers, puny defensive structures of which Major Foulkes was frankly contemptuous. A frigate, becalmed almost, lay out to sea in a setting so ineffably peaceful that it was difficult to imagine an embattled France not many miles away. Of course, everyone devoured the London papers, studied word for word official dispatches; and dwelt anxiously upon the fortunes of Sir Arthur Wellesley and his men, who had already landed in Portugal.

At Hythe the major seemed to grow in stature. Bellaby had been a place of sojourn where he was always restless, if not a little lost; now to the constant tramp of infantry, the slapping of muskets, the bawling of orders, the tapping of drums, he was in his natural element. Sue retained a vivid impression of the Commanding Officer's parade: the men in tunics of rich red, and yellow facings laced with pure white; the natty brass-plated shakoes of Austrian design, the white cross-belts, the black cartouche boxes; kits neatly strapped, side-swords suspended, muskets brown and shining. The captains and subalterns stood at the head of their respective companies – the Surgeon, Paymaster and Quartermaster to the left; the band, drummers and pioneers in the rear; and riding in at last, Colonel Pomeroy on his strawberry roan. In the background, wearing a grey habit piped at the seams with red, and flaunting in her hat a large orange plume, Mrs Foulkes on Felix patted her mount with a slender gauntleted hand.

But it was not the glow and glitter of the cohesive whole, though that was impressive enough, which held Sue's attention. She searched constantly for a face. Somewhere, framed by a chinstrap, shadowed by a visor, were the features of the elusive, unspeakable Harker. Alas, when her eyes ran along the ranks, it was almost impossible to distinguish one face from another; the men seemed alike as peas in a pod. She returned from the parade with a profound sense of disappointment. Had she expected too much?

As the days went by she found that she had little spare time at her disposal – the amount of sewing her mistress required was staggering – but during infrequent visits to the town centre, she scanned intently faces and hands of such members of the rank and file she encountered. This however, brought nothing but a measure of rude banter from the soldiers. She began to feel that she had either been shamelessly deceived by Mrs Bray, or that Jacob Harker had enlisted in another regiment. She dared not approach the Major, for though when not too preoccupied he exchanged the time of day with her, he remained upon his Olympian height. She did not in least wish Mrs Foulkes to know of her trouble. Anything but that. Once, when Sue had inquired if the post had included a letter for herself from home, her mistress had been frankly surprised. "Why," she exclaimed, "did you not leave your parents in perfectly good health?"

"Yes, Ma'm."

"They are not in the least anxious about you?"

"No, indeed, Ma'm."

"Then I don't see why you have occasion to worry," and Harriet turned indifferently away.

One day Sue heard the major refer to the "muster rolls" of the regiment:

apparently an official list of names. If only it were possible to examine this record, the problem of Harker's presence at Hythe would be solved. But where were such rolls deposited, and in whose hands? Once during the major's absence she rummaged through a number of his loose papers, but with no result. It was then that she remembered Stubbs, the Serjeant Major, who seemed to carry the regiment upon his own shoulders, for it was always Stubbs this, and Stubbs that, when the Major was in difficulties. Was he the god in the machine? The serjeant major was often in and out of the lodgings. A brash, cheerful fellow, six feet tall and broad in proportion, he was notoriously susceptible to feminine influence. His ogling eyes had often sought those of Sue, though in the presence of the Major that was as far as he permitted himself to go.

For some days the girl hesitated; Stubbs was not a man to whom she was attracted, and she was in no mind to become under an obligation to him; but a letter that she received from her parents during the weekend impelled her to second thoughts. The dreaded blow (she learned) had fallen: at York Assizes, where Robin had been sentenced to six years transportation in a convict settlement overseas. "Our only hope," concluded her father sombrely, "is that by God's grace he may one day be restored to us. For that we pray." Sue did not feel in the least like praying. She wandered into the garden where concealed by a shrubbery she dissolved in tears. When she recovered, still loath to leave the isolation of the garden, she could hear faintly, above the busy hum of the town the stentorian voice of Stubbs bawling out orders. As she listened it seemed to her that he, more than ever, held the key of the situation. She made herself presentable, and left the garden determined to approach him when he next entered the house.

But how? She was so seldom alone. A second family, members of which were constantly passing up and down the stairs, occupied two of the upper rooms, the rear premises being reserved for the landlady and her maid. Sue decided that she would have to seize the moment when Stubbs, having concluded his business with the Major, returned to the entrance hall to collect his shako and cane; an encounter, which would need to be accurately timed.

On the next two occasions of Stubbs' appearance she contrived to linger on the stairs, only to be disappointed, for the Major and Stubbs went out together. A third occasion however, offered distinct promise. Mrs Foulkes had departed for the circulating library, and what with coffee and general gossip would be away for the greater part of the morning; Sue too had overheard the Major remark that he had "mountains of paper work" to do. Thus she watched from an angle of the stairs as the maid admitted the Serjeant Major, who after placing his cane and shako on the table, knocked at the door of the room occupied by Foulkes and disappeared inside. Now! …Her heart leapt to her throat. Halt – on the lowest step she could hear a muffled conversation, the barrack square booming of the one, and the crisp incisive tones of the other. The interview seemed interminable. What were they discussing? Would Stubbs never come? As she waited, sewing in hand, with a feeble pretence at working, she felt that every detail of the green-washed hall, the oval mirror, the rich mahogany of the table upon which the Serjeant Major's equipment rested, would be etched on her mind forever. She heard the muted wash of the waves on the strand, the lazy inconsequential chatter of passing pedestrians. And still the muffled voices rose and fell ...

At last Stubbs appeared. To her intense relief he closed the door of the apartment, sealing off his superior officer. He had hardly taken two steps forward when Sue darted across, and snatching the shako from the table blew from it a slight film of summer dust, and with a polite gesture presented the headgear to its owner. "Why thank you, my dear," boomed Stubbs, distinctly pleased. Next, the cane. This was indeed service! His somewhat protuberant china-blue eyes swept her face and figure approvingly. "Look hafter me, Sally," he said indulgently, "and the time may come when hi shall look after you."

"That is kind of you, sir," said Sue with a little curtesy. "I should be grateful if you would answer me one question."

Stubbs drew himself up to his full height; an attitude apt to strike terror into the heart of the new recruit. "Hi will not commit myself," he said, "hi must first know the nature of your question, miss."

"Have you in the regiment a man named Harker?"

Stubbs blew out his cheeks with what might have been a disappointed gesture. "Before hi answer your hinquiry, "he replied, "he must know your intentions in so asking. He cannot allow hundue female interest hin the rank and file. Wouldn't do". His eyes swivelled. He intended a joke.

"The man is a relative."

"Hin what relation, may I ask – of a tender nature?"

"Oh no, serjeant major," she breathed hurriedly. (She could hear Foulkes in movement at the other side of the door.) "A kind of cousin."

"Then," conceded Stubbs, "hi will make hinquiries if I may steal a kind of kiss!" He extended his arms, but she eluded him.

"Not until you tell me what I ask."

"Surrender on terms!" Stubbs grunted. "That's it! Very well," he continued, though with lessened interest. "What was the name?"

"Harker – Jacob Harker."

"Hi don't recall such a name, but we have new men in."

"I am sure I shall be much obliged."

"That will do for me." He raised his cane in salute, grinned broadly and left ...

Two days elapsed before Sue saw him again. This time Stubbs' stay was brief. When she handed him his shako and cane, he frowned. "Did you—?" she began.

The serjeant major wagged a threatening finger. "You 'ad me on a wild goose chase. We 'ave no 'Arker. A Barker now – Jem Barker. Would that be the man?"

She shook her head sadly. Stubbs stood smiling. "'Aving gone to considerable trouble hon your account, young lady, hi must now claim my reward." As with pursed lips – a crudely comic figure – he advanced, she retreated until at last she stood with her back to the wall.

"No Harker – no kiss!" she said firmly.

"We're not 'aving that," he bantered. "Hi can see that you are a cruel deceiver, but no odds! A debt's a debt, and by the Markiss o' Granby, you shall pay."

She was saved from this awkward situation by the sudden appearance of the Major in the doorway. "Are you waiting for something, Serjeant Major?" he inquired tartly, looking from one to the other.

"Yes, sir – no sir," blundered Stubbs stiffening to attention. "Hi was about to take my leave."

"Very well."

Foulkes turned to Sue. "Have you no duties?" he asked severely.

"Yes, sir."

"Then please attend to them."

Disturbed by the implied reproof she darted off, mortified also that her first essay in detection should have ended so foolishly ...

* * *

"Upon my soul!"

The Major spoke, rustling his *Morning Chronicle*.

Harriet, who was playing Patience, looked up. "What is it now?" she asked.

"That fellow Wellesley!"

"Is he dead?"

"On the contrary! He is very much alive."

"You are most annoying vague."

Foulkes continued to read in silence, completely engrossed in his newspaper.

"Well?"

"All in good time," said Foulkes while Harriet waited more or less impatiently. At last he observed, "Here is Sir Arthur's dispatch," and began reading aloud—

"Vimiera, August 21st, 1808. I have the honour to report to you that the enemy attacked us in our position at Vimiera this morning. The village of Vimiera stands in a valley through which runs the River Maceira ... The whole of the French forces in Portugal employed under the command of the Duke D'Abrantes (General Junot) in person, in which the enemy was cer-

tainly superior in cavalry, and in which not more than half the British Army
was engaged, has suffered a signal defeat ..."

"Junot," explained Foulkes, "is Buonaparte's pet general. That's a blow for
the tyrant."

"I hope," said Harriet, "that this does not mean the end of the campaign."

Foulkes snorted at this expression of female ignorance. "Of course not. It
is no more than the first impact. A fine piece of work I must say; but my pleasure is more than tempered by the fact that while Wellesley's men are clothed
in glory, we are sucking our thumbs at Hythe." Out came the snuff box and
he sniffed indignantly. He turned to the paper for additional information. In
London the guns of the Tower had been fired, and the city enlivened by a
torchlight procession.

"London would seem to be enjoying itself," said Harriet, placing a king on
a queen.

The Major glanced darkly. "How can you concentrate on pasteboard with
so much impending?"

"If Drake played his game of bowls on the Hoe," she responded, "why not
allow your poor little Harriet her game of cards?"

"You are not poor," he rasped, "you are not little, and Drake has nothing
to do with the matter."

She accepted the rebuke with a faint smile, laying down her hand. "Now
tell me – if as Sir Arthur states, the French were superior in cavalry, what of
our own horsemen?"

Foulkes looked up again from the newspaper, surprised at her sudden
interest in the action, but he saw that she was quite serious. "You may be
sure," he said slowly, "that they would give a good account of themselves."

His answer conveyed nothing.

"If outnumbered one supposes that they would be in great danger," she
persisted.

"That would depend on how the army was employed; the lay of the land
and of opposing forces."

Harriet pondered his reply – again ambiguous. "To what uses are the
horsemen put?"

"In various forms," he answered patiently, "probing ahead of the main
body – pickets, patrols, supporting the infantry following up."

"So that they may be very near the enemy?"

"You may depend upon that."

She turned to her cards. Presently she spoke again. "What cavalry regiments are with Sir Arthur?"

"I am not certain. The King's German Legion, for one."

"Hanoverians?"

"Sound fellows, and some English dragoons."

"Oh."

He regarded her with a faintly quizzical expression. "Bye the bye, you remember your old Brighton flame, Anthony Harte?"

"Flame? Really, Percy!"

"A figure of speech," he hastened.

"A useful friend." She turned away her head, and began arranging the cards.

"I saw in the paper recently that he had been posted with a cavalry regiment."

"I noticed it too."

"You didn't say?"

"I did not consider the matter important."

Foulkes stared at his wife intently, but there was nothing in her bearing to suggest undue interest in the subject. She took up the Queen of Spades and waved the card gently as she might a miniature fan. He was about to add, "An impossible bounder," but in view of Harriet's attitude refrained. Instead, he rose from his chair. "The papers are just in," he remarked, "and as the Colonel may not know of this Vimiero business, I think it my duty to inform him."

"Of course," she said absently.

Briskly Foulkes put on his hat and went out …

Alone, Harriet gathered up the cards, stacked them, and approached a mirror surmounting the fireplace. Her cheeks betrayed a distinct flush, and she wondered if her husband had noticed. Remember Tony Harte? For the past three years she had tried her utmost to forget. Bored at Bellaby; having few social contacts of importance, she had elected to accompany Percy to the wars; but – though at times she had moments of doubt – the balance of decision had been tipped by the brief reference to Harte in the *Morning Chronicle*. Confronting the mirror, a sense of the past overwhelmed her, and with it the possibility of renewed association with one whom she remembered in a golden light. Hythe had strengthened the first nostalgic impulse. The warm, languorous summer nights, the rustle of silks beneath glittering candelabra, the lilting of violins, moonlight shimmering on the water – all this, and more, had revived the halcyon hours, when with Tony Harte, she had strolled along the Styne, or in haunts sufficiently romantic, had indulged their mutual taste for sketching. Percy, to whom artists were a race apart, had smiled indulgently when she submitted her drawings – billows engulfing stranded wrecks, trees surmounting savage rocks, crumbling manor houses, farmyard wains – for his approval. She noticed how his eyes had darkened when he heard that once again she had been squired on these excursions by the admirable Tony. At the same time he had been disarmingly complaisant. "Enjoy yourself, by all means," he remarked. "I am tied to Shorncliffe; and in any case the parade ground has spoiled me for the ballroom. I must meet Harte. Who is he? The third son of Lord Clancarty? A man of good reputation?"

The two men had met; an encounter not completely successful; Tony excessively polite, her husband stiff, constrained. But she assured Percy that her new friend was a model of discretion. "Then I leave you to your own devices," he said curtly ... As the friendship deepened, the implicit trust of her husband moved Harriet to grave dissimulation. She grew to relate only a part of what passed between Harte and herself – dalliance, secret assignations. Percy knew nothing of the letters, which passed between them, missives of romantic fancy where in Tony signed himself "Hector", and Harriet (who knew next to nothing of classical lore), "Andromache". Percy would have thought this conceit unspeakably frivolous – not so Harriet. To break the seal of a euphemistic note inviting one to sail upon the "wine dark" sea, or to dance in the "Olympian Grove", though the first was no more than the English Channel, and the second the crowded Assembly Rooms, was inconceivably thrilling. No trace of this correspondence remained; all letters had been destroyed on receipt; but a certain fragrance lingered. The break came when Tony was directed to travel abroad, she gathered on secret official business.

He wrote at intervals from Italy, Greece, Prussia and Sweden. The newspaper reference announcing his dispatch to the Peninsular had come as a complete surprise. She was not a little hurt that her whilom cavalier had landed in England at last, only to depart without a line of greeting. He may have been unable to do so, and it was easy to excuse him. There were the demands of Government, and of his own people; he would need to buy horses and collect equipment. Was there a tender attachment elsewhere? But she was not unduly vexed. They had to meet but once, she felt, and the old magic, like a mantle, would fall around them.

Back at the table she took up the cards and slowly reshuffled the pack. "I wonder how it will work out this time," she murmured, and was distinctly pleased when the first card revealed a king of hearts ...

* * *

Harriet wrote to Jane from Hythe—

"After the splendid news about Vimiero – which no doubt you will have seen in the public prints – we are all agog to leave. I am in great favour here. Colonel Pomeroy *insisted* that I attend the commanding officer's parade, to 'blood me' as he archly put it! He is pleasant in a rustic-bucolic fashion; but doesn't quite know if to treat me as a fellow officer, or a curious specimen of camp-follower ...

"He has no light conversation. The last time we met he enlarged – can you imagine? – on the subject of 'scale' flogging. Never would he go at one time beyond a hundred lashes! Deserters he preferred to shoot; hanging – when the rope refused its office – was so damned awkward! You had to swing on the fellow's legs, and men had a distinct aversion to it... I asked him how he thought the regiment would behave in the face of the enemy, and he replied, 'There is one secret I wish to impart – it is that every man should keep in step. Keep in step and you will fall to no harm. That's how we lost the American war damme! ... the forests, the trees, where men couldn't keep in step!' I asked Percy what he thought of Pomeroy; he answered, 'I don't think of him at all!' Obviously not in step! ...

"Susan Thompson shapes very well. I have provided her with several copies of the *Lady's Magazine* so that she may study coiffures and the latest modes. She is not so nimble with her fingers as Betty, whom I trust is making satisfactory progress. But I believe Thompson tries hard though I think I detect a certain hypochondrial strain in her nature; for hours she will sit without speaking, except to inquire about essentials. She brings me no gossip. One would have thought that the novelty of Hythe, and the cheerful bustle about her would have worked wonders. Still, I have her now, and it is of little use to yearn for the admirable Betty ..."

* * *

Marching orders came for September 1st: the regiment would take the coast road to Dover. Mrs Foulkes who intended to ride Felix, apologised when she informed Sue that the girl's place would be with the baggage. "I am sorry I can't do better for you, but in Portugal where we land, I will see that you have a mount of your own, a gentle mule, and after that we will ride together ... I am afraid we shall be in great trouble tomorrow. The women are to draw lots; all without exception wish to go, but that is impossible. The Major is sure that there will be painful scenes on the parade ground. You see how fortunate we both are."

Next evening Foulkes returned to the terrace swearing softly beneath his breath. The draw had been conducted; women in turn taking from a jar slips of paper inscribed "To Go", and "Not to Go". The rejected gave way to tears, hysteria, the tearing of hair. The banshee wailings of the Irishwomen had thoroughly upset their husbands who murmured sullenly in the ranks. Foulkes observed that he would rather tackle a dozen forlorn hopes than go through the whole detestable business again. "How many travel with us?" inquire Harriet. "Too many," he replied sternly, adding in a milder tone, "about sixty, not including children." He did not look at his wife, who found it prudent to withhold comment. "Carrying a nursery upon one's back!" he grumbled.

The auspicious morning dawned to a cool sea-mist, presage of humid hours to follow. Sue, awakened by drum-taps, dressed quickly. She arranged Harriet's hair, ate a hurried meal, and helped carry the valises including her own holdall to the parade ground where horses were already harnessed to wagons containing the fortunate wives and children. Sue halted beside a vehicle which seemed less heavily loaded than the rest, passed up the luggage, set her foot on the hub of the wheel, and climbed in. The driver thumped a package into shape so that she could sit in reasonable comfort. "T"is on'y the Serjeant Major's spare trowsis," he grunted, "you can press 'em for 'im." He reached forward to gather up what he termed "the ribbins", and reins in hand, gave her a friendly grin.

After some little delay, the Baggage-master appeared, shouted an order, and to a ragged cheer from men who had assembled to see their families off, the train rumbled out. Sue was spared the painful scene which came later when the regiment marched off – the despairing cries of the women who were left behind intermingled with the music of the band …

Jolting along at the rate of about four miles an hour, the train hugged the beach almost all the way from Hythe to Sandgate. For a time they rode in silence. Of the half dozen occupants of Sue's vehicle only the nearest, a sturdy apple-cheeked woman, a plaid shawl about her shoulders the corners of which were tucked in at the waist, ventured a remark. "You're Missis Foulkes' girl, aren't ye? Wheer ye from?" Sue informed her, and the subject dropped. As the others tended to speak only in whispers, the girl could not help but feel that as one in close contact with the officer class, she was somewhat suspect – in short might be a regimental tale-bearer. But this reserve was soon broken. After a time all were chatting freely. Sue turned to her companion.

"Have you been with the army long?"

"This is her third," interposed the driver, thrusting out his tongue and gazing at the sky.

"The third regiment?" inquired Sue.

"Imperant devil!" said the woman. "'E would mean if 'e could talk, 'at Rayner's me third 'usband. Not that it signifies. The others was unfortunate." A faraway look crept into her eyes. Sue wondered what Mrs Rayner meant by 'unfortunate'.

"No offence," said the driver. "I on'y shows you can't keep a good woman down."

"Me first was drownded," said Mrs Rayner, turning to Sue.

"In what?" asked the driver ironically.

"In the sea," responded the woman solemnly. "Me second just deed."

"I am sorry," said Sue.

"But Rayner is a good man," continued the other. "'E makes me a fair 'lowance. I could name a lot wuss." And she fixed the driver with an accusing stare. "What is Missis Foulkes like to you lass?"

"I can't complain," said Sue.

"You're lucky. Some nivver knows what they'll be wantin' next."

"She'll put the fear o' God into the French," said the driver.

"Which is moor than you'll ivver do," said Mrs Rayner.

"Do you want chucking off?" asked the driver lazily.

"Tek a better man than you to do that," said Mrs Rayner.

An agonised howl and a chorus of female voices interrupted the conversation. One of the children had fallen from a wagon. The train stopped. "My grief!" The driver spat in disgust. "What we 'ave to put up with!"

"You've nothink but a norse to look after," said Mrs Rayner scathingly. "You don't know you're born."

"Well," ruminated the man as they resumed movement – he slipped a quid in his mouth and softened the tobacco – "if the wives didn't want to be wi' the 'usbands, and the childer didn't want to be wi' the wives, it ud save everybody a lot o' trouble. It's all a game."

"What game?" asked Mrs Rayner.

"Nabbin' 'usbands. I've seed 'em i' 'Olland, their men shot down, a weepin' an' awailing' like billyho, jumpin' into the grave if you please; an' before you can say 'Jack Robinson' they've took the next man off the muster roll."

"What is a poor woman to do?" asked Mrs Rayner indignantly, "alone in a foreign land."

"Aye – what?"

"Never you mind."

"All right," said her tormentor, "let's all look forrard to Portygul, the land that is flowin' wi' milk an' honey – if it be but asses milk – which reminds me, I'm thirstly."

He produced a jar of ale, which he had taken the precaution to wrap in a wet sack, and with it a can. He poured out. "Down the sink!" he chuckled, waiting patiently until all had been served before he indulged himself.

By this time the mist had disappeared. Dew sparkled on the hedgerows; the sea lay barred with delicate greens and blues … Raising dust, they rumbled through the orchards and cornfields of Kent, until to the background of a towering cliff, the red roofs of Dover came in sight.

"Yon's the 'arbour," said the driver, pointing with his whip, "masts thick as bean poles, and – bless my soul! – " He shaded his eyes with his hand, "I vow I can see your very ship." When they asked him how he could possibly know this, he answered that the captain was his uncle, and that he (the driver) had been the greatest fool on earth not to have taken service with him. "Went down on his bended knees, 'e did for me to sail." But the women, their eyes fastened on the seaport, had no mind for his foolishness.

They drew up. The baggage master led the wagons to the quayside where all were ordered not to stray into the town on any account.

Later, to the strains of "Over the Hills and Far Away", the columns marched in, Mrs Foulkes in her feathered hat and grey serge riding dress, bringing up the rear with an air of escorting the whole …

CHAPTER V

The *Caledonia*, a brig of five hundred tons burthen, employed during the past thirty years in the Newcastle-London coaling trade, swung at her moorings. Coal-dust oozed from her seams, begrimed her yards and canvas, gritted underfoot on deck. Harriet who had expected the trim amenities of a first class frigate, a model of gleaming varnish and winking brass, was shocked when she learned that his execrable tub was to be their means of transport. She had prepared herself for a certain measure of inconvenience, but to be ferried (as she put it) to Spain "in a basket of coals", was quite intolerable. Creatures of dust and filth, in what condition would they land? As blackamoors? Colonel Pomeroy, she noticed, had found a better ship, and to the Major's annoyance implied that with the slightest initiative, he could have done as well.

She continued to fret and fume. When conveyed to the "spare cabin" – the officers being herded in the Captain's quarters – she emitted a strangled laugh, for it was no more than a cubicle with a hinged table and a bunk fashioned like a coffin. She called for the Captain. This gentleman who had just lost two members of his crew to the Press Gang, and was in no accommodating mood, appeared at last puffing at a pipe of rank tobacco, the smoke of which he did not scruple to send in her direction. When Captain Croker did not suck his pipe, he waved it like a baton. "T'is all planned by the Transport Board, Ma'm," he said stolidly. "If ye have a case, ye must inform London, not me. I can provide a pen and ink if ye would wish to write." Since the vessel was now clearing harbour and rolling to the Channel swell, this remark she considered a calculated impertinence. "But here," she protested, "is a hovel, a mere closet, positively reeking of bad bacon and tallow – not fit for a dog! I claim consideration." The cabin had indeed been a storeroom, now emptied for passenger accommodation. But when the Captain assured her that these were "healthy smells," she exploded. "T'is nothing but the Black Hole of Calcutta!" she cried.

"Never tied up there, Ma'm," said the Captain coolly.

"Oh!"

If, Croker continued, appearing to relent, the lady was dissatisfied with her quarters, she was at liberty to sleep with the officers in his own cabin. This suggestion, construed by Harriet as an additional mark of rudeness, was the last straw. "I've done with you!" she proclaimed, "quite!"

"As you please, lady," he said pulling at his hat brim, "but I can do no better." And abruptly turned away.

"The ruffian!" she cried. "The uncouth hound."

She was not really showing to advantage. The Major, whom she next sought out, gave little comfort. "You must be accommodating," he pleaded, "with the best will in the world we cannot transform the ship into an East Indiaman. What cannot be cured must be endured."

"If we are bandying proverbs," she retorted, "there are none so blind as those who will not see!"

"The Captain is absolute master of the ship," he explained smoothly. "He could put us all in irons if he wished."

"What nonsense!" she said. But there was nothing more but to move into the cubicle and make the best of it.

The rank and file had disappeared down the main hatch to a region darker and more malodorous than the quarters allotted to Mrs Foulkes. Stacking knapsacks and bundles among the stout, rough-timbered coal-bunkers, they accepted their lot with easy profanity and good humour. Hard living was in the texture of common experience. Many were drawn from the cabins and bogs of Ireland; others from insanitary country cottages, some from the tumbledown slums around Whitehall. Change and discomfort were the soldier's lot; but bare boards were a sight better than flinty stones. Here at least was shelter from the night frosts and rain. A few grumbled at the lack of straw.

Mrs Foulkes remarked, that when darkness fell, Sue would be required to join the rank and file. "I am sorry to thrust you into the crowd," she explained, "but I had expected a spacious cabin with room for two at least. It was not to be, so we must do the best we can. Rejoin me the first thing in the morning."

The convoy had made the open Channel when the long summer's day drew to a close. The sun set, throwing across the metalled waves a band of quivering fire. As the brig shouldered her way through the deepening night, her riding lamps contended with the stars. Dismissed by Harriet, Sue lingering for a time on deck tried to catch a last glimpse of the English coast; but she could see little, only a few widely separated points of light, elusive as fireflies. A gust of wind brought a strand of hair about her face, a dash of spray. She ran the tip of her tongue across her lips tasting salt...

She heard someone say that the wind was rising; the impression grew that she had been trapped. If only she could make her way to the deck again. A child gave a plaintive cry. Then a wave of nausea overwhelmed her. She lost all interest in time and place ...

Inert, her head sagging between her knees, she moaned. A woman beside her said, "Feeling bad, dearie?" "I should feel better," Sue gasped, "if only the ship were still." The woman sniffed. "We can on'y wait for dayleet," she said, and was silent. Sue gazed witlessly across the hold. A large number seemed not affected by the motion of the vessel at all. A voice, sadly ironic, lifted in a strain—

O a sailor's life's a pleasant life,
He freely roams from shore to shore—

a sentiment however, at once drowned in a chorus of protesting voices. A slight rustling behind Sue suggested the presence of rats. Rats always prepared to leave a sinking ship. Were they doing so now?...

Time dragged. Her head had become a dead weight on her shoulders; her legs were cramped. If only she could rid herself of the intolerable sour lining of her mouth! She yearned for water. Once she chewed the corner of her shawl, but the rough fibres only added to her thirst. "O God, how long!" she breathed. In a thin voice she inquired for the time. The question being overheard by a private, who owned a watch, evoked the response that it was one in the morning.

Through a haze of fatigue she observed others; the shoulder of the man who had ventured the time came within her line of vision. There was nothing extraordinary in that; but what brought her to attention was a hand poised stealthily over the recumbent figure – a hand bearing a scar! She caught a quick breath staring fixedly at the spot until the vessel rolled and the light of the lamp receded. When it returned however, the hand was still more or less in place, and faintly she could discern the scar. Forgetting weakness and cramp, she continued to watch. Stealthily the hand now slid across the tunic of the man with the watch. The sleeper stirred, and the hand half withdrew; but only for a few seconds. Then it moved again.

With a low snarl the victim of this incursion heaved up grabbing at the hand. A scuffle followed, a confused welter of arms and faces; then a fierce wrangle in which the man of the hand assured the owner of the watch that no mischief had been intended. At no time in the shifting play of light and shade could Sue catch more than a glimpse of the two faces. At length, after further bickering, both men resettled in their places, though the man of the watch she noticed, reclined with folded arms.

Sue still watched. She wondered if it might be possible to work into a position beside the two men, but the hold was heavily congested, and even if she did manage – what then? In truth she did not know. She closed her eyes, but not to sleep, conscious that in all probability she was now within a few feet of Jacob Harker himself. The old slattern of Tollgate had not deceived her; that he had assumed a name other than his own she did not for a moment doubt. For the time being therefore, she could only watch and wait.

Sheer tiredness supervened, and she fell into uneasy sleep, dreaming that in a quite unrecognisable domain she was riding a mule through mountains, and that when she tugged at the reins the animal turned its head, addressed her in perfect English, and lo! she found herself looking into the smouldering eyes of Major Foulkes …

* * *

When she awoke, a shaft of sunlight pierced the murk of the hold; the hatch had been removed and the Quartermast was ordering relays to draw rations. The sleep of exhaustion had left her heavy-eyed, stiff, aching. She hauled herself upright clinging to the bunker side, then because the brig was still rolling heavily she lurched towards the ladder, reaching for what little support she could find.

Though day had fully come, it was difficult to recognise surrounding faces. Overhead, the lanterns smoked, heavy with grime; but the light they shed was useless. She had by no means forgotten Harker; but her tongue paper-dry, and her mouth abominably sour, she felt that above everything else she must have water. And she was beginning to feel hungry ... After a time she secured her portion of beef and biscuit together with a pannikin of water, and with these settled in the first vacant place she could find. The meat, hacked into chunks, and army-style boiled in the copper, was tasteless and stringy; even so, it was better than nothing. The water tasted of tar, but she drank most of it, reserving a little for a "cat-lick" wash.

She had no sooner done this when she heard her own name called out insistently – "Susan Thompson ... pass the word for Susan Thompson!" It was the Major's man announcing that she was desired at once in the Captain's cabin. Combing her hair and smoothing out her rumpled skirts, she climbed on deck where she found Stubbs presiding over the hatch. "Ho," he said recognising her, "did you henjoy your beauty sleep?"

"Yes, Serjeant Major – did you?"

Stubbs growled. He had spent an uncomfortable night, partly wedged in a draughty sail-locker; and partly with the horses, one of which had smashed its makeshift stall like a matchwood. "You 'ad better be getting' half, young lady," he responded, "by which hi mean the rearwards part o' the boat." And he pointed towards the stern.

"Thank you kindly," she said.

"Sir! To you," he barked.

"I must have forgotten." The slightly mocking note in her voice made Stubbs stare fiercely. He opened his mouth to speak, but thought better of it. "All alike!" he muttered darkly, "all lip!" He turned and vented his spleen upon a luckless infantryman whose stock was a little awry.

As Sue made her way hand by hand along the rail, it seemed that the brig lay uncomfortably low in the water; but after so many foetid hours below the wind on her cheeks was welcome. For a few moments she watched the rush of foam-flecked waves alongside. Not too much distant, not too near, other vessels of the convoy curtseyed to the morning. That of the Commodore had run up a string of signals. Noting the vari-coloured scraps of bunting, she wondered what these meant.

She found the stern cabin and knocked lightly on the door. At once the Major appeared, his sparse hair snatched by the breeze. "You are here at last!" he growled. "My wife has suffered an accident. Attend to her will you?"

Sue entered. Three officers were grouped in one angle of the stern window. From behind a tarpaulin screen fixed across the other side came the impatient voice of her mistress, "Is that you, Thompson?"

The girl raised the flap of the shelter, and entered, dropping it behind her. "Oh, Ma'm!" she cried. Mrs Foulkles, who was half-sitting half reclining on a mound of blankets, said, "You may well be surprised; this is the gypsy tent to which I am reduced!"

"What indeed, has happened, Ma'm?"

"I was flung," answered her mistress resentfully, "from one side of the dog-kennel in which I was immured, to the other, striking my head terribly. And there I lay alone, half-dead – it must have been for hours. I fear I am disfigured. Please unpack my looking glass. The valise has been brought in."

Sue unbuckled the bag and produced the required article into which Harriet at once peered anxiously. She sighed angrily at a discoloured bruise above her right eye. "I was afraid so!"

"A piece of raw steak applied Ma'am," suggested Sue.

"Very well," said Harriet sarcastically, "go find a butcher!"

"A touch of powder, perhaps."

"Pah! It goes deeper than that. My head sings. Bring me the drops and a liquor flask. I must doctor myself."

The mishap had set the seal on Harriet's disillusionment. The squalid condition of the brig had appalled her; but the physical injury drove her to fury. At a time when she had hoped to grace a convivial board of attentive subalterns, the beast of a Captain (for who but he was responsible for the navigation of the ship?) had contrived her personal disfigurement. To be adorned with a monstrous black eye! She turned down Sue's suggestion of a rearrangement of hair with brusque contempt. It was quite evident that she was in no mood to be comforted. Two glasses of liquor moved her to action. She called her husband across. "Major Foulkes," she said firmly, "I must see that man."

"Whom do you mean – what man?"

"You know very well – Teach, Bluebeard, or whatever his name may be. The captain."

Foulkes was frankly puzzled. "For what purpose?"

"I have been injured aboard his ship; that should be sufficient."

"But—"

"You must send your servant to summon him immediately."

The Major winced, and muttered something beneath his breath. He was annoyed not only because her peremptory order had been overheard by others – his fellow officers had become significantly silent – but that she lacked the capacity to display a certain fortitude. It augured ill for the future. Thus he hovered indecisively, hoping she would sense his profound disapproval. But she was not to be denied. She must see the Captain.

Still embarrassed, Foulkes turned to his servant who was occupied in the background. "Find Captain Croker," he said coldly, "present my compliments, and ask if he will at his convenience, attend here on Mrs Foulkes. At his convenience, mind."

"Yes, sir."

The man saluted and left. Foulkes, who did not intend to be present during the proposed interview, murmured that he wished to look at the horses, and also passed out on deck ...

After some little delay, Captain Croker, massive in sea-boots and pea jacket lumbered in, confronted his passenger and bowed awkwardly. "Your pleasure, Ma'm?" he queried.

An image of injured propriety, Harriet eyed him coldly. As though to emphasise her plight, she touched her bruise and winced. "What are you doing with this ship?" she asked sternly.

The Captain beamed. "Just plain sailing, Ma'm."

"Plain enough to endanger life and limb!"

"That's the first I've heard of it," he responded cheerfully, "no complaints from any quarter, except if you would wish to make one. Have you fallen Ma'm?"

"I should not have suffered this if you had carried less canvas," said Harriet, repeating an observation by one of the subalterns.

The Captain's face reddened as he thrust his head forward like that of an angry bull; but he managed to restrain his temper. "A high-flyer" he told himself.

"I have never before sailed under such wretched conditions," she persisted.

"As to that Ma'm, I have no means of knowing – regarding the vessel I had orders from the Commodore to increase sail."

Checked, she turned a contemptuous shoulder. "I can only pray that you don't send us all to the bottom."

"Never touched bottom yet," he bantered, "leastways as far as I can remember."

When she concluded by announcing that she would report him to the owners, he retorted roundly that as he himself was the owner, her complaint would receive personal attention. In the meantime, while always her obedient humble servant, he must beg to be excused, and so departed. As he passed her on his way out, Sue heard him mutter between his teeth, "She, who don't know a ship from a shaving pan, a 'teaching me!"

Having given vent to her feelings, Harriet felt much better; later, when she presided at table it was with more than her accustomed charm. She played down her mishap, adding lightly that she was proud to have been the first casualty in the service of her country. The Major sat silent, immersed in his own thoughts. He reflected uneasily that Harriet's presence among them tended to restrict conversation, and that this was bound to continue. What would happen when they were united with Pomeroy? ... He thrust this speculation aside. Sufficient unto the day—

Sue now remained at Harriet's elbow. When not occupied by sewing she improved her knowledge by dipping into a volume of the *Lady's Magazine*, studying the fashion plates, concentrating mainly on coiffures. At Hythe, Harriet had effected a classical style – curls caught up and bunched at the back, but on shipboard she found it more convenient to have a single parting in the middle of her forehead, combed smoothly to the sides and curled back in a roll. She was so pleased with Sue's improved treatment of her hair, that Betty was quite unregretted. She set Sue making a "Spencer", the material for which she had purchased at Hythe. The girl had already cut out the woollen lining.

Sitting unobtrusively in a corner, Sue watched others. What a hunting squire the red-faced, burly Captain Daiches was! She could see him on frosty mornings, galloping at the tail of his pack, roaring over hill and dale, returning at dusk to a well-laden table complete with steaming punch. By contrast, Captain Harrod, perhaps because his features were pale and finely chiselled, seemed almost effeminate, something of a dandy, and tending in speech to drawl, he had been for a time of the Prince of Wales's intimate circle. He referred often – perhaps from the covert glances exchanged between his colleagues, a little too often – to "The Pavilion" and to "Carlton House", a centre of Whig influence. But he was, withal, an essentially good-natured fellow. Captains Creighton and Fairbank she saw as inveterate gamblers, marking gains and losses gravely in their pocket books. They handled little cash, dealing mainly in IOU's, with periodical grand accounting.

Of the junior officers, Lieutenant Suckly, was the only one with any pretension to reading. He carried in his immediate baggage copies of Shakespeare, Addison and Johnson. He had also brought aboard an issue of the *Political Register*, a journal which being perused by his colleagues, provoked violent debate. From this and succeeding altercations, Sue gathered that the editor, Mr Cobbett, was a man with whom no gentleman would willingly associate. Suckly however, partly redeemed himself by expertly playing the flute. One evening after having entertained the company with compositions by Scarlatti, he concluded with a piece which he announced the work of Frederick the Great. At once, the Major, who had hitherto listened indifferently, attended with the respect he felt was due to the victor of Leuthen and Rossbach.

The rest – Lieutenants James, Bird, Welldon and Carworth, were much of a piece, poured into the same social mould; students of horse-flesh, actresses and pugilists. Deprived for the moment of these diversions, they found solace in cards and the bottle. Sue, being fair game, was subject to occasional coltish by-play, though Harriet's presence remained a restraining influence. At times, tired of cards, they laid bets to a wider field: that one of their number would be the first to set foot upon Spanish soil; that Lord Sandwich would expire before the end of the year; that the next child born to Lady Ancaster would be a boy, and such like. On deck they hung over the stern-rail discharging pistols at floating bottles, or empty casks towed at the end of a rope. Ensign Waters, a pale gangling youth, completed the group. A schoolboy thrust into an adult world, Sue could not help feeling sorry for him. He was always on the fringe, too callow almost to defend himself, and certainly too poor to gamble at cards …

The war, of course, was an unending subject of conversation. At Dover they had heard of the Convention of Cintra, and were considerably perplexed thereby. That the defeated General Juno and his men should be allowed not only to depart, but to be shipped back to France in British bottoms, they felt particularly shameful.

"With the honours of war!" gloomed Creighton.

Daiches exploded. "We nab the fox, and by God he walks away laughing."

"The London City Council I note," said Suckley, "has demanded a court-marital."

"Small wonder!"

Foulkes pursed his lips, but said nothing. The youthful ensign inquiring please, where Cintra was, received no reply.

"What lies behind it all?" asked Harriet.

The Major feeling all eyes turned in his direction took snuff with some deliberation, dusted his tunic, and passed his hand over his eyes. ("Pray silence for the oracle!" whispered Bird to Carworth.)

"The Convention," began Foulkes, "from such information we have, would appear to be a sorry business, and I am not surprised at the outcry against it; but let us not jump to conclusions. There may be more in this than meets the eye." ("A lecture, begad!" whispered Carworth to Bird.)

With marked disapproval the Major waited for the whispering to cease. He had long formed an adverse opinion of Bird's capacity as an officer. "The French," he resumed, "though splendidly beaten had not lost the game. They still held a trump card."

"I don't see—" began Daiches.

Foulkes held up a warning finger. "Just a moment. They were in Lisbon remember, where they could have worked great destruction both to harbour and shipping. Now do we want Lisbon with all its facilities for transport, or do we not? We need all the means that we can get, so we let the French go."

"A golden bridge," murmured Suckley.

"Exactly. What port is there to equal Lisbon? The Portuguese are our long standing allies. We shall be more than welcome there."

"I still do not comprehend," persisted Daiches, "why we should butter up the French who were honourably copped."

"It is a time-honoured custom," said Foulkes, " for a defeated enemy to march out with drums beating and flags flying."

"Why?"

The Major raised his eyebrows slightly. "Tradition!" he replied curtly.

"A little out of date," grumbled Daiches.

"If you think so," said Foulkes, "some don't."

A strained silence fell.

"I gather, sir," ventured Suckley, changing the subject, "that the Peninsular is replete with old Moorish fortresses? May these be of use to the French?"

Foulkes settled himself anew, an eager look in his eyes, for Suckley, unwittingly enough, had touched upon one of the Major's pet enthusiasms – the art and practice of fortification. Under the table, Bird kicked Suckley's shins. The subaltern disliked all professional dissertations; but Foulkes was already speaking—

"Such works would not for long withstand modern siege artillery. On the other hand they may well be strengthened. The French are past masters at that kind of thing. French fortresses," continued the Major briskly, at the same time reaching for his tablet and pencil, "are more involved than you would imagine. Here, as you see—" Swiftly he sketched a many pointed star, and warming to his theme, explained that every angle and bastion was a self-contained fort, with its own guns and garrison; the line of each wall covered by a flanking fire of cannon and muskets. "This," he said, stabbing the paper with his forefinger, "is an outline – rough of course – of Vauban's Louvain." He raised his head sharply, and in doing so intercepted a wink intended by Lieutenant Bird for Carworth. A flush of cold anger took him. He shot a glance at Suckley, but that young gentleman was studying his fingernails. The culprit, who did not realise that he had been observed, sat stolidly impassive. "And," thought Foulkes, "such oafs are placed in command of men!"

He dropped his pencil as he continued: "To the best of my knowledge there are no Vauban fortresses in Spain; but if you were investing one, Lieutenant Bird, how would you proceed?" Pushing the tablet across to the startled subaltern, Foulkes placed his fingers together tip to tip, while Bird, who was shuffling a pack of cards preparatory to a game of whist, set these down again.

"I don't understand, sir," he said vaguely.

"Then allow me to make myself clear," rejoined his superior officer. "Assume that you were investing a Spanish stronghold, how would you drive your parallels?" The Major took a pinch of snuff, crossed his legs, and gazed fixedly at a beam overhead. The Lieutenant laughed sheepishly; he knew little of fortification, and cared less. That was the role of miners, pioneers. He was annoyed to catch a glimpse of Mrs Foulkes' enigmatical smile, and wondered what it meant. Frowning, he took up the pencil, managed to add a few lines to the diagram, scratched his head somewhat, added others, and hoping for the best pushed the tablet across. The Major scrutinised the junior officer's handiwork, and coughed dryly. "The damned pedagogue!" thought Bird uneasily.

"How do you advance your men?" inquired Foulkes smoothly. "Where are your communicating trenches? Please complete." He handed back the tablets. Bird, by this time his face almost as red as his tunic, tried desperately to improve his concept; but on receiving it again, the Major smiled sourly. "You would be wiped out by an infilading fire!"

"That is as I see it," muttered Bird sullenly. "What should I do?"

"Transfer to the engineers!" murmured Harrod.

"You really do not know?" insisted the Major.

"No – no, sir," Bird admitted reluctantly. To cover his embarrassment he began to shuffle the cards.

"An officer who would wish to advance in his profession," observed Foulkes icily, "cannot afford to wink at its problems."

So that was it! The Major had noted his gesture towards Carworth. "What a pettifogger – an old grandmother!" he thought, as he studied the queen of hearts which topped the pack in his hand. He raised his head to catch the flicker of a smile, not altogether unsympathetic, from Harriet, and Bird wondered what could have induced a woman so attractive to unite herself with an antique snuff box like Foulkes. With a faintly responsive smile, he lay the queen of hearts face uppermost on the table, not knowing quite why he did so. Harriet eyed the slip of pasteboard reflectively, and her smile faded.

Bird however was still denied a game. The Major put away his tablets, but some mention of the Prince of Wales launched Harrod into personal reminiscence. At first he spoke of Carlton House, the Prince's personal taste in furnishing; this led to a description of life in the fabulous Pavilion at Brighton, not without, he claimed, its moments of delicious comedy. "I well remember," drawled Harrod, "being at Brighton when the first news of Austerlitz came through in terms – if you please! of a French *defeat*. The Prince, naturally, was jubilant, and since he professed to know more about military matters than anyone else, must needs call for the largest map in the Pavilion to explain where the French line had broken, and how they would retreat. This, of course, was all humbug. He knew no more than the rest of us. Next day when the news came through proclaiming Boney's triumph, he was so mortified that he sat – literally sat – on the newspapers, and would allow no one to see them. Then followed the most delicious burlesque you ever saw, not bettered by Sheridan." Harrod glanced around the circle. "Any here acquainted, or have heard of, Tony Harte?"

Harriet lifted her head with a startled look. Her husband looked in her direction; conscious of his eyes she studied her rings. "Indeed, yes," she said in a low voice. The others were silent.

"In that case, Ma'm," continued Harrod, "you for one will not be surprised at the sequel. Or perhaps you have heard the story already?"

Harriet shook her head.

"Well, this man Harte," resumed the Captain, "who with others had listened to Prinny's exercise in fiction, produced the self-same map which had been used on the previous day, and with perfect gravity enlarged the story of the French defeat; here the French centre had been completely shattered, there so many guns had been lost, ten eagles captured – or was it fifteen? and three marshals taken prisoner. In view of this asked Tony, did not His Royal Highness feel that an instant peel of bells would be in order? ... Throughout, Prinny, who was in no mind to admit his limitation, fumed and fidgeted, until he could bear the prank no longer. "Damn my eyes!" he said, "Of all the miserable lies in Christendom, I swear that this is the worst!" And stalked away. Upon my honour I think that only a Tony Harte could have carried the thing off." He turned to Harriet. "So you know him?"

"We met during the season at Brighton." She was still occupied with her rings. In the uncertain light of the cabin it seemed to the Major that her colour had deepened.

"But not at the Pavilion, I'll warrant. The Prince had done with him from that hour."

"Elsewhere," she said, "- we drew together."

"Drew together?" Harrod repeated in a puzzled tone.

"I mean," she explained hastily, "that we were both interested in the art of sketching."

"Yes," rejoined Harrod thoughtfully, "I recollect that interest too."

The Major, suspecting a slight innuendo stirred uneasily, and the pang of jealousy which he had felt at Hythe returned. A pinch of snuff did not help to assuage this feeling. Also he was vaguely offended by the bearing of the anecdote; the frivolous treatment by Prinny and his circle, of a major military disaster. Men who had fought and suffered and died, ought not to be made the subject of parlour games. What a crew the Pavilion set were! – fribbles, dandies in ermine. Metaphors failed him as he continued to stare into the shadows ...

At last Harriet repaired to her cabin, this time taking Sue with her. Cramped as the quarters were, she decided that henceforth they would make do; but she was determined not to be left alone. Sue was glad to conform, though it would mean no more than blanket perhaps for covering, and a valise for a pillow. They did not undress. Harriet squeezed into her bunk; Sue sank to the floor in a sitting position, her back to the bulkhead. But the former could not sleep. Harrod's reference to Tony had moved her profoundly; the old yearning revived, and as the dark hours passed she dwelt upon the

future. It would be pleasant enough, exciting even, to discuss Tony with
Harrod; but on the whole, indiscreet. Better not. His discerning eyes might
read too closely into the workings of her own heart ... As the brig lurched
and rolled in the void of night, she continued to toss restlessly ...

Only a few feet away, half sitting, half reclining, Susan Thompson almost
wished that she was back again in the hold; there at any rate she would find
conversation. Her mind reverted to the fate of her brother. What did "transportation" mean? Vaguely she knew that it was associated with fever-haunted
plantations, slaves toiling under the lash; but in what distant country and
under what flag? One day (she decided) she should ask the pleasant, knowledgeable, Lieutenant Suckley for information. In the meantime she tried to
comfort herself with the assurance that Robin, industrious as he undoubtedly
was, would somehow pull through, and in due course be enabled to return
home. Suddenly reacting, she felt all speculation vain. She remembered an
expression often employed by the Major – "We must wait upon the event!"
It was one, which she never used herself, but she could think of nothing better now ...

The cabin door rattled incessantly; spray thrashed upon the panels, the
sails boomed, the spars creaked, water gushed and gurgled through the scup-
pers. She lapsed into a dimly conscious state, floating down interminable
avenues where from the shadows hands reached out towards her; hands
bronzed and gnarled, hands blanched and bony, hands matted with hairs,
hands searching, hands aggressive. If only she could win free of the hands! ...

* * *

When his fellow officers had settled for the night, Foulkes took from his baggage a well-worn copy of Plutarch's *Lives*, and opening the flap of a lantern
– he had no use at all for fiction – the eminent lives of Greeks and Romans
remained his invariable bed-book. He was attracted not only by the martial
content of the narrative, but by the statecraft, the intrigue, forays by land and
sea, the policing of frontiers, the commingling of nations and races. He liked
the sober unhurried style, the urbane observation. Steeped in Plutarch, you
had a grounding in almost everything. He had, of course, his favourite chapters, situations and heroes – Alexander and Julius Caesar, for example; the
latter above all. At times he had urged this reading upon his younger colleagues, but alas! without success. Suckly excepted, he could think of no one
likely to turn these pages. Officers stopped at the infantry manual, and a
good many knew little of that.

By chance Foulkes opened at a page in the career of Caesar where the
young patrician, Publius Clodius, rich, eloquent, but at the same time vicious
and profligate, was attracted by Caesar's wife. "Nor did she," Foulkes read,
"discountenance him. At the feast of Bona Dea, whom the gods called the

mother of Bacchus, an exclusive female celebration of which that year Pompeia was directress, this Clodius in collaboration with a maidservant stole in disguised as a woman. Discovered, he fled, but the affair made a great scandal in the city, so that Caesar immediately divorced Pompeia. Yet when called upon to give evidence at the trial, he said he knew nothing about Clodius. When asked why then had he divorced his wife, Caesar answered, "I would have the chastity of my wife clear even of suspicion." A master touch thought the Major, marking the place ...

He looked around. In one hammock flanking the stern window, wrapped in a boat cloak, Harrod was sleeping soundly, his handsome face (Foulkes thought) a little vacant in repose. One could not of course resent his acquaintance with Harte, nor blame him for raising the spectre of Brighton, but the Prince's familiars were all tarred with the same brush – silly, promiscuous, ineffective. Recalling Caesar, Foulkes smiled faintly. What more foolish than to make a mountain out of Harriet's Brighton molehill? "Not stupid Clodius," he murmured. "I must guard against suspicion, be patient too, under provocation." He was almost sorry now that he had admonished young Bird ...

He fell to wondering how a man like Harrod would behave under fire. He did not doubt the courage of Daiches, a no-nonsense fellow, would roar blindly into battle, nor that of Bird who would charge into the cannon's mouth like a bull across a meadow. Suckley, for all his flute, could be tenacious enough; but what of the drawing room exquisite, the lounging *flaneur* – would he screw to the sticking point?

The speculation remained unanswered. It was in this mood that Foulkes closed his book, took a final pinch of snuff, and after listening for a time to the blind, interminable rush of waters, composed himself to sleep ...

* * *

When next morning, Sue, who had been conceded the boon of "a little fresh air", walked on deck, she found herself surrounded by the women who had just come up from below. These for the most part had thrown off their sickness, and were enjoying the steady breeze, and the sunlight dancing on the water. She greeted Mrs Rayner, the much-married lady of the baggage wagon; exchanged a few words with sloe-eyed Margaret Higgenson, whose two children Tom and Janet, were by some miracle kept extraordinarily neat and clean; and found herself bantered by plump, rosy-cheeked Ada Jenks. This dame, who conducted a profitable side-line in usury, carried her cash in a satchel strapped to her waist, but hidden from prying eyes by capacious petticoats. This record of monies which she lent out at moderate interest, she kept in her own head; but woe betide the man who for this reason, tried to evade repayment. She was held in peculiar regard by all. "Shove her in t'watter," said Private Rayner, dwelling on the weight of metal she carried, "and she's sink like a stoan!" It was hinted that on more than one occasion she had come to the assistance of needy subalterns; but this may have been no more than campfire tittle-tattle. A certain Private Jenks subsisted in the background, but he had no part nor lot in his wife's financial transactions.

All the women were earnestly looking forward to the hour when they would disembark. They badgered passing seamen with the question, "When are you sailing into port?" A voice from the mast-head shouting: "Land ho!" brought them swarming to the rail. "Spain a'ready!" they cried hopefully.

"Aye, t'is all Spain now," said Captain Croker who had come up, narrowing his eyes at the horizon. "Yon's Corunna. Look careful now abaft my finger and you'll see the lighthouse."

"Shall we land today?"

He laughed gruffly. "If ye feel inclined to swim! We're bearing off."

They voiced disapproval. "Tell us when we land!"

"Some day," said Captain Croker.

"Oh – you!" They treated the Captain with scant respect.

For his part, he grinned, pointing to the *Commodore*'s straining canvas ahead. "When yon chap lifts his little finger! Another twenty four hours, and then we'll see. In the meantime get outer my way, ye're cluttering up the deck!"

He pulled down the brim of his hat and spat overboard ...

CHAPTER VI

Eighteen hours later the fleet hove to, standing off a rocky sunlit coast. Shrouded in mist, mountains loomed in the background, but to these heights no one – not even Captain Croker – appended a name. All he conceded was, "It's Portygul right enough – that's all we're after." While there was a good deal of busy movement between one vessel and another, they watched in vain for some sign of disembarkation. "It may be that we are awaiting orders to sail on to Lisbon," Major Foulkes suggested, "on the other hand it may be more convenient – strategically I mean – if we were to land here." But he was no less impatient than the rest. They noticed that for lengthy periods he stood watching intently the large three-master containing Colonel Pomeroy and the rest of the battalion.

At last, after a trip to the Commodore, Captain Croker reckoned that debarkation would take place at Maciera Bay off which they were now lying, an item of news received with emphatic groans by the young gentleman who had been looking forward to the fleshpots of Lisbon. But the mood soon changed; after so much tossing and buffeting on shipboard, they were willing to land almost anywhere. So they hung over the salt-encrusted rail, surveying the mainland where across a low-lying ribbon of rock, enormous breakers thundered in foam. Northwards a headland thrust its brown pinnacles into the sea; but of a convenient landing place, harbour, jetty, there was no trace. They would apparently descend on the beach itself.

Sue, fascinated by the pounding billows, considered the prospect appalling; but Captain Croker whose geniality seemed to increase as the time on board of his passengers diminished, spoke words of comfort. "That's not your worrit," he remarked. "What do you think King George, God bless him!" – and here surprisingly the Captain raised his hat – "pays his loyal seamen for?" Sue, who had never met the Royal Navy at close quarter, wished she could share his assurance. She continued to watch apprehensively as the rollers exploded along the half-submerged, saw-toothed pinnacles.

A few hours later a swarm of lighters appeared converging like water-beetles around certain of the ships. Men dropped down precariously hung ladders, and were ferried to the shore. Gathering speed they reached the line of breakers where they were steadied by sailors waiting waist deep in the water and hurried to the beach. A lighter carrying horses from one of the larger vessels emptied its cargo in mid-passage; the animals scenting vegetation had plunged overboard, swimming strongly until at last finding foothold, they trotted uncertainly, or rolled and kicked up their heels in the sand.

When the turn of the *Caledonia* came, the women and children were the last to leave. They clung desperately to the swaying rope ladder, until hauled off by main force, they were settled in the lighter. Captain Croker, puffing at his everlasting pipe smiled down at them. "'Tis plain, ladies, ye're not at all anxious to leave me," he rallied, "but I wouldn't have ye back, not for a thousand pun!" Sue, to whom immersion in the foam-flecked billows seemed desperately imminent, murmured the first few syllables of the Lord's Prayer, but the words were choked in her throat as the craft senselessly plunged and lifted. She grabbed at the nearest seaman's shoulder; gently he disengaged her fingers, grinning the while. The sailors in their striped trousers, and flat-brimmed shining hats, were uniformly cheerful. One, contemptuous of the unruly ocean, shot a jet of tobacco juice into it.

About a dozen soldiers completed the party. When they had scrambled down and settled themselves, muskets upright between their knees, the craft pushed off; slowly the space between the flat boat and the vessel widened. A midshipman straddling the stern, gazed fixedly ahead directing the oarsmen. The boat heaved and swayed, its blunt bows smashing heavily into the water. Spray splashed inboard. No one spoke, but all huddled closer, the soldiers interested in keeping their weapons dry. The sailors straining at the oars grunted rhythmically. One minute passed … two minutes … and after that … an age. Sue glanced at her mistress beside whom she was sitting. A trifle pallid, Harriet's face was perfectly composed. She lent the impression that if she were to be drowned it would be with appropriate reserve ….

But the girl had little time to ponder. The voice of the midshipman sounded shrilly over their shoulders, "Make ready! Here she comes! Pull away – away! Hold fast you landlubbers!" Carried on the back of an enormous roller the boat shot into a cauldron of foam. The sailors continued to pull hard. "put your backs into it!" screamed the middy, his voice breaking with excitement. Through the surge of waters Sue heard the muttered cursing of the seaman beside her. "If it be Thy will—" she breathed, but the words died on her lips as her eyes fastened on a hand gripping the gunwale immediately ahead. Sinewy, bronzed by the sun, glistening with seawater, it was transversed by a scar, a deep blue incision, ragged like a flash of lightning. Despite the flurry of wind and sea, the creaking of oars, the straining of arms to fore and aft, she had no thought now but for the hand. Her eyes passed to a tunic cuff, an arm, and a shoulder to the profile of a soldier sitting immediately in front. She glimpsed a pointed nose, a somewhat pronounced cheekbone, and a mouth the upper lip of which tended to overhang the lower – a mouth, she thought, at once presumptuous and cunning. Yes, here were the Harker family features. Suddenly, intent upon the approaching shore, the man turned his head away, so that now she looked at the back of a tilted shako, a fringe of jet-black hair, a knapsack topped by a rolled blanket, and the protruding muzzle of a "Brown Bess" musket. As it happened the act of recognition took place within a hundred yards of the beach. The boat rushed forward; the dripping head and shoulders of a seaman appeared in the water beside her, his hands gripping the side to haul it in. This fellow was joined by half a dozen others, until with a concerted, "Yo heave ho!", the craft grounded.

The man with the scar was amongst he first to splash ashore. Sue followed his every movement until she felt her own hand slapped smartly, but playfully. It was one of the sailors thigh-deep in water about to turn his back so that she could ride dryshod to the sands. From the tail of her eye she could see that Mrs Foulkes was being similarly invited. "Hurry up – we ain't all day!" jerked the seaman over his shoulder. She mounted awkwardly, clasping her arms about the man's neck. At all costs, she felt, she must not lose sight of her quarry, who by this time had stepped briskly some fifty yards or more up the strand. The sailor, who waded at an incredibly slow pace, seemed loathe to put her down; but she dropped to her feet at last, and with a breathless word of thanks darted forward. Now the soldier ahead was in grave danger of being lost in the motley crowd, which as other boats grounded, was being added to at every moment.

She plucked at the sleeve of a laggard infantryman who had landed from her own craft. "Soldier," she panted, throwing back wet hair from her brow and pointing to the object of her pursuit, "tell me – who is that?" The man stopped in the act of brushing sand from his breeches, regarded her curiously for a moment or two, and shaded his eyes against the sun as he followed the direction of her finger. "Why, that's Nick Raddock," he said.

"Raddock? Are you certain? How do you spell the name?"

The other scratched his head. "Now there you have me, lass," he replied. "I never was much good at spelling, and I never seed it wrote down. But half a mo' – it goes with haddock, if you can remember that."

"Raddock – haddock," she repeated.

"That's right," said the man encouragingly, "now if I may make so bold." But the voice of Mrs Foulkes cut across the conversation. It was a reproachful voice. Did Sue realise that this was no time for idle gossip; that her skirt was hanging about her like a kitchen dishrag; that a tent was being prepared for them by the colonel himself who would be furious if they did not at once appear? Had the business of landing so addled Sue's brains that she had completely forgotten her duties? Where were the valises? At the bottom of the bay? And much else …

Reluctantly Sue turned to follow her mistress; but her eyes strayed constantly in the direction of the infantryman who was known by the name of Raddock, though by now he had been swallowed up in the crowd of men who were stripping off their tunics to dry them in the sun …

* * *

Private Richard Raddock, late Mr Jacob Harker, was feeling tolerably well pleased with himself. Reclining beside a fire fed by splinters from one of the smashed landing craft, he had eaten his beef and biscuit, and was slowly bursting in his mouth grapes bought from one of the Portuguese vendors who had sprung up from nowhere. Wine would have been much more to Harker's taste, but he comforted himself with the thought that there would be plenty of the native liquor later.

Dusk was falling. Out to sea, a few riding lights marked the transports that remained. Enormous rollers still continued to pound the beach, running in swiftly, hissing foam. The firelight flickered across enclaves of scarlet tunics, winking brass, with muskets piled in the background. As far as the eye could reach campfires gleamed. Beyond the drifting smoke, a few windows outlined the village from which the vendors had come. Behind that lay unknown country; but few speculated upon its possibilities. All that mattered now were warmth and food and sleep.

Harker looked up as feet shuffled in the sand. It was a trooper in the blue and braided yellow of the King's German Legion, inquiring gutturally for his own unit. Among the first landed, he had swallowed more than his share of the local wine, but Harker who had half a mind to ask where he had found it, waved a vague arm to where rumbustious folk-song enlivened the middle distance. The Germans were there – always singing …

He dropped back to the sand his thoughts pleasantly employed with his own well-being. Thank God England lay in the past. That book was now closed. Never again would he breathe in the coal dust of the mine; never again look upon the winding gear and quiver to his finger tips as the bucket swung over the darkness of the void. Looking back, he regretted only the brief spell of employment as one of the Earl's stable boys. If only in that unlucky moment he had not borrowed the chestnut cob and cantered off to Doncaster races, breaking the silly beast's knees on the journey, he would have been on velvet in the stables now. He would miss some poaching per-haps; but that was a tricky business at best. His mouth twisted in a wry grin as he fingered the scar across his right hand, a souvenir of an encounter with the keepers. He would never forget the night when after being hit, he had crashed through Scholes wood, plunged waist-deep into the stream beneath the hump-backed bridge, and finally made the pit-yard where he had rubbed coal dust into the wound. His hand had healed, but the dark scar remained, aching when the weather changed …

He recollected Robin Thompson with no remorse whatsoever. The fool should have made his own dash for it. That was the result of book learning – no horse sense! He had seen in a newspaper, though he read with great dif-ficulty, that this Thompson was standing trial at York. "Bad luck for him!" he mused, "but good luck for me." Well, it would bring the chap no more than transportation; set the fellow up, make a man of him. Harker thrust his tongue in his cheek. Lucky too, that the old man had the pony and cart handy, and that the recruiting sergeant still lingered in Doncaster. All things had turned out for the best. He had always hankered after the army, and now here he was!

He turned his head keeping an eye on his musket; better look after that. The sergeant Major had warned them not to trust the natives, who were a light-fingered lot. "Have to get up early in the morning," he ruminated, "to do one on me." He finished the grapes.

Henderson, a private in his own company loomed out of the darkness and dropped beside him. "Hullo!" he said.

"Hullo," responded Harker, "what you want?"

"Don't want nothing."

"Soon served."

"I'm not a proud chap."

Henderson was smoking a slender cigar, a bundle of which he had lately purchased. He handed one to Harker, who took a splinter from the fire and lit up.

"Rather have a wet," said Harker ungratefully.

"Maybe," drawled Henderson. Then after a pause he remarked, "My word, you know how to do it!"

"Do what?"

Harker shifted lazily, allowing the dry sand to run through his fingers.

"Attract the women! Damme, if one wasn't askin' after you when we got off the boat!"

"Married wimmin!" said Harker indifferently, "is all spoken for."

"This one warn't."

"Which one?"

"The one I'm talkin' about. Mrs Foulkes' maid, I reckon."

Harker grinned, flattered. "I seen her – the red-headed gal?"

"Axed who you was."

"Should ha' told her the Duke o' Ditchwater."

"She seemed struck."

"They all are!" Harker laughed softly, his curiosity aroused. "Where's she from?"

"Dunno."

"M–m–m–" Abruptly Harker changed the subject. "When do we march?"

"Dunno."

Conversation lapsed. After a while. "These here cigars," said Harker, gazing out to sea, "is like smoking rhubarb leaves. Give me a quid at any time."

"Please yerself," said Henderson.

Tossing away the stub, Harker rose, and collected his musket. "I think I'll take me a stroll," he remarked. He did not invite his companion.

"Where ye goin'?"

"By the sad sea waves!"

Henderson laughed sardonically. "Good huntin'," he said.

Harker strolled to the water's edge trailing the butt of his musket in the sand. For a time he stood quite still watching the luminous action of the breakers rolling in. Overhead stars shone brightly, and a faint summer lightning played on the horizon – phenomenon in which he was not interested. Turning, he scanned the beach to right and left, and being satisfied that he was unnoticed by his companions, walked slowly towards the rising ground among the rocks where ridge-pole shelters had been pitched for the women and children. He padded softly across the intervening space until he reached a point just outside the circle of firelight. Among the silhouetted figures one or two faces were clearly revealed, but even so he did not recognise the girl Henderson had mentioned. Most likely she would be with Mrs Foulkes, he thought. Still, there would be no harm in making inquiry.

He recognised that he would have to proceed with caution. Women were uncertain creatures, and in company, aggressive. There was also a chance of being challenged by the baggage guard; perhaps even by a suspicious husband. He decided to take the risk, and to employ the veneer of manners he had acquired in the Earl's service. Women responded to deference. It flattered them, made them feel important. An oblique approach would be best; inquiry for a person whom he knew to be absent – Mrs Higgenson, for example, whom he remembered sitting with her husband, mending socks beside one of the beach fires. "Here goes!" he murmured. An ingratiating smile played about his lips.

As he appeared fully in the firelight someone cried, "The devil!" It was Mrs Jenks, who having just completed a small financial transaction, bent forward quickly to conceal the collection of coins in her lap, "What I do not like," she said loudly, "is folks that creeps an' crawls in the night! What d'you want, villain?" Unperturbed, Harker gazed around the circle of faces. "Good evening, ladies all," he ventured, "Mrs Higgenson hereabouts?"

"Not 'ere," said the women.

"Oh dear me!" murmured Harker anxiously.

"What do yer want?"

Harker improvised. "I thought I saw her little lad beside the water, but perhaps I was wrong. Shouldn't want him to come to harm."

"Nay, he's in there, fast asleep wi' the other childer," said one pointing to the shadowed interior of the nearest tent. "I seed him only a minute back."

"Then that's all right," said Harker in a relieved tone. "Must ha' been one of the little Portugeses. Now can you tell me if Mrs Foulkes' maid is with you?"

"Not 'er," said Mrs Rayner. "I heeard that they've gone aboard ship again. The Major's packed 'em off to Lisbon."

"Now isn't that a pity!" Harker stroked his chin ruefully. "I bring her a message, but I don't rightly recall her name. Would you happen to know?"

"I've heeard her called Sue," said Mrs Jenkins, who still held both hands over her money.

"And I've heeard, Thompson," said Mrs Rayner.

"So putting the two together it should be Sue Thompson. Very good."

Thompson? The name stirred an unpleasant memory so that he was impelled to question further. "There's a lot o' Thompsons about. Where would she hail from?"

"She was brought in by her missus," said Mrs Jenks sharply. The woman wished he would go. "Anything else you require?"

Harker laughed. "Not at present thank ye." He saluted. "Ah, well, "he said, shouldering his musket, "I can only say to you all, good night, ladies and pleasant dreams!"

Still smiling, he walked away, but when a burst of laughter followed, he grimaced darkly: "Brave, aren't ye when ye're in the pack, but let me catch you on your own!" The Jenks woman, he reflected, must have been handling all of two pounds. It would be a mercy to relieve her of a little. He wondered if her husband was of the gaming type. There were possibilities in that ...

So the red-head was named Sue Thompson? Returning to the water's edge he watched fold by fold the incessant movement of the waves. Thompson was a common name; there were almost as many Thompsons about the place as Robinsons or Smiths. And yet she had travelled down from Yorkshire with her mistress. He took off his shako and dropping his musket in the sand, smoothed back his hair. He laughed. The girl had been obviously attracted. What a pity she had been whisked away to Lisbon! But she would reappear – at least he hoped so. Talk of Spanish beauties? Far better a likely girl in the regiment, marching when you marched, and camping when you camped. There was time enough. He would await her return ...

* * *

Unexpectantly, Mrs Foulkes and Sue had left the encampment. The explanation was quite simple. They had no sooner settled in the tent provided for them when a message came, through the Colonel, from the admiral himself. A frigate was about to leave for Lisbon, and Mrs Foulkes, if she so desired, was welcome to a passage in it.

Harriet's reception of this offer was somewhat equivocal. She eyed her husband suspiciously. "What lies behind?" she asked.

"Nothing," said Foulkes.

"I wonder if the Colonel wishes to be rid of me?"

"Nonsense," said her husband. "I see no subterfuge at all. Meeting the admiral, Pomeroy as like as not, mentioned your presence with the regiment, and since the latest advices are to the effect that the port is now quiet, the

Admiral from the goodness of his heart felt that you would be much more diverted by the attractions of the city than the place where we now are."

"You would wish me to go?"

The Major combed what little hair he had with his fingertips. "You should weigh one lodging place against another. In Lisbon you will find markets, the shops, the opera, a good hotel, a comfortable bed; while here – the mosquitoes alone—"

Harriet winced. During the last few hours she had been stung abominably. The rocks and sand dunes stretched bleakly to right and left. Still, she awaited her husband's opinion. "What do you advise?" she persisted.

Foulkes hesitated. Jane's advice and that of Selman sprang into mind: "Take her as far as Lisbon, and by that time she may possibly yearn for home." Yet he did not wish to appear too eager for the proposed excursion. He said smoothly, "I leave the decision entirely in your hands."

"I will go," she said firmly.

"It was handsome of the admiral to consider you," he said.

"He is a gentleman," she replied emphatically.

Thus it was that a pleasantly excited lady, accompanied by her maid, once again rode pick-a-back through the surf to a waiting gig, and rowed out to the frigate *Alert*. As she stepped aboard the contrast between the new vessel and the *Caledonia* was quite breathtaking. The King's ship shone like a new pin, her decks scrupulously white, her guns glistening in the sunlight. Snowy canvas overhead shook out to the wind. Without exception, her officers were men of breeding, the seamen cheerful, attentive, respectful. From that hour Harriet, who had moved almost exclusively in military circles, began to feel that the Royal Navy had been grossly under-estimated; henceforward she would be loud in its praise. Throughout the trip, she was at her charming best ...

And how knowledgeable the officers were! They spoke of Naples, Alexandria, Port-of-Spain, and Buenos Ayres, familiarly, as a cockney would of Rochester or Margate. They outlined the attractions of Lisbon; although they explained, traces of the great earthquake which brought all Europe to its knees, were still to be seen. When she entered the Tagus however and saw the honey-flushed, pink-washed houses climbing to the citadel, she caught her breath in wonder. A dream city, one of complete enchantment, she thought. No trace of ruin here; the quays so crowded with masts, that she wondered if the *Alert* would be able to tie up at all. She need not have been anxious; the navy took over. An engaging lieutenant brought them to the Square of Commerce, and with the utmost ease found places for them at the Hotel du Corpo Santo. Their baggage followed, and they booked in.

The hotelier, an expatriate American, spare as a bean-pole and clad in a long linen housecoat and striped pantaloons, was most attentive – a thought too attentive. He was so insistently curious that Harriet in a whisper warned

Sue to keep a close watch upon her tongue. "On no account make mention of the regiment; its numbers, or anything pertaining to military business at all. For all his glib English, he may be a French spy."

"Say," he drawled, "what part of the old country do you hail from?"

"From the north. What is your place of origin?"

"South Car'lina. Do you aim to stay long?"

"That depends. Have you been long in Portugal?"

"'Bout ten years. Guess you're an army wife?"

Harriet regarded him warily. He must have noticed that their baggage was stamped with the regimental markings. "In a manner of speaking," she said reluctantly.

"Your people coming later?"

"That I cannot say. Are you a married man?"

The hotelier shrugged. "Shucks, no!"

"Why not?" She raised her eyebrows archly.

"Wa-a-l," he drawled, "ah reckon ah never saw a girl ah could cotton on to."

"Why did you leave your native country?"

The hotelier eyed his interrogator sharply, and shifted his gaze. She felt that she had touched a tender spot. At last he said, "Ah guess I was a natural born wanderer."

"And you wandered here?"

"That's right, Ma'm. Say—" As he realised that he was giving out much more than he was taking in, he began to scrutinise his cigar with unusual interest.

"What is your name?"

"Bradley – Eli Bradley, Ma'm."

"Well, Mr Bradley," said Harriet bringing the conversation to a close, "we should be very pleased to inspect our rooms."

"Surely Ma'm."

"That will teach him," whispered Harriet as they followed Mr Bradley upstairs, "that we are by no means to be trifled with. Eli – wasn't he a prophet?"

* * *

At first sight, Harriet's room, furnished with an old wardrobe, two solid, but somewhat worm-eaten, chairs, and a bare four-poster bed, made her shudder. In compensation the sheets however, were of good linen, and the pillows muslin-frilled, quite clean. She examined the room closely for vermin, but for the time being could find none.

Sue, directed to a garret under the eaves, found a mattress stuffed with wooden shavings. The walls, flecked with ominous brown patches, one or two of which were ringed by pencil marks, looked none too inviting. A curious sickly odour pervaded the room, so that, having dumped her holdall, and standing in the bed, she forced open the skylight to admit fresh air.

When in a little while, the two women descended to the public dining room for a meal, Harriet issued a further warning. "Now that we are alone in Lisbon, although thank God our people are taking over, you had better stick to me. On no account wander. We don't want our throats cut. Do nothing without prior consultation."

After this dark assessment, Mrs Foulkes was a trifle disappointed when their presence at the common table evoked only passing interest. Their fellow guests – merchants and travellers apparently – after bowing to the two Englishwomen, applied themselves to the dishes placed before them, and drank their wine with no attempt at conversation ... At first Harriet was repelled by the coarse cloth upon which cellars of brown salt were set at intervals; but the first course, a greasy mess of fish proved oddly palatable; boiled chicken followed, and an ample dessert of fresh plums and peaches. The waiter, a youth who sported a curious amalgam of Portuguese and American English, kissed his grubby fingers at the ceiling and assured the two English ladies that he loved their nation to distraction. "Did you love the French also?" inquired Harriet sceptically. The youth shrugged indifferently. He opened and closed his fists. "Take all – give nothing," he said. Harriet, who had expected a violent outburst of anger against the late invaders, murmured doubtfully. "That is what he says, but watch him," she told Sue. "He has shifty eyes."

Late afternoon, the two ventured out into a street which stank to high heaven. Harriet, her romantic conception of the city badly shaken, held a scented handkerchief to her face. "Faugh!" she cried, "of all the abominations! A garden city in a cess-pool!" These intermittent odours however, did not prevent them from exploring the markets where the banked flowers, the piled-up fruits, the rainbow fish and crayfish, were an unfailing source of wonder. Sue pitied the patient donkeys, incredibly burdened. She eyed the obsequious priests who thrust collecting boxes under their noses, with heretical distaste; and as for the Portuguese women leisurely hunting for lice in each other's hair, she had no words to express her disgust ...

After a time it was a distinct relief to drop down to the Tagus, drinking coffee in a waterside café, they watched the ferry boats arrowing the broad blue waters, and the brown lateen sails of the fishermen glide athwart the black hulls of Russian men-o'-war ...

That same evening, Harriet having changed a few guineas into Portuguese currency, the two visitors went to the Opera, where they saw a ballet, in which a beautiful maiden was rescued from a grotesque villain in French uniform, by a hero in an ill-fitting scarlet tunic – presumably British – to the pronounced satisfaction of all. "Unspeakably crude!" observed Harriet.

Next day she ventured out alone, not only to report her presence to the

Town Major, but also to ascertain if any ladies with whom she might possibly be acquainted, had come in. The harassed officer, newly appointed and inadequately staffed, was none the less a model of patience. "My dear Madame," he said, "I have no social register of any kind. The only lady I have heard of is the Quartermaster General's wife, and a female cook brought in by one of the General officers. With the latter you need not be concerned, but where the former is to be found, I have no more idea than fly. All will adjust itself in time. If in the course of a day or two you were able to call again, I might have something of interest for you. In the meantime be careful what you do and say – there is still some feeling against the British because of Cintra."

She inquired where the cavalry headquarters were placed, and at this the Town Major exploded. "I wish, upon my soul, that they were established in hell! They must think I can make horses. Already the Prince Regent's stables are drained to the very last mule, and still they bring me requisitions. Down they come from Quelez—"

"Quelez?" inquired Harriet.

"That's their little den. Really it's a palace away up yonder," and he gestured vaguely towards the hills. "I had Captain Harte yesterday demanding forty mounts – forty, mark you! All I had was a couple of foundered mules."

"Captain Harte?" asked Harriet quickly.

"Yes. Do you know him?"

"He is a friend of mine."

"No offence I assure you." The Town Major spread out his hands. "Nothing personal, you know."

"Of course not. He was in yesterday?"

"And off again. If he picked up half a dozen horses he'd be lucky; but there are people of consequence with stables."

"You say that he came from Quelez?"

The officer nodded. "Is it possible for me to convey a message?"

"No, thank you; but I should like you to inform Major Foulkes, my husband where I am lodged." She wrote down her address. "You have been most kind, and I must not trespass any longer on your time."

"A great pleasure," said the Town Major politely. He saw her out …

She left with a disappointed sigh. The elusive hour had passed. A day earlier and they might well have met, perhaps upon the very steps of this building. The Town Major had mentioned Quelez. She gazed towards the distant heights wondering how many miles away the palace could be, and how one managed to get there.

Returning to the hotel she questioned the proprietor. "Wa-a-al," he answered, "ah guess this Quelez palace is about two leagues ride into the hills – mebbe more. Having no truck with royalty, never been thar mahself. A fine place they tell me, but mighty queer."

"In what manner?"

"Bewitched, I reckon," he said with a furtive look. "The old Queen lived tha. Went plumb crazy, Ma'm. Ran around all day long a'snarlin' and a'screamin', beatin' up her ministers, poor devils, and generally raising hell's delight. The pink palace of the mad queen they call it, and I guess they were right."

"Is she in residence now?"

"Not if you don't believe in sperrits."

He spoke with much feeling. "Look, what happened to that General Junot after he lodged there. It's a house of dam bad luck." When Harriet was prompted to inquire if he believed in ghosts, he spat, and at once craved her pardon. "Friendly sperrits, yes, Ma'm; spiteful critters, no! We had a nigger ghost once on shipboard that was always trippin' people up. No good in it."

He ran on, and Harriet listened with what patience she could muster; but she had secured the information she wanted …

The next time she wrote to Jane, she said little about the *Caledonia*, but a great deal about Lisbon. "I have to tell you of hanging gardens, spacious squares and collonades; my dear you have no notion of the climbing streets and cobbles that bite into one's feet! The natives range from mahogany brown to deep yellow. In the café's they sing what is called the 'fado' – songs of unrequited love: a man admires a girl, but he is old and she is so young; or she is noble and rich, and he alas! is very poor …

"Our hotel is reasonably comfortable. But the beds are a torment, hard as iron and stuffed with wooden shavings. You toss uncomfortably all night, and instead of being awakened by bird song, you are deafened by the yelling of fish-women in the street below. Every house has its attractive balcony. What a pity that English architects never considered this …

"Both Thompson and I have had stomach trouble, due I believe to indulging in too much luscious fruit. But one may tire even of Lisbon where there are so few people whom one knows. My urgent requirement for the present is needles. There is fruit, fish, flowers, mantillas, cats, dogs, monkeys and guitars in great profusion, but not a single needle to be had. Be a darling and send me a fair packet of all sizes care of the Town Major here, who will – if I be not at the hotel – send it after me …"

* * *

"Can this," thought the Major as he gazed up at the rusty grilles and the peeling façade of the Hotel du Corpo Santo, "be the turning point?" Riding down from the hills on a mixed commission, including certain necessaries for the Colonel, and for himself the purchase of pistols, he had not been greatly preoccupied by his domestic problem. Now, however, it would have to be faced. Tossing his reins to the orderly, he prepared to confront Harriet. He screwed up his eyes wondering in what condition he could find her – too much to suppose that so soon she had relinquished her purpose. But one never knew. Perhaps she had found the mosquitoes of Lisbon more ruthless than those of Maciera Bay! He hoped profoundly that she would decide to stay in the capital; he would certainly do his utmost to persuade her. But no head-on assault, he concluded, as he climbed the stairs …

He carried letters from home; and when Sue opened the door to his knock, he was pleased to be facetious. "Only the post boy," he announced cheerfully as he entered. Harriet greeted him in the same lively spirit. "Behold our deliverer!" she cried.

He cocked an appraising eyebrow as he looked round the apartment. "I must say that you are pretty comfortable!"

"So much that we are ready to go," she replied with feeling.

"Go, where?"

She did not reply instantly; for Foulkes the interval of waiting became intolerable. Then she said: "To the regiment, of course."

His heart sank. "We are," he said ruefully, "encamped on the lower slopes of a mountain – a damned windy, meagre, rocky site." He shook his head. "Most inhospitable."

"You are looking quite well."

"I can't do otherwise."

"Well, for our part," she said, "we have exhausted Lisbon. Ten days is quite sufficient. A fortnight would be intolerable."

He did not speak.

"Are you absolutely in the wilds?"

Foulkes hesitated. He would not lie. "There is a fishing village," he said reluctantly, "close by."

She smiled in triumph. "Good! We will find accommodation there."

"It will be difficult."

"Not for you," she rallied in a tone which suggested that all things were possible for the senior major.

"I shouldn't wish you to exchange the frying-pan for the fire."

"This place is boring." Her gesture of distaste embraced not only the room in which they were sitting, but the whole city.

"You would go further and fare worse."

"I am prepared to risk that," she said stubbornly, and for a few moments he was silent. When however, she inquired after the regiment, he warmed a little. The men were in fine fettle, and excited by the arrival of Sir John Moore, whose headquarters were at Quelez.

"Moore at Quelez?" she said slowly.

"For the time being."

So matters stood. Foulkes wondered now if he ought not to reopen the question of her return home; but decided not. Anything would be better than renewed acrimony. Hard days and rough going might be more efficacious than verbal argument. At length he promised that in a day or two he would send a wagon down to bring them and their belongings to Paco d'Arcos; if Harriet cared to ride, Felix would come also. "If," he concluded, "you change your mind and decide to stay in Lisbon, you have but to say the word."

"You may be sure I shall," said Harriet with an air of indifference.

"Here then, are your letters." These he placed on the table, and after waiting a little further to learn what they contained, left to complete his business in the city …

* * *

The packet of letters included one for Sue from her parents, enclosing a pencilled note, which they had received from Robin. Scrawled upon a scrap of paper, torn it would appear form the end pages of a prison prayer book, the message was terse, poignant, dramatic. "My dear father and mother (he wrote) I have been brought to the convict hulks off Greenwich, being now lodged on the second deck, the lowest being reserved for the worst offenders. My day's labour is from 5 in the morning until 5.30 at night, after which we clean cells, pots, pans, etc. By day we go ashore, some to shipbuilding, some to painting, some hauling timber and some cleansing the river of mud. I have had a little fever, but the surgeon has given me some opium pills. We do not work Sundays, for then the chaplain preaches. I do not know how long I shall remain in this condition; they say until a convoy can be assembled. My money all but two shillings, has been taken away from me. I buy bread and vegetables at three-pence a day. I hope you are both in good health. Please pass this news on to our Sue. If I can – "

Since the letter had the appearance of being suddenly interrupted, the girl wondered by what means it had been smuggled out – possibly by a prisoner who had served his sentence. She slipped the paper in her bodice, but the lines so lingered in her mind that she tended to neglect her duties, and time and again Mrs Foulkes called her to attention. "Really, Thompson," she protested. "You must be sickening for an illness or something – I don't doubt from the wretched oily food we eat." And she insisted upon the girl taking some of her own tablets.

So Sue steeled herself to routine, but her eyes hardened as she thought of Harker at ease in freedom, jesting with his companions, while her shamefully bamboozled brother languished in irons. Was there no justice in the world? Had God turned His face away? Long after silence had fallen on the public rooms, and the last guitar had struck its unbearably plaintive note, she tossed restlessly upon her mattress awaiting light and leading. But none came …

CHAPTER VII

Half a dozen mules adorned with black and yellow worsted tassels drew a wagon to the entrance off the Hotel du Corpo Santo. Tethered behind, saddles, sleek and shining, was Mrs Foulkes' chestnut, Felix. Two privates had been detailed as bodyguard, and with them, but mounted on his own horse, was Mr Simms, a young assistant deputy commissary, who on victually business in Lisbon intended to use the vehicle for this purpose.

Both women were more than ready to leave. They waited awhile until the commissary brought up his goods. These loaded, trunks and valises were heaved aboard, and after a little farewell speech and wave of the hand from the American – who had generously presented them with a basket of fruit – Mr Simms, followed by Harriet in a high white linen stock and jaunty plume, led out of the city. She occupied a place in the wagon with the two infantrymen. The driver, a Portuguese, sat with hunched back apparently in deep contemplation.

Busy until the last moment with this and that, Sue had caught no more than a passing glimpse of the military escort, but climbing up she was startled to look into Harker's subtly mocking eyes, so much indeed, that she almost lost her foothold. When, with some ceremony, he arranged a little throne of sacks for her to sit on, she could only stammer a word of thanks. The ogre she had so often conjured up in her imagination, appeared in the flesh disarmingly affable, smiling often, his teeth white against the bronze of his skin. His grey-green eyes, sardonic and watchful, were never still. He dropped into a place beside her, adjusting his firelock between his knees, and – though whether by accident or design she could not know – set one hand upon the other so that his scar was concealed. He introduced himself immediately. "No reason for not being friendly," he began with a swift grin. "The name is Raddock, and that article," nodding towards his companion with scarcely veiled contempt, "is Jack Turnbull."

"Pleased to meet you, missy," said Turnbull, extending an enormous hand. Sue winced as her fingers crushed. Turnbull evidently did not know his own strength.

"A chawbacon," whispered Harker, "from the plough tail."

Sue, at a complete loss for words, stared straight ahead. She struggled to maintain composure, bracing herself against his honeyed brashness. "The name Raddock," she repeated to herself – "Raddock". On no account must she forget.

Silence fell in the wagon. Hooves padded, starting dust. The mule bells jingled. As the wagon bumped over the uneven road, the musket butts of the two men beat a faint tattoo on the floorboards. Ahead, Mrs Foulkes laughed heartily at some observation made by Mr Simms. At times, stress of traffic in the narrow streets compelled them to halt; but entering the suburbs they continued at an even pace through the dark beauty of orange and lemon groves – vistas of olive green and gold. In to her circumstances the girl might have yielded herself completely to the bright sunshot air, the radiance of the morning. But not now. She held her breath as she considered future action.

With a watchful eye on Mrs Foulkes, Harker produced a flask of wine, and offered it to Sue. When she refused, he was not in the least offended, but took a long pull himself, and passed it over to Turnbull, who drank noisily. "Talking makes you thirsty," said Harker with a comic side-glance. Stooping, he selected a straw from the litter at his feet, slipped it into his mouth, at the same time pushing back his shako to reveal a fringe of black stubbly hair. He rolled the straw over on his tongue, and without removing it, spoke again. "Enjoying yerself?"

"Yes, thank you, Mr Raddock."

He laughed. "My friends call me Dick."

"Do they, Mr Raddock?"

"Dang me!" he rallied, "we can do better than that. Where you from?"

"England," she said curtly.

He started in mock surprise. "You don't say!"

He stared ahead. Fascinated, she watched the oscillating tip of the straw, awaiting his next remark. She wished that she had Mrs Foulkes' gift of language, her attitude sometimes of wordless reproof. "I mean," he resumed quietly, "in what town was you born? Don't speak – let me guess. I should say Lincoln way."

Sue hesitated. "No," she said briefly.

"Bad shot! From Lacasheer?"

"You are quite wrong." Impulsively she decided to tell the truth. "I was born," she said watching him closely, "at Tollgate in the county of York."

Calmly, Harker took out the straw, and regarded it thoughtfully.

"I am a fooil," he remarked, "I should ha' known that from your twang." He slapped his knee triumphantly. "As it happens I have an uncle what lives in that very place." He had no doubt now that the girl sitting beside him was a relation of the Thompsons he knew. There was a daughter who went away. "An uncle on my mother's side," he explained.

"In that case I should know him," she rejoined.

"Name of Harker. Never seed much of the old brad myself."

"I've seen him around," she said.

"I don't talk about him much," he said with a distasteful grimace. "Not tit for tat – your name I make out to be Thompson?"

"How do you know?"

"A good looking lass i' the regiment must expect to be noticed," he answered lightly. "Your name's no secret."

"Tit for tat," she said quickly, "where were you born?"

"Miller's Dale," he grinned. He was beginning to enjoy himself.

"I've often heard of Miller's Dale," she said smoothly. "What was your occupation?"

Harker chuckled, placing his hand familiarly upon her knee. She edged away. "Working for the miller," he replied. He cast an approving glance at her curls now aureole in the sun, and at the roundness of her arms.

"Grinding?"

"A bit," he laughed. The little simpleton!

"You grind corn," interposed Turnbull, who felt he had been left out of the conversation long enough, "wi' big gert millstones – upper and nether. Stones does grinding."

"Well—" began Sue.

"'E don't know nowt about millin'," continued Turnbull, pointing a scornful finger at his companion, "a pick an' shovel's moor in his line."

"Speak when you're spoken to, "snapped Harker, "you don't know a beanpole from a bayonet."

"Ar?" challenged Turnbull, but his attention dawn to a passing girl leading a goat, he broke off and waved his hand. The girl smiled and waved in response. In her rusty tattered black dress she walked with a certain regal grace. Harker's eyes followed the lithe upright figure. "There she goes," he murmured admiringly, but Turnbull's homely face had become serious.

"Aye," he rumbled, "but you moan't go too far wi' em. Yesterday one o' them Portuguese wimmin shoved a knife through a sapper's 'and – pinned it to the table, she did, like a lump o' butcher's meat. Carry the mark to 'is dying day, 'e will!"

"Shut up!" growled Harker.

"Couldn't pull 'is 'hand away – like steak on a choppin' block. I seed it."

"All right – you seen it! But keep your trap shut. We have a lady present."

"You're the on'y one that speaks in this cart," muttered Turnbull.

Sue noticed that Harker's right hand had slipped from sight; he appeared to be half sitting on it. He turned towards her.

"You must forgive my poor friend," he explained with mock gravity, "he doesn't know his own ignorance."

"I know what I know!" said Turnbull darkly.

"About hogs?"

Turnbull lowered his head as though to cut his tormentor, but thinking better of it, sat gazing over the wagon side, his great hands splayed over his knees.

After an interval, Harker whispered, "You got a lad?"

Sue averted her head.

"Bless us," he smirked, "you needn't be shy wi' me."

"I'm not shy!" she said indignantly.

"You'll not need to be," he remarked, "wi' what's coming."

He brought out the flask again, and raised it in the air before drinking. "Here's to short days of fighting, and long hours of pleasure." He swallowed hard, and ignoring the avid eyes of Turnbull, replaced the wine in his pocket. To Sue's relief, Turnbull, annoyed by this denial of liquor, began an argument concerning the identity of a rising bird, contending against Harker's assertion of a woodcock, that it was undoubtedly a partridge. The two wrangled for a time until both fell into sullen silence. Once, noting a flurry of glossy tail-feathers behind a boulder, Harker raised his musket, but thinking better of the matter, lowered his weapon ...

The wagon continued to jolt through stretches of grey granite and heather. As the two riders walked horses ahead, the roadside verdure they crushed emitted a certain aromatic odour, bitter-sweet in the nostrils of those who followed ...

Meanwhile Harriet Foulkes was much more pleasantly engaged with Mr Simms. He was young – not more she would have guessed than twenty-five – freshly complexioned, intelligent, attentive. A man of parts. A pity, she reflected, that he should be of the civil arm; but in his closely fitting blue coat, brass buttons, nankeen breeches and grey beaver, he made an acceptable escort.

Simms responded to her quizzing with easy good humour. He needed little inducement to dwell upon his own profession; the collecting of fodder, beef and biscuit, the uncertain hiring of muleteers, the importunate demands of quartermasters.

"I am quite certain," she observed, "that you do not allow yourself to be overwhelmed."

This flattery, enforced by a glance from a remarkably fine pair of eyes, pleased Simms.

"One manages to keep out of Newgate," he said sardonically.

"I perceive," observed Harriet gravely, "that if I am to be well-provisioned in camp, you are a gentleman with whom I must remain on respectful terms."

Simms bowed slightly from the saddle. "I can assure you, Madam," he replied, "that we shall not let poor Nellie starve." Later, he regretted the impertinence of his rejoinder; but if Harriet did feel resentment, she gave no sign of it.

"One thing I do promise," she said, "that unlike your quartermasters, I shall not appear at the crack of dawn."

Her curiosity was insatiable. Was he a married man? Were his parents alive? Did he like Portugal? Did his commission work take him far afield?

He developed the last point. Scouring the countryside was the greater part of his burden. It called for a horse with wings.

"You have much more liberty of action than a regimental officer?" she suggested.

"To be sure – with much less pay."

"Do you visit headquarters?"

"At times."

"Where are these?"

"At Quelez, for the moment."

Harriet was all attention. "Do tell me about Quelez," she said eagerly.

Simms informed her that it was a most attractive place; the Versailles of Portugal. Junot had lodged there, and after the manner of French commanders in occupied territory, had lifted everything portable – the choicest silver, pictures, furniture. When Simms added that he would be visiting the palace in the very near future, she inquired if by chance, he had encountered a friend of hers, a certain captain Harte. Surprisingly, Simms had; not only so, but the animal he was riding, a grey white-stockinged mare, had been secured through the good offices of that gentleman.

"Which makes a bond between us," she murmured. Immediately, changing the subject, she pointed with her riding switch to a mud-coloured ruin which crowned the horizon. Was not that an old Moorish castle? And how long had the infidels remained in Spain? Simms did his best to answer. Thereafter conversation turned to La Mancha, a province she erroneously supposed to be very near. Once again, Simms, who knew his *Don Quixote*, put her to rights; he was particularly gratified when, towards the end of their journey she confessed that seldom had she found a conversation more interesting. "And I," he replied, "a companion more charming." But he rode away with a furrowed brow, acutely conscious of his inferior station as a Deputy Assistant Commissary.

As for Harriet Foulkes, she dismounted with a slight smile playing around her lips. Certainly she must keep in touch with the affable young gentleman. Quelez? She had the feeling that Mr Simms would come in useful ere long.

The wagon drew up, and Sue climbed down. How attentive the soldiers were! Harriet could hear one of them, crying, "Allow me, Miss Thompson. Whatever you say! At your good pleasure, Miss Thompson!"

Everyone seemed most helpful ...

* * *

At Paco d'Arcos the Quartermaster had found accommodation for Mrs Foulkes and her maid with an apothecary, whose squat stone house, littered as it was with dusty bottles, drying herbs, children and cats, appeared the ante-chamber to Bedlam; but after an excellent dinner of chicken cooked with sage, thyme, onion, parsley, tomato and garlic, rounded off with sweet cakes and coffee, Harriet revised her opinion. When she found that the beds were scrupulously clean, she became almost reconciled to this bizarre menage, though she never quite took to Manuel, the apothecary himself. His beaked nose and deeply set glittering black eyes conveyed a certain brooding, occult impression. She saw him compounding with equal ease, death-drops and love-philtres. There were so many mysterious bottles without labels at all, and he never spoke until spoken to.

She had expected much from Paco d'Arcos, but soon the place bored her. Men drilled regularly on the rising ground above the village, the vivid red of tunics contrasting boldly with the soft green pastel shades of the background. The incessant bawling of orders, the slapping of musket stocks, and the stamping of feet, became oppressively familiar. The sea broke silver on the strand, but for the time being she had had enough of the sea. She visited Cintra, and after the manner of tourists marvelled at its groves and mansions; but on her return, she sighed almost for Lisbon. As some kind of relief she turned to sketching, but harassed by chattering hordes of children she shooed them away and sought refuge among the granite boulders of the hillside. Here monotony returned. No gleaming tower, no crumbling castle appeared, to enliven her romantic fancy. Perversely the colours ran; flies, a greater nuisance than the children settled on her hands and face, and beneath the scorching sun she regretted not having brought an umbrella from England. Finally she packed her brushes, and thoroughly discontented, returned to the musty herb-laden atmosphere of the apothecary's house, where beside an open window she tried to read *Tom Jones*. After yawning hugely over its pages, she set the novel down, and decided to write letters.

A discursive transcript to Jane she dashed off with comparative ease. She drew a sketch, comically satirical of her host, and enclosed that. After a somewhat shorter letter to her father, she prepared to write to Anthony Harte.

She cut another pen, took a fresh sheet of paper, indited the address, the date, and paused irresolute. After so long an interval of silence, she was at a loss for words. To frame formal sentences would be absurd. The thought struck her that the letter might well go astray. What then? Supposing some person returned it to the Major?

She decided to fall back upon the euphemistic conceit they had used at Brighton. But even now her pen faltered. The time, the place had changed. Some magic had been lost. The bell of the little pink-washed church began to toll mournfully. The harsh crackle of musketry practice from the heights beyond cut across the sound. She waited patiently for silence, the white page blank.

At last the bell stopped, and after pacing thoughtfully for a time, she took up her pen and attempted a few lines. These displeased her. She tore the paper into tiny pieces, and thrust them in the brazier. She began again, and at length contrived a note which she felt would serve. Even so, she scanned it frowning—

Dear Hector (it ran), I am here in Portugal at Paco d'Arcos with the regiment. Lodged with a dispenser of ineffectual potions I am dying of ennui. To whom shall I turn for deliverance if not to my old friend? Are there no palaces, no gardens with arbours where we may meet and talk again?

Andromache

By the hand of Mr Simms, the commissary, to whom you may safely entrust a reply.

Addressing the letter to Captain Harte at Quelez, she folded and sealed it carefully, and summoned Sue. "I wish you to seek out the Commissary, Mr Simms, whom you must know is quartered at the end house of the village. Hand him this with my compliments for delivery the very next time he rides to Quelez." She took up *Tom Jones* and fluttered the pages with studied indifference. As Sue reached the door, Harriet added, "One moment. The letter deals with a private matter, and must be delivered to the officer in question by Mr Simms alone. You understand?"

"Yes, Mrs Foulkes."

The girl's face was inscrutable. Harriet turned away her head, but after the maid had gone; almost in panic, she wondered what would happen if the young Commissary and her husband were to meet en route. Would Simms be impelled to mention the matter? … Deriding her own fears, she dismissed the idea as highly improbable; if any officer rode over to Quelez, it would be Colonel Pomeroy himself. The chance however, would have to be taken.

* * *

Sue had no difficulty in finding Mr Simms who was sitting at a table outside his depot paying off Portuguese drovers. She stood aside while the carts screeched and rumbled before him. From a bag of dollars at his elbow, he allowed one coin per cart, and tossed it to the man. Sometimes he flicked the money into the body of the vehicle where the Portuguese darted to retrieve it. Imperturbably Simms kept the tally. He paid out the last dollar and turned towards her.

"Is there none for me?" she asked, smiling.

"Payment only," he said gravely, "in respect of service."

She was not certain what this implied – his lips were set, but his eyes were smiling. She watched him with a leathern thong around the neck of the bag, and drop it under the table touching his foot for safety. This done, he grinned, and taking from behind his chair a basket of grapes set these upon the table. "Help yourself," he said. She came forward and broke off a few. "Take more." He waved a spacious hand towards the fruit. For his part he lit a slender cigar, blew a jet of smoke into the windless air and murmured, "Well Miss, what can I do for you?"

His tone, at once nonchalant and friendly, pleased her. Sitting at ease with outstretched legs, he looked much younger than when she had last seen him riding with Mrs Foulkes. His lively grey-blue eyes and tumbled brown hair; and a smile that trembled at the corners of his mouth betrayed an inherent good nature. He was if anything, a little overweight, but this he would have claimed a natural advertisement for his profession.

Sue, handing over the letter, did not fail to convey Mrs Foulkes' compliments, to which Simms grunted, noted the address, scanned the reverse side of the missive, and dropped it on the table. He tilted his hat over his eyes regarding her keenly from under the brim. "I sometimes wonder," he observed, "where my duties begin and where they end. Sit down." He pushed forward a stool which had lately been occupied by his clerk. The girl obeyed, still gazing curiously at the man before her.

The Commissary was no stranger to Portugal. Before the outbreak of the war he had been employed by a London-Oporto firm of wine merchants, but the house being ruined by the French invasion, he had joined the Commissariat where his knowledge of Portuguese proved invaluable.

She broke off one of the grapes. Simms now helped himself, contriving to eat and to keep his cigar going at the same time. "Since the fair lady employs us both," he began, ejecting a pip, "we must become acquainted. What is your name?"

Sue told him. He blew smoke into the air, watched it convolve and vanish. "Well Susan," he resumed, "now that we alone – for to be forewarned is to be forearmed – what is the relation between your mistress and this Captain Harte?" He tapped the letter.

"That I cannot say."

"Is it – of a delicate nature?"

"You are asking too much," she said.

"And you are imparting too little."

"I have nothing to impart – it is no business of mine."

"You have a point there," he said soberly, "but carrying this makes it my business. I only wish to protect myself."

"If I knew what you had in mind—" she began.

"There are friendships, and friendships," he suggested.

But she was not to be drawn. He eyed her darkly for a few seconds.

"What do you think of the Major?" he asked abruptly.

Sue hesitated. "I don't see much of him."

"Do you like him?"

"Don't you?"

Simms frowned. "I wish I could give you a straight answer, but I can't. I like officers to be free and frank. You know where you are with the Colonel, who outs with everything he has, but Major Foulkes is different. He always thinks twice before he speaks once."

"Is that a bad thing?"

"It may be. The Colonel damns and forgets, the Major remembers."

"What for example?"

Simms' mouth set grimly. "The inconvenient particular. I don't like people who jot little things down in pocket books for further reference." He shook his head sadly. "When I consider that I was passing rich on a hundred pounds a year, all found, drinking the firm's wine, and drifting in the sunlight on the broad bosom of the Duoro, the honoured servant of a beneficent company, and reflect on my present lot, I could weep tears of mortification." He closed his eyes against the thought.

She said dryly, "You have my sympathy!"

Simms opened one eye. "Thank you! Now I must be about my official business." He began to buckle on his spurs. "Take the rest of the fruit if you will. My compliments to Mrs Foulkes, and assure her that her commission will be faithfully executed."

"She will be grateful, I am sure."

"No doubt," he commented wryly. "I need not ask you to regard my own loose chatter as confidential."

As she nodded in response, he rose, bowed slightly, took up his bag of dollars, and shouted for his horse ...

* * *

Thereafter, Harry Simms, called often at the apothecary's, carefully timing his visits (Sue noticed) to coincide with the Major's absence. He had always some interesting item of news to impart, nor did he ever appear empty-handed. The two women lacked neither fresh fruit nor meat while they remained at Paco d'Arcos. His knowledge of the language was especially useful.

In due course he brought an answer to Harriet's letter. With the best will in the world (wrote Harte) Hector could not arrange to meet Andromache within a week as he would be on reconnaissance; after that she was at liberty to ride over to Quelez, though again ..., his movements might be uncertain. He would try to keep in touch ... Frankly, she was disappointed, feeling that the note should have been less brief, less matter-of-fact. But, she reflected, Anthony must now be a very busy man indeed, the more so from staff duties. In the meantime she would have to wait with what patience she could muster ... The hours continued to drag, and once again she turned to her painting.

One day while Mrs Foulkes was out sketching, Simms discovered Sue alone, re-reading her brother's letter. She tucked the scrap of paper away as he entered, but nothing that he could say or do dispelled the dismal mood into which she had fallen. Puzzled by her attitude, he wondered if by chance he had given offence, and said so, upon which she shook her head dumbly, turning aside that he might not observe the tears starting in her eyes.

"You are unhappy," he said gently. "Is it that you pine for England?"

"No," she murmured.

"What then?"

"I don't know. I cannot say."

He was touched by the underlying pathos in her voice.

"I may be able to help you?"

If he had rejoined with banter – as well he might – she would have remained withdrawn, but the sympathetic bearing of his last remark released in her the pent-up anxiety of many weeks, and before she was quit aware, she was pouring out the story of Robin's misadventure and its sequel. Confused, at first, she tended to omit relevant particulars; but with judicious questioning Simms managed to bring the narrative into some sort of order. When the picture was clear in his own mind, he lit a cigar and smoked for a little time in silence. To Sue his studied calm was impressive. For once the house was still, though a faint clinking of bottles came from the dispensing closet showed that the apothecary was busy. Gazing fixedly at the burnished foliage of a giant chestnut which spread its boughs over the little garden, she wondered if she had confessed too much. So that waiting for Simms to speak became additional torment. "I cannot expect—" she began, but he checked her with an upraised finger.

"First things first," he said. "You believe your brother to be absolutely innocent?"

"Of course!"

"Ah!" He watched the smoke of his cigar drift lazily through the open window. "I do not for a moment doubt your version, but Harker must be *proved* guilty. I mean," he added hurriedly as Sue bridled, "in the eyes of the law."

"Harker is beyond all question a scoundrel."

Simms made a deprecating gesture. "The army is a sink of scoundrels – men whose past will not bear looking into. In that case no useful purpose would be served by exposing Harker's real name to the authorities. If the rascal marches well, keeps his musket trim—" The commissary threw up his hands in a hopeless gesture, "they ask no more."

"Then we can do nothing?" she said faintly.

"Out of nothing, nothing comes," said Simms oracularly. His chin on his chest, he was silent for a while. "War," he resumed, "is a lottery, a gamble – I mean as far as private lives are concerned. Our man may have his head struck off by a cannon ball, succumb to a fever, fall into enemy hands – in short disappear completely. We would wish him to remain, and surviving, appeal to his better nature, or by other means compel him to speak the truth."

Sue looked questioningly.

"The best we can hope for," continued Simms, "is a confession properly drawn up and signed before witnesses, but what chance is there of that?"

"It would be a miracle," she said.

"Miracles have happened. In the meantime we must keep him well in sight."

Sue did not speak. The problem baffled her.

"Does he know who you are?"

"I think he suspects."

"Then he will be on his guard, though such gentlemen often through self assurance and vanity over-reach themselves. Give me leave to consider the matter a while. I should like to sound the man personally. I have ways and means."

"I am sorry that you should be burdened by all this," she murmured.

"Think nothing of it," he replied cheerfully. "We are poor things if we cannot assist our friends."

He tossed the stub of his cigar through the window, and with a broad grin departed. But as he entered the village street his face sobered. "The poor lass," he thought, "has one end of the string in her fingers, though God knows where the other may be. There would be no harm however in looking more closely at Private 'Raddock'."

Later, as Sue overhead Simms cursing a crowd of drovers, she wondered, if with numerous duties, he would be able to redeem his promise. At the same time she was relieved to have found one confidant, for in spite of their brief acquaintance, he had every appearance of being sincere ....

* * *

Simms was not the man to forget. A rib of pork in the right quarter, and on the following evening Private "Raddock" was detailed for bullock duty at the compound adjoining the commissary's depot.

The infantryman obeyed with a reluctance qualified only by the thought that "pickings" were more likely in the region of the depot than anywhere else.

In due course he reported, saluted Simms, and grounded his firelock. "Present for duty, sir." He was not compelled to "sir" the commissary, but felt it advisable to do so.

"What is your name?"

"Private Raddock, sir – awaiting your instructions, sir."

"Well, Private Raddock," said Simms motioning towards the compound, "you will look upon every one of these bullocks as members of your own family. There are forty at present – a good round number, easy to remember. At daybreak I shall expect the lot intact."

"Never been a herdsman, sir."

"You are not asked to be," said Simms. "All you are required to do is to prevent the local lads herding where they have no business. We lost a beast last night, dragged over the wall we think with a rope around its horns. You see the rising ground beside the wall," said Simms, pointing to the Westward corner, "that's one weak spot. There may be others. Cover them."

"I can't be on all side o' the compound at the same time, sir," said Harker.

"Which means that you must keep in movement. Challenge every sound. Remember – forty on the hoof!"

With that, Simms strolled back to his quarters.

"A clever devil?!" muttered Harker, as after fixing his side-sword he glanced with a poacher's eye at the thin shaving of the moon. "She'll not be with us long," he reflected. The dark bulk of the mountain shouldered the sky; that would not help. "Cat's eyes you want for this work," he grumbled. In the waning light he studied the two massive doors of the gateway, hung within an arch of stone; and held in place by a wooden baulk. "Should ha' been three chaps on this job, I reckon I'll be a runnin' dog all night." Thoroughly disgruntled, he cursed the compound, the animals, the serjeant, and the deputy assistant commissary all in one breath. After that he rested on a stone.

Away to the left, broken somewhat by a projecting spur of the mountain a string of bivouac fires glowed and flickered. Only the occasional barking dog or the braying of a baggage mule broke the silence, although distantly, he fancied, he could hear the pounding of breakers on the beach. He conjured in his mind's eye the convivial circle grouped around his own fire; the turkey which Henderson had that day "found". The bird would be sizzling now, golden brown on the spit, and not a morsel, not a lick for a poor devil sequestered at the compound!

Dusk deepened into night. After a leisurely perambulation of the walls, Harker returned to his post at the gate. Nothing here, nothing anywhere, except the vague outline of a girl who approached from the village street carrying a basket. As she drew near, Harker had no difficulty in recognising the Thompson wench, and he whistled softly as he slipped into the shadow of the archway and knocked upon the commissary's door. In a moment or two she was admitted. "So ho!" he breathed, "that's the game!" Sorely tempted to eavesdrop, he decided that on the whole it would be better to stay where he was.

After the ride from Lisbon – though he remembered her vaguely as a girl of fifteen – Harker had no doubt at all that this was Thompson's grown-up sister; she had the family resemblance, the carroty hair, the slightly tip-tilted nose, the hazel eyes of her brother. Yes, she was from the same stable. He continued to watch the glowing slit in the shutter, behind which, no doubt, the two would be having fun among the biscuit barrels. When, after what seemed a very long time, she reappeared, and was escorted some little way down the village street by Simms, the lone sentry drew a sardonic breath. "That's right," he grinned, "don't have nothing to do with strange men after dark!"

He spat. Apart from one or two raggle-taggle drabs haunting the fringes of the camp, there were few girls available at Paco d'Arcos. The slightest word in their direction, and papa and big brother were reaching for their knives. He sighed impatiently as he began another round of the walls. Approaching the corner especially pointed out by Simms, he fancied he heard the slightest padding of feet on the turf. He stopped – listening. A cat perhaps. There were droves in Paco d'Arcos. "Puss, puss!" he called endearingly, but to his surprise he was answered by a girl's low laugh. Was it the voice of Susan Thompson? He waited tensely, his musket at the ready. At last he cried, "Come out – let's have a look at ye."

A female figure broke from the shadows into the faint moonlight so softly that he guessed the newcomer's feet were bare. She was of middle height – no Thompson, this – lithe, slim, elusive. As she swept her hair from her brow her eyes glittered mischievously. A gypsy like as not. "Senor Inglese," she whispered, "vino – much good, damme!"

So that was it! He grounded his weapon with a chuckle. "All right," he responded, "what's the price-o, money-o?" The girl giggled, extending a bottle, but as he reached out his hand, she drew back again substituting an empty palm. Pay first, apparently; the goods afterwards. After rummaging in his pocket he found something that resembled a coin but which was really a tunic button hammered quite flat, reserved for such a transaction as this. "Fine Inglese dollar," he explained, "me buy plenty." Grabbing the button she handed over the flask; whereat Harker satisfied with his part of the bargain, propped his weapon beside the wall and drew the cork. He drank deeply, with relish; the wine was good. He wiped his mouth with the back of his hand. "What's your name?" he asked, "namo – callo?" Such argot being beyond her comprehension, she shook her head, pointing to herself. "Much vino," she repeated, "damn good, by God," phrases she must have picked up during the past few weeks.

"You said that once," he remarked, and took another pull; but when at last he lowered the bottle, to his amazement he saw that she held his weapon in her hands, and before he could make the slightest movement to restrain her, had fled with it into the darkness.

The flask splintered on the stones at his feet. He let out an agonised cry, the prospect of losing his musket so appalling that he charted into the darkness waving his arms wildly. Remarkably agile, the girl sprang like a cat from boulder to boulder, her dark dress merging with the deep shadows of the hillside. For the first fifty yards he did not gain a foot, until darting behind the ridge of granite outcrop, she disappeared completely.

Baffled, he halted, listening. "Come back," he pleaded, "give you much more Inglese dollars!" though even as he spoke he knew that the words were vain. He fancied he heard a mocking laugh, followed by the mewing of a cat, and rushed in that direction; but he was quite mistaken. Far to the right, on what must be more level ground, he could hear his firelock being dragged across the stones, then a clatter as though the weapon had been flung aside. Had the girl fallen, or alternatively was it possible that she now found the piece too heavy to handle? Fortunately it did not discharge. He darted forward in the direction of the sound, his feet tangling in the dry, wiry heather. Then, almost by instinct, he came upon his precious musket, cutting his hand on the bayonet as he did so. He sagged to one knee panting heavily. "If I'd ha' caught her," he snarled, "I'd ha' strangled the little bitch!" But he addressed only the quiet hillside.

In panic he remembered his duty at the gate. Stumbling back to the compound entrance, his worst fears were realised. The wooden baulk serving as a bar lay on the ground; and the padding of feet down the road implied that he had arrived only just in time to prevent disaster. Breathing heavily, he stared into the cool, velvet darkness. He could have sent a shot after the intruders, but this he realised would alert the Commissary, if indeed he had not already overheard the scurrying of feet. The girl, of course, had been a decoy, and he the veriest of fools to be so taken in. The best he could hope for was that the intruders had been disturbed before they would handle the bullocks.

Inside the compound one or two animals moved restlessly. He tried to count their outlines, but this proved impossible. Using all his strength he replaced the bar, and after that attended to his wounded hand which he bound up with a strip of rag from his cartridge pouch. There would be blood on his uniform, but that would dry and perhaps be little noticed by daylight.

He was still chafing inwardly when half an hour later, Simms strolled up whistling softly between his teeth. By this time the moon had completely disappeared, and Harker was thankful that the darkness concealed his bloody hand. "How goes the night, soldier?" asked the commissary cheerfully. "I thought I heard some movement." Whereupon Harker gave a garbled account of the incident, omitting all mention of the girl and her wine, and of course, the attempt on his musket. He calculated that he had routed at least half a dozen cattle thieves, and taking a long chance swore that Simms would find the cattle intact. "Good work!" said the commissary, "now you may eat." He produced a portion of bread and cheese, and leaning beside the gate-post smoked as Harker chewed voraciously. The commissary's easy attitude puzzled the infantryman. He waited suspiciously.

"A glorious night," Simms observed.

"If you want glory," said Harker.

"What was your name?"

"Raddock," said Harker, "same as before."

"Raddock – Raddock?" mused Simms. "An odd name."

"What's so odd about it?" asked Harker.

"It would appear to be a little – fabricated"

"Fabricated?" said Harker. "I don't understand."

"Contrived – concocted," Simms drawled, "but let it go. There are many men in the army with queer names."

"I've nowt to hide," said Harker defiantly. "My parents died when I was young. I was browt up by my owd granddad, who was a butcher of Lincoln. You can get sick of guts and hides, so being in the militia I listed. And the name is still Raddock."

"A good straightforward story," said Simms, "simple, graphic and to the point. Is Lincoln a sizeable town?"

"No kind of place."

"Large say – as Hythe?"

"'Bout," said Harker hesitatingly.

"A fine church there, I'm told."

"Never noticed none."

"No church?"

Harker shook his head.

"You'd be more familiar with the jail perhaps?"

"Have your little joke, sir."

Simms chuckled. "Your turn may come."

"I can wait," rejoined Harker. Simms would get no change from him!

"The army," resumed Simms musingly, "is clogged with men escaping magistrates warrants, poor clods unable to return to their own place. I've often wondered what it must feel like to be hunted, trembling at every footstep, ready to run like a scalded cat at the clap of a hand." Here Simms brought one of his own sharply on Harker's shoulder. "Don't you agree?"

Harker scowled, releasing himself. "You will have your bit of fun, sir."

"Fun, you call it? Fun?"

"You're making me feel real nervous, sir."

"I wouldn't do that for the world," said Simms. He felt the conversation was leading nowhere. With half a mind to raise the question of poaching, he refrained. The man was too cagey. He began to move away. "Remember the reckoning!" he called over his shoulder.

"Reckoning?" repeated Harker.

"The bullocks, soldier – and let the tally be complete."

Harker swore gently as he watched the commissary walk away and disappear through the doorway of his house. Magistrates warrants? Reckoning? He could not help feeling that there had been a purposive trend in the conversation, a probing element inspired no doubt, by the Thompson girl. The reference to a magistrate's warrant touched him profoundly. Was it possible that way back home one had been issued against him? Had the old man, always loose in his cups, betrayed him? He tried to recapture every movement on that fateful night, until with an angry gesture he effected to dismiss the subject altogether …

But it was not easy. As he resumed his pacing of the outer walls, he laughed softly, but without mirth. The reference to his assumed name still rankled. What did it all amount to? Precisely nothing. The silly girl and her jack-in-office acquaintance had no power whatsoever. "You sit tight, my lad," he told himself, "that is all you need to do."

As Simms wriggled into his sleeping bag, he was far from satisfied with the late encounter. The fellow was undoubtedly glib, inventive, and something of a liar. No church indeed, in Lincoln! But how to break through the screen, and at the same time to do a service to Susan Thompson and her brother, Simms for the moment had not the faintest idea.

CHAPTER VIII

Quelez – at last! With an indrawn breath of wonder Harriet Foulkes drew rein before the royal palace of Portugal. Framed in low-lying hills and surrounded by a high white wall, this Portuguese "Versailles" was much smaller than its French counterpart. You took in with a single glance the gleaming façade of white and pink and green; the central stroke lifting two storeys above the rest. The whole effect was at once elegant and charming. It had an air. You must almost hear the rustle of silk and brocade within, the tapping of dainty heels, the lilt of violins across the shining parterre. A house of dalliance.

But scars remained of the French occupation. Across the garden she saw that one of the statues was minus a head; that two others had broken arms. There was a gap in the yew hedge where carts had been run through, and unswept animal ordure still littered the approach. Junot had left much, but he had carried away considerable tapestry, furniture, silver and pictures. The Portuguese were bitter that under the screen of the infamous "Convention", Napoleon's darling general had filched so much of the national treasure.

Harriet's eyes were more anxious for personal reasons. She did not in the least expect to meet her husband (Percy and his fellow officers would be busy with Sir John Moore, who was that day inspecting at Paco d'Arcos); but where was Captain, the Honourable Anthony Harte? As she rode forward at a walking pace, she could see numerous red-coated figures, members of the headquarters staff, moving about the lower rooms of the mansion; but of he whom she sought, no sign at all. Her heart sank as she reflected that he might have been ordered away on some stupid mission. When a harsh, derisive laugh came from an unseen quarter she was reminded that this had been the residence of the mad Queen Donna Maria. Was it possible – as the American had suggested – that her crazy spirit, still haunted the building? She shivered, feeling strangely alone. (The invaluable Mr Simms escorting her to the gates had gone to the stores depot, which had been set up at the approach to the park.) She felt herself the target of a hundred curious eyes.

An officer of Dragoons appeared in the doorway, stared hard, consciously stiffened himself, and approached with so firm a step that she felt he must be the bearer of a message from Tony. When she halted her mount, the jingling impact of the officer's feet on the flags was the loudest sound in the quiet afternoon. She patted Felix's neck, speaking softly to the animal, at the same time shaping a sentence with which to receive the newcomer. That moment, to her intense relief, she saw that Tony Harte was running down the steps to meet her. She gave a little cry of pleasure. With a significant, but good-humoured glance, the Dragoon officer turned away.

Tony seemed not an hour older than when they had last parted in the glittering ballroom at Brighton. If anything his cheeks were of a deeper bronze, but the cleanly-cut features, the crisp chestnut hair, the jaunty lift of his chin were exactly as she had remembered. His eyes perhaps were a trifle more anxious. How handsome he was in the gold and blue of his huzzar uniform: the slung jacket less a cloak than a drape of adornment. "We meet again," he said simply, to which she responded tritely, "And in circumstances so very different." Nervously she smoothed out her riding skirt ...

He summoned an orderly who led away her horse, and at once suggested that the Dutch Canal was a place where they might conveniently walk and talk. Was it possible (she fancied) that she detected a certain diffidence of manner, the slightest touch of embarrassment as he drew her towards the screen of dark enamelled leaves and still shining water? She checked the reproach that he had withheld from her the date of his return to England. That could wait. Sufficient now that they were together alone; that the air was filled with aromatic odours, the singing of birds, the gentle rustling of leaves.

When later she tried to analyse their conversation, she found it strangely aimless. Of course, he listened attentively as she related something of her journey to the Peninsular, her life at Bellaby, her domestic pursuits; but how insipid it all seemed as with a touch of that glancing irony she knew so well, he spoke of his own adventures – the night when lodging at a Grecian inn he had found a corpse in the second bed; how in apostolic tradition he had been cast ashore on the coast of Asia Minor; how eluding French patrols in Switzerland by masquerading as an artist, he had eventually been denounced by artists in Florence as a stupid philistine. "My way of life," he smiled, "has been one of constant dissimulation. Now it is all virtue and honour."

"You appear committed."

"I am – to my vocation, and of course to Sir John."

She laughed ruefully. Always Moore. Like her husband, Tony had fallen under the spell of the new commander-in-chief. Still, she reflected, the army made its own demands.

He took her arm, and they paced slowly. "It was quite surprising to learn that you were here," he said. "Why did you come to this—" He waved his hand towards the rolling hills beyond, "to Spain?"

"The attraction was irresistible," she rejoined.

"Adventure?"

"It may be." A mischievous light shone in her eyes. She waited for the next observation; but he did not pursue the matter.

They walked for a few paces without speaking. Then, "How on earth do you fill the time?" he asked.

"Eating, drinking, reading, sketching – and looking up old friends," she said lightly.

"Old friends?" he mused. "You know Harriet, I have always remembered you with affection." He spoke with an oddly detached, a vaguely reminiscent air.

"And you were often in my thoughts," she said.

There was a brief deep silence. She hoped that he would continue, this time with some expression of warmth, of profound feeling, but she was to be disappointed. Inconsequentially he pointed to the orange grove. "Apples of gold in a screen of olive – how like a tapestry! There should be classical figures, huntsmen, hounds and deer ... How is your husband?"

She answered briefly that he was well. "A worthy fellow, and what is more to the point, a conscientious officer."

She murmured vaguely, and dismissing the subject, suggested that it would be pleasant to view the interior of the palace. Her companion hesitated, explaining that one wing had been devoted entirely to hospital cases, and the other to the staff. "Not a spare inch anywhere," he said doubtfully.

"It is of no consequence," she said flatly, but noting her disappointed tone he rallied, "No – no indeed. We will do our best, though I warn you the lower floor bears less the appearance of a royal residence than a counting house."

They returned to the main entrance. Thereafter he whisked her down corridors and through rooms where she caught a glimpse of the Napoleonic bees and eagles introduced by the French; Watteau-like conversation pieces, the throne-room with its massive chandeliers, vistas of silken panels and velvet curtains. Staff officers glanced at them curiously. Once a general officer with eyes of flint stared hard – it was Crawfurd – but passed without remark. In a short time they were out in the open again. She noticed that there had been no introductions.

Later, seated in the garden, conversation often lapsed into silence; but she was content. Enough (she assured herself) that they were together again. More than once he consulted his watch; time for both of them was limited. At three he called for her horse, assisted her to mount, and paced slowly beside her until through the gate they caught a glimpse of Mr Simms, waiting dutifully at the end of a row of huts.

"We must meet again?" she said.

"There will be opportunity."

"When?"

He shrugged. "That depends – on Sir John and the French."

The note of hesitation in his voice, of evasion even, touched her, but she gave no outward sign.

"I am not now," he explained, "my own master – a will-o'-th'-wisp, riding here, riding there."

"A veritable Pegasus!" she smiled.

"Not quite."

She raised her arm signalling to the commissary.

"I will contrive to communicate with you," said Tony, his voice suddenly warm and reassuring. "In the meantime send me your sketches." Simms came forward. "I leave you now in the hands of this good gentleman. Au revoir."

"Au revoir," she responded brightly.

As she wheeled her horse looking back, she saw that the bright façade of the palace had fallen into shadow. She shivered slightly, but responded to Tony Harte's final salute with a gay flourish of her switch. For a moment or two the captain watched the slowly pacing Felix and the lithe swaying figure of its rider, until clasping his hands behind his back, he walked thoughtfully through the gilded gates of the park …

* * *

That evening the Major said, biting his words off primly, "I hear from your woman that you have been to Quelez."

"Yes," said Harriet, with a little laugh, "Mr Simms was riding over so I took advantage of his company. I was much impressed."

"By Mr Simms?"

"Don't be ridiculous – with Quelez, the palace."

"You might have mentioned that you were going."

"It was quite on the spur of the moment. You were much occupied. Don't frown so. One would think I had committed the unpardonable sin."

"Sir John was with us," he replied sharply. "I wished to introduce you to him – a most convenient opportunity. I came expressly to collect you."

"And I was not there!" She threw a commiserating glance.

"You were not!"

"Was the gentleman disappointed?" she asked archly.

"That is not the point. We must observe the proprieties, to say nothing of being in touch with the Commander-in-chief."

"I am sorry, but I thoroughly enjoyed myself. I was fortunate in meeting Tony Harte, who did the honours and showed me round."

With deliberate action Foulkes took a pinch of snuff, and brushed a few grains from his tunic. "They don't know how to mix snuff in this country," he exclaimed petulantly.

"You should turn to cigars," she observed, "there are plenty available." She wondered if her colour had risen, and averted her head.

"I must have a supply sent from England," he continued, "but one has to wait so confoundedly long." Then he faced his wife squarely. "Reverting to Quelez – on the whole, excepting only an invitation from Sir John, I should keep away in future."

"Why?" She raised her eyebrows in mock surprise.

"Because of danger lurking."

"Danger?"

He smiled strangely. "I might lose you."

"Come now," she teased with rapidly beating heart, "you would never miss me!"

"Make no doubt of that." He paused, running his thumb over the lid of the snuff box, regarding with close attention the inlay pattern of the surface. "There is, you know, a grave danger of infection."

"I am proof against that."

"No," he said firmly, fixing her with his eyes. "A palace, which is at the same time a hospital for dysentery, is no place for a woman."

"Is that the only reason?" she laughed.

"One could be dead within twenty four hours."

"You needn't fear."

"Harriet," he said gravely, "I, and I alone, am responsible for your welfare; if anything were to happen to you I should never forgive myself."

"I ask only to be buried with full military honours!" Again, the flippant rejoinder.

His eyes rested on the burnished surface of the snuff box as though to read a riddle there. Then, looking up he said firmly, "I don't intend to lose you at all."

* * *

Harriet wrote to Jane—

"I am still quartered with Don Quixote's apothecary, who remains as elusive a figure as when I first set eyes on him. He denied to Mr Simms that he compounded love potions, but why, if this be not so do village maidens steal in after dark and exchange coins for phials which they immediately secrete on their persons? ...

I must tell you of my visit to Quelez – of all palaces the most amazing. Words fail to express its magical elegance and proportion. Square hedges line gardens where cypress trees are bent into arches, and bushes clipped into varied shapes; and fountains, cupids, nymphs, and double-tailed mermaids without number ...

Inside, one walks on brick polished like parquet. There is a ball-room, *salle de glaces*; and everywhere intricate floor patterns, mirrors and curiously reflected light – one could linger for hours. Incidentally, who should I meet but Anthony Harte, my old Brighton friend, of whom you have heard? He is more charming than ever ...

Colonel Pomeroy – old badger – has joined us here. He is as polite as he can find in his nature to be, but his compliments have the tang of ill-sweetened rhubarb ...

We have now assembled 30,000 muskets and sabres – you see how easily I adapt myself to military nomenclature!"

* * *

Sir Hew and Sir Harry, the notorious "convention" mongers had returned to England leaving Sir John Moore at the head of an army more formidable in strength than any landed on the continent since the days of Queen Anne. The new commander-in-chief had served in America, the Low Countries, Corsica, Sicily and Egypt. At home his new methods of training had attracted universal attention. He had formed and equipped the Light Infantry with the improved Baker rifle. In all his dealings he was considerate, humane, authoritative. No general officer commanded greater respect.

But his appointment brought complication. Moore was a Whig, and ministers were Tory. His own party had for years maintained steady opposition to continental adventures, and Spain was no exception. Thus if he were to fail in the campaign he would be subject to a galling crossfire at Westminster. The opposition would not cease to harass the government, and for their part ministers might be lukewarm in his defence. Moore did not intend to fail, but clouds darkened the horizon.

If however, he had left England with mistrust, he had much more reason to be anxious in the new field of operation. The country rang with patriotic exhortation; but where were the armies with which he was expected to unite? Where were La Romana, Castanos, Blake, and other Spanish commanders? No one could say for certain; but from what little information trickled through, Moore gathered that great numbers of Spanish cavalry were without horses, gunners without powder, the rank and file ill-clad and poorly armed. A Supreme Junta ruled, but its writ ran adventitiously. Dispatches from Mr Frere, the British Minister in Madrid, reflecting every shade of Spanish hopes and fears, did little to clarify the situation. One factor did remain constant – the French controlled overwhelming forces. Soult and Ney alone lay at Burgos with 40,000 men, and more were constantly streaming through Bayonne. Moore was not afraid of the French, nor of the rumour that Napoleon himself had entered the field of operations, but in the council of his own mind he had decided that the defence of Portugal was virtually impossible. A year later, two years at most, when *guerilleros*, ambushing convoys and cutting communications, compelled the French to distribute their forces, the situation altered. But that lay ahead. For his part Moore would be compelled to probe and thrust and thus by vexing the French, relieve pressure upon the disunited Spanish armies.

Transport was the immediate problem. Apart from a few vehicles of the Royal Wagon Train, he was entirely dependent on local mules and ox carts – the latter with drivers hired from village to village. Mountain country had to be traversed; information concerning highways amounted to very little. Main roads thinned into stony tracks, and after torrential rains dried up water courses became raging torrents. Guns, no doubt, would have to be man-handled across gullies and ravines. Baggage would have to be reduced to a minimum.

The first General Order issued on October 9th, required officers to make their equipment ready for inspection. All heavy baggage was to be left behind, at which those who had collected many creature comforts for the campaign cursed roundly. The rank and file were warned against excessive drinking. It contained finally a charge to the women, which brought the Major hot-foot into the apothecary's parlour.

He entered and took a seat beside the charcoal brasero, for the air had begun to sharpen, and the rooms of the old stone house were chilly. Harriet, who had just received an English newspaper from Lisbon was reading extracts aloud. She looked up. "You are not listening," she said.

"I have good reason," he said. "Put down your paper. I have something more to date."

"What is it?"

"A General Order, which since it concerns Thompson as well, I will read aloud."

"Dear me!"

He shot a glance, which imposed silence, and read in a firm, level voice—

"As in the course of a long march the army is to undertake, and where no carts will be allowed, the women would be unavoidably exposed to great hardship and distress, commanding officers are desired to use their endeavours to prevent as many as possible, particularly those having young children, or such as are not stout or equal to fatigue, from following the army. Those who remain will be left with the baggage of the regiment. An officer will be charged to draw their rations, and they will be sent to England by the first good opportunity; and when landed they will secure the same allowance which they would have been entitled to if they had not embarked, to enable them to reach their homes."

The Major folded the document slowly allowing the full import of the message to sink in. "That," he said, "is the General's feeling."

Harriet dropped her newspaper and sat very still, her hands folded in her lap. The stark official sentences lingered in her mind – "the greatest hardship and distress" – "to prevent as many as possible" from marching forward. Moore's shadow brooded in the room. But she remained composed. "The order," she said quietly, "enjoins persuasion by commanding officers. Why did not Colonel Pomeroy present this himself?"

The Colonel preferred that I should raise the matter with you."

"Gallant fellow!" she cried.

"No," continued her husband patiently. "He conceived the matter to be a purely domestic affair." (We arrive now, he thought, at the specific turning point. She cannot possibly flout and official order. At the same time he realised that he would have to employ all his power of persuasion). He added bluntly, "There it is."

Harriet who had been meditating with half-closed eyes opened them suddenly. "What response is there?"

"From the women?"

"Yes."

The Major hesitated. "The returns are not yet in."

"But such as you have."

Foulkes frowned. It was not in his nature to hedge. "Very little," he answered reluctantly.

Harriet smiled. "I am not surprised."

The Major shifted uneasily under his wife's gaze. "This is a serious statement," he said. "The question is – what do *you* intend to do?"

"To do?"

She spoke with a pained expression. The repetition, her air of serene detachment, irked him. He thought, at all costs I must exercise patience. Best keep the document before her. He opened the order and scanned it again. "So far you have travelled in comfort," he said.

"I should not have thought the *Caledonia* comfortable," she retorted.

He allowed the remark to pass. "In Lisbon you were fortunate in a good hotel, amid pleasant urban surroundings. You have been well-cared for at Paco d'Arcos. Now, I am afraid, it must end. You can return home from this place in perfect safety. If not, then I am bound to say, that Sir John will make no preferential treatment for ladies."

"I ask none. I shall ride with the regiment."

"Don't forget that I have my duties."

"Have I ever kept you from your duties?"

He winced as he listened to the calm unhurried words. She had not. He would have welcomed some display of emotion, but this was ominously absent. Sharply he turned to Sue, who during this conversation had retired to a corner of the room, and beckoned her forward. He tapped the paper in his hand. "You understand girl, that here is a general order of the Commander-in-chief advising all women to return to England?"

"Not all women," corrected Harriet, "only those not equal to fatigue."

The major ignored the interjection. "How do you feel in the matter? Think well before you answer. On the one hand you may go home. Your passage will be provided, and I myself will give you ample means to reach Bellaby. On the other hand, your well being, indeed your very life, may be at stake. You understand?"

"Yes, sir."

"Well, make your choice."

Sue passed from the stern gaze of her master to the more relaxed and meaningful eyes of her mistress. Harriet's lips curled slightly in amused disdain. From this the girl took her cue. "I should wish to be with my mistress whatever happens," she said.

"How could you expect anything else?" observed Harriet. "Things being equal, what would *you* wish me to do?"

"As man and husband I would wish you to stay; as a soldier – and I trust I am unquestionably that – I think it your duty to return to Bellaby."

"A Daniel come to judgment," she murmured as she crossed to the window.

"That does not help," he rapped.

"Sir John leaves the matter open, does he not?" Her eyes were fixed upon the misty slope of the mountain. "I have no wish to appear inconsiderate, Percy, but I must ask for a little time to reflect. I will give you an answer tomorrow."

"Very well."

He slung his cloak over his arm, his spurs jingled on the flags, they could hear him speaking sharply to someone – perhaps an orderly – and he clattered away …

* * *

That evening Harriet slipped through the apothecary's door – alone. A few lights glimmered in the windows, but the village had already disposed itself for sleep. Across the shoulder of the mountain bivouac fires pricked the darkness. Towards these she went.

She had never paid much attention to the regimental women; on shipboard she had been almost entirely withdrawn, and Lisbon had taken them away. Now she decided to seek them out. They would, of course, receive the Major's wife with deference, but would they speak freely, naturally, and not consciously to please? She wished for a frank opinion of Sir John's manifesto. Percy had implied an equivocal response. If she could refute this her own position would be strengthened.

She met with a challenge, but her peremptory, "Don't be a fool man!" brought the sentry to order. Around the fires men lazily conversed or gambled with dice and cards. Woodsmoke drifted, and once caught in a choking swirl, she stopped with both hands covering her face. Moving more in darkness than in light, Harriet was comparatively unnoticed. She listened for female voices and presently found the fire from whence the sound came. There was a tendency for married groups to cling together.

She appeared in the firelight where half a dozen women flushed with heat were sewing, mending socks, and chatting the while. One was breaking biscuit into small pieces for a dog.

"Good evening," said Harriet pleasantly.

The women looked up. Her sudden entry reduced them to silence. At last one said, "Why, 'tis Missis Foulkes."

"Indeed," said another. The women stopped their work waiting for Harriet to speak again.

"You look quite comfortable."

To this commonplace opening the woman who had spoken first said politely, "Thank you kindly; we make do." The rest murmured assent. They were awkward, abashed in the presence of the Major's lady. Harriet remained standing.

Again silence. One woman – a Mrs Branscombe – rose from her seat, a swan-off log, and said, "Won't you sit here, Ma'm?" she dropped to her knees on the turf which was quite dry.

"You are very kind," said Harriet. She took the place offered, and pointed to the half-darned socks. "Don't you find the firelight trying for your eyes?"

"Oh, no – no," they chorused, though Mrs Branscombe ventured that she was used to spectacles, but unfortunately had lost them.

"I am sure you do splendidly," said Harriet. She examined one sock closely. The darning was neat and firm. "I don't know how the men would do without you." She looked inquiringly around the circle. "I suppose you have been discussing the general's new order?"

The women did not answer. Why had the lady come? To enforce the regulation?

"The General's order now," repeated Harriet. "Do you like it?"

"Haven't considered it much," said Mrs Branscombe, who seemed to be mouthpiece for the rest.

"But surely—?"

"Don't see that it applies. We come by agreement, so we sticks by our men."

"Accordin' to reg'lation," said one.

"Has Colonel Pomeroy addressed you?"

"He did that – called us round his tent, but only one, poor soul, gave in. She was six months gone."

"You were all of a mind then?"

"'Deed we are," they chirped.

"Don't know what our poor Joe would do wi'out me." The assertion was made by a stout woman with apple-red cheeks.

"You don't by any chance," said Harriet smiling, "carry his musket?"

"Mrs Foulkes, lady," rejoined the woman, whose name was Favell, "I'm speaking God's truth when I say that I've carried that man on my back afore now."

"Metaphorically speaking."

"I don't know about that," said Mrs Favell, "but i' Sicily – an' there is those here present that knows I don't tell a lie – what does he do but break his ankle when on march, with no carts, no mules, no nothing – so I ups him on me back and carries him three solid mile."

Harriet stared incredulously.

"He's as thin as a lat," explained Mrs Branscombe.

"Which makes no difference," said Mrs Favell. "I carried that man three miles, an' I'd do it again."

"You were very brave," said Harriet.

"You've got to buckle to, haven't you?" said the woman. She squared her formidable shoulders, as though to hoist the burden again.

"I take it you are all prepared to go forward?"

"No doubt o' that."

Harriet rose. "Well, I expect to share your company. If you should need help – it doesn't matter when – don't hesitate to approach me at any time. But I can't promise to carry your husbands for you!" And she turned to the doughty Mrs Favell. The company laughed …

"Pity we 'aven't a tasty bit for you to eat," said Mrs Branscombe ruefully.

"That's kind of you," said Harriet, "but thank you very much, I am not in the least hungry."

She passed to the next fire where three younger women were reclining with their husbands. As she approached they stared curiously, but in a composed manner. "Have you a moment?" inquired Harriet.

"Certainly Ma'm," said one of the men. He nudged the girl beside him. "'Tis the Major's wife!"

"I know," she whispered.

Here the seats were more makeshift; all were lying on mounds of heather. To give Harriet room, one of the girls shuffled closer to her man. The newcomer sank upon her knees.

"You have heard of the General's order?"

They nodded reluctantly, sensing like the others, that she had perhaps been sent to influence their decision.

"Do you propose to return?"

"Back home?"

"It is proposed."

"I should be sorry to disagree wi' you ar the General Ma'm," said the nearest regular, a lean fresh-faced Lowland Scot, "but where I go ma wife goes wi' me."

"Let her speak for herself," said Harriet.

"I will," said the girl who was leaning on the infantryman's shoulder, her clear grey eyes fixed upon those of her interrogator. "'Tis not for naething that I tramped the tract o' the Lowlands frae Glasga, and the long length o' England to join him i' Doncaster, the which 'cept for a mile or two, never a lift did I get till Boroughbridge, an' ma feet red-raw wi' blisters! Do you think I mind now the stony roads of Spain? Och – no!"

"You walked all the way from Scotland?" asked Harriet incredulously.

"That I did. Sir John, or no Sir John – an' he bein' a Scotsman, I speak with respect – here I am and here I stay." She cocked a defiant chin.

"A girl of spirit," said Harriet. "What say the others?"

"The same," said the second to the right. Across the fire the third woman nodded approval. "Let the General find us a tidy bite and he'll have to cause for worry."

Harriet laughed, turning to the indomitable Scots girl. "A bite of porridge?"

"Aye, a bit porridge."

Harriet rose to her feet. She had heard enough. As she retraced her steps and regained the still, moon-lit street of Paco d'Arcos, she smiled tightly. "The wine is drawn and must be drunk," she decided ....

* * *

She did not wait long in conveying a decision to her husband, reading by candlelight until Foulkes appeared. He had been dining with the Colonel and Major Daiches, and since the prospect of marching had heightened the spirits of all in camp, he shared the prevailing good humour.

Harriet had already marshalled her argument. "Sir John," she said, "excepted all who where not stout and equal to fatigue. Now, apart form a little indisposition in Lisbon – which I lay to excessive fruit – I am perfectly well. Besides, how can I, the wife of a senior officer hold back when Mrs Binks and Mrs Jenks or whatever, will follow their husbands?"

"I am bound both by obligation and example. You see that, do you not, Percy?"

"If you put it so," he said.

"I do indeed."

"Your sense of duty does you credit," he commented dryly. "You argue well. "A nerve began to twitch in his cheek. "That is your final decision?"

"Yes"

He sat, hands on knees staring at the thin spiral of smoke lifting from the lamp container ... and could think of nothing which had not been said many times before. He sighed. "We will manage as we can. Is Felix well-shot?"

She thought that he was.

"Your girl will need a tolerable mule. That will be difficult. We seem to have drained the district, but I will see what can be done."

Harriet murmured her thanks, and wondered what he was really thinking. He was staring over her shoulder abstractedly ...

* * *

The ridge-pole tents were struck, all shelters abandoned, and in a few hours time Portuguese peasants poked among the blackened stones and scattered brushwood for remnants left by the army. Now the upland resounded with the steady tramp of the infantry, the jingling of horsemen, the crashing and squeaking wheels of the ox-carts. The pace of these vehicles was painfully slow. "Arrivo! Arrivo!" yelled the Portuguese drivers – not that it made much difference. The oxen held to their own pace, and the wheels continued to complain excruciatingly.

The army splayed out in four probing columns – Beresford by Coimbra, Frazer by Ciudad Rodrigo, Paget taking Alcantara, and Hope with the artillery in a wide eastern sweep via Talavera. Sir John rode soberly; many days would pass before they reunited at Salamanca. Before Hope arrived at that destination, for the Talavera route while being the best for wheeled transport, was the longest way round, the army would be without heavy metal, no general action would be considered. It was a chance that would have to be taken. Moore hoped that the French were as little aware of his movements as he was of theirs.

Colonel Pomeroy rode in advance of the regiment. To his annoyance he carried almost the same number of women and children with which he had landed at Maciera Bay. "Like a damned gypsy horde!" he muttered as he turned to see some women marching with their husbands. "I tell you," he protested to Foulkes, "when action comes, they'll be running around and blubbering in every quarter of the battlefield, to the distraction of all concerned. We saw it in Holland, and in Sicily."

"They must stop where they are stationed," said Foulkes.

"Might as well stop monkeys."

"It's our burden," rejoined Foulkes with feeling.

"As if we haven't enough to carry!"

Steadily the columns, threads of crimson-grey, wound through the expanse of heather and granite outcrop. "One might think oneself in Derbyshire," reflected Foulkes ... His wife brought up the rear on Felix, attended by Sue on a mule. This animal, which except for a crack in one of its hooves (made good by a neat metal staple) was in excellent fettle. The beast carried not only Sue and her holdall, but in addition, two valises, one balancing the other, and a sizeable bag of fodder. After a few hours riding the girl, lamenting her aching joints, decided to buy – though how she had no means of knowing – a pair of trousers to wear beneath her skirts.

It was clear to all why Sir John had sent the bulk of the artillery round by Talavera. The roads of the region were little better than cattle-tracks over which the wagons and carts lurched like vessels in a storm. They jolted into ravines, skirted gullies and precipices, poised goat-like on mountain crags. At times a thick mist concealed the depths beneath, until the marching men seemed suspended between heaven and earth. By night, to the pervading odours of dung and garlic, the snuffling of animals and the clucking of hens, they quartered in miserable hamlets, heaping up heather for beds or resting on the stark stone floors. Sue finished the day by cooking scratch dishes for Mrs Foulkes, and washing and mending for both mistress and master. This done, she slept the sleep of exhaustion.

The Major held towards the rear. His eyes followed the column when, as often, it vanished for a time and reappeared among the crags, noting where the files thinned and broke. Thank God they were in no danger of a flank attack. As he balanced his snuff box (what on earth did the merchants in Lisbon grind – oak leaves?) his mind ranged freely over campaigns in the remote past. Caesar had made his early reputation in Spain, perhaps among these very mountains. He wondered how present equipment – musket, ammunition, blanket, pouch, and various impedimenta – compared in weight with that carried by the Roman legionary. Not much in it perhaps, including the armour ...

Glancing towards the baggage train, he was pleased to see that Harriet rode with complete assurance. Her conduct at times was distinctly irritating, though he could point to nothing that called for direct censure ... For the time being the regiment had no real mess; but when she did join the circle of offices, she flattered the Colonel shamelessly. For his part, Pomeroy, who still felt her presence an intrusion in his male world, displayed commendable forbearance. He had, of course, knocked about too long to be swept off his feet by female blandishments. Foulkes wished this could be said of the younger officers. When she inveigled Lieutenant Suckley into reproducing bird-song on his flute, the farce went on so long that only an immoderate amount of grunting and coughing in Pomeroy's part brought the performance to an end. When Carworth had drunk more than he ought, she persuaded him to sing. Foulkes winced as he remembered that. Nor could he easily forget the time when she invited Lieutenant Bird to an exposition of the noble art of self-defence. Pomeroy's face as that young gentleman demonstrated the hook, the jab, the half-cut, the upper-cut was a study in baffled exasperation. The fool could not see that he was being led by the nose! She intervened with polite but persistent inquiries into purely military matters. "Do tell me, for I am appallingly ignorant" – until the Colonel, his patience exhausted would rise before his time, saying, "Well, gentlemen, we have a long hard day before us tomorrow – by your leave Ma'm," and break up the circle ...

* * *

Only once during the long march had Sue been brought face to face with Harker. When the ranks broke into bivouac, the women invariably joined their husbands, but in these groupings Sue had no place. On the uplands of Spain she was as closely tied to Harriet as she had been at Hythe, indeed more so. Sometimes passing infantrymen were curious about the ridge-pole tent erected for Mrs Foulkes, but having no business there none lingered.

Always at the day's end there was a certain ranging afield for brushwood to feed the fires, and although this was not Sue's duty, late one evening noting that the fire had died down, she set off in search of fuel. Within a circuit of perhaps fifty yards she was fortunate enough to find a withered bush the branches of which being brittle snapped off in her hands. She had gathered an armful and was about to return when she noticed half concealed by the shadow of a rock, the silent figure of a man. Having heard no footsteps she concluded that he must have been watching her throughout.

It was Harker. He carried a bundle of tough, wiry heather, so that his general purpose was clear, but what did he now intend? Half a dozen throbbing seconds passed. She wondered if he would speak. The two however, remained rooted where they stood in complete silence. She could find nothing to say. Perhaps he too was at a complete loss for words. As she turned away, he moved also, but it was in the direction of the company's fire ...

* * *

The weather broke. Rain fell in torrents. It seemed that the very heavens had opened. Shakoes and knapsacks streamed water, cloaks hung soddenly; even Mrs Foulkes' new English oilskin was no proof against the downpour. Horses and oxen steamed in the rain; even the mule bells were muted. In places the track became almost impassable, mud axle-deep bogging and binding the wheels. Campfires attempted in the lee of enormous boulders, flickered, sputtered and died away. The dwarf oaks gave no shelter. Any flea-infested posada would have been welcome, but never a cattle-shed made its appearance. So they crouched in rocky crevices with blankets alone for cover. Darkness came, and still it rained ... and rained ... and rained ...

After a couple of drenching days, the columns entered Guardia. Billeted at a house on the plaza, the two women dried their clothes, and ate a substantial supper of quail and partridge. They had arrived early in the evening, and it was not long before Harriet, who felt she had been deprived too long of social diversion, produced a pack of cards, proposing a game. At Paco d'Arcos she had taught Sue to play whist, but her husband being absent at headquarters, she cast around for other partners. With a murmur of satisfaction she recalled that Lieutenants Bird and Carworth had been lodged in the room opposite. Why not invite them both? Overhearing a voice in the corridor, she darted to the door, and opened it to discover Lieutenant Bird himself, cloaked and hatted for the street. Bareheaded, Carworth loomed just beyond his friend's shoulder. Using all her gift for persuasion, Harriet invited the two young officers to share a game. Carworth was willing enough, but Bird reluctant.

"At any other time, dear lady, I should have been honoured to oblige." She wagged a knowing finger. "You have a tender assignment!"

"One," he grimaced," that I could very well do without. I am on duty at eight."

"Duty!" she exclaimed indignantly, "after all we have marched this day!"

"None the less, to duty I must go." He spoke without conviction. The glowing brasero, and the bottle he glimpsed on a side-table were all too tempting.

"'Tis not yet eight," she pleaded, taking the damp cloak between her fingers. "Give this a chance to dry."

Still, Bird hesitated. The siren voice was warm, compelling, and he never could resist cards. He had, it was true, a little time in hand. After all (he thought) there was still a deal of confusion in the town; men were still settling in, and what with one thing and another it would be easy to cover a few minutes delay. So he was induced to enter, warning Harriet that he would be compelled to play by the watch. This, as a mark of conscience, he set upon the table. Less than half a minute later, the four were seated, and the young officer dealt the cards. "If we keep the stakes low," said Harriet, slipping Sue a small coin or two, "we shall none of us be ruined."

"Mother of God," said Bird, "I am that already."

"But luck will take a turn," said Harriet confidently.

"Let's hope so," he said.

Sue fingered her cards nervously. She was quite certain that her parents would have disapproved. She recalled her father's frequent reference to the "Devil's Bible", but there would have been no point in raising the matter ...

No such inhibition affected the other three ... Below the windows the tramping of feet continued, rain hammered on the shutters, the spouts cascaded on the plaza stones, but all was peaceful in the upper room where four intent faces were outlined by candlelight.

Bird did not notice that his watch had stopped at seven fifty-seven ...

* * *

Meanwhile, a few hundred yards away in a convent, drinking mulled wine and smoking cigars, sat the Colonel, the two majors, the paymaster and the commissary. Saddlebags had been dumped on the floor, and swords decorated convenient brackets. After the long day's march, the austere room provided that haven of peace and comfort to which they had all looked forward. They were being well-served. The Colonel saw that the beautifully chased cups of silver-gilt, for the priests had produced their best, were constantly replenished. "One ought to keep an eye on these," he thought, "so many people in and out, so very tempting. One mustn't have trouble with the Fathers."

The five chatted easily, relieved to learn from Simms, who had explored several miles ahead, that they could anticipate a less difficult road on the morrow. Turning to more general themes they discussed for a time the confused nature of the Spanish problem, the possibility of government forces retaining Madrid, and – although they had only rumour to work upon – the strength of the French armies. At last, the Colonel smothering a yawn announced that it was time to turn in.

"Blessed be he who first invented sleep," said the paymaster, quoting Sancho Panza.

"Sleep," capped Simms, "that knits up the ravelled sleeve of care, the death of each day's life, the balm—"

"Hey, what high-falutin' rant is this?" growled the Colonel, who was beginning to feel out of his depth.

"Quotation, sir," said Simms, to point the moral and adorn the tale."

"Humph!" Pomeroy blew out his cheeks and reached for his cloak. As he did so heavy feet pounded across the forecourt, and fists interspersed with a few hearty kicks, thumped on the outer door. Voices arose – the smooth, unhurried inquiry of the porter almost drowned by an imperative request to speak with the commanding officer. "What in God's name?" grunted the Colonel, raising himself to his full height, "this is no way to behave in quarters." But before he could speak again, Serjeant Major Stubbs, enormous in a dripping oil-skin thrust in, sprang to attention, and saluted. "Colonel Pomeroy," he gasped, spent with running, "hi 'ave to hinform you that large numbers of our men are rollin' beastly drunk, hincluding the guard and pickets, sir, and that hif something is not done immediate, though hi am sorry to say so, the rest will go to pot!" He sagged slightly, his glistening rain-wet face quivering with excitement. Never had those present seen the Serjeant Major so shaken. The effect on the Colonel was equally striking. Pomeroy, turning from one to another of his companions, seemed bereft of speech. He dropped his cloak, swallowing hard, struggling for words. "What's this?" he barked at last. Stubbs again explained. "But, God in heaven," cried Pomeroy turning on Simms, "you told me that there was no liquor available in town!"

Simms shook a bewildered head. "The alcalde said not."

"Then he's a damned liar!"

"The coach house by the river, sir," said Stubbs, "is full of brandy."

"But how?" bellowed Pomeroy. He meant by what means had the store been raided.

"The men who wanted water for soup, sir," said Stubbs, "went to the quayside, seed the casks through a chink hin the door, broke through the roof, and 'elped themselves. Hi go to hinquire, and find the corporal and 'is men spread out like flat-fish, dead drunk to the wide."

"I'll drunk the poltroons!"

Livid with rage the Colonel snatched up his cloak again. "The scoundrels shall be thrashed from here to Salamanca!" He bit of the words savagely.

"Who is the officer on picket duty?"

"Lieutenant Bird, sir."

"Where is he?"

"Cannot say, sir."

"Let him be found at once," ordered Pomeroy. "Come, Foulkes!" And out he stamped, shouting for a detachment of "decent, honourable soldiers, not the filth of the Old Bailey."

Led by the sergeant major, the little party hurried through the archway of the convent, and taking a narrow street leading to the river, were caught up in a laughing, vociferous crowd moving in the same direction. The news of "liquor for all" had spread like wildfire. One oaf, throwing his arm around the Colonel's shoulder babbled of delights to come, but was flung off with a hearty curse. Simms behind, smiled tightly. All cats were grey in the dark!

Leaving the street, they arrived at the quay, where beside the dark, silently flowing water stood a squat stone building, on the flat roof of which infantry-men were swarming like monkeys, those above drawing up kettles which in turn were to be filled by their comrades inside. "Here – lend's a light!" An Irishman snatched at the Serjeant Major's lantern, but was hurled aside. "Be jasus," he shouted resentfully, "do ye want it all for yerselves?"

Stubbs, in a voice that had rattled the windows of many a market square, proclaimed the advent of Colonel Pomeroy, but his words were lost in a pan-demonium of shouting and horse-laughter. Still, Stubbs persevered. His "Tenshion! Tenshion!" broke out again and again. As this was of no avail he struck out at delinquents within reach of his cane. Pomeroy, no less active in his own fashion, thrust through to a cluster of those who were manipulating the kettles. "Where is Lieutenant Bird?" he roared. "How much longer must we wait for decent reliable soldiers?"

The sweating subaltern, sword drawn, marched in. Musket butts crashed on the flags. "Round 'em up!" ordered Pomeroy. "Book every man-jack, Serjeant Major. We'll have an accounting they won't forget till the Day of Judgment."

Steadily order was restored. Those who could stand were herded together and hustled off; dead drunks hauled into cars. The majority of the tipplers made off under cover of darkness. Two men blundered into the river and were drowned.

Pomeroy's smouldering anger constantly burst into flame. "A regiment of toss-pots!" he stormed, "damme, if I'll take 'em a step further!" Once, Foulkes heard him mutter under his breath, "I'll sell out or exchange.." He called for the Alcalde, requesting Simms to stand by as interpreter.

The town dignitary, his sixteen stones, quivering with concern swore by all the saints in the calendar that he did not know the casks – which were the property of Lisbon merchants held rum. "Indeed Excellency," he explained, "it was my belief that the storehouse contained only oil."

"Oil be damned!" rejoined Pomeroy, "put a guard at his door."

It was as well that the Alcalde did not understand English, for by this time he had recovered his balance, and was inquiring with a certain hauteur why this uniformed stranger should address him so. Foulkes, who was standing by intervened. "You know, sir," he said, addressing Pomeroy in a low voice, "we must continue to live and work with these people. I don't doubt that the man is telling the truth." Pomeroy blinked, still fixing the Alcalde with a basilisk stare. "Say," whispered Foulkes to Simms, "that we regret our part in the disturbance."

Simms did so, trusting he said, that relations between the British and their allies would ever continue to be harmonious. As commissary he had greater need of the Alcalde's goodwill than the Colonel ...

The hubbub took some time to die down for the streets had filled with curiosity-mongers. A cry arose that *afrancesados* had attempted to fire the granary. In the arcade immediately below the room where Mrs Foulkes and her maid were lodged, the wrangling of intermingled English and Portuguese voices continued. Harriet, whose pleasant little party had been broken up by the hasty exit of Bird made a gesture of annoyance. She turned to Sue. "This is intolerable. Go down and send them about their business."

"What shall I say?" asked Sue doubtfully. Harriet threw up her hands. "Anything! Threaten them with General Frazer. Use your tongue!"

The mission was by no means to Sue's liking. Throwing a shawl over her head, she groped downstairs feeling that the best she could hope for would be the intervention of a passing officer. Unfortunately Carworth had left the lodgings, but there were bound to be responsible Englishmen within earshot. When she lifted the latch and peered out it was to discern only a few gesticulating outlines, cloaked figures grouped a few feet from the doorway. To her immense relief a drift away was beginning to take place, so that in a matter of only a few moments the area emptied. Partly from curiosity, partly to draw in a few breaths of fresh air after the smoky atmosphere of the room she had just left, she walked a step or two along the arcade. Through the darkness the town stirred uneasily. The fitful glare of torches shone across the plaza, by whom these were carried, military or civilian, she could not tell. Almost all the houses were shuttered. One doorway alone emitted light. Men passed in and out. The General's headquarters perhaps.

But she was in no mood to linger, and returning to the half open door found her entrance barred by the housedog, which must have been released during her brief exit. She stepped forward, but was greeted by so savage a growl that she stopped in her tracks. She extended a friendly hand, and spoke endearingly. Teeth clashed only inches away, and she found the corner of her shawl dragged. A devil was in the beast. She pulled loose, leaving some of the fringe in the mastiff's mouth. Helplessly she gazed to the window above. If she shouted, would Mrs Foulkes hear? She stepped back into the arcade.

"What am I to do?" she murmured helplessly. She moved again and an ominous growl came from the doorway.

As she hovered uncertainly a man detached himself from the shadows, the glint on the metal plate of his shako indicating that he was one of her own countrymen. "Hey," he growled, "what's up?"

"The dog," she said curtly, "won't let me in."

"Oh, it won't, won't it!" The newcomer bent over peering into the aperture, in no way perturbed by a warning snarl. "I see you," he said, "good dog – good dog!" Then with a sharp stride forward and fierce "Geroam!" launched his foot in the animal's ribs, where the hound with a pained yelp decided to make off. "That's put an end to his mischief," said the soldier. "It's the only way to talk to 'em." Sue stood quite still. Already she had recognised Harker.

"Ain't you goin' to thank me?" he inquired.

"Indeed I do, "she said.

Peering into her face he gave a low whistle of recognition. "By gum," he breathed, "I thought I knew that voice." He moved as he spoke into the vacant doorway, and leaning on the side obstructed her passage. Certainly the dog had gone, but here was another nuisance. "I have already thanked you for your service," she said in strained tones, "now – if you don't mind?"

"Ships that pass in the night, eh?"

She caught a whiff of liquor. The truth was that he had had his share of the storehouse brandy, but though he carried his liquor well, he was stirred enough to be awkward. "Everything comes to him that waits," he said.

"Does it?"

"I know you, my dear."

"What of that?" she said tiredly.

"I mean I know who you are."

"And I know who you are," she rejoined bitterly, "only too well."

"Who am I then?" he mocked.

"You are the man who destroyed my brother."

Harker's tongue clicked deprecatingly. "Fancy that now!"

"Please allow me to pass."

"No," he said hoarsely, "not until we've had this thing out. You might be wrong you know."

"I am not wrong."

"Who are you to say? Was you there at the time? No. You was miles and miles away, and you know damn nothing at all."

"I can believe my own people."

"Pah!"

"Who are honest at least."

"Honest!" he scoffed. "What's that worth? Listen – I've nowt again your brother. He was unlucky, that's all."

"You planted your guilt on him."

"It wor a mix-up, I tell yer."

"And who mixed it? A fine dish I must say!"

"All reight, "he conceded heavily, "we'll let it go at that. But I'm not going to be talked about."

"Who has been talking?"

"You – to that Simms."

She was silent.

"I can put two and two together, you know."

"You have only to confess your wrong-doing," she cried desperately, "to say the word."

Harker drew a deep breath. "God a'mighty," he exploded, "now look here girl, I bear ye no ill-will, but from this time forward you keep your mouth shut and I'll keep mine."

"I've nothing to be ashamed—"

"Ah," he interrupted, "gently – gently now. What would Mrs Foulkes be saying at her having a maid who is sister to a jailbird? I can split that on ye."

"You wouldn't dare!"

"Just try me."

"I can tell you this," said Sue firmly, "that upstairs yonder, Mrs Foulkes will be wondering where I am, and if you keep me longer there'll be trouble for you."

Harker dropped his arm from the doorpost. "All right," he said, "get in, but remember, no more talk."

"That's as I please."

"We'll see, young lady."

"A man who was a man would confess."

He gave a snickering laugh. "Who to – the priest?"

"You could write it down with your own hand."

Harker winced; she had touched him on the raw. He could read a little, but that was the extent of his scholastic achievement. "If I can't write and I never could write," he snarled, "so that horse won't run!"

He moved away slowly, dragging his feet on the stone flags of the arcade floor. With a kind of bitter exultation he cried over his shoulder, "Can't write, thank you!"

With a throbbing headache, Sue stared after until his outline had melted in the shadows of the plaza. She hurried upstairs expecting to be reproached for having delayed so long. But this was not so. Her mistress was poring over a pocket map of Spain, tracing the thread of road which ran from Albuquerque to Alcantara, the route – she understood – taken by the cavalry ...

* * *

Next day, sentenced by drum-head court-martial, nine rankers were flogged; and Lieutenant Bird, mercilessly grilled by Pomeroy, resumed his duties with a pronounced hangdog air. The subaltern had, of course, made no reference to the unfortunate game of cards, pleading only – which was true enough – a stopped watch. But he was no sort of company for his colleagues during the week that followed.

Neither Mrs Foulkes nor Susan Thompson saw the official punishment parade – the crossed Halberds, the fall of the lash as it thudded on the quivering flesh of the culprits. Formed in a hollow square, silent and sullen, men watched the laceration of their comrades. Under a lowering sky, the Colonel lashed them with words of shame. "I thought I commanded soldiers," he rasped, "not rapscallions of the pot-house; warriors eager to confront the enemies of their country, not undisciplined wretches, fit only to lie in the gutter. Let this punishment be a lesson to all concerned, not only on this day, but for all days to come!"

Rain fell, so that the savage thongs dripped both water and blood. "See, the heavens themselves weep for you," added Pomeroy. As the punishment proceeded, one by one the stumbling figures were led away for treatment – salt rubbed into the weals by the surgeon's assistant ... For hours afterwards the Colonel glared askance at the slightest observation, indeed was barely civil to the senior officers. A report would be submitted to General Frazer, and from Frazer would go to the commander-in-chief. Already (when next they met?) the Colonel could feel the cold, contemptuous eyes of Moore fixed upon his own, hear scathing words of reproof. "The dogs," he announced, "shall march out of town in disgraceful silence. They shall have no music. I'd drown the band rather!"

Foulkes, dwelling upon his superior officer's violent reaction was sorely troubled. He himself detested – always had – the brutality of flogging. Some other form of punishment, he felt, should have been devised. Pomeroy, of course, lacked flexibility of mind; he was an old dodo really, a relic of Fontenoy and Dettingen. Foulkes wondered what the devil the Colonel would do if placed in broken country among dry walls and sunken roads; or like the stupid Whitelock at Buenos Ayres, trapped in a maze of streets and alleys. He was at best a barrack-square commander. "The fellow is out of step! But keep in step and we shall triumph!" That was the extent of Pomeroy's military perception. But was it enough? ...

CHAPTER IX

They entered Spain through a countryside dotted with dwarf oaks and cork trees, marching steadily until at least the medieval walls and thickly encrusted towers of Ciudad Rodrigo came in sight. Presently they crossed the Agueda bridge and entered the town.

Light was trapped in the narrow tortuous streets – the iron grilles before the windows reminding Sue all too poignantly of prison bars. Rodrigans stood around staring at their new allies with an oddly detached interest, as though the red-coated strangers pursued some secret purpose of their own. The full impact of the Napoleonic venture had not yet touched Rodrigo. They were to drain a bitter cup to the dregs ere the final tide had passed.

"Now heaven bless all quartermasts!" Thus Harriet unexpectedly as they settled in the substantial house where they were billeted. The carpeted rooms, the spotless linen of the beds, the walls bright with tapestry, the furniture of rare woods, and tables replete with glittering silver and glass, were after so much tough living an uncovenanted blessing. The dining room fireplace displayed the armorial bearings of Don Benito de Mendoza, their host. All underlined the status of an ancient hidalgo. Yes, Harriet felt she would like Rodrigo.

That evening, together with her host, his wife and three daughters, she relaxed before a cheerful log fire. A second guest, whose Christian name she recalled as Miguel, a man of about forty, with weather-beaten face and blue eyes suggesting somehow contact with the sea, completed the circle. To Harriet's surprise he began to speak English, explaining at the outset why this should be so. "You regard with some curiosity that I speak your language? You need not senora, for I owe it to your own countrymen. In short, I fought and was captured at Trafalgar, and subsequent became a prisoner in your province of Norfolk, England. I did not waste my time. Need I say more?"

"Only that you do very well, senor."

He smiled faintly, and with a touch of ironic humour spoke of the flat and watery lands of East Anglia.

"You still find your English useful?" she asked.

"As a commercial agent, indeed yes." As he began to roll a cigarette, she noticed that two fingers were missing on his right hand, but he managed deftly, and with a twig from the hearth lit up. "I need not tell you," he resumed, "how happy I am to converse with a lady so charming as yourself, the more so in that we are bound by a common cause. That is well. But there are other times, senora," and here he frowned, "when I wish that I knew no English at all." He placed his hands dramatically over his ears.

"Why so, senor?"

"I listen to words which do not please me."

"I fear," said Harriet, "that I do not understand."

"Then I will enlighten you," said Miguel. At the same time she noticed that her host made a deprecating gesture. Did Don Benito know a little English? She could not be certain. The man of Trafalgar, however, continued. "Sitting in the wine shop I cannot help but overhear your countrymen – you agree that they speak loudly? – discussing our people, their habits and their courage – or should I say, their absence of courage? I hear them proclaim that we Spaniards care so little for the cause that we run like rabbits at the first crack of a musket!" Miguel's voice rang indignantly. "In a word, senora, that we are cowards, and what is even worse – traitors! It is more than enough!" He crushed his newly rolled cigarette and flung it in the hearth, turning to her. "As one patriot to another – for who but the truest patriot would follow her husband to the wars? – is such language to be borne?" His eyes challenged proudly. "They forget," he said firmly, "Saragossa."

"Saragossa?" repeated Harriet in a puzzled tone. The name meant nothing to her – was it a province, a town, a distinguished Spanish soldier? She waited.

"I speak of the famous siege," he said tensely, "which this at least—" raising the hand from which two fingers were missing, "will not permit me to forget."

"You were present I take it?" So Saragossa was a town.

"Yes, senora – in Saragossa I fought, I suffered, I endured. Your countrymen should know that for many weeks humble Spaniards, men, women and children, untrained in the art of war, defied a proud French army. Madness, you say? So it would seem. None the less we transformed churches, convents, houses into forts; we saw that every place had its sharpshooters, every streets its artillery. When one house fell we broke through the party wall and defended the next. Imagine that in your cherished London! Day and night we fought, awake and sometimes half asleep. And the women, senora, passed the lead and powder, filled the sandbags, rolled the bandages, tended the wounded and buried the dead. They were magnificent." Miguel threw up his arms. "When the great powder magazine exploded, it made no difference. The French siege guns raged and roared, but we laughed in our cellars. The churches were the citadels of God. I have seen the smoke of powder enfold both Mother and Child, but still the babe was upheld, and gently the Holy Mother smiled through the tumult … You are a woman. Very well, I will speak of your own sex – a mere girl." Miguel paused and raised his chin proudly. Harriet threw a swift glance around the circle. It was certain that the Mendoza daughter knew no English, but the passion, the feeling investing the speaker's voice – the frequent reference to Saragossa – held them breathless. Only their father sighed.

"Agostine Zaragoza was her name." Here Miguel spoke almost reverently. "A maid whose lover, an artillerist, had been struck down before her very eyes; but who in that awful moment, snatched the lighted match from his hand and fired a twenty-four pounder cannon into the oncoming French. No time for tears! Tell me – would you do that for a lover, for a husband? ..."

"French columns fought their way in, and we fought them out again. Surrender? 'Over our dead bodies alone,' said Joseph Palafox, for he you must know, was our leader. And so it was. Our slain lay unburied; we fell sick of the pestilence; but if we were exhausted, the more so our enemy. Then one day – after many days – the French camps thinned; we saw their stores in flames, and we knew that they were beaten. Away they went. The brave city had triumphed."

The narrator's voice fell, and he muttered something which Harriet did not catch. He stared into the glowing logs still reliving the grim hazards of the siege. He ended by addressing Harriet personally. "Madame," he said, "Englishwoman – I know that being of the quality you associate with men of great influence – when you hear the ill-disposed, or it may be the grossly ignorant, among your fellow countrymen, speak of Spanish inertia, of cowardice, of craven leadership – forgive my emotion – recall I beg of you, the nameless dead, the humble citizens of Saragossa, the girl Agostina, the man Joseph Palafox, the Captain General of God, that they may be confounded." Miguel glanced apologetically towards his host as he added, "I fear that I have spoken too much?"

"By no means," said Harriet faintly. She shivered through the room was warm enough, for the Spaniard with the sea-blue eyes had lifted a curtain upon a reality which so far she had apprehended through mere gossip and rumour. The thunder of the guns, the crash of falling masonry, the excruciating burden of blood and tears, seemed uncomfortably close in the sumptuous dining room of Don Benito de Mendoza. She reflected that she had not yet heard a shot fired in anger ...

* * *

The British did not linger in Rodrigo. About noon of the day following, Sue stood in the shadow of the arcade, looking out across a plaza crowded with men and carts all ready to go. Saddled and bridled, Felix pawed the cobbles, while Sancho the mule stood alongside, a symbol of dedicated patience.

Sue sighed. All was not well between the Major and Mrs Foulkes. Harriet had been particularly fretful that morning, complaining that she had been denied a real opportunity to view the town where she had hoped to buy a present for her sister Jane. This had led to sharp exchanges between husband

and wife, during which the latter had been sharply reminded that the campaign had not been organised for her convenience. She rejoined that being human, she was entitled to a little consideration – a mine touched off when she alluded to the attention she received at the hands of others. Incautiously she mentioned that Lieutenant Bird had obliged at cards. "Where?" at once asked the Major.

"In Guardia," she said.

"The night indeed," he flashed, "when the brandy casks were broached by the river, and Bird, your familiar, should have been attending to his duty!" Acidly he implied that Harriet was responsible for the subaltern's negligence, and consequently for the whole wretched business.

"For the sake of a nail the shoe was lost," said Harriet flippantly," for the sake of a card the brandy was lost!"

This reply moved Foulkes to swear that for two pins he would have it out with Bird. As he spoke he knew that he would not, and he knew that she knew he would not, but the observation drove her into a cold fury. "So that is how your mind works," she said bitterly, "you and your two pins! Go to Pomeroy and inform him that your wife is corrupting the regiment, but she, having no mind to bring the campaign to disaster, will take a vow of silence and confine herself to quarters."

"I did not say—" he began.

"Accost the lieutenant," she cried, her eyes snapping indignantly, "and a fine fool you will make of yourself. I thought you were above such petty meanness, but now I see that it is not so. In future I will do nothing to reduce these young men to misfortune. If Lieutenant Suckley obliges with his flute, he shall be made conscious of his danger!"

"What on earth has the flute to do with it?" cried the exasperated Foulkes.

"No man shall address me without your permission. *You will have to see Major Foulkes*," she mimicked.

"This is beyond all reason," he protested.

"It is indeed! In future I shall ask of you only the barest necessity."

"Don't be a fool," he muttered.

"Of the two—" She faced him with dangerously flickering eyes, but turned away abruptly.

"This can't go on," he said lamely.

"No?"

He became silent studying her expressive back. She moved to the window gazing out ... Quite half a minute passed when to his extreme surprise, she faced him murmuring, "I – I am sorry—"

"Say no more," he said curtly. "We had best forget—"

"I am afraid, Percy," she continued in a level tone, "I tend to misunderstand your position. I have been thoughtless. You shall not have occasion to complain again."

There was an uncomfortable pause. Foulkes stood with half open mouth wondering what she would say next. Was it possible that she had decided to return to Bellaby?

But no. With a studiously detached air she examined the contents of her satchel, while for want of other action he took her place at the window. "I should be out on duty," he thought, "not lingering here." At last he said abruptly, "Much on edge myself lately -I owe you an apology." And he bowed slightly. There was so much of formality in his attitude that he might have been addressing his superior officer. He cleared his throat and in a more accommodating tone observed, "I must remind you that we march within the hour."

Harriet inclined her head. "I shall be ready," she replied.

* * *

Echoes of the domestic storm troubled the girl as she hovered in the arcade. She would be relieved when they were in movement again.

Her interest began to centre upon a dragoon in conversation with a serjeant of the regiment, who was pointing apparently directly at her. She continued to watch feeling that somehow she was being discussed, and yet the trooper was a complete stranger.

The dragoon, spurs jingling, and sabre hitched in the crook of one arm, strolled across. He was a burly, freshly featured, square-jawed fellow, with tufted side-whiskers. He saluted easily. The crest of his helmet towered above her.

"You Sue Thompson?" he inquired, "the Major's woman? – or as I should say," he added hurriedly, "the Major's lady's girl?"

"I am so," she answered, "and who may you be?"

"No names, no doghouse!" he grinned. "I have a message for you of a kind." He groped in his pouch. "It don't amount to much, but here it is."

The scrap of paper he produced was folded in four, having on the outer side her name and the number of the regiment. She took the note cautiously and opened it. Scrawled unevenly, perhaps with a scrap of charcoal, were four words in her brother's handwriting—

"Primrose Van Deemens Land"

That was all. The dragoon waited, silently watching.

"How did you come by this?" she inquired.

"Can't tell you a deal," replied the dragoon, "'cept it was handed to me at Portsmouth by a poor lad in chains."

She caught her breath. "Did – the prisoner say anything?"

"Nobbut a word or two. We was embark' you see. Their boat bumped into ourn – matter of fact we smashed an oar and they two – but before we drew apart a young chap pushed this i' my hand, saying, 'Message – girl in Spain – do this for a poor devil!' It wor all over in a second or two, and I thinks well you never know what you may come to yourself someday, so I kept the paper till the day I come up wi' the army. So now you've got it. Wish it could be something better." He eyed her with compassion, under the impression that the unfortunate convict was her lover. "Must be on my way," he concluded hurriedly. "Come up from Lisbon with remounts. My respects." And almost before she could thank him, he had clanked away leaving her staring at the grimy paper. What could the message possibly mean – that Robin had embarked? The four simple words, and the circumstance in which the note was delivered implied that; but she could not be certain. Primrose? Van Deemens Land? She knitted her brows, studied the writing once more, and finally thrust the paper into the bosom of her dress. At the first opportunity, she decided, she would consult Mr Simms, though here she hesitated, for she had seen little of him since Paco d'Arcos ...

* * *

They marched across the plain beneath a low grey ceiling of cloud. For Harriet Foulkes, Rodrigo had been profoundly disappointing. She had hoped to meet Tony, but all that she gathered from a fellow huzzar officer, was that he had been sent forward on "Intelligence". The perpetual intrusion of military duties disturbed her. The fact that she had never been invited to headquarters where they could have met and conversed, rankled also. The Commander-in-chief's indifference to women was well known; but need that preclude the exercise of common courtesy? If the campaign went well; celebration balls and soirees were bound to follow, and from these she could not be excluded. Only wait, Sir John? She smiled secretly as she pondered the snub she would administer. As for Percy, inflating Bird and the wretched brandy into a major episode – he was more than ever an intolerable bore. The delinquency of his own servant that night had compelled the appointment of another. ("Just as the drunken fool had become accustomed to my ways!") He had been irritated by that, but why make the lives of others unbearable?

When they exchanged words at the first halting place, relations were still strained. When she inquired what route they were taking to Salamanca, Foulkes answered curtly that the Colonel had not as yet seen fit to communicate marching orders. This had put him out; but she too could be awkward, so that when Lieutenant Suckly approached in a friendly smiling manner, she wheeled her horse away ostentatiously, leaving the subaltern mystified and her husband scowling. She walked Felix through a stretch of scrub to the top of a sandy knoll, where she surveyed the countryside alone, a model of classic isolation. Suckley did not deserve such treatment, but Percy would comprehend the gesture. She moved only when the column had started again.

After that she unbent when later Mr Simms brought his nag alongside. He raised his hat and bowed.

How many miles to Salamanca, sir?" she inquired.

"About fifty." He explained the difference between Spanish leagues and English miles. "Tomorrow," he remarked, "I put the matter to the test when I shall push ahead."

"You are fortunate." She eyed with disaster the shabby undulation of scrub and rock through which they were marching. Noting her expression, he laughed softly. "Is it so amusing," she asked.

"Why should you put up with this?" he rejoined. "You have no regimental duties."

Harriet raised her eyebrows. "You mean that I leave the column?"

"Why not? We are in friendly country."

"Yes – why not?" she mused, gazing ahead.

"I should deem it a privilege to escort you to Salamanca."

"That is kind of you, Mr Simms, but—"

"It is out of question?"

"On the contrary, I am much attracted. Assuming however, that I push ahead of the division, how do I lodge in Salamanca?"

"Ah, that is a problem for the Assistant Quartermaster General," said Simms. "He will find you a billet. It would give you ample time to explore the place before the rest arrive."

Harriet nodded. "The more I dwell upon the suggestion, the more I like it, Mr Simms."

"Then I am at your service."

"But I must first consult my husband."

When however, she flicked Felix with the switch, the commissary raised a cautionary hand. "Do not," he said, "lay the inspiration to me!"

She shot a meaningful look. "Don't worry!" And shot forward to acquaint the Major …

"When she had gone, Simms checked his horse, and allowed Sue who had been riding behind, to overtake him.

He greeted her cheerfully. "Good morrow, stranger!"

"Good morning, Mr Simms."

Her tone was distant, her manner cool. A week had passed since their conversation at the apothecary's. She felt that in spite of his numerous duties, he could have found some moment to speak. Unable to account for this apparent neglect, she kept her lips tightly closed.

"How are you faring?"

He was altogether friendly, but she looked away. "Well enough," she replied sharply.

"You have your own mule now?"

"Yes."

"Is it a sturdy animal?"

"Yes."

He glanced down as, apart from these monosyllables, she maintained an obdurate silence. "A girl of few words," he remarked.

"I would not wish to trespass on your time," she said.

"Now what kind of talk is this?" he quizzed.

"You are a busy man, Mr Simms, and I must not detain you."

"I suspect irony here," he replied, "but in spite of the fact that I am very busy indeed, I did manage to get a closer look at this Private Raddock. Not that I gathered very much; but I found that he was brash, shifty, and something of a liar – which would be in accord with your own feeling. I have seen nothing of him since."

"I have," she said.

"When?"

"In Guardia."

"Did he molest you?"

"Not exactly, but he knows – or thinks he knows – that I have been in touch with you."

"How right he is," said Simms.

"He told me not to discuss his business with anyone."

"The devil he did!"

"He said that he had been the victim of a real mistake, and that if I didn't heed his warning he would split to Mrs Foulkes about my brother."

"A touch of blackmail, eh?"

Simms gazed sternly ahead. More involvement! He looked down at her, the mule's head rising and falling rhythmically, the worsted decoration of the bridle swaying.

"We must continue to watch him," said Simms. "He may lay himself open in some way, though how God alone knows. In the meantime, any news of your brother?"

"I had been waiting to show you this." She produced the note transmitted by the dragoon, and held it up. "You may read it."

Simms took the paper, and scanned it reading aloud, "Primrose Van Deemen's Land." After explaining how the note had come into her possession, she invited Simms to interpret the four mystic words.

"Why, everyone knows—" he began, but hesitated, biting his lip. "How can I tell you the poor lass," he thought, "that it is a brutish convict settlement? Yet, sooner or later—" Aloud he said, "Primrose, I should assume the name of a vessel."

"I thought that too," she said quietly, "but what is the Van Deemens?"

He sighed deeply, and in some effort to soften the blow, said, "I am sorry – it represents your brother's ultimate destination." It was possible that she had never heard of the place, and her next question confirmed this.

"A long way off?"

The nag stumbled almost to its knees, and Simms thankful for the brief respite patted his mount's neck. "Such roads!" he grumbled, "one would have thought that a main highway – Quite a distance," he said reverting to her inquiry.

"Farther than America?"

It became difficult to find words. "I cannot rightly say – a long voyage at least, but not so far that your brother, who I take it is a healthy fellow, may not return in due course, you may depend upon that." Job's comfort at best! Convict ships were notorious death traps. Sue's brother would be fortunate to survive the voyage out. "One can only enjoin patience," he said.

"It is a hard fate," she said, "almost beyond enduring." Her figure drooped as she rode, the reins loose on Sancho's neck.

Simms said, "There is much cruelty in the world, sometimes beyond man's understanding, but there is courage also and the will to endure. One must not lose heart."

"I will try," she murmured. "I – I did not intend to trouble you."

"No trouble," he replied, "I would wish you to." He smiled. "Although I am a poor father confessor."

A mounted officer broke free from the column ahead, and rode towards them. "Here comes my father confessor," observed Simms, "farewell."

Pricking his nag, he trotted forward to meet Pomeroy …

* * *

Sue overtook her mistress at a small village a mile ahead to find Harriet in high good humour. She had consulted her husband on the matter of pushing forward, and the response was not unfavourable. He suggested referring the proposal to the Colonel, who for his part reacted emphatically. "By all means go!" he grunted, "and good – er good fortune go with you!" Then feeling that perhaps he had agreed with unseemly haste. Pomeroy added, "Always provided that you are attended by a suitable guard, and remain in the company of Mr Simms."

So all was arranged …

When next morning, through air nipped with frost, Foulkes saw his wife away, her colour was high, the lilt in her voice pronounced. Every gesture denoted the pleasure she felt on leaving the column. She pecked dutifully at her husband's cheek ere he assisted her to mount. Turning in her saddle, she saw him standing hands on hips to a background of piled arms and smoking fires, quite motionless, and she waved her switch gaily with a downward flourish which might well have been a gesture of dismissal.

She united with Simms, and O'Connor, his Irish servant, a hundred yards or so down the road, and the party set off at a brisk trot. The mule bells jingled as Sancho cantered after. The air stung deliciously. The clear duck-egg blue of the sky; the mist that wreathed the woods of evergreen and oak, the melting dove-grey horizon; the creaking and clinking of harness, the rhythmic impact of hooves on the iron ground – all contributed to the mood of intense release. Freedom – at last! For no reason at all except that the tune flashed suddenly in mind, Harriet began to hum a strain from M.Rousseau's *Devin du Village*, an operetta which she had last seen in London—

J'ai perdu tout mon bonheur,
J'ai perdu mon serviteur ...

They cantered easily along a track rutted by forward contingents of the army, stopping only once when Simms with departmental prudence dismounted to retrieve a horseshoe cast on the verge.

He was a lively companion, replete with curious, out-of-the-way information. Was Harriet aware that smugglers always made the best of guides? ... That Spanish travellers hung on their necks scraps of priestly writing to ward off lurking demons? ... That in approaching Salamanca and Valladolid she would be in the country of *Gil Blas*? ... Had she not read *Gil Blas*? ... When Harriet assured her cavalier that she had not, then he must needs recount the trials and distresses of that much travelled young gentleman. She quizzed and laughed constantly. Sue, jogging behind, could only marvel at the transformation of spirit revealed in her mistress. It seemed to her that Simms had completely fallen beneath the spell ...

Midday they halted for refreshment. Simms carried food for all, but hoping to help out the ration of cold beef and biscuit, stopped at a wayside posada and smartly clapped his hands to attract attention. In response an old women appeared eyeing the travellers suspiciously. Simms said, "Senhor Commisaris des Tropoa Ingleses!" A few sentences followed, Simms doing most of the talking. At the end of this altercation he turned an abashed face to his companions. "The old crone says she has nothing – neither eggs nor sausages; nothing in a village of chickens and pigs!"

"Nothing at all?" cried Harriet as a cook stalked through the doorway.

"She says Inglese soldiers have already eaten her out of house and *home.*"

"Perhaps they forget to pay?"

"I don't know – not unlikely."

By this time the old woman had retreated through the door, though they could see that from the shadows she was watching closely.

Simms, his professional pride at stake, dismounted and sought her out. "Senora, you are not so miserably poor that you have no pan for chocolate, nor a can even of water!"

The woman replied sharply and turned away, her attitude such that Simms wondered what it was she had suffered at the hands of passing troops. He turned to the others. "She says she will provide a pan, but nothing more. Please dismount."

Thus, in the foetid, smoke-laden atmosphere of the posada, they consumed their rations, and drank chocolate from their own horn cups. "Well, Senor Gil Blas," bantered Harriet, "what have you provided for the next stage of the journey?"

"The road," he replied curtly. As they left he threw to the woman the smallest coin he could find. "My only wish for you," he remarked, "is that the next batch of Ingleses you entertain will be braw Scotsmen, and heaven have mercy on your soul!"

"You pay somewhat niggardly, Mr Simms!" said Harriet. "The dame was obviously poor."

"Such poverty," retorted Simms, "is nothing to go by. The peasants are cunning. See that?" and he pointed to a run half-concealed in the rear of the building, where at least, a couple of dozen fowls were pecking. "No eggs, if you please!"

On the outskirts of the village, O'Connor, who carried a carbine, brought it to his shoulder and at a distance of about fifteen yards let fly at a turkey. He aim true, he instantly dismounted and crammed the twitching bird into his saddlebag. Simms, effecting ignorance of his servant's action, gazed steadily ahead.

"Plenty of wild fowl around," he remarked casually. Uneasily he cocked his chin upon his shoulder, half expecting an indignant outcry. O'Connor, he knew, had erred, but now the deed was done. "Push on!" he said. Still listening for some shout of remonstrance, he increased speed; it was not until they had cleared the last of the scattered stone huts that he heaved a sigh of relief. The men of the village, he concluded, would be beating the woods for acorns.

The countryside now became level, uninteresting; the road a thread of drugget drawn across dull vistas of greys and greens and browns. Once they stopped a muleteer, from whom they inquired the direction of Salamanca. He raised the brim of his hat and screwed up his eyes suspiciously as he noticed the colour of Simms' frock coat – French uniforms were blue; and as it happened, O'Connor's red tunic was concealed by his cloak. However, the peasant informed them that at the next crossroads they should bear east.

"Did he give any idea of distance?" asked Harriet.

Simms shook his head. "These people work by rule of thumb. Is it far? you ask. Yes, it is far. A day's journey? It may be. A two day's journey? Perhaps. And it goes. We had better watch out at the crossroads. There may be other travellers."

As the day wore on, the four strained their eyes for the first glimpse of the outer walls and spires of the city. Shadows began to lengthen. For want of confirming advice they had taken the eastern fork at the cross-roads; and after a time, it was Simms, who in a savage undertone protested that the muleteer had deliberately misdirected them, and that in consequence they might be compelled to spend the night in the open. He was of a mind to push further. Soon, if no posada offered, they would have to make do with the best shelter they could find.

They still held to a beaten track, though this at times dwindled to a mere thread across the turf. Simms, who was anxious for the safety of the two women entrusted to his care, said little. His face cleared when a light some distance ahead pricked the gathering dusk. It disappeared immediately, but the Commissary lifted his nose and sniffed. "That may or may not have been a marsh-light, an *ignus fatuus*, he exclaimed; but I do know, and am certain of, the difference between woodsmoke and brimstone. Follow me."

He forced his way for a time through tangled grass and scrub. They had now left what little track there was and presently rode across closely cropped turf. The light to which he had referred did not reappear; he began to whistle uncertainly.

"A rustic shelter of leaves and twigs—" began Harriet, when she was checked by Simms stabbing the air with his forefinger. "Look yonder," he said, "and tell me what you see." The four riders drew to a standstill. About a quarter of a mile distant, beyond a grove of cypress stood a mansion which with its numerous chimneys, conical towers and slit windows, might have been transplanted from the banks of the Loire; its walls, touched by the after-glow, gleamed pearly-grey in the half-light. "The big house, be Jasus!" cried O'Connor, speaking first. "Say rather," Harriet murmured with a singularly rapt expression, "a castle of enchantment!"

"Board and lodging," said Simms.

"You are much too earthly minded, sir," said she.

A few more paces forward and he ventured the opinion that the smoke had drifted from a small village, the roofs of which he dimly discerned at the fringe of the grove. "Providentially," he observed, "we have now a choice, between the great house on the one hand, and the village on the other. Which shall we take?"

"The house, by all means," exclaimed Harriet.

"So let it be."

Drawing near, their progress was checked by a high wall, and around this for a spell they were compelled to ride until they gained the main entrance. Here, though the gates were wide open, there was no sign of life. The travellers passed through, but had no sooner entered the park when the sound of scurrying feet to the rear impelled them to turn in their saddles. Two men who had been lurking in the deep shadow of the wall, were running full speed, their ragged cloaks flying, in the direction of the village. "Now what is the meaning of that?" asked Simms uneasily as they listened to the dying footfalls. But he made no further comment. His eyes were fixed on the house.

The drive was thickly carpeted with fallen leaves. A bat winged across their faces and disappeared in the dusk. The great mansion had every appearance of being deserted; its windows empty, dead. No smoke lifted from the chimneys. O'Connor began a mumbled incantation, whereat Simms turned sharply upon him. "Stop that heathen farrago instantly, or I'll send you back – alone!" They came to the main door, and dismounting he picked his way through a litter of stones, until halting, he gazed at the elaborately carved armorial bearings overhead. He signalled O'Connor to join him. A pull on the bell-chain produced a muffled clangour, but after that – silence. They waited, listening.

I am almost tempted to believe, " said Simms, "that the place is empty." So saying he set his shoulder to the door and thrust vigorously, surprised when this gave suddenly and he staggered into the hall. He recovered his balance immediately, and cupping his hands to his mouth hailed the circumambient darkness, "Hola there! Who lives here?" But beyond the echo of his own voice reverberating down empty corridors, there was no response. "All very strange," he muttered. Ordering O'Connor to bring the lantern he habitually carried, Simms returned to his horse and took out his pistols. "One can at least parley with these," he grinned.

O'Connor, having nicked steadily with flint and steel, the lantern was lit, and the two men moved forward into a void which the tiny flame did little to dispel. Gradually they discerned outlines: a double staircase with an elaborately wrought iron balustrade ran to the first floor; on either side massive mahogany doors admitted to the lower rooms. "We'll take the right hand first," said Simms, and turning the handle entered a chamber containing in the centre a long table empty save for a decanter and a single empty dish. Five chairs oddly awry, and some broken pieces of a sixth, surrounded the hearth. The room, heavy with dust, had evidently been unused for some time. "Nothing much here," commented Simms, "we'll examine to the left."

They crossed the hall and pushed open a door where the lantern light fell upon rows of gilt and calfskin volumes. An ancient globe stood beside a table littered with prints. This room seemed in much better shape than the one they had left. "The library beyond doubt," said Simms, "but we need something more to our immediate purpose; in a word, the kitchens."

They left the library, crossed the hall, and through a door behind the staircase, entered a stone corridor, which, after sundry twists and turns, brought them into a sizeable vaulted chamber, evidently the main kitchen. Here was further evidence of neglect, of destruction. Pots and pans were scattered in all directions. The two men crushed beneath their feet earthenware shards and quantities of broken glass. The ashes in the hearth being dead, Simms ordered his servant to kindle a fire – afterwards to pluck and roast the turkey. The Commissary then lit a candle stub, and leaving his none too happy servant alone, rejoined the women who still waited at the main door. "Please dismount," he said, "you will find a somewhat dilapidated mansion, but we are furnished at least with a roof – for the rest we must take pot luck."

"What of the beasts?" inquired Harriet.

"All in good time," he answered. "There are bound to be stables, but since we must keep a close watch on our property, the animals had better to be brought into the hall. We will kindle a fire in what appears to be the dining room. Enter, tread with ease, and take the door to the right."

The two women came in, Sue bringing the turkey which O'Connor had shot. "Make certain that it is drawn," warned Simms, "or that servant of mine will cook it whole." He escorted Sue to the kitchen where she was left with O'Connor; but before settling down, Harriet and Simms explored further. In the writing room a fine Sevres panelled bureau had been broken open, its contents scattered on the floor. Silver sconces had been torn from the walls, and candle-ends lay among the papers. Harriet shuddered to see such vandalism, but Simms, always practical, collected the candle-stubs for future use. "I fancy," he remarked, "that if we return to the library we shall find some indication of the owner's name." So off they went, and Simms taking down a volume from the nearest shelf, opened it and scanned the bookplate. An elaborately engraved label proclaimed that the book was the property of one Joseph Medoza y Taboada, "Such," said Simms, "is the gentleman to whom we are indebted for shelter, though who he is, or where he is – if alive at all – remains the supreme mystery."

Returning to the dining room he started a fire with pieces of the broken furniture. "Putting two and two together," he observed, "we can only conclude that Don Taboada is a local grandee serving on the central Junta or some other legislative body, and that in his absence peasants, or roving *guerrilleros* have been making merry at his expense."

"Guerrilleros?" she questioned.

Simms shrugged. "Patriotic bandits- the terms are interchangeable. They may return, and take a patriotic fancy to our horses. We can at least make fast the doors."

"They may have other means of entry."

"There are not so many doors in a house built for defence. I will straightaway see to it."

He went out with a candle and shot the massive bolts. After what seemed to Harriet an unconscionable time, he returned. "All snug I think. Now we will attend to our dumb companions." He unsaddled mule and horses, dropped fodder for them, and after that dragged saddles and blankets across the floor to the dining room where he proceeded to build up the fire. Harriet watched him closely. "I commend your efficiency, Mr Simms," she said.

Th commissary, to whom praise in discharge of his duty was something of a novelty, murmured that he tried to make do.

"I must really note you for promotion," she continued.

"If madam," he said roundly, "you were the wife of the Commissary General – which heaven forbid – I should avail of your interest."

"The chance may come."

She smiled dazzlingly. Until that moment Simms had not realised how completely seductive Harriet Foulkes could be: the hint of coquetry in her voice, her cheeks flushed in the firelight, her eyes mischievous, her lips eager and slightly parted. He had seen her often enough during the past few weeks, but always in the company of others. Now, *tete-a-tete*, a subtle intimacy prevailed. She was no longer the senior major's wife, nor the friend of the elusive Captain Harte, but a disturbing presence, which could not be ignored, the gracious lady indulgent to her squire.

"Why are you not married?"

The question embarrassed Simms; it was as though she had penetrated to his most inmost thought. He dropped a chair splinter on the fire, and watched it wrap with flame before he answered. "Because," he said, "I should not wish my wife to share a gypsy existence of this kind."

"As I do?" she said swiftly.

He turned his head. "You are especially favoured."

"But if the lady were willing?" She bent forward so that he could feel her breath upon his cheek.

"Love doesn't sprout on bushes," he said bluntly, "besides I am much too impoverished."

She took one of his brass coat buttons between her finger and thumb with a movement strangely intimate. "You could exchange these for commissioned ones."

"Impossible," he said.

She gazed inscrutably. "Means could be found."

"Means?" he repeated. Six hundred ... a thousand pounds – A sense of their isolation, of being alone with her in the empty echoing house, came upon him. He recalled how closely she had clung during their brief exploration of the rooms, and laid it to natural apprehension of darkness, of lurking danger. "By whom?" he inquired.

"By one who might well be your friend." She smiled with raised eyebrows, her hand on his arm. Simms sighed. The fine lady, whimsical, impulsive ...

Sue Thompson entered, and the two moved apart. Simms announced that it was time to see what O'Connor was doing, and left immediately. Sue, who had found cloths in the kitchen, began clearing litter from the table, and making it presentable for a meal. For her part Harriet gazed fixedly into the flames. "A strange house, this," she remarked. "One feels that anything may happen at any moment."

"Yes, indeed Ma'm."

A sudden numbness of feeling almost choked Sue's voice. The *tete-a-tete* she had interrupted disturbed her. Not that she had any claims on the affection of the young commissary – far from it – but that he would be attracted to another of her sex, and that person Harriet Foulkes, her mistress was thoroughly disconcerting. In a word, she disapproved, the more so since with sharp intuition she felt that Mrs Foulkes, subtly artful, was frivolously involving Simms. For the first time she regarded her mistress with severely critical eyes. "Why does she not stir herself to something useful," the girl thought. There was much to be done.

"Yes, indeed Ma'm," mocked Harriet. "Here we are, lonely wayfarers by night, thrust into the most romantic of situations, sole occupants of a Gothick mansion, and all you can do is to indulge in monosyllables! Have you no secret yearnings – no flights of fancy?"

"I am not employed for that purpose, Ma'm."

With a pity smile Harriet strolled into the hall where she could be heard softly speaking to Felix. "Yes, you are good at that," thought Sue ...

The turkey – although a small bird – took longer roasting than they had expected. When, blotched with smoke it did at last appear, such was their hunger they ate without restraint. After clearing away, the four, using cloaks and saddles for pillows, settled down to sleep. But it was an uneasy bedchamber. Draughts from a rising wind rippled the tapestry. Remotely the chimney boomed, and from time to time jest of smoke shot across the recumbent figures. The occasional clicking of a shoe upon the pavement of the hall reminded them of the patient beats. Simms, who – catnapping – attended to the fire, was mostly awake. Hands clasped behind his head, he studied the relaxed faces of his companions – that of Harriet Foulkes in particular, classically moulded, self-willed, the upper lip faintly disdainful. Of what? The world in general? She appeared less attractive now, less impulsive, less dangerous. In more than one sense he was relieved that they were not travelling alone. Beyond her, half concealed by shadow, O'Connor's button nose and scruffy jowl showed faintly. The Irishman, always something of a lout, was useful, but could be a distinct liability. To help matters he was beginning to snore ...

Simms turned his attention to Sue Thompson who reclined with head resting on the crook of a smoothly rounded arm. Once she raised her head and a pair of enigmatic eyes challenged his. He smiled, but she closed her eyes in instant dismissal. For a moment, he felt ashamed that he had accomplished so little on her behalf, yet with the dice so loaded what could one do? ... He continued to study her face, until after a long bout of yawning, his own eyelids drooped ...

* * *

He sat up listening, broad awake. On windy nights these great houses were the devil – tapestries rippling, chimneys sobbing, window frames creaking, door latches clicking, a hundred unaccountable murmurings from every quarter. The leafless branches of the trees in the forecourt twittered and squeaked like banshees. In one momentary silence, Simms fancied he heard a sharp peffing cough from the direction of the hall. "The mule belike," he muttered, and although not entirely convinced, fell back upon his elbow.

Again the cough. Simms sat up and reaching for his pistol. "An animal with two legs!" he decided. He rose quietly, and moved to where O'Connor lay, touching him lightly on the shoulder. Fortunately the Irishman opened his eyes without a sound, and Simms holding a finger to his lips cocked his head towards the door. He then pointed to the lamp, and O'Connor taking the hint, lit up. Meanwhile, the two women slept on.

His weapon cocked, the commissary eased the door open and stepped into the hall. The mule, he saw, had found a resting place on the floor, but the three horses, which were standing, shifted uneasily. As O'Connor elevated the lantern, a shadowy outline flitted towards the staircase and disappeared through the archway leading to the kitchens. "A demon!" breathed O'Connor. "Man or demon," said Simms, "we must know who he is!"

He led the way across the hall, but confused by the abysmal darkness, and through the archway, unfamiliar turns in the corridor, at last entered the kitchen they had discovered earlier. "He most certainly came this way," said Simms, casting the light around. "You man, check the outer door, I'll examine here."

The great fireplace proved empty. Simms wrenched open cupboard doors, peered under tables, but without success. The Irishman beside the outer door reported that both bolts were in place. "Then" said Simms, "the creature, assuming that he is of flesh and blood is still with us. There is still the oven." Together they peered into the cavernous depths, but here too the shadows were still. "'Tis a leprechaun," mumbled O'Connor, "the black witch o' Balleyhooley cellar?"

"In that case we will catch him by the tail," said Simms. He cried loudly in Spanish, "Show yourself – we know you are there!" But there was no response.

Simms had already decided that the strange being had disappeared through a secret passage, when a cough – the same dry peff which he had heard in the hall – sounded from a large jar resting on its side in a remote corner. He strode across, but before he could reach it, a man's head emerged from the mouth. With a thrust and a wriggle a body followed at once rearing upright on a pair of grotesquely diminutive legs. "Mother of God!" cried O'Connor crossing himself, "'tis a creature of the woods – a man ape!"

A dwarf stood before them. With an elaborate gesture he bowed almost to the floor. His broad leathery face creased into a smile, and he croaked in Spanish, "Good evening to your excellencies. You come on a wild night."

"Wild enough," said Simms dryly, rolling the jar away with his foot. "I think Don Diogenes we will discuss the weather in a more convenient place. Bring him along."

Seized by O'Connor, the little man raised himself to the full four feet of his height, calmly disengaged the Irishman's fingers, and announced with impressive dignity that he was not accustomed to such treatment, indeed it would be his pleasurable duty to lead them himself back to the dining room. Thus the curious procession returned to the firelight where the women awakened by their entry, sat up anxiously. But it was the dwarf who did the honours. "Pray be seated, all of you," he said with a ceremonious wave of the hand, "you have nothing to fear from me." The Spanish words conveyed nothing to Harriet and Sue, but the gesture by which they were accompanied was plain. They both sat.

The dwarf remained standing. In the shifting light his hairless skull shone like polished ebony; his cheeks drooped in greasy folds to the corners of his negroid mouth; his restless liquid black eyes regarded them with a certain melancholy. Clad in a lengthy coat of orange velvet frogged with black, he appeared to have no legs at all. His left hand, they noticed, was bound in a dirty rag. "Have we the honour," inquired Simms politely, "of addressing Don Taboada?" The irony of the question did not for the moment strike him.

The dwarf shook his head sadly. "Alas, no. My master is absent in France with the King himself whom you must know is held in duress by the cursed Napoleon." He drew himself up an inch or two and threw back his head. "I control during his absence."

"You lodge in somewhat restricted quarters, senor," said Simms dryly.

The other smiled deprecatingly. "If you refer to the humble jar in which you discovered me, I can assure you that the accommodation is one of necessity. These are strange times, and one must protect oneself as best one can. I wear the major domo's coat for example. It is not mine, but it serves a useful purpose."

"I do not understand," said Simms.

"My master, as I have told you attends to our thrice unfortunate king. Branded as a traitor because of his continued absence – though no man more loyal to his country – and inflamed by scoundrelly *guerrilleros*, the villagers attempted to sack his property. They beat up the servants, who fled; applied torches to the furniture, so that the whole building would have been destroyed had I not beaten out the flames. They would have done more, but one of their number having swallowed a goodly portion of my master's brandy, fell over a balcony and broke his back. Another, fooling with a pistol, shot himself through the head. This quieted them. When I cursed them in gypsy language they fled in some terror, howling for the priest."

"And you remained – alone?"

The dwarf nodded. "How could I forsake a master with whom I have lived for forty years, and from whom I have received nothing but kindness? When the *guerrileros* come, I make the jar my humble place of refuge. Ah, senor, I know little of the high affairs of state – the great ones and their ways – but I have grown with this house, and while a turret stands, here I shall stay." The dwarf's eyes shone with complete devotion. In his tarnished splendour he loomed almost heroic. With a comprehensive gesture, embracing not only the apartment in which they were standing, but the mansion itself, he said, "Here you see proud and noble Spain in the hands of despoilers, vagabonds and strangers."

"The last of whom we form a part," observed Simms.

The dwarf smiled easily. "I see that you intend no harm – it is of others that I am thinking!"

"The men of the village?"

"Yes. They will summon courage when they have found a priest to follow."

The dwarf laughed strangely. "To shrive Beelzebub! But the man they seek is trailing a musket in the mountains. He will not return."

"How do you know?"

"I do know."

With an exclamation of dismay, the odd major-domo cried, "What a neglectful dolt I am! You require wine, and that at least I can provide. Your pardon senora – your pardon senor." He ambled off, and in a very short time returned with a flagon and glasses. "My master would assuredly wish me to do this." He poured out, inquiring as he did so their destination. Salamanca? Ah, he knew the city well. Perceiving his intelligence, Don Taboada had sent him to a seminary in that place, and afterwards he had become his master's secretary-librarian. "Perhaps you may have noticed, senor, how excellently well the library is kept? The villains scattered the books, but these I gathered together again, repaired as best I could, and arranged the whole as before." If he talked too much, they must remember that he has not spoken to a living person for many days. In the morning he would do his best to set them on the road to Salamanca ...

A gust of wind brought smoke swirling about them, and when Harriet coughed he apologised profoundly. "The chimney has crumbled badly and cannot be repaired. It is beyond me."

But he made no attempt to withdraw. Simms who had been watching him closely, said, "One thing continues to puzzle me, senor – the villagers are many, and you are alone. Why did they not return?"

The dwarf smiled darkly. "I have already explained."

Simms looked askance. "I am never-the-less intrigued."

"They believe I have the evil eye." The little man faced the commissary squarely. "Do you think so, senor?"

"What little I know of you is good," said Simms. "More than that I cannot say."

"They know that I am gifted with second sight, but what of that? The saints also had second sight."

"Second sight?" repeated Simms vaguely. "You mean that you are a necromancer – one who foretells?"

"I inherited so much from my mother who was a gitana — yes, indeed, but that did not make her a limb of Satan." He turned his head slowly, listening. Simms recalling the peasants at the gate, wondered if any were lurking much nearer the house. "It is the animals," said the dwarf at last," only the animals." Listening intently, the commissary could hear only the droning of the wind.

At intervals, Simms had translated briefly for the benefit of his companions a sentence or two from the dwarf's conversation. When Harriet, who had been listening with a certain detachment heard the reference to "second sight" she became broad awake. In past days she had patronised the salon of the celebrated Madame Melopar of Bond Street, so that she was not unacquainted with popular clairvoyance. She sat up, regarding the dwarf with peculiar attention. True the little man was less personable than Madame (who for her part had no pretension to beauty) but what of that? The spirits employed the oddest of mediums. The dwarf's eyes, liquid, mysterious, held promise of revelation. If only one could preview the coming days, the fortunes of the campaign, and more particularly her future with Tony Harte. At Quelez she had detected a certain reserve, an affinity from which the bloom had vanished. Was she committing the great mistake of her life in riding towards Salamanca, indeed in remaining with the army at all? The dwarf might draw aside the curtain. She turned eagerly to Simms. "Do ask him to tell us more concerning this second sight."

Simms confronted the dwarf. "Madame," he said, "who is most interested in your power of reading the future, would like to pursue the matter."

The dwarf glanced from one to the other, and shook his head. "Such powers," he said, "tend to come and go. I am as a leaf in the wind. And that is all."

Simms turned to Harriet. "He seems disinclined."

She smiled invitingly at the little man in crumpled velvet. To Simms she said, "Do your utmost to persuade him."

The commissary looked doubtful. "We had better let him go."

"To please me!"

"Easier said than done," reflected Simms. "Madame defers to you," he said aloud. "At the same time I suggest that it would be courteous to accommodate the lady."

The dwarf stared into the fireplace clasping an unclasping his hands nervously. "How so?" he said softly, "I cannot expound as from a treatise."

"A treatise? Come, senor! ... you have other means."

The dwarf gazed fixedly at the floor, sitting very still as though listening to the creaking of branches outside. At last, after what seemed a very long time indeed, he said in a low voice, "Does the senora possess what you would call sympathy?"

"You would wish her to be perfectly amenable?"

The dwarf sighed. "Without that, all is vain."

"He wonders if you would be sufficiently receptive," said Simms to Harriet – "able to attend completely."

"Assure him," she replied eagerly, "that indeed I will."

"She agrees entirely," said Simms translating.

"Then be pleased to draw near," said the dwarf," and allow me a little time to compose myself."

He closed his eyes, folded his hands, and in a low voice added, "The time, the place, and the spirit concerned may not be propitious, but I will make the attempt. I promise nothing however, for in this I am not my own servant, being at the governance of another." With this he buried his face in his hands, and (in words incomprehensible to Simms) murmured an incantation. Then exposing his face he turned to the commissary saying, "You shall be the first. Set your hands in both of mine, look into my eyes, and think of – nothing."

"Nothing?"

"Yes. Erase from your mind all measure of thought, dwell wholly upon a void, a frame in which there is no picture – an empty circle. This effect slowly, in your own time."

Simms, at once attracted and repelled by the melancholy of the dwarf's eyes, placed both his hands between the brown leathery fingers extended towards him. "Swearing fealty to a medieval chief," he thought … but concentrating closely as his mentor indicated, he sensed nothing except in his ears a faint humming which was certainly not that of the wind, when almost imperceptibly he felt drawn as it were to the inner circle of a whirlpool. He heard the dwarf whisper, "Empty of all thought … empty … quite empty …"

Both men sat perfectly still, while the others watched hardly daring to breathe. Later, trying to recapture the experience, Simms remembered drifting light as a feather, weirdly incorporeal, while beside him the firelight continued to flicker, the wind to moan in the chimney, and the dwarf's sing-song voice to intermingle oddly with circumambient sound. Words came as from a great distance. "I see a snow-covered plain affording shelter to neither man nor beast …" For Simms a wind blew bitterly cold. His feet numb in the stirrups, for he was mounted, and the beast he bestrode curvetting and wheeling madly … "I see you with a wagon train … a company of women in great haste to be gone …" The voice continued level, detached, unhurried … "I see a musket smoke, first the flash and then the report… I see dark shadows on the snow… men cry out in fury and anguish … the plain empties, but there are still shadows and blood stains on the snow …"

The dwarf shuddered, released Simms' hands, and at once covered his own eyes. "I could have told you more," he said reproachfully, "but the circle was not empty. It may be that the fault was mine."

More smoke billowed from the fireplace. "The fire is inconvenient," he said, "I am sorry."

"What did he tell you?" inquired Harriet of Simms.

The commissary shook himself like a swimmer emerging from water. With numbed fingers he rubbed his eyes to bring himself awake. His feet were still very cold. The wood fire on the hearth expanded and contracted rhythmically. "Give me a moment," he gasped. He ached, almost saddle sore as with the effort of riding hard.

"What happened?"

Gradually for Simms, the room, the fireplace, the surrounding faces fell into normal appearance. "I seemed to be in a confounded scrape with a baggage train," he panted … "draught animals … troopers … blood on the snow"

"Oh!" Harriet seemed disappointed. "Please ask him to consider me." Her hand fell to her satchel as though to open it.

"Don't offer money," said Simms sharply.

She raised her eyebrows. "How do you know he will not accept money?" But she did not insist, and regarding her hands with a faintly whimsical air, extended them towards the dwarf who drew back with a muttered word or two and a gesture of disapproval. "What does he say?" she asked.

"That you must take off your rings."

"Is that all?"

She took these off and handed them to Sue.

"Now," instructed Simms, "when he takes your hands in his you are to look into his eyes and clear your mind of all thought."

"Gracious!" Harriet settled herself before the Spaniard, who sat awaiting impassively.

"Close your eyes briefly," said Simms, "concentrate, then look directly into his."

Harriet, who had by now become completely responsive, followed the commissary's directions. At first the deep lines in the dwarf's face held her attention. After that the liquid eyes became so compulsive that she felt herself yielding. The room about her faded, and she found herself rising, poised, drifting almost as it were over an abysmal void. Faintly, intermingled with the soughing of the wind, she could hear the dwarf's voice. She wished that he would speak louder, for although she could not understand his language, he was the only human contact she possessed. Steadily even that sound diminished, until both wind and voice lapsed into an aimless whine …

She had drifted from her former position. Now she looked over a vast waste of mountains, icy cones lifting to the distant horizon. The whole expanse was lifeless; snow powdery and wind-blown, interweaved in the valleys below …

She descended slowly into brighter light, into a blissful aura of sunshine. Now she discerned tree-tops, which as the wind teased them, broke into a misty silver grey. Her feet gently touched a road surface. Ah, here as sub-stance, the normal world! She would be content if she were not so unutter-ably tired!

She halted beneath a tree beside the grassy verge, and reached out to touch its friendly strength, but in doing so her fingers encountered not the warm flecked bark, but a face with eyes of stone and hair thickly matted with moss. A cry froze on her lips; it was the face of Anthony Harte. But the eyes of stone were lifeless, and the lips of stone, dumb ... She flung her arms around the tree clutching at the obdurate surface, but this was vain. Anthony was at one with the tree. She cried for help. None came – the road was quite empty. Alone in this petrified world, she shouted until her voice cracked from the effort, until whimpering she uttered words without meaning. Then to a long way off, crying, "That is the end?" ... The end of what?

The road, the tree, faded. She was still clutching something tightly but now it was the arms of her chair. She looked up in the face of Simms. "It is all over," he said gently, "do you sit still for a moment. Our friend is also over-come." She saw dimly that the dwarf had collapsed and was bent forward, head between knees. In a daze she watched Simms pour out a measure of wine and bring it to the lips of the medium. Susan Thompson was at hand with a glass for herself. Harriet's hand trembled as she took it. "I had expected," she said tremulously, "something ... I don't know what ... some-thing quite ... different ..." She swayed. As the room clouded over once again, the fire misty as a dying sun, once more she saw the crystal cheeks of Tony Harte. Then complete darkness overwhelmed her ...

When she opened her eyes again it was to find Sue and Simms hovering solicitously; she heard the girl's compassionate, "You are very, very tired – you must try to rest."

Harriet raised herself on her elbows. "Where is he?" she cried poignantly.

"The dwarf?" inquired Simms.

"No – no," she moaned, falling back, "not the dwarf ..."

* * *

A pitiless morning light filtered through the dusty, smoke-dimmed heraldic emblems in the windows, exposing the sad havoc of charred hangings and broken furniture to which the darkness had lent enchantment. Simms doused his face in a water trough, and afterwards went about whistling cheerfully. O'Connor grunted and hissed as he rubbed down the horses; the mule's mousy coat he ignored.

Harriet, struggling with a splitting headache, tried at breakfast to put on a cheerful front. One had to admit that the dwarf did well, providing goat's milk, white bread and a stew of rabbit. He was all attention, concerned only

for the Ingleses safety and comfort. No mention at all was made of the previous night's excursion into clairvoyance, but always (Harriet noticed) he
evaded her eyes.

She heaved a profound sigh of relief as they mounted and rode away. The
forecourt was still deserted. A vagrant chestnut leaf fell, brushed her face and
rested clammily upon her hand. She shivered, somehow impelled to look
back. In the doorway stood the grotesque little man, his velvet coat more
shabby than ever, his black melancholy eyes fixed on her own.

Simms also gave one last look. "Another castle in Spain!" he said lightly.

Harriet remained silent …

CHAPTER X

Beyond a low range of hills, golden brown in the late autumn sun, they viewed the crowded convent and college roofs, the pinnacles and towers of Salamanca. Watering their horses below the old Roman bridge, they entered by the river gate, where Simms inquired for the house, which the Assistant Quartermaster General had made his headquarters. In the Plaza Mayor, they were told.

They rode through into a finely arcaded square, and at last found the officer in question. He occupied a splendidly furnished room, and was easing the rigours of the campaign with a dish of sweetmeat, roasted chestnuts and wine. He was however, most attentive, insisting that they shared his repast. When they introduced the subject of billets his mood changed. He groaned aloud. "My dear compatriots," he exclaimed, "the place is crammed to the eaves. If we could clear out the priests and the students we could oblige everyone. I personally, would have no compunction in doing so; but I am neither the Captain general nor the Pope, so we must do the best we can. I have chalked a convent for your regiment. You may go there if you wish, though my advice is that you await your people and move in together. In the meantime take pot-luck. Now let me see."

He consulted a well-worn record book, flipped over a few pages, ran his finger down a column, and with a grunt of satisfaction scrawled an address on a scrap of paper. "Apply," he said, "at this house, which you will find across the square. I have no doubt they will take good care of you." He turned to Harriet. "I should be honoured to escort you personally, Madam, but as you see I am chained to my post."

So they left him to the elegance of his room, his papers, wine and chestnuts.

But if they had expected to enjoy the elaborate décor of the Assistant Quartermaster's lodgings, they were son to be disillusioned. A bronze door was opened to them by an ancient serving man, but a drift of cigar smoke over his shoulder, and a babble of contending voices across the hall indicated that other guests had preceded them. A card game was in progress, and the shouting and laughter by which it was accompanied augured ill for a quiet evening. When Simms explained that the lady he presented was the wife of an important British officer and would require especial accommodation, they were shown into a sizeable upper room, and the servant disappeared to acquaint his master of their arrival.

Presently, their host, a courtly hidalgo in an old fashioned wig, a green velvet coat with ruffles at the neck and wrists, a sprigged yellow satin waistcoat and black satin knee breeches, entered tapping his cane and bowing as well as his creaking joints would allow. After exchanging a few words with Simms, he bent over Harriet's hand. The only two words she retained from the consequent flow of Spanish was "Senora Generalissimo!" – whatever that might mean – and she bowed her head in acknowledgement. Another low bow and the old man withdrew. "Short and sweet," she observed to Simms. "The old boy was really quite friendly," he explained. "You are to regard the house as completely our own. He trusts that the bells will not disturb your slumbers." Harriet cocked her head listening to the hubbub downstairs. "The bells," she said, "will be the least of our problems!"

Simms laughed. "He assumes you to be the wife of the Commander-in-chief himself."

"No harm in that," she remarked. "We must live up to it."

The servant returned for further orders. O'Connor was relegated to a corner of the kitchens, while Sue remained with her mistress. Late though the evening was, Simms excused himself, went out in search of the central depot, and did not reappear until morning ...

* * *

The two women retired early, but what with the roistering officers below, the rumbling and squeaking of ox-carts in the square, and the tolling of bells from half a dozen churches, Harriet dozed fitfully. She could not dismiss from her mind the séance of the previous night, the road of crystal where she had walked alone. What did the tragic tree portend? Dreams, she remembered, went by opposites, but was the harrowing adventure into which she had been wafted a dream at all? A transcript rather of time to come? If so, what possible action could she take? Return to England might break the spell; in that case she would not see Tony again. She felt that somehow she had been touched by evil. How foolish to have had any connection with the mis-shapen little man at all? ...

She heard a distant clock strike one ... and after an age, almost ... two. Turning restlessly on her couch, she decided that during the coming day she would find the cathedral, and within its sacred precincts exorcise the taint. Anglican though she was, she wondered if she might be allowed to make confession, but she had no Spanish and the priest in his turn, no English. What then? Submit a fervent prayer? ... This she would ... At last, her mind disposed, she fell asleep ...

* * *

Next day she was up and about early. The novelty of wandering around the arcades, fingering jewellery, combs of ivory and jet, shawls and mantillas – two of the last she bought, one for Jane and the other for herself – did something to expunge the torment of the midnight hours. But not completely. Approaching the old Cathedral – for strangely enough Salamanca boasted of two – the impulse returned, and instructing Sue to remain within the porch, she entered alone.

The huge building was icy cold. To right and left in dim recesses ancient bishops and grandees lay in marble and alabaster. Above them, chattering indifferently, masons on tall ladders were repairing windows. A few suppliants sat awaiting their turn at the confessional boxes. She could hear half-whispered snatches of supplication, and the droning almost nonchalant, responses of the priests.

Harriet, approaching the altar, moved towards a pillar where surrounded by elaborately fashioned ornaments of gold and silver, precious stones and gleaming brass, stood a snow-white figure of the Virgin. How still she was, and how serene her features! And how gently the candles burned. Harriet closed her eyes against the massive panoply of the high altar, but the form of prayer she had considered in the isolation of the bed-chamber somehow would not come. She tried to remember the familiar phrases of Anglican worship, but without result. At last she managed to mutter, "From unholy thought and purpose, Thou good Lord deliver us! From cold and hunger, danger and death, good Lord deliver us! From all evil spirits deliver us! ..."

The murmured words came to an end. She could no more. But was that enough? With bowed head she lingered, and with a final glance at the graven, but wholly compassionate figure before her, rejoined Sue who coming forward a step or two regarded the elaborate gilding, the splendid effigies and the ornate carving around her with a doubtful non-conformist eye.

On the steps Harriet dropped a coin in a beggar's cup, only to find herself immediately surrounded by a clamouring mob of the maimed and blind, children of unnatural growth, some exposing sores, but all whining for alms. Repelled, and not a little frightened, she had thrust through the press when a hunchback, his pendent arms almost sweeping the ground, linked himself with her. She recoiled violently. "Leave us, for God's sake!" she exclaimed, striking out with her fist. But the man clung like a shadow, snatching at her dress.

Sue forced herself between the beggar and her mistress. "Get thysen whooam!" she cried, falling into her native dialect. She confronted the mendicant squarely. "I shan't tell thee a second time!" Whether it was the emphasis in the girl's voice, or the appearance of two British officers on horseback, which freed them from his attention – whatever the cause, the dwarf fell behind and they saw him no more.

"Faugh," breathed Harriet in disgust, "revolting! Misshapen in body as in mind!"

"I suppose," said Sue, remorseful that she had spoken so rudely, "the poor things must live ..."

"Live?" responded Harriet darkly, "for what purpose? Tell me that!"

* * *

The regiment marched into the convent twenty-four hours later, piled arms, shed equipment, and settled in for the night. Soon fires smoked in the courtyard, and rations were distributed. The monks had vacated their cells to the officers, and straw heaped in the corridors made tolerable bedding for the rank and file. They had been warned that as guests of a community devoted to the religious life, exemplary conduct would be required, and for some times this order was obeyed. After that, for no ostensible reason at all, red-coated figures could be seen in the most unlikely places. Pickings however, were few for the convent was as bare as a bone. A few soldiers peered hopefully into the brilliant little chapel itself, but the Father Superior, wise in his own generation, had posted relays of the brethren there. The heretics were politely but firmly turned away. "Go with God!" murmured the monks.

Colonel Pomeroy was delighted to have his own officers brought together at last into some sort of Mess, though at the outset the Father Superior tended to mar the general impression by presiding in robe and cross. Enormously fat, he seemed to overflow the arms of his elaborately carved chair. The Colonel occupied a seat to his right; Harriet Foulkes, who in the course of the day had been put in one of the guest chambers, that on his left. Gracing the company in point lace and ivory satin – albeit somewhat creased from prolonged packing – she was more than adequate to the occasion, responding graciously to the inclined head, the neatly turned compliment, the glance of admiration. The scarlet uniforms, brought light and colour to the scene, a glowing frame to the silver and glass of the table. Using her beringed hands eloquently, she related – not without significant omissions – the adventure of the deserted mansion. There was no check to the free play of her imagination, for Sue was in her appointed cell, and Harry Simms, stamping his numbed feet on the stone flags of the buttery, which had been converted into a stores depot, working late.

The refectory meal dragged on, partly because in hesitant French helped out by a little Latin, the Father Superior persisted in discussing at length, the relative characteristics of Spanish and Irish peasantry. Service was slow; the Colonel shuffled, and drummed on the table with his fingers; Harriet, bored by the conversation, yawned. The younger officers groaned, and rolled bread pellets. When at last, with a murmured apology, the loquacious ecclesiastic lumbered from the chamber, the door closed behind him to an audible sigh of relief.

During the uneasy silence, which followed Foulkes, shot more than one

significant glance at his wife hoping that she too would withdraw. But
Harriet showed no signs of doing so. Ignoring his gaze, she studied with
intense interest the finely chased goblet before her, wondering aloud if it
could be of Renaissance workmanship. Harrod intervening, thought Cellini.
"He was much employed by the Pope, you know, accomplished, but an arrant
rascal for all that."

"Cellini, begad!" Foulkes fumed secretly. "She knows – she must know –
that it is desirable for her to leave." Aloud he said, "You must be more than
a trifle fatigued, my dear."

"Not in the least," she answered blithely.

Foulkes slumped, hoping that Pomeroy would enforce the observation,
but in this he was disappointed. The Colonel, who had thought of the matter, refrained. ("Ungentlemanly to dismiss a lady!") At the same time he
gloomed a little; on the balance he wished too that Harriet were absent. It
was not habitual to discuss military problems at Mess, but conditions were
such at Salamanca that something ought to be said.

The strained silence was broken when Foulkes posed a question, which
was uppermost in the minds of all present. "Are you able, sir, to inform us
where we stand?"

Eyes turned on Pomeroy, whose florid cheeks deepened.

"What? – What's that?"

Foulkes repeated the question.

"Ah – yes – yes."

Pomeroy cleared his throat loudly, and twirled his wine glass before speaking. Although he had lately come from headquarters, where he had gathered
a certain amount of information, he had forgotten much of the detail – place
names, for example, eluded him. Fortunately an outline remained; he would
do the best he could. As a preliminary he cleared an open space on the table
before him, intending by a simple arrangement of glasses, bottles and the
like, to convey some idea of the strategic position of the army. "Gentlemen,"
he began, "and – ah, yes – you Madame, you know as well as I do that the
army is not yet concentrated. At present—" and he pushed a dish to the centre of the clearing he had made, "here some of us are in Salamanca." He drew
a deep breath as he considered his next move. "Salamanca," he repeated
gravely. The listeners – with the exception of Harrod whose thoughts were
still fixed on Cellini – eyed the receptacle as though at any moment it would
sprout a host of towers and pinnacles, until Pomeroy slid a second dish to the
table's edge. "And this is Baird marching towards us from Corunna. Where
he is at present we do not know. He may have reached Astoria – Astorga, or
some such place, though you may assume that his rear – mountain roads and
all that – will be miles behind."

"Where is Astorga, sir?" inquired Daiches.

"To the north – to the north," replied Pomeroy testily. "Don't bother me with details! Consult your map. Now, as I was saying before I was interrupted – we are awaiting Baird, whom you see represented by the dish."

The Colonel then slid a wine decanter to the right. "This is General Hope taking the roundabout road through the something mountains – dammit, I forget these outlandish names."

"The Escorial pass; the Guadarama," said Foulkes.

"No doubt you are right, Major," grunted Pomeroy. "Where were we?"

"Awaiting Sir John Hope."

"Very well."

The Colonel measured the distance between three strategic objects with his eye, shifted Salamanca an inch or two, and at a short distance arranged a bottle. "Valladolid," he jerked, pointing. "Mark the place well; forty thousand Frenchmen, horse, foot, and guns, are there, three marches from where we sit at the moment, while Hope is six away at least."

"Thus," said Major Stanton, "the enemy is three marches nearer this place than General Hope?"

"That is so."

"What conclusion do you draw, sir?" asked Foulkes.

The Colonel did not respond, and silence fell.

"While there's life there's hope," said Harriet cheerfully.

"Say rather," drawled Harrod, "where there's Hope there's life!" It was doubtful if the Colonel had noticed the quip.

"In the meantime," continued Pomeroy, "I would draw your attention to the matter of public behaviour. Let there be no – ah – indiscretions. I need not remind you of the wine shops, of which there are far too many. No more Guardia!" he rapped, glowering in the direction of Bird. "The Spaniards too are jealous of their females. Tread lightly there. Seek your quarters early, and in respectable condition." He stared across at the young gentlemen sitting at the lower end of the board, who for their part assumed attitudes of impeccable propriety. "Very well!" he concluded, pouring out wine for himself.

After the Colonel had finished, conversation became general. When he rose to leave the chamber, a little off balance, he caught his toe in a rush mat and fell heavily across a settee. He recovered himself quickly, and with his hand pressed to his side in obvious pain, snapped that it was nothing – nothing at all. "Don't fuss!" he jerked and stalked away.

Foulkes watched his superior officer thoughtfully as the broad back disappeared through the leathern curtain of the door. What if the Colonel were to fail, to collapse even, under strain? He had seen his best years, and the road to Salamanca had been unusually trying. Was the age of portents past? But Foulkes at once dismissed the speculation. "No honour," he reflected, "in waiting for dead men's shoes!"

* * *

Later that night Foulkes remarked to his wife, "By the way, I have a new servant, Raddock by name. Look out for him. An excellent fellow. Anticipates
everything. He tells me that he was for a time valet to Earl Fitzwilliam."

"Then how comes it then that he is in the army?" asked Harriet. "He is
probably lying."

"If so, he is a very accomplished liar," replied her husband, "for his attention to clothes, boots, accoutrements, to creature comforts generally, is all
that could be desired."

"If you are satisfied," she responded. The subject was to her not one of
particular interest ...

* * *

She wrote to Jane from Salamanca, enclosing a sketch she had made of the
regiment on the march. "This I trust you will find more expressive than
words. The bulky man in the tilted cocked hat – forgive the horse's legs
which I find difficult – is Colonel Pomeroy, and spaced behind him calling
for no more than a few up and down strokes is Major Foulkes, no less. The
reins hang loosely because he is balancing his snuff box. The third horseman,
somewhat undersize, is Major Stanton of whom Pomeroy ventured to Percy
that the "man grew more like a ferret every day." The officer with sunken eyes
and heavy chin, trudging on foot, is Lieutenant Suckly who plays the flute
divinely, though not of course when on duty. The sturdy figure more to the
rear, his cheeks blushing vermilion, is Lieutenant Bird, a familiar of mine;
while the man with a Grecian profile is Captain Harrod, who carries a large
umbrella on his pack mule ... The porcupine quills touched with Chinese
White, represent musket barrels glinting in the sun ...

"I regret I cannot include the women who straggle behind. On the whole
they do very well; so far not one has fallen out. In billet and bivouac they do
some cooking for the men, wash clothes, darn socks, sew boots with twine. Of
course they chatter like jackdaws, but there is little quarrelling among them,
and so far I have heard of nothing of scandal with other men. One matron,
however, approached me yesterday complaining that her husband had formed
an attachment with a woman of the Ninety Fifth. Of course I referred her to
the Quartermaster! Who am I to judge between husband and wife? ...

"P.S. Do not on any account allow the enclosed sketch to leave your possession. If it were to be inspected, particularly by the *warriors* concerned, I
should be the subject of a drum-head court martial!"

* * *

Next morning, brisk, trim, saluting with deference, Harker entered the guest
chamber of the convent, bearing a number of newspapers under his arm. Sue

who was unaware of the new appointment, caught her breath in surprise. He managed to give her the faintest wink before addressing her mistress. "Major Foulkes' compliments, Ma'm – he sends you these public prints, and requests that you will be good enough to look them over before you venture out, as he would like them to be circulated to others."

"Thank you," said Harriet. "You are the new man I take it?"

"Yes, Ma'm – Raddock the name." He cast a side glance at Sue.

"Well, I am certain you will take good care of the Major. See that his undergarments are always aired, and that he does not miss his meals." Foulkes, she knew, was too often content with wine and a scrap of biscuit.

"It will be my pleasure, Ma'm. Is there anything I can do for you?"

"Not now."

She turned away, and Harker left, closing the door gently behind him. "Seems a most obliging man," observed Harriet, but Sue, who had watched the performance with fascinated eyes, could only marvel at the smooth deference the man displayed, and at his correct form of speech, though he would be repeating exactly the Major's own words. She bit her lip, feeling that no good would come from the new appointment.

Leisurely, Harriet unfolded the newspapers – *The Morning Chronicle*, *The Morning Post*, and *The Political Register* – scanning the columns rapidly. There were County Meetings, transcripts of windy, interminable speeches: in *The Register*, Cobbett railed at length against the public emoluments of the Wellesley family. People everywhere were still denouncing "Cintra". She lingered a little over the art sales at Mr Christies. The Duchess of Westmorland's masquerade engaged her attention. It seemed that plans had been made for rebuilding the burnt-out Covent Garden Theatre. A certain lady of the town had been involved with one in very high authority – a member of the Royal Family – over the sale of army commissions, the matter to be raised in the House ... After studying the advertisements, and making note of "highly recommended calomel and opium pills," she tossed the papers aside, remarking that Sue might peruse them if she wished.

The girl took up *The Morning Chronicle* indifferently. She was not interested in politics. The gossip of "The Town" concerned persons who were complete strangers to her, so that after reading a few advertisements, she was about to lay down the sheet when her eyes caught the word *Primrose* printed in italics. As she read on the passage chilled her—

"Advices from Portsmouth indicate that during a violent tempest off the coast of Spain, the merchantman *Primrose*, being dismasted, fell away from the convoy of which she formed part, and being last observed drifting shorewards in a sinking condition, may be presumed lost. On boat were a number of unfortunate convicts bound for New South Wales."

That was all. She sat numbly, while Harriet scribbled on her tablets. After a few moments, the girl rose quietly and leaving the room entered the corridor where in the shadows with her back to the cold stone of the wall, she was alone in her distress. Ws this the last link in the tragic chain of Robin's misfortune? Overhead a bell began to toll in a measured, melancholy iron-bound note. A funeral knell? ... A flood of horror overcame her. The sea, of which she retained the most vivid recollection surged through her brain, washing mercilessly in and out of her consciousness. She saw Robin submerged in the cruel water, thrashing vainly with fettered limbs, sinking in the dark green depths, until at last all life extinct he rested on the swaying weed of the ocean floor. Overwhelmed, she covered her face with her hands.

Moments passed ... A monk emerged from the shadows and shuffled by without so much as a glance in her direction ... a chair scraped in the guest room ... she could hear her mistress moving. With an effort she composed herself, contrived to re-enter and to resume her duties. She gathered up the scattered newspapers and set them aside, tidied a workbox, and folded once again the gown of ivory satin and point lace which Mrs Foulkes had worn the previous evening ...

Harriet had hardly noticed Sue's absence, for having finished her shopping she was at a loose end. She had been told by Harrod that the ceilings in the University were well-worth inspection, but who on such a fine day would wish to stare at ceilings? The convent was dull to distraction. Felix, she knew, was champing in his stall, and while it was all very well to exchange pleasantries with Suckley and Bird, they were not available as cavaliers. The horse needed exercise. Her husband being at headquarters where he had found old friends – what on earth did they find to do there? – would probably stay and dine. Thus she was prompted to approach the only person with whom she could find diversion. She decided to communicate with Tony. She dismissed Percy's disapproval with a shrug. No mention had been made of Harte since Quelez. What more natural in the course of an easy ride beyond the walls, than a chance meeting with him? In order to assist this hazard she dashed off a note—

Dear Hector (It ran) I seem to have exhausted the attractions of Salamanca, and intend to proceed at 2 o'clock in the direction of Alba de Tormes. If not confined to your tent, is it possible that you also will be riding in that direction?

Andromache

Alba de Tormes, she had discovered was a small town upon the river bank well worth visiting for its palace fortress and Jeronomite convent. It was possible that Tony might be involved with some stupid reconnaissance, but the chance had to be taken. She calculated upon two to three hours in which she could be completely her own mistress. As for Alba and its convent – she might look in. She would see ...

After re-reading the note she sealed it carefully, and sent it by Sue to Simms for transmission to the cavalry headquarters. Simms being busy, and in his present mood indifferent to Harriet's affairs directed O'Connor to the task. A reply came more quickly than the lady expected. On a leaf torn from his notebook, Tony had written "It is probable."

In due course Felix was saddled, and Harriet in grey riding habit crossed the Tormes Bridge. The river, swollen by the rains swung in an easterly direction, but riding diagonally across country she calculated that she would meet it again near Alba. The landscape, now a dull November brown flecked with shabby sage green, was broken only by skeleton pines. A keen wind blew from the hills so that she was glad of the thick woollen fabric of her costume; but her cheeks tingled freshly, and she rode with the composure of one having time in hand. The ten miles between herself and her objective offered no difficulty; there would be ample time to return ere darkness fell. Occasionally she passed bullock trains bringing supplies into the city, and while the object of some curiosity, none halted or questioned her purpose. Once a dragoon, caked to the eyes with mud, clattered by, and she wondered if he might be a courier bringing news of Hope. But that was Sir John's business, not hers ...

She rode on ...

* * *

Meanwhile Sue, preoccupied, gloomy, donned her shawl and wandered restlessly around the plaza. In no mood for sightseeing, she soon returned to the guest chamber where she decided to sew. She was due to write to her parents but the thought of conveying the latest news of Robin agonised her. How could she withhold information, which sooner or later they would learn from other and less sympathetic sources? Her eyes filled with tears. She pricked at the cloth mechanically.

She was still so occupied when Harker returned to collect the newspapers he had left earlier. Noting the absence of Mrs Foulkes he pushed forward with brash assurance. Sue, her face averted, pointed to the several journals, His presence was the last straw. She hoped profoundly that he would take up the papers silently and at once withdraw. But that was too much to expect. Calmly he seated himself on the settle arm and swung a loose leg. She watched the polished toe of his boot as it came within her range of vision. "Yes" he observed, following her glance, "these boots belonged to the Major, who being a gentleman, passed 'em on to me."

"Please go," she said in a tiny voice, "the Major may come in."

He chuckled archly, shaking his head. "Oh dear no! His High Mightiness will be away for four hours – he told me so – and her ladyship has rode off on her fine chestnut horse, which means that the lower orders may do as they please."

She did not reply ...

Harker dropped into the seat and crossed his legs. "You didn't expect to find me in this position, did you?"

An icy contempt welled up within her. She was on the point of thrusting before his hated eyes the paragraph in the newspaper beside her, but on second thoughts refrained. Why should he be enlightened, when the chances were that he would rejoice in the final disappearance of his victim? She steeled herself to speak. "I expected nothing," she said, "but I warrant you won't last long."

"I shall last as long as it suits me," he drawled. He lit a cigar from the brasero. "The Major won't regret."

"Not till he counts his spoons."

Harker laughed sarcastically. "Har – har!" he grinned, "now that was nasty – quite out of turn seeing what we have in common."

"Too much!" she said bitterly, bending to her task.

"These here cigars," he observed, ignoring her remark, "is full of what I am too polite to mention. Give me a thick quid any day. Look ye here – isn't it time we be friends?"

She made a gesture of distaste. "There's the door," she said.

"I have been thinking," he mused, "what a lot we could do to together, you an' me – the Major's man on one side, and the Lady's maid on the other."

"You can think again!"

"Go softly," he said reproachfully, "I do mean it. Why look here, I've brought you a souvenir of Salamanca. Found it this mornin' and' the first thought in my mind was – that's just the ticket for Sue Thompson!"

Unable to restrain her curiosity, she turned her head and saw that he balanced in his hand a pearl-hafted stiletto, encased in a tooled leathern sheath. Slowly he bared the blade. "Now ain't that a beauty," he purred. "Toledo steel, which I may tell you is of the best. Bends like a willow wand." He ran his thumb along the edge. "Sharp as a needle too – pick your teeth with it." He jabbed the blade in the table top where it vibrated gently, "It's yours. You'll find it useful for a hundred things."

She faced him scornfully. "I don't want it."

"You might be in need."

"For what?"

"'Gains't them as would interfere with you." He laughed softly.

"So long at you don't turn it agin me – which being a nice quiet girl you wouldn't dream of doin'."

"Please put it away."

"Very good Madam," he said. "Always willin' to oblige. I'll save it up for you. Back you go, you little rascal," he murmured, addressing the blade as he returned it to the sheath. "P'raps you'd like a nice gold bracelet with bangles?"

"I want nothing from you at any time. Please go."

He regarded her with a mock serious expression – was silent for a moment or two. He spat out a fragment of tobacco leaf. "Don't think you've got Simms," he said bluntly.

She looked up startled. "Mr Simms to you," she replied coldly, but she found herself flushing.

"Well then – Mester Simms."

"Please leave him out of it."

Harker thrust his tongue in his cheek. "You don't know enough. You ask him how many senoritas he had in Ciudad Rodrigo. Ask him about the tailor's niece at Paco that he fitted up with ration beef."

"I won't listen to your stupid gossip," she retorted, stung.

"Not all that stupid." Harker shook a reproving head. "I keep in touch. You'd be surprised what I pick up. A little bit here – a little bit there."

"Much good may it do you."

"That is as it may be," he said smoothly. "I know, for instance that your lady sends notes to a gentleman at headquarters."

"None of your business," she said curtly.

"It is what I choose to make of it."

"Burn your fingers if you want. Take the papers and get out of this room."

Unabashed he brought his heels together. "Well, you can't say the black bile is on my side. No hard feelin's. Think over what I say, girl – you and me together – and God go with you as the Spanish say."

He picked up the newspapers, saluted, and marched off, breaking into a whistle as he set off down the corridor.

When his footsteps had died away, chilly though the room was she flung open the window to let in a little fresh air. The encounter had left her stifled, limp. She pressed both hands to her brow in a torment of speculation. If Harker carried a guilty conscience it was with consummate ease. Or was he culpable after all? It was not easy to understand. Was this part of the chameleon front he displayed in presenting himself to Mrs Foulkes that morning? Sue was particularly irked by the slander – for slander she felt it must be – on Mr Simms' affairs; nor was she unmoved by the subtly sly reference to Mrs Foulkes's acquaintance with Captain Harte. Here again the Commissary was involved if only as an accessory. For a moment or two she wondered if by becoming more friendly with Harker it would be possible in some manner to anticipate his machinations; but it was not in her nature to dissimulate. So the problem remained. Ostensibly harmless, cheerful, willing to oblige, she felt certain however, that given opportunity he would strike. Sometime – sooner rather than later – both Mr Simms and her mistress ought to be apprised of his malice ...

CHAPTER XI

Following the road through Arapiles, Harriet Foulkes entered Alba de Tormes, alone. She crossed by the bridge, looked into the gate posada, but finding only drovers and such, went forward and slowly circled the square. She was followed by many curious eyes. A Spanish officer in white uniform from the garrisoned fortress stopped in his tracks, and twirling his moustaches gazed after her.

She bit her lip impatiently. Tony must have been detained by some pressing duty, and reflecting that by now she had used up more than half her available time, she decided to return. The late autumn day drew quickly to a close, and she had no mind to be caught on the wrong side of Salamanca city walls ere darkness fell … She turned her horse's head, recrossed the bridge, and for a little while cantered at a steady pace, her eyes on the deepening purple-grey of the horizon. Already in the deep belt of forest, which upon her left hand stretched from Arapiles to Alba, shadows were deepening. The sooner she made Salamanca the better.

"It is probable," he had written. Increasingly her mind dwelt upon the terse ambiguous reply. What did he mean by that? Was there in the few brief words an element of withdrawal? Professionally, of course, he was anything but his own master, but the lack of warmth, of impulse on his part drove her into sombre speculation. She was beginning to regret now that she had communicated with him at all. She had sensed reserve at Quelez. What a fool she was!

Leaving the rutted road she took to the verge where the turf, smooth and cushioned, lay invitingly. Here she brought Felix to a gallop.

Harriet was a good horsewoman, but she had no eye for ground, and the verge in places was thoroughly deceptive. Swerving much too near a scrub oak, the horse caught its left hind foot in an exposed root and crashed heavily. Harriet, flung over the animal's head was stunned …

When she came round, Tony Harte was bending over her, and a peasant who had come up with an ox-cart was holding Felix. She murmured a few incoherent words and fainted again. Finally, when she did recover consciousness, it was a head humming like a beehive, and a shoulder so heavy with pain that she felt it must be broken. Assisted to her feet, she was appalled to see that her skirt was torn from hem to waist. Fortunately her face, protected somewhat by her hat, had not suffered. Nor had her gloved hands. Tony was saying that she must take things quietly; that in a few minutes all would be well. She bit her lip against a flood of tears, and with trembling composure announced that she felt in a fit condition to ride. She detached the buckle from the feather in her hat and made a rough repair to her skirt, but it was with fumbling fingers.

Now a further complication arose. Quietly, Tony informed her that Felix was quite unrideable; and that (except for the peasants' cumbrous vehicle) there was no alternative but for her to take his (Tony's) mount, while he led the disabled Felix. In the meantime dusk had deepened, and five miles lay between the scene of the mishap and Salamanca.

They set out. The pace conditioned by poor Felix's limp was painfully slow; indeed at times her injured mount could hardly be persuaded to walk at all. In spite of her own discomfort, Harriet's heart was wrung to see the faithful beast in such a condition, and the thought that he might have to be destroyed appalled her. At last a trooper overtook them, and this man lending the Captain his own horse, promised to follow with Felix. It was a sad end to a blithe excursion. The great iron bell of the cathedral tolling in the distance brought only foreboding.

Indeed, there were further embarrassments to follow. When through the murky streets they arrived at last at the convent, to Harriet's dismay – for she had hoped against hope to slip into her room unobserved – there was her husband waiting in the company of Captains Harrod and Daiches. All three stood motionless in the gateway with the exception of Foulkes who perfunctorily returned Captain Harte's salute. As the Major listened to a brief account of the accident the other officers moved away, though still within earshot. Foulkes helped his wife to dismount, and without a word to her late escort, accompanied her to the guest chamber. In an atmosphere heavy with impending storm, Harte rode away.

The Major had spent a couple of anxious hours. Returning from the Archbishop's palace where he had dined, his first inquiry had been for Mrs Foulkes. Sue, whom he first approached, could give him no satisfaction. He pressed questions. What time had his wife left the convent? Was she mounted? Had she an escort? Or received any kind of message? ... Sue's negative attitude he regarded with intense suspicion, inferring that she knew much more than she cared to tell. He eyed her darkly. "I am sure that I shall find the truth," he snapped.

Off he went in search of the orderly who had saddled up Felix, but was no further enlightened. He returned, moving about the room restlessly. "My wife out riding," he exploded, "in a country infested with gypsies, and God alone knows what riff-raff! Anything may happen, especially after dark. Utter madness! Of all the scatterbrains!—"

So he ran on, his snuff box in full play; he sneezed and choked, went out again ranging the streets, at last hovering in the doorway of the building. Harker appeared, and Foulkes sent for his cloak. When the Major had donned this he noticed that his servant still lingered. "Anything I can do for you, sir?" asked Harker.

"My chief concern is for my wife. Have you seen or heard anything of her?"

"Well, sir, I don't know for sartin', but "' Harker broke off in mid-sentence.

"But, what?"

"There may be nothing in it, sir, but I did hear O'Connor – the same that is Mr Simms servant, sir – remark that he had conveyed a note from Mr Foulkes to the cavalry headquarters, sir – for an officer, sir."

"What officer? By what name?"

"I don't rightly remember, sir – Smart – something like that."

"Would it be Harte?" asked Foulkes tensely.

"Might be, sir."

"Might be! Might be!" said Foulkes pettishly. "Go find this O'Connor and bring him to me. And ask Mr Simms to come too."

Harker saluted and vanished in the darkness, but neither Simms nor his servant were to be found. At last, when Harriet did arrive, lamentably dishevelled and accompanied by the inscrutable Harte, the only remark she ventured was, "There is no more to it than that I fell from my horse." A pretty story, forsooth! Foulkes wondered what Daiches and Harrod were thinking...

Pomeroy called him, and he was glad of a respite which would allow a little time to compose his nerves before the inevitable inquest with Harriet. When the Colonel had finished, Foulkes' anger had subsided somewhat, but with stern resolution he decided to see the thing through. He hesitated only lest Harriet might be in such a mental and physical condition as not to discuss the incident at all.

Thus he allowed an hour to elapse before he re-entered the guest room where Sue was still in attendance. Harriet was resting, but when he inquired how she felt, she replied in a level voice that apart from bruising she was quite well. At once he suggested that the girl should withdraw and go to bed. Sue glanced questioningly at her mistress who observed, "She has still something to do." Indeed, Sue was already mending the torn riding skirt. "Better finish that," said Harriet, "there is no knowing how soon I may need it." The Major, being in no mood for small talk, attended to certain papers.

Time dragged on for the better part of an hour ...

When Sue left, the Major took snuff with an assumed air of indifference. "Feeling better?" he inquired. He fixed his eyes at a small ivory crucifix suspended on the wall beyond his wife's shoulder.

"Yes, thank you. Nothing that a good night's rest will not repair."

"I sincerely hope so."

A pause followed broken only by the tolling of the convent bell. Waves of iron sound reverberated through the building.

"Midnight Mass?" she suggested.

"Something of the kind," he answered curtly.

"I suppose their worship becomes mechanical."

"It serves a purpose," he said.

He waited for the tolling to cease, took a seat, clasped his hands and said quietly, "What made you venture out on the Madrid road?"

She folded her riding skirt and flung it carelessly over a settle. "I was bored with this place, so thought I would look in at Alba de Tormes."

"Was the town interesting?"

"Yes, indeed. I was particularly struck by the church."

"Well?"

"Well, what?"

"Tell me about it."

She made a little gesture of surprise; he was not ordinarily interested in sacred buildings, but as she had not entered the church, she improvised. "The usual lay-out – an altar, candles, a crucifix, the effigy of a saint."

"With a ring through his nose?"

"If you are pleased to be facetious—" she began.

"By which, I suppose, like most men, he might be led. And was that all?"

"All what?"

"Don't fence." He was still gazing at the crucifix on the wall.

"I went alone – if you mean that."

"So it would seem!" He laughed sardonically.

"I don't know where all this is leading," she protested. "The incident happened precisely as I related. Leaving Alba, foolishly I galloped Felix on a length of treacherous turf, and down he went. I was knocked senseless. By a lucky chance Captain Harte appeared."

"Quite the good Samaritan!" he taunted.

"I don't know what I should have done without him" she answered sharply. "He ought to be thanked a thousand times."

Her husband's mouth twitched. "By whom? I wish I could believe you Harriet."

"Believe what?"

"That you met by chance."

"We did." She tried to assume innocence.

"The same chance, I suppose, that brought you together at Quelez!"

"Oh!—" With an impatient gesture she began to draw off her rings.

"But I at least do not intend to be controlled by chance."

"I repeat the meeting was quite accidental."

"Not altogether. Now listen to me, Harriet," he continued sternly, "I know that you were in communication with Captain Harte."

"You know nothing. Indeed, there is nothing to know."

"I have my own sources of information," he rejoined, "the how and the where of it does not a matter of the moment. What does matter is that you appear belatedly in Harte's company alone, obviously distressed, your skirt disgracefully torn, riding if you please, the fellow's horse – with Harrod and Daiches looking on."

"Who invited them to look on?" she said contemptuously.

"It will become common gossip through the convent tomorrow, and a pretty tale they will make of it."

"They should mind their own business."

"We are too closely bound for such things not to become a scandal. I did not wish you to follow the army in the first place; but now this! I waived Guardia and your thoughtlessness with Bird; but I must ask you from this moment to behave as becomes your station. I tell you this—" She saw that his lips had blanched from the intensity of his feeling, "if it were not for these" – and he touched an epaulette, "I'd call him out tonight. If—"

"Why hesitate?"

"If, I say, it were not for my own position. I could shoot the fellow down like a partridge, but it would damn me with Sir John." She knew as he spoke that her husband was not boasting. He was an expert shot.

"You must not," she taunted, "ruin your career on my account."

He rose from his chair and stood over her quivering with indignation. "That is a devilish thing to say, and only one having taken leave of her senses would have been capable of it. But that you seem to have done. I warn you I will not have my name a byword. You must learn to behave yourself decently."

"Is that an order?"

He sat down again, and when he spoke again his voice had lost something of its edge. "It would be better for both of us if you were to return home. I have my duties, and I am not made of iron."

Suddenly, his face, white and drawn, moved her. She hesitated before she replied. But she would not yield.

"I have my own life to live," she said stubbornly.

"Then go back to your sister," he pleaded. "The road to Lisbon is still open. What kind of existence is this – for both of us?"

"I am satisfied with the army, and will not be dismissed like a child."

"If only you would behave less like one."

"I promise," she said quietly, "I will become a burden neither to you nor to the regiment."

"I will call him out," said Foulkes grimly, "and we shall go home together."

She laughed strangely. "I think you will not, Percy."

"Oh, won't I!"

As he clasped and unclasped his hands he knew – and knew that she knew – he would not.

"We shall see you Colonel yet."

"Incorrigible" he cried.

"Insanely, stupidly jealous," she retorted as he strode from the room …

* * *

Salamanca lay tranquil in the frosty moonlight, but beneath its silvered roofs and towers the flow of life went on. Grandees and their ladies chatted over raisins and wine; tutors scratched at lectures with their quills; students in dingy ill-ventilated garrets dreamed less of gowns and texts than of military adventure, the tuck of drum and the beat of marching feet.

Wine flowed in the bodegas where British red-coats tippling to their heart's content, wrangled over cards or wagered on flea and beetle races. The literate few indited letters and journals, preserving campaign impressions for the benefit of those at home. From darkened alleyways, light fingered gentry, scavengers of the night, converged upon the plaza where among the parked wagons and ox-carts the unregarded bag of biscuit, the stray trenching tool, a bag of fodder even, might be had for the lifting. But all traffic had stopped. The walls were sealed.

Few wayfarers marked the window in the Marques de Canralbo's palace behind which by candlelight, Sir Jon Moore was writing up his diary. The fine head with its unruly chestnut hair, the frank open brow and expressive eyes bent diligently over the page, for Moore was a dedicated man, and his diary a working journal. Here were no musings on art, no tender personal confidences. He had loved only once in his life, but because of a pronounced difference in age – he was so much older than she – had renounced his suit. His name had been associate with that of Lady Hester Stanhope, niece of the late Mr Pitt, but this had been a platonic relationship; nothing more. Devoting his life to the army, he had lavished on that service all the gifts at his command. He had never evaded responsibility; was not given to "councils of war". Now, confronted by an increasingly difficult situation he confided in his diary—

"Wrote to Lord Castlereagh upon the 25th and 26th stating the critical situation in which we were; that Spain was without armies, generals or a government; that I saw nothing of being able to resist the attack being made upon her ... I was not in communication with any of her generals, and neither knew their plans nor those of her government. No channel of communication had been opened to me, and I had no knowledge of the force or situation of the enemy but what as a stranger I had picked up ..."

The door opened and an officer entered placing a sheaf of papers on a side-table. He was about to withdraw when the General said, "Ah, Colborne!"

The tall and handsome military secretary halted with a word of apology. "I thought you were busy, sir."

Moore smiled wryly. "I was." He turned to the diary. "Listen to this," and read aloud the last few sentences he had written. "Did you ever hear the like?"

"Incredible, but true, Sir."

"The worst of it is," continued Moore, "that our masters over yonder—" and general though the reference was, Colborne had no difficulty in assuming that his superior officer meant not the Spanish Juntas, but Ministers in

England, "orating, resolving, amending, rejecting, expect wonders. The tri-fling matter of roads, transport, imperfect intelligence, unfaithful allies, to say nothing of enemies incomparably more powerful than ourselves, is the least of their troubles. Is that an overstatement?"

"I think not, sir."

"All we need is a magic wand which Ministers in their prescience have failed to provide." Moore lifted his head. "What is the feeling here?"

"Feeling?" Colborne pursed his lips. "You mean in Salamanca?"

"I mean generally – among the officers, the rank and file. I think some-time I am told only that which I would wish to know."

Colborne sighed, disinclined to speak. He knew the answer would not please Sir John. He had heard chanted that day by an officer who should have known better—

The far famed General Moore
Had thirty thousand men;
He marched them to the heart of Spain
And marched 'em out again!

"There is some dissatisfaction, Sir John."

"In what sense?"

"Our present inaction."

"So that is how the wind blows!" Moore pushed the Journal to one side, but his face showed no trace of feeling. It was only what he had expected. "The men will get a bellyful before we have finished. If one were compelled to deal only with the rank and file the task would not be too easy; but it is with the more important gentlemen, the amateur strategists, persons who try to run my business for me, who are the bugbear. One such—" (Ho-ho! thought Colborne, the British Minister in Madrid for a ducat!) – "urges me to rush forward and to succour the capital. What folly, with fifty thousand Frenchmen almost on my lines of communication."

"Mr Frere, I suppose?"

Moore glanced darkly, contenting himself merely by saying, "A civilian in high places. We should be shattered to the winds, and your humble servant – assuming he survived – would be brought to court-martial. Well, I intend neither one thing nor the other. If I could see with the eye of my Maker, all would be well. Being mortal I must do the best I can. Of one thing I am assured – I do not intend to be trapped, though we must work on the assumption that the French are likely to be everywhere – two hundred thou-sand bayonets across the Pyrenees. It makes one think."

The Military Secretary was silent.

"Did you ever see a bull fight, Colborne?"

"Yes, sir, and a bloody mess it was."

"You are right, but do you remember the fellow with the cloak who played the bull, teased him this way and that?"

"I remember that he skipped like a dancing master," said Colborne.

Moore smiled. "He had need too, and believe me if we trail a cloak before the Gallic bull we must do the same."

"You mean, sir—?"

"I mean not to be trampled in the sand, not to be outmanoeuvred. Enough for tonight. You must be dog tired."

"Not more than you, sir."

"I shall turn in now. Good night to you."

"Good night, Sir John."

The Military Secretary withdrew, and Moore turning once again to his Journal indited a few more lines: "I was occupied in uniting the army, and could determine nothing but that. When that was accomplished I could see what was to be done."

There was a knock on the door. An aide appeared bearing a dispatch having "Hurry! Hurry! Hurry!" scrawled on the cover.

Moore broke open the seal and read: "Beg to report Generals Castanos and Palafox heavily defeated at Tudela by Napoleon. Calculate on no effective support from this province ..." The general frowned. When news did arrive it was of this nature. In his mind's eye he could see the Spanish formations scattered like chaff, their white coats bloodied and torn, the survivors in harassed groups straggling towards the hills. And Napoleon in person! What of Madrid now, Mr Frere? What indeed!

He sat very still, his handsome face pale in the golden flame, until, taking a pair of compasses he unfolded a map, placed one tip of the instrument at Salamanca and the other on Corunna. He made a swift calculation of distance, then swung the tip over to Lisbon. Corunna, Lisbon, Vigo? At one port or another he could depend upon the ships, but more than mountains lay between. What next? ...

* * *

Sue Thompson thoroughly detested the convent. The building was as cold as a tomb; the floors as hard as flagstones could be; the great bell tolled like death. The cell that she shared with a certain Mrs Crawley was barely furnished – not even a rush mat. After leaving her mistress alone with the Major, Sue was in no mind to retire, but it was not the bleakness of the lodging place, which gave her pause. Harker's reference to Captain Harte and Mrs Foulkes linked as it was with the late mishap, filled her with foreboding. Simms, she felt ought to be warned. She knew little of regimental authority, but sufficient to realise that there were ways and means for a senior officer to make life uncomfortable for a Deputy Assistant Commissary.

The magazine of provisions was in a chamber leading off the Buttery. She entered diffidently, for while the majority of the monks were lodged temporarily in the chapel, a certain number prepared food. Here half a dozen gowned figures lingered in conversation, and although they watched her covertly as she made her way to a slit of light which indicated the chamber controlled by Simms, none questioned her passage. The advent of a young and attractive woman must have been for them a rare occurrence.

She found Simms, who had almost finished for the night, muffled to the eyes. He looked up from his inventory, surprised. "Why so pale and wandering?" he observed.

"I must speak to you – at once," she said in a low voice.

"Here?"

"Yes – alone."

Simms still looked askance, but did not question further. He dismissed his clerk, and waited silently until the young man had disappeared. Sue shivered. "I am not really cold," she said.

"That be damned for a tale!" And drew a tot of rum. "You will think this queer stuff," he grinned, "but down with it, and await the result."

She took the cup, eyed the contents doubtfully for a few seconds, swallowed, gasped and choked. He patted her on the back. "You'll feel better in a minute," he said comfortingly, "when it's done its work."

She agreed that she could find the spirit tingling almost to her finger tips.

"That's what the man intended. In the meantime take a chair." He indicated an upturned keg, rolled up another, and together they sat. He sniffed expressively. "I seem," he said, "to scent trouble."

"Trouble it is," she said soberly. "Mr Simms, a storm is brewing which concerns Mrs Foulkes and may well concern you. I have just left the guest chamber, where Major Foulkes almost pushed me out. In a word Mrs Foulkes had an accident today while riding with Captain Harte."

Simms frowned. "Go on."

"I feel he suspects something."

"You mean my playing post-boy for the lady?" Simms took out a cigar and lit up. "How would he know?"

"Mr Simms, you must be aware that Harker is the Major's new servant?"

"It has not escaped my notice. What of that?"

Sue then related the conversation of that morning, omitting the personal aspersions on Simms. When she had finished, the Commissary slapped his thigh. "The leak – if leak there is – must have been through that ass O'Connor; he it was who transmitted the note. I should have known better than to use him, but the damage is done now. Wait here a moment."

He strode away, his footsteps striking sharply across the buttery floor. Presently he returned, a mystified O'Connor trailing at his heels.

"What would ye be wantin', sorr," mumbled the servant, "with the sleep in me eyes. Tis late."

"Late enough!" rejoined Simms grimly. "Do you happen to know Private Raddock that is Major Foulkes' servant?"

"In passin', sorr."

"Have you conversed with him?"

O'Connor scratched his head. "A word or two – nothin' more."

"What kind of words?"

The servant screwed up his eyes in an effort to charge his memory, gaped, but made no response.

"Come now – think!"

"Faith," said the Irishman at last, "I call to mind he spoke well of the work we did."

"Spoke well?"

"Why, sorr, the witt'lin' of the men – the grand way that we fill their bellies. He was loud in your praises, sorr."

"No doubt. What else?"

"We talked this way an' that." O'Connor shook his head sleepily.

"Cudgel your brains!"

"He said you must be a busy man, sorr."

"Never mind the soft soap," jerked Simms impatiently. "Did you by any chance mention that you carried a note from Mrs Foulkes to Captain Harte?"

O'Connor shuffled. "Oy did since I wus standin' with ut in me 'and."

"Good heavens – why?"

The Irishman glanced towards Sue. "He bein' the Major's sarvant, an' one ye might say, of the family—"

"The family!" exploded Simms angrily. "You utter fool!"

"For why, sorr?" O'Connor was genuinely aggrieved.

"Be off with you, dolt, and in future keep your mouth shut."

"Thank ye, sorr." The Irishman shambled away.

"It's clear enough," said Simms frowning, "that yonder simpleton blabbed to Harker, and Harker acquainted the Major. The fault is mine. I should never have employed him. Well, to be forewarned is to be forearmed."

"What will the Major do?" asked Sue.

The Commissary eyed her darkly. "What can he do? Nothing ostensibly. It is a domestic mater; but you may be quite sure that he will lay a rod in pickle, a note on his mental tablets, and when a hitch occurs, a breakdown in supplies maybe, he'll whisper in the Colonel's ear of the Commissary's incompetence." Simms smiled strangely. "I shall not be loved."

"I am sorry," she said.

"You have no reason for reproach. This comes of playing cupid for a regimental charmer! I should have stuck to my last."

Sue watched his face closely as he continued to pull at his cigar. Frank, undissimulating, was this the man who from town to town played havoc with the local maids? Attractive enough, perhaps he had been tempted; but he broke into her thoughts by observing, "You saw Harker this morning – did he behave?"

She smiled dubiously. "After a fashion, friendly like. He finished by offering me a present."

Simms sniffed. "The voice of Esau, but the hand of Jacob! Did you accept?"

"How could you think that?"

"I beg your pardon." He looked away quickly.

On the point of relating something of her own distress at the time, the loss of the *Primrose* and all it implied, she decided otherwise. "The poor man (she thought) has enough to shoulder without my burden." She would inform him later – perhaps. But Simms was resilient enough. Quickly he changed the subject, and contrived to make her laugh by relating the oddest stories of the wine-shippers of Oporto ...

* * *

Pierre Laborde, a lay brother of the convent, left the new cathedral whence he had been to pray. A touchy Navarrese, his duties were of a menial character: the care of mules, the transporting of fuel and grain, and sundry other jobs calling more for muscle than brain, although to Pierre all work at the convent was one of dedication.

To announce that he had been disturbed by the admission of soldiers to the institution, which he loved, would be to understate. Profoundly shocked he had seen the sacred precincts handed over to a horde of polluting red-coated heretics. The brethren had even been compelled to sleep in the chapel. Hour by hour the holy peace of the cloisters had been broken by irreverent chatter, profanity and lewdness of tongue. As though upon a common heath, fires had been lit in the courtyard itself.

Writing home, he complained bitterly. "Things have happened in this sacred house the like of which have not been known within living memory – the sanctuary desecrated to the confusion of the devout and the extreme distress of Our Lady; blasphemy uttered both by night and day. Women have been brought in more abandoned than the men. The heavens remain without a sign. Who shall deliver us from the body of this sin? ..."

The passing days brought no relief to Pierre Laborde. The Father Superior seemed as one bewitched; the lesser men helpless as those set in authority over them. But (reflected the tortured lay brother) the meanest vessel might be accommodated to the Lord. As God had spoken through the ass to Balaam, had lent purpose to David's prentice sling, so he, Pierre might become an agent of deliverance. That day as he knelt in the cathedral it seemed to him that the crown of thorns had pressed more closely in the Saviour's brow, that the gashed wounds were more extended. Of his own strength he could not confound this intrusive legion of devils, but their leader, the commander of the whole, the serpent's head of the British, the florid haughty Colonel remained. In days gone by – for the lay bother was not without some scraps of knowledge – the Prince of Orange had been removed from the earth by the consecrated hand of Gérard, and the wicked Valoid king by a humble priest. Was a colonel of English redcoats more sacrosanct than these?

Thus Pierre Laborde, his mind a ferment, his eyes smouldering fanatically, hurried through the streets of the city. "A deed must be done," he concluded, "lest I be damned amongst the damned!" A bright light suffused his very being. His fingers reached for and grasped the haft of his knife …

* * *

"Good night – good night to you!"

Leaving General Frazer's headquarters, Colonel Pomeroy drew his cloak together, pulled the cocked hat towards his nose, and with a casual gesture acknowledged the sentry's salute. Warmed by several cups of excellent punch, he had decided to walk to the San Francisco convent, only a street or two away.

He dwelt upon the late conversation when he had discussed with certain members of the staff, hunting in many lands. At last they turned to the wretched Cintra convention, and the awkward position of Sir Arthur Wellesley. Sir Harry and Sir Hew they decided, were plainly culpable, but not the victor of Vimiero. Would Sir Arthur be exonerated? Opinions being divided, Pomeroy had placed with Colonel Frame a bet of ten guineas that Sir Arthur would not suffer. It was a sizeable stake, and now Pomeroy was beginning to feel that he had been too venturesome. One never knew what those fellows at the Horse Guards would be up to. However, the bet had been booked, and that was that … He stood aside grudgingly to allow a tipsy infantryman to pass; being dark the man had not recognised an officer. "Good night, senor," the semi-drunk mumbled as he felt for the wall. The Colonel grunted disapprovingly. Men should not be denied their liquor, but enough was enough. He recalled Guardia …

Pomeroy bent his head to the wind. Of all places he detested these narrow Spanish streets – wrought iron at the windows, the houses withdrawn, buttoned up. God help a regiment trapped in gullies such as this! Fancying he heard footsteps behind him he quickened his pace. The Spaniards were too fond of long silent knives, of stealing around in the dark.

He halted in a doorway listening until the footsteps died away. Now the street was empty, a vista of dimly outlined shadow, the only light shed by a guttering oil lamp in the archway of a house opposite. In a moment or two he moved forward again, and as he did so a figure broke from the forward pool of darkness, and almost without a sound to the nearside wall. The

Colonel gave the newcomer a fair clearance, but as they passed the stranger lurched towards him, and as though in hearty good fellowship delivered a slap on the back. "What – damn you!" cried Pomeroy stumbling, but these were the last words he would speak. A blow in the ribs, and a searing stroke of pain brought him to his knees. After that he doubled over, coughing blood on the cobbles. The assailant moved off as silently as he had come; but the Colonel groaned where he lay, and in a matter of moments was very still. The long knife had done its work ...

Pomeroy's body, discovered half an hour later by an orderly of the Fifty Third, was carried into an adjoining house, and afterwards transported to the convent ... Thereupon torches flared, patrols clattered up and down surrounding streets, fists hammered on Spanish doors, but the miscreant had vanished as cleanly as a pebble tossed in a pond. At once, Major Foulkes reported the crime to headquarters ...

The Junta passed a resolution charged with horror and indignation – *Afrancesdos* (they declared) were responsible, nor would they rest until the scoundrel had been arrested and punished. Meanwhile, Sir John, interviewing Major Foulkes was pleased to appoint him brevet-Colonel in command of the regiment. As for Pierre Laborde, he continued to grease his harness and lead his mules through the convent doorway, fervent always in prayer, and (his fellows noticed) strangely elated ...

* * *

It was still incredible. Foulkes, sitting alone in the dead man's room, and taking snuff incessantly, tried to adjust his mind to the situation. He had often regarded promotion as a kind of lottery, but now that the wheel had swung in his favour, he was thoroughly disconcerted. Pleas and protestations, fuming in antechambers and courting the highly placed – "Your obedient humble servant" – had achieved nothing. He was indebted now to the stroke of an unknown assassin. It was odd – damned odd! ...

Sir John had been most kind, announcing that the new Colonel had his every confidence. Yes, he remembered Foulkes in Sicily. For his part the new commanding officer responded formally, deploring the great loss that the regiment had sustained. He wondered if in justice to Pomeroy he had said enough, but Sir John being busy Foulkes was soon out in the square again. Turning over the late Colonel's papers, using Pomeroy's notebook and silver pencil, his portfolio, it was almost with a sense of guilt that the new Colonel began an inventory of equipment. Like a delinquent schoolboy surprised by his master, Foulkes was ready to jump at the sound of that familiar voice. He took a pinch of snuff and began to feel better.

He had looked forward to promotion ardently, but somehow the gilt was off the gingerbread. A few days time, and the blow would be received by

Pomeroy's widow, a patient little woman living in the heart of Shropshire, and upon the two sons of whom the dead man had been so proud. Foulkes made a note on his tables. He would need to write immediately. In the meantime cold and chill under his army cloak, Pomeroy lay in the chapel awaiting burial. Foulkes would have looked upon the familiar face again, but he was in no mind to disturb the monks. A funeral with military honours would follow – the measured tread, the slow drum-taps – and after that the melancholy auction of effects; horses, harness, weapons, field canteen, shaving case, spying glass – everything.

He leaned back in his chair allowing his mind to dwell on some of the problems by which he would be confronted. Daiches would step up, and Suckley, but what of the rest? Pomeroy in his blustering fashion had been too easy with the younger men; the rough edge of his tongue for them one day, indifference the next. No more of that! He – Foulkes would introduce a thorough brisking, a keener sense of duty.

When, with the assistance of the clerk, he had gone through Pomeroy's valises, and received the adjutant, he relaxed and tried to review what he always considered "the principles of command." But it was an elusive task, and before long he was considering more mundane matters. He wondered, for example, how much Pomeroy had made from clothing contracts; not that it mattered much, but perquisites had to be attended to. By taking over some of Pomeroy's horses he would add to his own equipment. Harriet needed a new mount to replace the unfortunate Felix …

Yes, there was still Harriet. Her comment on his appointment had been, to say the least of it, equivocal. "Indeed, Percy, you have done everything you possibly can to gain the honour." Promotion would not, of course, ease their strained relations, but it meant highly increased authority. Over whom? Simms, for instance. The clue conveyed by his servant had been invaluable; the more Foulkes considered the situation the more he detected between Simms and his wife a sustained collusion. It was Simms who had brought up Harriet from Lisbon; Simms who had escorted her to Quelez; Simms with whom she had decided to ride to Salamanca, and Simms who still acted as her running footman. The young upstart could not be removed without just cause, but from now on he should have a tightened rein. Henceforward let him keep to his official kegs and tallies! As the brevet colonel listened to the sombre tolling of the convent bell he did not decide to take the first opportunity possible of putting Simms in the wrong, but there were changes and chances enough in military life to cover almost everything …

Still, Harriet remained.

He sighed …

* * *

Partly because he was out with his wife, but most because he wished to be alone. Foulkes slept in the late Colonel's quarters. The second night Harker had brought him biscuit and a tot of rum – Spartan fare. Warmed by the liquor he undressed, put on his gown and nightcap and sank to the palliasse; but not alas to dream of armies triumphant and cities stormed. Instead he found himself leading his regiment in column of march across a treeless plateau. He could hear the tramp of feet behind, rhythmic as on parade. Hours passed, and still they marched ... Then, from nowhere, conjured from the shadows a general officer and his staff appeared, so that Foulkes reined up and braced himself for the encounter. It was Sir John himself. Formal salutes were exchanged, but through the circumambient haze the Commander-in-Chief spoke in the sternest of tones. "Colonel Foulkes," he demanded, "why did you allow yourself to be cut off?" ... Foulkes turned in his saddle, and to his horror found that he was riding alone, his men vanished, the quivering level of the plain empty. "Colonel Foulkes," again the terrible accusative voice, "where are my legions?" Speechless, still staring into Moore's reproachful eyes, the new Colonel gave a heartrending cry, and awoke bathed in perspiration ...

The room was still; the darkness intense. A bell vibrated in the tower, and a low monotonous chanting began in the chapel. He heaved a profound sigh of relief, but did not dare to close his eyes again lest the shattering incident be repeated. He groped for the flint machine, lit a candle and for a long time watched the thin spiral of smoke as it mounted to the ceiling, thankful for the first glimmer of dawn ...

CHAPTER XII

For all ranks the weeks spent in Salamanca were charged with frustration. Daily, regiment by regiment the men marched to exercise on the esplanade outside the city, but the emotions were automatic. They were bored. Had they been brought to Spain for this?

Slowly Harriet Foulkes recovered from the effects of her fall; she had been more bruised and shaken than she had at first supposed, thus much of her time had been spent in bed. Isolated, self-immured, she read, played cards with Sue, and wrote long letters to her relatives at home.

Foulkes saw his wife daily, but their intercourse was brief, indeed formal. He would not unbend; she was equally cold and withdrawn, but the outward semblance of domestic harmony was preserved. She was hurt when Tony Harte made no effort to communicate with her, or as far as she knew, did not inquire concerning her welfare. She could only conclude that his duties had taken him far afield, but she would have cherished a word, a line of writing.

When sufficiently recovered, she appeared at mess, where all members seemed unaffectedly pleased to see her. More than once she had been tempted to open a conversation with Harrod about Tony, but she was afraid of his drawling comment and his ironical gaze. After overhearing a snatch of conversation between Harrod and Daiches one evening, she was thankful that she had not. Standing concealed by the high back of the Father Superior's chair, she heard Harrod who lounged at the table with Daiches, remark, "Of course, Tony stayed much longer than he ought in Sweden – I am told on account of a ravishing Countess, a true Nordic beauty. I suppose there were diplomatic involvements ..." And Harrod smiled. That instant Suckley came from behind and greeted her. At once the conversation between the two men broke off and they went out ...

The incident plunged her into gloom. A Swedish countess? Hedda – Helda – or some such name, with braided, corn coloured hair? Evidently Harrod had a source of information denied her. How much more did he know? She sat at the table crumbling bread pellets abstractedly, speaking only when spoken to. What a fool of impulse she had been! ...

* * *

Doubts of a different kind assailed the mind of General Moore. Through the ornate doorway of the palace headquarters trooped the fervent patriots of

Spain with news good, bad, and indifferent, and mostly unreliable. They spoke of phantom armies straining to succour Madrid; of stores and transport which never materialised. Tomorrow ... tomorrow ... always tomorrow!

Moore was not impressed. At midnight, November 28th–29th, he informed his divisional generals that he intended to retreat – Baird, marching towards them was to fall back on Corunna, and Hope on Ciudad Rodrigo where he would be followed by the bulk of the army.

The general officers listened, gloomy, silent, resentful an attitude later reflected in the rank and file. With incredible effort they had struggled through the mountain passes, had entered the broad plains of Leon, merely to sound retreat. What would be the effect on Spanish opinion, to say nothing of the people at home to turn tail without a shot being fired!

But, while many cursed and questioned, further news now gave Moore pause. Madrid was actively preparing to resist the French, and at the same time the Marquis La Romana, who assisted by the British fleet, had escaped from the Baltic with troops was marching forward – these, and other factors impelled the harassed General to a different line of action. Taking the offensive, he would drive his thirty thousand men to Valladolid, the great road junction between Burgos and the capital, thus cutting the French line of communications.

Events moved ahead of news. When, on the day following, Hope arrived with the guns, Moore learned that Napoleon had swooped and occupied Madrid. In spite of this the British general still adhered to his plan. Now the Emperor's communications were to be threatened – a few tail feathers plucked from the imperial eagle himself.

Beneath a cold winter sun – scarlet and grey the columns of the line, dark green the Riflemen – the army wound out of Salamanca. A few students in shabby gowns followed hopefully, though what role they expected to play in combat it is difficult to say. In the thin bright light, faces were turned to Ledesma, a small town on the riverbank famous for its sulphur baths. Peasants in draggled black coats and laced breeches; women, handkerchiefs about their heads, stood watching the columns pass. A few windmills broke the rim of the horizon. Wild hawks darted upon the fields.

Harriet Foulkes on her new mount, a dapple grey – the unfortunate Felix had been shot in Salamanca – followed the rear ranks. Noting her outward poise, no one who saw her riding with loosely dangling switch, would have suspected her division of mind. She kept to the rear, but in advance of the baggage.

Foulkes himself moved with a new air of authority, subtly enjoying his new command. He was now more than usually anxious for his wife's comfort. He could afford to be indulgent, forgiving. No further reference had been made to the bitter exchanges at the convent; time (he felt) would erode the memory and all would become as before. Compatible with duty, he would

meet her every requirement. Promotion, in more senses than one. He would
be the first to turn a new leaf.

Before leaving Salamanca he had summoned a parade of all ranks when,
after a respectful reference to Pomeroy, he delivered a general charge. It was
not a long oration. "Give me of your best," he said, "and I will not only be
your commanding officer, but a father also. Anything less than your best
however, and you will wish you had never been born. We are moving out to
meet the French. I am assured that when we do come to grips we shall beat
them; but each soldier must play his part, and nothing less." Knowing the
men with whom he had to deal he had not minced his words, and when
Daiches called for cheers for the new Colonel, he was gratified with the
response. His nickname henceforward was to be "Daddy Foulkes".

Like everyone else, Foulkes was glad to be rid of Salamanca; the aura of
the city had dimmed. During the weeks of inaction he had shared the hopes
and fears of officers and men. Now, riding ahead of the column he was
delighted to note a new buoyancy of spirit, a renewed sense of purpose. It
augured well. Soon he would draw aside to watch the men pass. He was quite
certain that he did not intend to emulate the parade ground rigidity of
Pomeroy, who would have checked the buckle of every knapsack, the slope of
every musket. Firepower it was that mattered, and he wished that it were
greater. The old "Brown Bess" was good for a barnyard door at twenty paces,
but the new Baker rifle- what chance was there of having that? – was so
much better. The old forms died hard – too hard for comfort.

There was the moral aspect too. Men mattered. For the most part enlisted
men were like children, crying out with hunger, or moaning in pain, but
thank God, lions when roused. One thing he decided. There would be less of
the lash, and greater officer attention to welfare ... He began to feel a trifle
guilty, riding as he did, on his fine bay horse. Caesar had stepped out with his
men, but nowadays (for obvious reasons) one could not do so. It was important that the commander should move freely to be seen by all.

Simms, the young Commissary clattered by, riding across country on
some mission of his own. The fellow had too much liberty. A steely glint
entered Foulkes' eye. Harker had already pointed to the indifferent quality of
the meat which was being issued. "Not fit for the kennels!" That would need
looking into. Simms must not be allowed to get away with it ...

* * *

Matters came to a head one evening outside Zamora. Marching through the
town they had pushed eight or nine miles beyond to a grove, where they
encamped beside a stream. Fires were started, but by the time these were
burning strongly, men were still waiting with empty kettles. The ration beef
had not been issued. It was still in the carts – but where were the carts?

Within earshot of complaining voices though effecting not to hear, Foulkes paced backwards and forwards in cold fury. The men had covered twenty miles and were famished. Where was Simms the dispenser? And where his train?

It was not until another hour had elapsed that the Commissary and his vehicles put in an appearance. The young man exhausted by incessantly harrying his team forward, for he too was conscious of delay, was summoned to the presence. One glance at Foulkes' face was enough. The Commissary was in for trouble.

"I presume," began the Colonel acidly," that you have an explanation of this disgraceful business? The kettles empty – the men starving. Is this your notion of duty?"

"If you will allow me, sir," said Simms.

"Very well," responded Foulkes with a glance, half disdain, half disgust, "but be quick about it." He was obviously in no mood to listen.

The Commissary explained that he had been held up in the town by a religious procession. When this had passed, and they prepared to resume their journey, another procession more important than the first, came up. This included the provincial bishop, a dignitary to whom the drovers declared they were bound to pay reverence. Abandoning the vehicles, they had so intermingled with the crowd that afterwards they were collected with only the greatest difficulty. Some drovers had drifted to the wine-shops; two had vanished completely.

"You were provided with a guard," said Foulkes severely.

"The guard was helpless." Having no mind for father complications, Simms did not add that the guards had been as foot-loose as the drovers.

"You should know how to impose discipline," snapped Foulkes. "I am tempted to believe, sir, that you are unequal to your duties."

Simms flushed angrily. "But sir, with respect, you know the religious habits of the Spaniards – how devout they are. What more could I have done?"

"You should have employed means."

"Shot a couple!"

Foulkes' mouth tightened at the sarcasm. "Impertinence will not help. Another repetition of this and I shall report you to your superiors."

"Report and be damned!" thought Simms. He said with emphasis, "Thank you sir."

And left the tent blazing with anger. "The old story," he muttered, "no meat for the camp-kettles, so string up the Commissary!" The delay of the train was, in the circumstances, quite unavoidable. Everyone knew how the Spaniards cherished their religion, and devotion apart took every opportunity to desert. If Foulkes was not aware of this then he had been singularly blind during the course of the past six weeks. Of course he knew. Simms had no

difficulty in putting two and two together. This, he concluded, was the natural outcome of his association with Mrs Foulkes.

Dog-tired, he had no sooner settled in his sleeping bag when an orderly
shook him by the shoulder – the Colonel wished to see him immediately.
"Here beginneth the second lesson, "He grimaced as he made his way to the
headquarters tent. Foulkes sitting on a stool was waiting. "Bring me a full
tally of stores, Mr Simms," he said curtly; so back the Commissary had to
trot for his portfolio, and returning, wait – standing if you please! – while his
High Mightiness checked the figures item by item. "Doesn't know a thing
about it," fumed Simms as he watched the admonitory pencil pass from entry
to entry. "You have an inadequate supply of spirits," said Foulkes at length,
"there should be a third of a pint for each man per day. Calculate requirements for three days ahead, and give me your total."

The Commissary numbered on his tablets – no easy task under that
basilisk eye – and making a mistake, had to begin all over again. To crown all,
the secretly smiling, obsequious Harker hovered in the background.

The inquest had almost finished when Foulkes pounced on a discrepancy in
the amount of fodder allowed for horses and mules, forgetting that the latter
were apportioned only half the ration of the former. Simms explanation was
received in complete silence. No word of apology. The result was that Foulkes
ordered an immediate transcript of the whole; so that on returning to his tent
Simms wakened his clerk, and the two scratched pens into the early hours of
the morning. Next day when he presented the paper, he was mortified to see
the Colonel toss it aside as a mater of minor importance. "He means mischief,"
thought Simms, "but I'll be damned if he catches me a second time." A vain
hope, he knew; much might happen in the course of a day's marching.

Later, he looked up Higgins, the Paymaster. The two were on friendly
terms, and as they rode together, Simms broached the subject of the
Colonel's conduct. He inquired if his friend had noticed a marked change in
Foulkes' character since assuming command. Higgins laughed. "Who hasn't?
He's playing with a new toy; if anything I find him extraordinarily polite.
Does something worry you?" Whereupon Simms related what had happened
in the business of the delayed supplies. "I shouldn't lay too much to that," said
Higgins comfortingly. "The new broom, you know. He's jealous for tip-top
efficiency."

"I wish I could agree," said Simms.

"It would be strange if it were not so. He'll bed down. You'll see."

But whenever he dwelt on Foulkes, Simms hardened. The devil in the
cocked hat should have his due, but not a fraction more. Henceforward he
(Simms) would be perfunctory in the extreme; concede only essentials. "Let
the galled jade wince," he told himself, "my withers are unwrung!"

* * *

Through the days that followed Simms began to wonder who the galled jade was. Complaints were levelled at every march. Now it was a keg of mouldy ship's biscuit; how a flash of wine turned sour. "Ask Mr Simms when he had taken to issuing vinegar?" The observation was conveyed through Harker, and sarcastically Simms inquired if the Colonel had said anything else.

"Yes, sir," replied Harker, "he said that if you smoked fewer cigars you might have a clearer brain."

"He did not."

"Call me a liar, sir," said the other airily. "I heard him say so to Major Daiches."

"Cigars are my business; let the Colonel stick to his pouncet box," said Simms incautiously. It was a foolish remark to make, for nothing was more certain than that servant would relay the observation to his master. And so it was. When the Commissary and Foulkes met again, Simms was cut dead, and thereafter the two communicated only by writing. Notes like, "Attend to fodder – horses feeding from scrub oak leaves," and "rations inadequate" became commonplace. Simms adopted a uniform, "Will attend," in reply, a brush-off, which annoyed Foulkes exceedingly.

But a deeper pitfall awaited. After the regiment had marched into Toro, Foulkes tethered his horse outside the church marked as their billet. The interior presented an appearance strangely at variance with its religious purpose – muskets had been propped against the tombs, men squatted or lay full length on the floor. The confessional boxes were crammed with grain, every available corner being used in one way or another. The Commissary's office was in the house adjoining; outside the premises half a dozen drovers awaited to unload their vehicles.

In Lisbon, Foulkes had bought a pair of pistols of which he was extremely proud; weapons expertly and curiously inlaid with a Moorish pattern in silver filigree. He was in the habit of boasting that if he carried back from the Peninsular nothing more than these rare weapons, he would be perfectly satisfied. The pistols he now left in the holsters as he intended spending no more than a few minutes inside the church. He entered, and was having a few words with the adjutant, when Harker came up and stood to attention. "What is it, man?" Foulkes inquired.

"May I take the liberty, sir, of asking if you brought your pistols in with you?"

"Here? Of course not. I do not intend staying."

"Then, sir, I regret to report that the weapons are not in your holsters."

"Nonsense! I left them only a moment ago."

With a swift glance around, Foulkes hurried out, Harker following. Darting to his horse the Colonel thrust his hand into the holsters which were indeed empty. "By God," he breathed, "they *have* gone!"

"You are sure you had them with your, sir?"

"No doubt about that."

His face set grimly, he turned to a knot of Spanish drovers, who with swart impassive faces were lounging beside the carts. "I have been robbed in broad daylight!" he exclaimed. With a quivering finger he singled out the foremost Spaniard. "Who are these men?"

"Mr Simms' lot, sir," said Harker.

"Simms!" shouted Foulkes imperatively, "where are you? Come here at once."

Hearing the Colonel's voice Simms appeared in the doorway of the depot. "Can I be of assistance, sir?" His markedly quiet tone in marked contrast with the brusque nature of Foulkes' summons did not ease matters.

Foulkes pointed to the drovers. "Are these objects yours?"

"You mean the men, sir?"

"Don't quibble – of course I mean the men. Let me inform you that my pistols have been stolen – both of 'em – five hundred dollars worth under your very nose. You will secure the weapons and return them."

"But I know nothing about your pistols, sir."

"No, but I warrant your precious scoundrels do." And Foulkes glared round the semi-circle of Spaniards who watched with some amusement the comedy now being played between the two English officers. Strange beings they were! "Estos Ingleses," they muttered, and shrugged.

"Bring me the sergeant major," ordered Foulkes, "and until he arrives you will see, sir, that no man moves from this spot. You can stand by to interpret."

After a few minutes a file marched in, surrounding the now sullen Spaniards with a hedge of muskets. Each drover was searched, but there was no trace of the missing weapons. Simms harangued the Spaniards vigorously, but without avail. To help matters. Harker ventured the opinion that he had seen a drover patting the charger. This prompted Foulkes to demand a full muster of all Simms' men from every quarter. But all the subsequent hubbub, bustling and bellowing of orders, accomplished nothing at all. Foulkes announced that he would stay no longer. "You will hear more of this," he threatened.

"Do you suppose I have secreted them?" said Simms contemptuously.

"I hold you responsible."

"For what?" protested the other. "I was occupied with my tallies as the clerk will tell you. My men have been mustered, searched to the shoelaces and you have found nothing. What more can I do?"

"We have bandied words enough," said Foulkes turning.

"*Traga la perro!*" said Simms softly in Spanish, meaning, "Swallow that you dog!" One or two of the Spaniards laughed.

Foulkes faced about. What was that you said?"

"Nothing."

"Some impertinence, I'll be bound."

"As you please." Simms shrugged and looked away.

Without a further word, Foulkes left him, and returned to the church, where in a moment or two he could be heard sharply berating the officer on duty. Harker, who remained standing beside the Colonel's charger brought his hand gently down the glossy chestnut flank, and threw a flittering glance in the direction of Simms who still lingered outside his own office. There was an air of sleazy satisfaction in the servant's attitude. If he had spoken, if instead of the sinuous movement of the hand on the horses flank, he had made an unfriendly gesture, Simms might have dismissed the Colonel's servant as an innocent bystander. Now he could not be sure. Harker knew something. There was in his silky restraint a touch of triumph. It was impossible to believe that Foulkes had deliberately rigged the affair; but had Harker? Uppermost in Simms' mind as he returned to his duties was an impression that Honest Iago had a finger in the pie ...

* * *

Colonel Foulkes was not one to waste time. That evening when Deputy Commissary Kearney, Simms' superior officer, rode in, the Colonel raised the question of the young Assistant's ability. "This man," said Foulkes, "is neither use nor ornament – quite unreliable. As a special favour I wish you would make other provision for him."

Kearney rolled his comfortable body in the chair, and frowned. There were incompetent, even dishonest, commissaries on the staff whose conduct caused scandal. Investigations were always thorough and lengthy, involving much checking of accounts. A tedious business. Did this imply another such inquiry? "Chopping and changing," he rumbled. "Strange, I have no complaints hitherto. Simms has been with us since Vimiero."

"I speak," said Foulkes, "from bitter experience." As he plied Kerney with wine, he recounted Simms' many sins of omission. "I must insist on a transfer."

"You may go further and fare worse," said Kearney.

"No," said Foulkes decisively.

"Suppose we have the man in to talk things over?"

"I have quite made up my mind."

Kearney sighed. His staff was stretched to the uttermost; but reflecting that one had to work smoothly with commanding offices, with ill-grace he yielded. "Very well," he said at length. "I have Proctor, just up from Lisbon. I had intended sending him back to Zamora where we are baking biscuit for the Benevente magazine. Simms shall take his place. If the fellow can't attend to a set of ovens, then he is no good anywhere."

"You can dispatch him," said Foulkes, "to the devil so long as he doesn't stay here to torment me." And away he went, still irked by the loss of the pistols, lovely weapons which had once belonged to the Duke of Alva. All things considered he had no difficulty in persuading himself that he had every justification for the step he had taken ...

Simms reacted sharply to the blow which Kearney tried to soften by explaining that at all costs he must have a reliable man at Zamora. The change, Simms felt, had not been due to Kearney's own volition. He pointed out that his accounts were in order, that he had been on excellent terms with the quartermaster, but watching the expression on Kearney's stolid face, realised that further words would be useless. Zamora it would have to be ...

* * *

Simms' translation from commissariat duties in Toro to the depot at Zamora was neat, swift, effective. Proctor, the new man, came in that evening, and after a necessary briefing of his successor, Simms packed and prepared to leave at dawn.

This arrangement allowed no time at all for visiting farewells. As it was he had no wish to contact Mrs Foulkes – enough fat (he reflected) had been cast into that fire! Indeed, he had not exchanged a word with either mistress or maid since leaving Salamanca. Now that the thread of their acquaintance was broken, they would be unlikely to meet again. The most he could do would be to leave a note for Sue Thompson. He did not wish to say much -one never knew into whose hands the writing might stray—

Dear Sue (he wrote) I am sent to Zamora as pastrycook – in a word, baking biscuit. Don't ask the why and the wherefore. It is a puzzle within a puzzle which you must read for yourself. The fortune of war, I suppose. But we shall meet again. In the meantime keep yourself free.

Yours affectionate friend,

H.S.

"Exit of the whipping boy!" he thought ruefully as he rode across country to Zamora. At no time, even by a single word had Foulkes betrayed the slightest knowledge of the part that he (Simms) had played in the Harriet-Harte liaison; but in his bones the Commissary felt that this was the mainspring of the Colonel's action. Yet how could one have behaved otherwise? He was annoyed that in addition to professional injustice, he was riding away from the enemy. Civilian though Simms was, he had looked forward to the excitement of the battlefield. He jogged the reins resentfully. Now he must dree his weird in the little walled town and await the day of deliverance.

He covered the distance in rather more than half a day, and soon with a fellow Commissary, one MacTavish by name, was checking the golden brown bread of the region as it was drawn from the ovens and dispatched immediately to Benevente on the Corunna highway. Seated beside the indispensable brazier after the first day's work, moody and silent, he continued to dwell upon the circumstance by which he had been compelled to leave the regiment. He could not help feeling that Harker had had a hand in the loss of the Colonel's pistols, and oddly Sue's wistful face continued to haunt his mind. Fate had linked them both with the baleful personality of the Colonel's servant. And the day of judgment seemed a long way off ...

* * *

Had he been privileged to be present, Assistant Deputy Commissary Simms would have been intensely interested in a little comedy then taking place at Toro, for by a fortunate circumstance, apparently by his own initiative, Harker recovered the Colonel's pistols. Surprised and delighted, Foulkes listened to his servant's story, a colourful narrative garnished with appropriate detail.

Harker had continued to keep his eye on the drovers – two in particular, "One having a red handkercher round his forehead, t'other all in black." That morning he had seen them "looking this way and that" as they peered into a little box fixed under the axle of one of the carts. "Uncommonly secret they were in movement, so I thinks ha – ha – I'll watch a bit further. Sure enough they takes out an object wrapped in a cloth, and red hanky nodding to black, off they goes across the square to a little posada in the corner. I says to myself these for a ducat are the gentlemen – I beg your pardon, sir – the sneak thieves in question. Putting two and two together, I reckon they contemplates a deal with a third party. Well, sir, I takes the bull by the horns so to speak, picks up a likely fellow of the Ninety Fifth, and enters the place which was not better than a pig sty to find red hanky and black drinking and laughing like mad with a little Jew, and the pistols laid on the table afore 'em."

"The villains!" exclaimed Foulkes.

"Bad through and through, sir. Well, I accosted 'em instanter—"

"Did you employ violence?"

"A little prick with our side swords, sir – that's all."

"And you arrested them?"

"Sir – I wish I could say so, but while we was examining your weapons, overjoyed as you may guess – the miscreants made a dash. Run – I never seen the like; we lost 'em in the alleys. You know how they turn and twist."

"But if they belonged to the commissary's train you could have traced them."

"Give me leave to have thought of that, sir. They must have got back to their carts and made off."

Foulkes almost caressed the pistols; what lovely weapons they were! "That was unfortunate," he said. "At the same time I am immensely grateful to you. I never thought to handle these again." He took out his purse. "Here are two guineas – one for yourself and one for the other fellow."

"What other fellow, sir?"

"The man of the Ninety Fifth who assisted you."

"Oh, yes, sir – certainly, sir."

"A useful piece of work, Raddock."

Harker took the money. "Thank you kindly, sir. Your pleasure is my duty. Shall I relieve you of the wrapping, sir?"

"Please do, and thank you once again. I am much obliged to you."

The servant saluted and withdrew. "What a tail our cat's got!" he chuckled as he pocketed the guineas. "The swiftness of the hand deceives the eye!" Amazing, he decided, what you can slip into a knapsack …

* * *

At Toro, Harriet saw little of her husband. He was often at Divisional Headquarters, or inspecting men who had been withdrawn from the church and billeted in outlying farmhouses. Proctor, the new Commissary she thought a sorry substitute for Simms. He had no conversation, and when spoken to would lean forward slightly as though to impart a confidence, although of course, nothing ever happened. A Cornishman, she concluded that he must have descended from a line of wreckers, an aspersion altogether unjust, for poor Proctor's father was a burgess of Truro, a worthy citizen, and the proprietor of a small pottery.

No news came from Tony Harte. He had drifted beyond all reach and knowledge. As it was, the hours dragged with leaden feet, the weather was bitterly cold, and by this time one Spanish town looked pretty much like another; the same peeling colour-washed walls, the russet pan-tiled roofs, the over-decorated churches, the cobbled plazas; Spanish women carrying water pitchers, and their men-folk like hooded owls stalking from one arcade to the next.

To employ time she turned to reading *Tom Jones* which was one of the few books she had brought with her. After the barren country through which they had passed – the scrawny tees and fields of stubble – it was a relief to recapture if only from the printed page a glimpse of English lanes and meadows, of sweetly smelling inn parlours and manor houses. She followed the fortunes of Tom and Sophia Western with nostalgic zest. Though by no means stooping to discuss her secret impulses and emotions, she realised intuitively that her servant had long been aware of her feelings towards Anthony Harte. For her part the girl often sighed as she pondered the situation, but it was not in her place to propound a solution. The problem was one for Mrs Foulkes alone.

The transfer of Harry Simms had touched Sue more than she cared to admit. He was the only man in whom she had ever confided, and apart from her own family, the only male it was pleasant to remember. His removal had left a gap in her life. It was, of course, possible that they would meet again, had hopefully she looked forward to a day when he would reappear. She liked to recall that he had left at least a written message which was half-promise. Thus she preserved the note carefully, reading the brief jaunty sentences until she knew them by heart. "Keep yourself free," he had written. Free for what? Only time would tell …

When Harriet recalled that Sue "knew her letters", she invited her to a shared spell of reading *Tom Jones* aloud. They took alternate chapters, skipping it must be confessed, the literary and philosophical digressions of Mr Fielding, in order to come more to grips with the plot. It was Sue's turn to read when they arrived at the point where Sophia implored her father to be relieved of the impending marriage to Blifil – "Oh, sir," murmured the girl with intense feeling, "Oh, sir, not only your Sophy's happiness; her very being depends upon your granting her request. I cannot live with Mr Blifil. To force me into marriage would be killing me." "You can't live with Mr Blifil," says Western. "No upon my soul I can't," announced Sophia. "Then die and be damned," cries he, spurning her from him …

Sue's voice trembled, and she swallowed hard to control her emotion.

"Poor Sophia," murmured Harriet. "It is most effecting. Please read no more for the moment. We will finish the chapter later."

As Sue made a dish of chocolate she turned to Harriet. "Do you consider, Ma'm, that Miss Sophia will marry Mr Blifil?"

"Of course not," rejoined her mistress sharply. "Mr Fielding would never permit such a misalliance. Such things happen only in daily life, but you may be sure that she will suffer before her adventures are complete."

As Harriet sipped her chocolate, a horseman clattered beneath the window, and setting down the dish she hastened to look out; but it was only a dragoon orderly in crested helmet – a stranger.

"It would be dreadful it she were not to escape," said Sue.

"You mean Sophia?"

"Yes."

Harriet's eyes surveyed the room which formed their temporary lodging place, regarding distastefully the tousled straw matting on the floor, the once white walls adorned by a flecked mirror, a small engraving of a saint, an oxtail bearing a single comb, and a crucifix beneath which stood a bowl of holy water. "She will escape," said Harriet firmly. "It must be so."

In the town that day, moved by a sudden impulse she bought an ebony snuff box, the lid inset with figures of the Three Graces. She had felt for some little time that Percy needed a new one, though she had no intention of making him a present now. She placed it in her valise. A convenient time would come – but not just yet …

* * *

They set out again on ice-bound roads where the animals floundered, carts lurched and skidded, and across the frozen ruts men found it difficult to march. Despite this, the rank and file sometimes sang so that Colonel Foulkes' thin lips more than once relaxed in a smile. A good healthy spirit prevailed. They grew to listen for the beat of the French drums. Soon the army would be at grips, but the River Garrion ran somewhere between their present position and that of the enemy. They were told that when darkness fell they would halt in or near the town of Sahagun ...

At the outskirts snow began to fall, large damp flakes, which caught by the wind, drove full in their faces. A few Spaniards who were in the streets trudged by with hats pulled low and chins buried deep in their cloaks. Mules and horses tended to halt and turn their hindquarters to the storm. It was almost impossible to see across the plaza, where in the Benedictine Convent Sir John Moore was lodged. The town lay on the cold pilgrim road to Santiago, but here were pilgrims of a very different kind.

The regiment however, marched through the town to a position facing the river, where the men found shelter in three large granaries, the officers in the adjacent farmhouse. Advance sentries were posted on the south bank among a stretch of tumbled rocks screened by overhanging trees. With stones and broken branches, they improvised shelters against the inclement night.

The officers were thoroughly dissatisfied with their quarters. Instead of reasonable billets in town they were led to a house the owner of which had never at any time been preoccupied with comfort. A fire certainly blazed on the hearth, but planks balanced on kegs were not the best of seats, and the straw provided for beds had made an all too obvious acquaintance with the stable. After a mess of strongly seasoned pottage, Harriet decided that late though the hour was, she would do much better in Sahagun. By this time the snow had stopped, and Foulkes recognising the force of his wife's argument, the two women accompanied by an orderly rode back into the town.

But out of the frying pan into the fire! The Quartermaster, muttering under his breath at the vagaries of women, was brusque, almost impolite. Finally he placed the two with an old lady who had been excused billeting on account (among other things) of extremely defective eyesight, though the dame had no difficulty in recognising the silver dollar that Harriet thought it prudent to display. The old crone, after a prolonged bout of hawking and spitting, led them to a room into which she brought a small charcoal brazier. Later, a slatternly girl served soup so stiff with lentils that the spoon stood upright in the bowl. "Pilgrim fare indeed!" said Harriet ironically, already beginning to regret the farmhouse fire, "but beggars can't be choosers."

The soup was hot enough and tasted better than it looked. After eating it there was nothing better to do but to make the best of the damp, mildewed room. They did not undress – wrapped in cloaks and blankets they huddled together for warmth ...

Dawn broke; the maid brought in cakes and coffee. Chilled to the bone they moved about the room stamping feet and thrashing arms in order to restore circulation. "I pray that this may be a fine day," said Harriet, "for of one thing I am quite resolved, and it is not to spend a moment longer in this charnel house than I am compelled."

So after breakfast they went out into the streets to find the English talking of General Paget's notable affray with a body of French cavalry. The enemy had been handsomely beaten; prisoners taken. Some had been brought in, and were now fastened in the plaza cellars, singing lustily and jigging to tunes by their own fiddler. "It would appear, Ma'm," said Sue as they paused to listen, "that they are almost glad to be taken."

"They are but poor ignorant conscripts," replied Harriet, "thrashed no doubt, into battle by their officers. Exchanging one servitude for another, what are prison bars to them?"

CHAPTER XIII

By noon a misty sun had struggled through with a hint of thaw. This, more than anything else, moved Harriet to propose an outing.

"To the camp, Ma'm?" inquired Sue.

Harriet smiled disdainfully. "Certainly not – some quite new line of interest – anything in preference to this horrible ice-house." She gave no further information, except to add that they would be using the animals.

When the convent clock struck one, Sue ventured through the kitchen to an evil smelling stable, where – though she had difficulty in forcing the bit through the closely clenched teeth of the grey – both beasts were harnessed. She led these round to the plaza door.

When they set out, Harriet in her little round hat and grey cloak might well have been mistaken for a civil officer, though there could be no mistaking the identity of Sue mounted on Sancho. "In what direction?" she inquired. "We shall follow our noses," said her mistress enigmatically. Really, she did not much care.

So they clattered along splashing gouts of melting snow. The sky was reasonable clear, the sun a ball of misty red. At the town gate an officer of the guard detained them. "I would not interfere with your pleasure, Ma'm," he ventured, "but I must warn you not to go too far."

"What distance do you give me?" asked Harriet.

"Well –" the young man stroked his chin doubtfully, "not beyond the cavalry vedettes. Our people are patrolling, but they are only here and there. A couple of miles perhaps."

"A couple of miles?" she commented derisively, pointing to a slushy track which wound into the middle distance, "Does that lead to the Carrion?"

"The river, yes Ma'm."

"Then we shall give it a wide berth. And over yonder?" She pointed to the misty eastern hills.

He screened his eyes. "Open country I should say – thinly populated. You might come across a farm or two."

"Then we will ride in that direction."

"Again I must give you warning," he persisted. "We are pretty well screened, but there are gaps, and the French patrols probing—"

Harriet laughed. "We have eyes – and I carry a pistol."

A pained expression crossed the young officer's face. A woman with a pistol matching herself against French cavalry! Her assurance was amazing. He could do no more than shrug. "I have done my duty," he said ruefully.

"Very well indeed!"

She touched him on his shoulder with her riding switch – an almost regal gesture, an accolade. His eyes caught her slightly amused and mocking ones, but he was flattered. She brought the switch to the flank of the grey. "Hup!" she cried, and before the officer could make further comment, rode on. As Sue drew alongside however, he said sharply, "Keep her within reasonable distance." And he stared doubtfully after both riders wondering if he had been sufficiently firm.

As for the two wayfarers it was delightful to leave the town behind, to be rid of tramping feet, the incessant squealing of cart wheels. Nor was going difficult. The level snow-covered fields offered good riding. If cavalry patrols were to appear, they would be quickly sighted; but the possibility of danger added spice to the outing ...

Soon, leaving the road, they passed a farmhouse where a woman's inquiring face appeared at one of the windows, and a Spaniard in a tattered brown cloak stopped herding his swine to watch the riders go by. Mother of God! – two completely strange women riding across the fields in mid-December! ... A sleek grey animal darted towards a clump of trees making a slender trail in the snow. A fox perhaps. "What a pity," said Harriet, "that Sir John has no thought for hounds." (That moment Sir John was reading a dispatch from his liaison officer with General Castanos to the effect that the Spaniards about him, lacking shoes and weapons were in a desperate condition.) When a little later a long-drawn howl came from the distance, Harriet was not so certain that she had seen a fox. That might have been a wolf cry. She felt for her pistol ...

Brought up by a small ravine through which a stream ran silently, they descended the bank, broke through the thin ice at the verge, and splashed to the other side. Climbing, they still faced open country. Pale sunlight touched the clouds, gilding ethereally the distant hills of Leon. About a quarter of a mile to the east upon rising ground, stood a windmill its latticed arms raised in mute appeal to the windless sky. To the west a feather of smoke arose from a cluster of farm buildings half buried in snowdrifts. Impelled by a common thought the two women glanced at each other, though Sue waited for her mistress to speak first. "I think we ought to see what creature comfort the place offers," said Harriet. When Sue reminded her of the officer's warning she exclaimed impatiently, "Yes – yes – but not until we have had something to drink."

Apart from a drifting spiral of smoke there was no sign of life in or about the squat huddle of buildings; but as they drew nearer a horseman left the central archway, and paced slowly towards them. He wore a long cloak and a battered hat, but his horse had the clean lines of a cavalry mount. "Must be one of ours," said Harriet with hopeful assurance. "I cannot think otherwise."

The man approached, still walking his horse. He appeared unhurried, and both watchers heaved a sigh of relief as they detected beneath his cloak the bright blue tunic of the huzzars. When he did draw abreast they were startled to see that he was a young trooper, whose face waxen pale from loss of blood, was swathed in a bandage. He swayed slightly in the saddle as he muttered, "Are you English?"

"What is it, soldier?" asked Harriet anxiously.

He continued to mutter through what appeared to be a set of locked teeth. From his disjointed sentences, they gathered that he had been involved in a skirmish with the French, and that in the farmhouse beyond he had left a companion in distress, a badly wounded officer. Meanwhile, he was pushing through to Sahagun for assistance. As she listened, Harriet came to a swift decision. "Do you," she said to Sue when the trooper had finished, "see him back to town, while I look in at the farm." Hearing this, the young trooper, probably because he did not wish to be assisted through the pickets by a woman, protested vehemently that he was well able to look after himself. "No – no no!" he cried with such violence that Harriet desisted. "As you please," she said reluctantly, "but be careful to stick to our tracks. Follow these, and presently you will come to the high road; after that you should have no difficulty."

"I'm not dead yet," the trooper muttered stubbornly. With a feeble salute, he jerked his reins and the two women watched him go. "I don't like the look of this at all," said Harriet. "How long have we been away?"

"About two hours."

"I would have returned with the poor fellow, but if there is a second unfortunate, we had best make inquiry."

They rode forward …

At the main building, the farmer, a sturdy, bandy-legged fellow, who had been watching the newcomers closely, appeared in the doorway scowling. He scrutinised his visitors from head to foot, every line in his body suggesting that they were unwelcome. He tried to stare them out, but something in Harriet's high patrician attitude touched him and he weakened. "She is of the quality," he thought, "and, who knows, may have influence." He bowed slightly with a gesture that they might enter, but did not attempt either to take their animals or to help them dismount. It was a conditioned welcome. They dropped to the ground, and he stood aside for them to enter the main room, half hall, half kitchen.

Harriet cast a swift glance around. A groined ceiling melted into the shadows, but there was light enough to perceive a man, his body half-covered by a blanket, stretched upon a straw mattress at the farther end of the room. A slung jacket draped a chair, a sabre being balanced on the seat, while saddlebags and a single riding boot had been dropped beside the wall. As Harriet went forward a premonition that the inert figure might possibly be that of Tony Harte seized her, and through discounting the impulse – for there were many officers on the cavalry arm – she trembled. Why should it be he?

Then, all doubt was shattered. A feeble, but all too familiar voice came from the recess, so that she halted a moment or two quite still, before she darted forward dropping to her knees. Even so, she could only stammer a word or two, repeating his name almost incoherently. She had hoped to look into his face, but to her dismay she found that she was speaking to a mask – his face had been so thoroughly bandaged that a vent had been left only for nostrils and mouth. Ominous stains showed about the eyes and forehead.

"Who ... is there? You will have to speak up. I can't hear."

Harriet rose to her feet staring wildly at Sue. The scene embodied all the elements of nightmare. War brought death and wounds, but never to those one loved and cherished! "I don't understand," she whispered, though even as she spoke the truth was plain. Then, realising that she was in the presence of others, she controlled herself, and stooping with lips close to the bandaged face, said clearly, "It is I – Harriet."

"Everything," he said sighing, "seems a long way off."

She spoke more loudly. "You know – Andromache."

"Dreams ... hallucinations," he murmured.

She laid her hand on his shoulder. "No hallucination," she said gently. "I am with you – here in this room." She found his hand and pressed it.

After a pause, he said, "I understand. By whom are you accompanied. Have you marched hither?"

"I am alone, except for my maid, Susan Thompson. We were riding by."

"I would not have laid a thousand guineas that we should meet so –" His voice tailed off. "Incredible ... Ramsden, the trooper, did you meet him?"

"Outside – riding to Sahagun."

"A staunch lad."

"I instructed him to follow our tracks, but what of your own injury?"

"A nasty sabre cut across the face," he said, "blinded me for the time being."

"It seems awkwardly dressed." The bandage consisted of a couple of neck clothes bound tightly around his head. "I am certain it could be adjusted."

The wounded man raised a restraining hand. "Please do nothing of the kind. To start bleeding would only worsen matters. I need a surgeon with needle and thread."

"We have a needle case," she said.

"No doubt," he responded dryly, "your intentions are of the best, but this is not your kind of embroidery?" She felt that he must be smiling faintly. "I – I think I should like something to drink."

His voice cracked, and he sank back tiredly. In response to a signal from Harriet, the farm's wife brought a cup of wine so full that she drank a little before she placed it to his lips. He took it gratefully. "That's better," he breathed, then after a moment's silence, "I have no doubt that you are wondering—"

"Please don't talk if you'd rather not," she said.

"No indeed – it is quite a relief to speak to someone – I mean in English. We were on reconnaissance when the French came from behind a wood – the neatest ambush you ever saw – cutting, thrusting, wheeling about. It was all over in a couple of minutes. Somehow, I got this. I don't know where the blow came from, but Ramsden beat the man down and managed to hurry me away. Not very heroic – I mean my own share. What became of the others I do not know. To crown matters – no blame on Ramsden — I fell off and broke my leg. And that is the woeful story. Now enough of myself. Tell me how you happened here."

"I think," she said, "by the intervention of Providence."

"Then by the same token," he urged, "you must leave immediately. You are in great danger."

"We can share it."

"Indeed no. You must get away."

"Where did you meet the French horsemen?" she asked.

"A couple of miles away."

"Then we are safe for the time being."

"Not," he said emphatically, "while there are tracks in the snow."

"It is thawing," she rejoined triumphantly.

"Tracks remain."

"Time to be quiet," she ordered. "You have talked enough."

"I do beseech you," he pleaded, "return to Sahagun at once. The farmer's people are quite attentive, and I have no doubt about Ramsden's ability to bring help."

Harriet averted her head. It was heartrending to see him laid by, so thoroughly helpless. "I will not be shuffled off," she announced. "I have every intention of staying." She turned to Sue. "The Captain, as you see is badly wounded, and I shall remain here until he receives proper assistance. Will you stay with me?"

"Yes, indeed," answered Sue.

"Good girl," nodded Harriet taking off her hat and cloak, and moving to the doorway, with signs induced the farmer to stable the animals …

* * *

Harriet found a stool and seated herself beside the alcove while the farmer's wife assisted by her daughters, prepared a meal. At times the Spanish females addressed each other sharply, but there was no clue to the trend of their conversation. "Why did I not," reflected Harriet bitterly, "spend some part of my idle hours at Lisbon and Arcos learning the language?" But it was too late now for self regret. The locust hours had been eaten.

She sensed a certain tension in the air. From time to time the Spanish woman shot questions at her husband, only to receive curt answers. He moved restlessly in and out of the premises, his footsteps making a beaten track to an observation post beyond the arch. His anxiety so impressed Harriet that once she proposed making the best of their resources, and with whatever difficulty, getting away. "I am quite willing to make the effort," said the Captain, "if only I could find a crutch." But when he began to raise himself he fell back with a half suppressed groan. He had attempted too much. Sometimes he spoke, though so faintly that she had to strain her utmost in order to catch what he said. She gathered that he had been sketching the lay of country on the left bank of the Carrion. He regretted that the plans were still in his saddlebags – these he should have sent on with Ramsden, but his head like a ringing pot, he had omitted to do so. "In the event," he said, "which I pray unlikely, of an enemy approach, take out the sketches and burn them. They will not give the French anything they do not know about their depositions, but that is not the point. They are best out of the way ... I am all in darkness," he concluded quickly, though (she noticed) he spoke without self-pity ...

"I will do as you say."

Harriet went to the door and looked out. The sky had darkened. Heavy with impending snow, she prayed that the fall would be sustained, obliterating all tracks to the farm. At home during drought they had often prayed for rain to revive the parched fields, a religious exercise to which she attached little importance. Now, with all the intensity of her being, she craved for Divine intervention. "Oh God," she muttered, "if it please Thee, make it to snow."

She returned to her post.

The first few flakes began to flicker in the dusk. She was more relieved now. Darkness and snow would draw a protective veil around the farm, give Tony time to collect his strength, and herself to speculate upon the next step. There was also a chance that Ramsden would lead back a rescue party – that must be allowed for ...

It was almost dark when the farmer, who had been absent for some time, entered, and with a savage word and a gesture that included every person in the kitchen, pointed across the fields. He worked his two fists before him in a rotary movement. Horsemen were coming!

Harriet's heart leapt joyously. Here was the expected deliverance; but a savage glitter in the Spaniard's eyes checked the impulse. Already he was helping the women to take down the few hams which hung from the ceiling, and as these were dropped through a trap in the floor, her worst fears were realised. The newcomers must be French. The farmer confirmed this impression by drawing a finger across his throat, and pointing from Captain Harte to a door built in the opposite wall leading, she guessed, to the stable. The English officer must be removed at once! She dropped to her knees beside the pallet. "Can you hear me?" she inquired tensely. "The French are coming, and we must move you to a place of safety. At once. You understand?"

The wounded man motioned with his hand, and to her inexpressible relief answered that he would try. He raised himself on his elbow, and as she grasped one arm, Sue was at hand to take the other. "It will have to be a peg-leg progress," gasped Harte. "We'll manage somehow," said Harriet; but it was not until the farmer came to their assistance, that they were able to bear the Captain through the inset door into darkness humid with the odour of animals and decaying straw. They staggered to a corner knee deep in fodder upon which they lowered their burden. "We shall cover you up," said Harriet, "but it may be only for a little time."

"I shan't wander," said the Captain dryly.

With quick afterthought the Spaniard hurried back bringing the jacket and sabre. When he returned for the saddlebags, Harriet followed, and recalling Tony's reference to the sketch plans, took them out. She motioned the farmer to conceal the bags, and cast a brief glance at the papers. The drawings were in pencil outlines of terrain, arrowed and annotated. She thrust these for the moment in her satchel, which hung from her waist-belt, and at once directed Sue to occupy the pallet vacated by the officer. "Disorder your hair and effect illness – by that means I will try to explain our presence here. Whatever happens," she cautioned, still improvising, "don't speak – groan if you like. Play dumb from sheer exhaustion!" For herself she intended to draw upon her rusty knowledge of French, acquired when as a girl she had taken lessons from an émigré in Richmond. She might manage to pass herself off as a much-travelled Spanish lady, though here another difficulty emerged. What if the soldiers invited her to translate their language into Spanish? It was too much to hope that she would be ignored completely.

There was not time to speculate further. The trampling of horses, the jingling of bridle chains, a barked word of command, sounded outside. She remembered the papers secreted in her satchel, and to her consternation saw that the fire had burned low, so that even if she were to try and destroy them some time would elapse before they burst into flame. Too late! Now men were stamping feet on the threshold. A fist hammered on the door. She could do nothing more than drop on the stool beside Sue, wondering if her hair was in order. She would have hated even in these circumstances not to be presentable. At all costs she must keep her head …

* * *

A dragoon officer in a slow plastered cloak and crested horse hair helmet, entered. A young sprig, his smooth almost girlish cheeks tanned by the weather were adorned by slight side-whiskers and a jaunty moustache; his uniform that of Lasalle's Dragoons. Taking in the kitchen with a sweeping glance, he drew off his gloves, at the same time addressing the farmer in halting Spanish.

He was followed by a second officer, a tough veteran of war, with an eagle's beak of a nose and moustaches much fiercer than those of the young man who preceded him. In spite of his age he was apparently junior in rank to the other, whom he addressed as Captain. He too eyed the room keenly, and there was no mistaking the flourish with which he indicated a ham, which the farmer had judiciously left suspended from the ceiling. Looking around quizzically he smiled, as if to infer that there were others if mine host cared to produce them. The two Frenchmen then fixed Harriet with a long and curious stare; but having other business to attend to did not attempt a conversation. The Lieutenant barked out an order, and the rest of the patrol, a dozen in all, entered. It was evident that the company intended to stay.

Soon the great kitchen enlivened as the fire was replenished and urged into flame. The troopers chattered noisily forming a solid barrier round the hearth, one broken only when the Spanish woman pushed her way unceremoniously through to drop eggs into a pan. Her husband, savagely intent, sliced away at the ham as though he would have been better pleased to have used the knife for a lethal purpose. Harriet noticed that the Spanish girls had disappeared, though where she had no means of knowing.

As the meat began to cook an air of well-being prevailed, but there were significant overtones. The two officers questioning the Spaniard closely evoked only sullen replies. After that they seated themselves at a table somewhat removed from the men. The Captain laid a pistol beside his platter; his sabre propped between his knees. The Lieutenant took no such precaution, but there was a rough and ready assurance in his every movement. Served at last, both men ate with relish, while covertly Harriet watched. So (she reflected in a detached moment) these were the "enemy", the "Johnny Crapaws" of vulgar English parlance! How lively they were in movement, in gesture; how self-assured and human. Yet they were to be feared, and somehow thwarted.

Up to this point Harriet had been almost ignored, but she had little doubt that her turn would come, perhaps (she felt) at the end of the meal. She murmured at times a few words to Sue – irrelevancies on dress and fashion – play-acting to simulate concern with the invalid, but for both women the minutes dragged leadenly. At last, stroking his moustache gently, the young officer strolled across, his manner galante. Unconsciously he imitated his General Basalle. He bowed and addressed her in his own language. "Madame is not of the household?"

"No, M'sieur." She smiled charmingly, hoping that her accent would not fail.

He glanced at her hair, her slender white hands, her rings. "A lady of quality."

"You may say so, M'sieur."

"To meet such a one," he continued, waving an expressive hand, "in a Spanish hovel is – somewhat unusual?"

"Yes, M'sieur."

"And so?" He cocked his head archly. As he awaited an explanation, his manners were perfect.

"I am a traveller," she explained, "but as you see, my maid indisposed, I halted for assistance."

He nodded sympathetically. "But you are far from the main road?" He asked the question smoothly, with a hint of banter, still stroking his moustache.

"We were confused by the snow."

He clicked a sympathetic tongue. "Ah, the demon weather! But perhaps we may be able to assist you. Where is it you would wish to go?"

"Alas, my maid is unable to move."

"Assuming that she were?"

Harriet thought swiftly, trying to recall place names on her little map. "We were travelling to Burgos."

He frowned. "A long way."

"Yes, M'sieur."

"And you hail from—?"

"Salamanca," she said reluctantly. Ought she to have replied, "Madrid?" She felt she was being drawn into a web.

"No?" His surprise seemed genuine. "Then you must have seen the English?"

"I have seen them, M'sieur."

"Are they in excellent condition?"

"Soldiers," she said lightly, "do not interest me."

"Madame!" He drew himself up reproachfully. At once she made amends. "I referred to soldiers in general – not in particular."

"That is better. May I see your maid? Is she pretty?" His hand stretched towards the alcove, when Sue now lay very still.

"M'sieur!" said Harriet sternly. His hand dropped.

He stood silent, his eyes upon her face. Then almost guilelessly he asked, "Where did you acquire your French?"

"I was taught—" She stopped, biting her lip.

"In a convent doubtless?"

"Of course."

"In England?"

It was no use. She might have claimed American nationality, but that implied further complication. She answered quietly, "Yes, M'sieur."

"Le Capitaine," he added.

"I am sorry – Le Capitaine."

So the cat was out of the bag! She looked away conscious of his intent gaze.

"You are indeed English?"

"Yes, M'sieur le Capitaine?"

"So I presumed."

Now that the lingering doubt had been removed, the young officer nodded gravely. At this point the grizzled veteran who had been standing within earshot came forward. "English!" he glared, his moustaches bristling ferociously. As the two Frenchmen confronted her, Harriet realised that here were two distinct national types – the first, a cadet of an aristocratical family, once émigré perhaps, but now conforming to the requirements of the parvenu Empire; the second, a relic of the Revolutionary armies, a man of Valmy, Wattignes, Jemappes, promoted from the ranks, accustomed to smelling out aristos by instinct. He continued the interrogation where the Captain had left off.

"Your name?" he said abruptly.

"Why should I tell you?"

He smiled darkly. "In case – shall we say, that misfortune befalls you. You would wish your friends to be informed?"

She took the point. "I am the wife of Colonel Foulkes," she said coldly.

"Of the English forces?"

She shrugged.

"Where is your husband?"

"That is my secret"

"And with reason," he said slyly. "It may be that you have no husband at all!"

"As you please." She turned away indifferently.

"I do please," he insisted. "It is my pleasure to believe that you are here for no innocent purpose."

"What other purpose?"

"To gather information."

"Do I look a spy?" she said proudly.

"I have seen ladies as fine who were."

In other circumstances she would have answered with contempt, but she held her peace. The young man turned upon his colleague sharply. "Lieutenant Garraud," he said firmly, "there is no occasion for insult." And as the other drew back with a disapproving snort, "The French do not make war on women." Turning to Harriet, the Captain bowed, "Perhaps you will honour us by taking a cup of wine?"

Harriet inclined her head. "With you," she said significantly, "it would be a real pleasure." She stiffened on her stool as she thought she detected a smothered cough beyond the door admitting to the stable, and relaxed as the two men before her seemed not to have noticed.

The Frenchmen moved away. So far, so good. "How much longer must I stay here?" whispered Sue. "I am almost stifled."

"Until the animals are fed," she said ironically. "Be still, my poor one," she said in louder tones, "you shall come to no harm."

Wine served, Harriet seated herself beside the Captain who introduced himself as Armand de Rolle. With nice discretion he made no reference to the late conversation, and markedly attentive tried to make amends for the boorish behaviour of his colleague. He inquired how she employed her time in Spain – sightseeing, of course? Was she interested in art, in literature or in music? The Lieutenant, whose teeth had been cut on revolutionary pamphlets and speeches, affected indifference and gazed stonily ahead. When she mentioned that a present she was reading *Tom Jones*, the Captain laughed loudly, explaining that "Poor Tom" had long been a favourite in France, but – he was impelled to inquire – Monsieur Jones a man of spirit; would not M. Fielding's hero have profited enormously by remaining with the army?

"Naturally," smiled Harriet.

It was, the Captain contended, a matter of *la gloire*. "Why descend," he argued, "to footpads and wayside *canelle*, when one may grapple bravely with the enemies of one's country?"

"In that case," rejoined Harriet, "poor Jones would have been plunged into civil conflict."

The Captain frowned. "How so?"

"With the Young Pretender?"

"Pretender?"

"The Chevalier St George," she explained.

"Ah – Prince Charles!"

She laughed at his quaint pronunciation, but the internal politics of Great Britain being somewhat outside his range of interest, the Frenchman shook a puzzled head. Immediately he changed the subject, beginning to speak in a wistful tone of his native Perigord, and of the ancestral chateau, now alas, a shell, a blackened ruin … The Lieutenant stirred uneasily. In his time, perhaps, he had flourished an incendiary brand …

Time passed. Harriet, making her excuses, contrived to share a portion of bread and meat with Sue, who for an invalid ate with uncommon relish. When the farmer brought them a candle, his eyes glinted strangely and he gave them a significant smile. He seemed elated, possibly because the Frenchmen were relatively well behaved.

A trooper relieved from vedette duty entered, and as the man made a hurried meal, the Captain more than once consulted his watch. He said something to the Lieutenant, who nodded curtly. Presently the younger officer strolled across. "I regret we must leave you Madame. Au revoir, and a safe journey whithersoever you may go."

She gave an intense sigh of relief, and nodded graciously.

"And you also, M'sieur le Capitaine." Chivalrously he was leaving her to her own devices. "I trust," she added, "that we shall meet again in happier circumstances."

"It is possible."

Erect, confident, he turned away to issue orders. In one minute – in a few minutes, they would ride away. She could hardly credit her good fortune, and that of the wounded man, who by now must be half suffocated in the straw. Troopers were already clustering round the doorway. But if the Captain had finished with her, the Lieutenant had not. After a few words with his superior, who stood doubtfully biting his lip, Carraud fixed her with a gaze so hostile that anxiety returned. He came up, his moustaches fiercer than ever. Reluctantly, the Captain followed, but it was the Lieutenant who spoke. "Madame," he said bluntly, "your story is doubtless true, and you maybe all that you say, but we have no proof of your identity, your good faith. Where are your papers?"

"In our country we do not carry papers."

"But you are not in your own country. You have a passport – a credential?"

"No."

The Lieutenant stared incredulously, and Harriet smiled faintly. It did not strike her that the Frenchman would demand a personal search, but she was soon to be enlightened. He pointed to the satchel at her waist. "We will begin with that," he said sharply. For her part she did not move, but looked appealingly at the embarrassed Captain who had acquiesced in his colleague's implacable sense of duty. "We should go, Carraud," the young man murmured, "it is of no consequence."

"Yes, we should go," repeated the other, "but the consequence here may be more important than we imagine. I must ask Madame to open." And again he indicated the satchel. She remembered now the sketches, which earlier she had transferred from the saddlebags to this very receptacle. What folly not to have disposed of them sooner! But the eyes of both men now upon her, it was to late. She opened the catch, and contriving with her thumb to hold the papers in place, shook the contents of the satchel in her lap – a few Spanish dollars, a comb, a small embroidered case containing needles, and a phial of opium pills. "There, M'sieur," she said. Gently, she snapped the catch, and with an air of complete indifference glanced aside. Carraud took up the needle case, opened it, and finding nothing but glinting steel, put it back. His keen eyes were however, fixed on the satchel, and he pointed a quivering finger. "What do I see?" he cried, and to Harriet's horror indicated a scrap of paper which had caught in the rim. "If you please," he said, smiling tightly. "Come now, we have no time to waste."

There was no alternative but to concede to the ogre what he wanted, and with a feeling that a cold stone had dropped to the pit of her stomach, she watched the two men bring their heads together over the incriminating sheet of paper, studying the diagrams closely. "Ah! cried Carraud triumphantly, "see, here is the river, and here our depositions—" He looked up, addressing her with sinister calm. "Is this your work?" Harriet hesitated. To assent would be fatal; to dissent would do Tony no harm. "It is not," she replied.

"Then by whom?"

She shook her head.

"You do not know!" he taunted. "No doubt the pixies contrived it – creatures of air – but that is not so. See!" He crackled the paper in his hands. "It has substance. It is mortal! You are certainly an enemy agent, the more loathsome for your fine manners. You must accompany us, Madame le Colonel."

"Impossible," she said weakly.

He grinned with relish, triumphant now that his early suspicions were justified. "You shall come all the same – fine ladies with your combs and frills and your delicate noses!" He spat in disgust. "Assume your cloak and we will bring round your horse."

She swayed a little. A sudden wave of sickness engulfed her.

Swooning will not avail you."

"I cannot forsake my maid," she muttered.

"That shall be accommodated," rejoined Carraud as he hauled a protesting Sue in the candlelight. "At the cart's tail, by the look of her! Pretty travellers! Ladies indeed!"

The young Captain still hovered indecisively. He was not devoid of sympathy for the Englishwoman, but in the face of the incriminating papers, he had by his earlier complaisance, been made to appear both dupe and fool. Now he could only murmur that judgment was difficult. But Carraud tapped the plans triumphantly. "Here is the judgment. What more do you ask? A million devils, we have waited long enough."

The Captain shrugged hopelessly. Had he been alone, the sketches would have been confiscated, and Harriet allowed to go free. Who in any case wished to be hindered by women, and in such weather! But Carraud's venom was overwhelming. Addressing Harriet, de Rolle said, "I assure you we will not try to make the journey arduous, and Marshall Soult is not without compassion—" But there was no conviction in his voice. Then with a resigned air he took up his pistols. "Prepare to leave – if you please."

It was the final irony. "Put on your cloak," she said to Sue, "they are taking us with them."

"Where?"

"God knows – to their camp, I suppose."

She was disturbed to see that the farm was now under guard, suspect no doubt, on her account. She wondered if she would be shot. As surrounded by curious, half-mocking faces, the two women awaited the next move, Harriet's thoughts moved freely. So far Tony had been saved, but what of his condition were she and the farmer to be taken away? At the same time she envisaged her husband, pale with anxiety interrogating orderlies, the town guard at the gates all to no purpose. If troopers were to enter the stable for the mounts, would they make another captive? The thought appalled her.

She resigned herself to the inevitable; watched as the troopers donned their cloaks. She thought nothing in that period of suspended time of a muffled cry that came from outside, but which made the officers glance sharply at each other. A scuffle followed, a stifled groan. Then, before either Captain or Lieutenant could make a movement, the door was flung violently open and a gust of wind brought snow across the floor. Swarthy Spanish faces and musket barrels crowded the threshold, and a voice in bad French cried, "you are lost – drop your weapons!"

For two or three seconds silence reigned. The surprise was complete, the more so as the French in the Peninsular were at this stage not accustomed to meeting peasants in arms. Later, it was to become a commonplace of Spanish resistance, savage and all pervading.

With a savage curse, Carraud was the first to move. He drew his sabre, but before the weapon cleared the scabbard, a shot rang out and he fell groaning, doubled on the flags. Harriet could see through the acrid smoke, which swept inwards that De Rolle, had a pistol in his hand; but a second shot crashed, and the young man staggered backwards clutching at his shoulder, still eyeing the doorway incredulously. Spaniards pushed into the room with the menace of their weapons herding the dragoons like cattle into the farthest corner. Before this overwhelming strength the Frenchmen began to throw down their weapons. The farmer, now released was smiling broadly. Harriet could hardly believe her own good fortune.

The chief of the guerilleros touching the body of the prostrate Carraud disdainfully with his foot, strode into the centre of the room. In his sugar-loaf hat, striped cloak and leathern gaiters, he dominated the scene. Shaking snow from his shoulders he addressed the farmer familiarly by name, and with a smile indicated one of the daughters, who with bedraggled skirts appeared to have accompanied the band. Harriet wondered if she had acted as messenger.

After the Frenchmen had been tied up effectively, the chief motioned in the direction of the two Englishwomen. Who were they? Did they belong to the French? When the farmer explained, the Spaniard's face relaxed. "Ingleses!" he exclaimed, clapping a hand over his heart. "Gomez a friend, damme!" The only English he knew, it was amply sufficient. Harriet, hovering between laughter and tears, nodded vigorously. "Yes – yes, we are all friends!" She noticed that the chief's eyes seldom left his prisoners, but when she pointed in what she believed to be the right direction and cried, "Sahagun – Sahagun!" he inclined his head comprehendingly. Turning to the farmer she indicated that Tony was not to be forgotten, but she need not have been anxious, for the farmer eager to be rid of his guests, as they were to depart was already moving towards the stable door. In a short time the half bewildered Tony was brought from his hiding place and given a restorative.

With many hands to assist they were soon mounted and in movement; the Captain hoisted on Sue's mule being upheld by a couple of Spaniards, while the grey took a double load. Guerilleros mounted the captured horses, with the exception of one, which bore the inanimate body of Carraud. The rest of the hapless captives with pinioned arms were hitched to a stout rope and dragged ruthlessly along. The young Captain came last. As he was hustled past Harriet he murmured ironically, "*Fin de la guerre!*" The end indeed! A bitter smile on his face he was dragged after his men. Snow continued to fall. Soon all tracks would be obliterated …

Mile after mile through the flurried darkness the motley band trailed towards Sahagun, where the convent bell struck ten as they hammered on the gates. But only the Englishwomen and the disabled captain passed through. The Spaniards and their captives wheeled off to an unknown destination. Harriet and Sue left in charge of Tony hardly noticed their departure. A few whispered words from Gomez and the darkness swallowed them.

Harriet saw Tony safely through the doors of the convent hospital where an orderly undertook to arrange for a surgeon. With a start she remembered the survey sketches, but these had been lost for good. Carraud had stuffed them in his pocket, but where was the unfortunate relic of Valmy and Wattignes now?

She returned to their lodging off the plaza, hammering for a long time on the door before being admitted. The ice-cold room was as they had left it – quite empty. Harriet had expected to find – she knew not quite what – an orderly instructed to await and report her return? – an anxious husband, pale as the avenging angel himself, pacing the board? Instead a neatly folded note lay on the table. She took it up and in her husband's writing read—

"This by the hand of Pt. Raddock. Be prepared to move out at any moment – I mean in respect to everything, your baggage, etc. I trust you find Sahagun sufficiently interesting."

Harriet dropped the note and laughed. "Sufficiently interesting!" she repeated. She continued to laugh helplessly, hysterically, all the pent-up anxiety of the last few hours released in spasms of emotion. "It is too – too much!" she gasped, and went off again, "What is it, Ma'm?" inquired Sue, who watched her mistress with increasing wonder for she had not read the note. "Oh dear!" choked Harriet, "he trusts – he trusts!—" Again the laughter, until unable to resist the infection, Sue began laughing too. The old woman of the house overhearing the disturbance thrust her head through the door, only to be motioned away. "He trusts! He trusts!" gasped Harriet more weakly. On the edge of nervous prostration, she stopped as suddenly as she had begun, and sank limply to a chair. Amazingly she had not been missed, so dispensable was she to the life of the regiment …

At the same time she had no regrets. Tony had been saved, she felt, by her intervention, although the affray would have taken place had she not been present ... For a long time she could not sleep turning over in her mind snatches of conversation, the harsh phrases of Carraud, the deadly glances of the Spaniards, the bewildered faces of the dragoons. The features of the young and friendly French Captain rose before her. What had happened to him and his unfortunate companions? She decided that when daylight came she would seek him out, and perhaps with some little service alleviate his wretched plight.

Dawn filtered in grey and frost-laden. The two women arose, and after breakfast sallied out. At the infirmary Harriet learned to her relief that Tony's injuries had been attended to. She did not attempt to see him, but went back to the square to make inquiry about the prisoners taken at the farm. The officer in charge of the detention cellars stared at her blankly. No overnight prisoners had been brought in. When she explained that the French officer in whom she was interested had been captive in the hands of the guerilleros, she was informed that the gentleman in question would be damned lucky to finish with a bullet in his head. "The Spaniards," observed her mentor with crushing understatement, "do not like the French!"

She had no answer to make, and left sadly. As for her own position, the least said the soonest mended. The Colonel's man finding her absent, would assume that she was somewhere in the town and report accordingly. No British troops had been employed to succour her. She wondered if Ramsden had managed to reach his headquarters. She could not know that the hapless lad lay still and silent on the bank of the stream they had crossed the previous afternoon ...

CHAPTER XIV

Though the impending action kept Colonel Foulkes on stretch, Harriet had not been absent from his mind, thus the alerting message delivered by Harker.

That gentleman nothing loath for a diversion, requisitioned a mule and set out for Sahagun. Throughout the whole army no man yearned less for battle than the Colonel's servant. The campaign had been a real disappointment; the buttered words of the recruiting sergeant – "Fame and fortune, high living and rich booty" – were as ashes in his mouth. Apart from the two guineas he had collected from the Colonel through the pistol trick – of which only a shilling remained – his pockets were as empty now as when he had landed in Portugal. Pay was in arrears. His acquisitive honour had been touched. "God rot it," he grunted, "the game ain't worth the candle!"

He took a pull at a flask of the Colonel's wine, and felt a little better. "Not much of a place," he thought, as he came within sight of the town walls. There was however, the chance of a bite and sup at Mrs Foulkes, after which he would take his time and look around a bit.

He found the house beside the convent without difficulty. When the little maid opened to his knock, and he flourished the note crying, "Dona Inglese," the girl stammered incoherently. A passing priest stopped, smiling. "I have a little English," he said, "tell me your purpose and I may be able to assist you."

The priest obliged, and the girl allowed Harker to enter. Ushered into Mrs Foulkes' room and finding it empty, he decided not only to take his ease, but to call for drinks on the house. He smiled endearingly at the girl, pointed to his mouth and tilting an invisible bottle, said, "Vino – pronto!" She stared suspiciously and withdrew; a little later he could hear her voice raised in altercation with that of an elderly person downstairs. He waited impatiently, chafing the cold from his hands. "Here we come," he grimaced, "risking life and limb to rescue such from the heathen French, and what happens – they grumble at a sup of wine." He laid the note on the table.

He gave the room a quick look over, but what he saw – a table, three chairs, a bed, a chest, and a few pock-marked engravings on the walls – brought a derisive curl to his lips. He lifted the lid of the chest, but as this contained nothing but an old dress and a rusty lamp, he shut it again. He picked up a novel which had been left on the table, flicked over a page or two, and thrust it aside …

The girl entered with a pewter jug, and went away. There was to be wine after all. Seating himself, Harker toasted the absent women and drank greedily. He opened the book again, but being unable to decipher more than a word or two, closed it noting that the girl had shut the door behind her, he tip-toed over and brought it open a couple of inches, the better to hear approaching footsteps.

He continued his examination of the room. The only objects of interest now were female clothes folded on the bed, and baggage dumped in a corner. As Harker regarded the latter he wondered what articles of value this might contain. The Foulkes' were well to do. No doubt of that. there would be brooches, rings, bracelets, money perhaps. He had often noticed rings on the fingers of the Colonel's lady, and since these were changed from time to time a jewel case there must be. What place more likely than the bottom of a valise? Here – a certain sign that he was thinking deeply – Harker stroked his nose. "This," he breathed, "calls for inquiry."

He drank again, and nodded sagely. "In and out, pack and unpack, here today and gone tomorrow – that's the way it goes." In circumstances of constant removal, a missing ring would never be noticed, and even if it were Mrs Foulkes would probably lay it to her own carelessness, or possibly to light-fingered people at the billet. On the march again, you couldn't turn an army back to find a ring. The more he considered the prospect, the more assured he felt that a safe prig could be managed.

He bent over the valises, unbuckled the strap of the larger for there were two, and slid his hand gently among the tightly packed contents taking care not to disturb the lay of the clothes. What a mort of lumber the women carried! He worked his way to the bottom, and at length whistled. His luck was in. His fingers touched a flat ebony case. "Some people," he grinned, "go asking for trouble."

He took out the case and opened the pearl inlay lid. Eight or nine rings gleamed before his eyes, but these were intermixed with silver chains, bracelets and cameo brooches, a medley so confused that a person needing to check the contents would be compelled to empty the whole box. As he viewed the collection, a further possibility entered his mind, and his grin widened. Since Salamanca the red haired wench had treated him with undisguised contempt. Why not in taking one ring, secrete another in Sue Thompson's own baggage, so that if Mrs Foulkes were to discover her loss a search of immediate equipment would start a false trail? Not only so, but the girl herself would "suck the mop". "That ud larn her," he thought. He was amazed almost, by his own ingenuity. At the same time the ring in his own possession could be turned into cool cash later.

Carefully, he selected two rings, one set with a cluster of diamonds which he dropped in his pouch, and the other—? He paused listening. Steps sounded on the stairs. It was the maid returning. "Of all the devils in hell!"

he breathed. Darting to the table he seized the empty pewter jug, and block-ing the doorway so that it was impossible for her to see into the room, thrust the receptacle into her hands. He waved her away, and to his profound relief she obeyed. Harker waited until her footsteps had died away, then, "Pronto lad!" he exclaimed. Nimbly he took the second ring set with a curiously set ruby and thrust it to the bottom of a holdall, which he guessed belonged to Sue. This accomplished, he stood listening. Was that a faint familiar voice from the square? Perspiration broke out on his brow. He dumped the valise and holdall in their original positions. It was time to go.

Placing the note from the Colonel in the centre of the table, he tiptoed to the door. From somewhere near the bottom of the staircase came the inces-sant clatter of a pan. "That girl," he murmured, "springs from the gypsies. Same everywhere. Not to be trusted." He let himself out.

Arriving at camp he reported that Mrs Foulkes was taking her pleasure in town ...

* * *

When darkness fell, Foulkes decided to visit one or two of his outlying pick-ets. For the first time his men were, so to speak, within bayonet length of the enemy, and from long experience he knew how apprehensive especially by night a young soldier could become; a swaying bush so easily conjured up a horseman, a gnarled branch a sharpshooter. Nerves might be frayed by the incessant rustling of leaves ...

Foulkes decided to go alone. Before setting out he ate frugally of biscuit and meat, and placed a flask of rum in his pouch. A nip would be useful later.

He left the farm in a tolerable good humour whistling a bar or two of *Malbrook sen vat guerre*. He had no difficulty in following the farm track to a ford which had been marked for observation. The road ran black and stark into a haze of snow. At times the gaunt arms of trees reached towards him. More than once had he not been careful, he would have been unhorsed. Borne on the wind, he heard (he thought) a long-drawn howl – that of a wolf perhaps, but since he carried pistols he was in no way perturbed. As he approached the top of the rise, he tried to envisage the lay of the river bank as he had reconnoitred it by daylight, the pronounced loop where one might easily be surprised.

He reached the top and with close rein cautiously descended the slope. his mount, he knew, was surefooted, but in these conditions he was taking no chances. What a savage irony it would be if he were to be disabled before a shot had been fired. His eyes, by now adjusted to the darkness, managed – though only just – to trace the outline of the farther bank. No surprise attack in such weather. Still, one could never be certain ...

At the bottom, challenged by Private Higgenson, he gave the countersign.

The sentry, who had built for himself a rough shelter of brushwood in the crevice of a rock, was numb with cold. When Higgenson half-apologised for the shelter, Foulkes smiled. "All that matters," he said, "is that you keep your eyes skinned. Have you heard them challenged on the other side -*qui vive*, or any sound like that?"

"No," Higgenson replied, "nobbut once a clatter o' stones. The trees squeak a surprising amount, sir. Listen!"

Foulkes cocked his head towards the bare boughs creaking in the wind, and laughed. "I'm afraid we can't do much about that," he remarked, as he brought his horse to the water's edge and watched the dark swirl disappearing into the night. He returned to Higgenson, and gave him a nip from the flask. "You'll be relieved ere long. Keep your limbs in motion."

The man saluted. "If I might take a great liberty, sir?"

"What is it?" Foulkes reached for his flask again, expecting a request for more rum.

"May I, with due respect, inquire what your Christian name might be?"

"My name?" There was no hint of impertinence in Higgenson's voice.

"Begging your pardon, sir, my wife is expecting again, and we thought that if it were a boy – we call to mind you said you would be father to us all – we would christen him the name of the Colonel of the Regiment, sir."

So that was it! Foulkes drew a surprised breath in the darkness.

"Begging your pardon, sir," said Higgenson.

"No need to," said Foulkes heartily. "I should take it as a great compliment. Name the boy Percy, and I'll give you a guinea to wash his head."

"Thank you, sir."

Foulkes chuckled. "That I take it, would make me the lad's godfather!"

He was still smiling as he rode on. He could hear that Higgenson had set down his musket, and was thrashing his arms on his sides to restore circulation. It was a cold, lonely vigil …

Picking his way carefully along the bank, Foulkes was soon challenged again, this time by a young soldier named Bates, who had been posted at a point when he might easily have been overrun. Foulkes said nothing as again he took out his flask and gave the man a swallow. Interrogated, Bates answered only in monosyllables. "The trees—" he muttered, "the trees—"

"What of the trees?"

"They are allus shifting."

"That is as may be," said Foulkes dryly, "but don't challenge until they begin walking towards you. Things might be a good deal worse, you know. Now if it were fog—" And he related how, as a young subaltern on active service in Holland he had walked through a very thick mist straight into the enemy's lines. "How would you have liked that?"

"Shouldn't have liked it at all, sir."

"No more did I, but I didn't lose my wits. I was cloaked, and since as we say, all cats are grey in the dark, I mumbled a few words of French and strolled back the way I had come. It was as simple as that. Mark you, I was lucky. Now you had better fall back a little. If you were to see where you stand by daylight, you'd be surprised. Good night."

Foulkes sighed as he passed on. The old story – night phantoms, fear of the unknown. But, of course, they would harden.

Jenks, the third sentry, had with some ingenuity, arranged before his position at a distance of perhaps twenty yards a trip barrier of rope, dead boughs and precariously balanced stones. "They'll none surprise me, sir," he boasted. "A step into that lot, and down Johnny Crapaw comes."

"What if you are taken in the rear?" asked Foulkes.

"I'll watch out."

The man was overconfident. As the Colonel drew away he heard from behind, a whistled tune. He returned. "Are you asking for a pot-shot?" he said sternly.

"I am sorry, sir."

"Keep your whistling for the camp-fire."

"Yes, sir."

"Remember. Good night."

Hardly conscious of the wind that whipped his numbed cheeks, Foulkes climbed the bank and halted for a few minutes facing directly east. He stared intently as though by an act of will he would pierce the flurried darkness. Across the river lay the traditional enemy – Soult and his gaudy generals; masses of blue-coated infantry, and cavalry attired in all the colours of the rainbow. Foulkes had not seen the French at close quarters since Maida, now three years ago. They had courage enough, but he reckoned that when they did attack, they would follow their usual tactics: a screen of tirailleurs darting about like jack rabbits, followed by solid columns of infantry waving shakoes and shouting like mad for the Emperor. Thus they had broken Austrian, German and Russian formations. His own men would confront them in line, and let loose volleys to bring them to a stop. He wondered what artillery Soult had. The French were renowned gunners …

It was time to turn in, for his men were to march at dawn or as soon after as may be. As he resumed his journey to headquarters he remembered the conversation with Higgenson, and slapped his thigh good humouredly. "Damme!" he chuckled, "I'll warrant he'd never have asked that of Pomeroy. Good lad!"

But the last words were addressed to his surefooted horse …

* * *

"By your leave, Sir John."

To the flickering light of flambeaux Moore prepared to mount, but as an aide hurried across the courtyard towards him, he drew off his gauntlets and waited for the officer to come up. "A Spanish courier to see you immediately, sir – intimates he is from the Marquis la Romana."

"Let him come forward."

The Spaniard, travel-weary, caked to the eyes in mud, doffed his hat and presented a dispatch. Moore took the somewhat crumpled, but otherwise intact paper, called for a torch in attendance, and read where he stood. "Your Excellency (wrote Romana) I have the honour to inform you from agents in whom I have every confidence that all the French forces in the direction of the Escurial have turned northwards and are now crossing the Guadarrama."

Moore frowned. The information conveyed by the Marquis meant that Napoleon at the head of sixty – perhaps eighty thousand sabres and bayonets was marching to overwhelm him. The news confirmed rumours brought in during the last few days by muleteers and other travellers, that much food and forage had been ordered to be collected by the enemy in the villages west of Palencia. So that was the truth of it – an all out drive by the Emperor himself. The bubble had indeed burst! ...

That hour Moore countermanded all orders to advance. If Hope's division and Alten's brigade had gone forward, they were to be stopped. Couriers swung into the saddle, clattered through the forecourt and vanished in the night. For every man it meant retreat.

The order checked columns already preparing to cross the Carrion bridge. As they turned about face men threw down their muskets in disgust. So this was the end of all their hopeful, their heroic marching – to run like rabbits before the French! But the weapons were picked up, and sullenly the troops returned to the high road. Orders were orders, and had to be obeyed. The general informed his senior officers that he wished to be at least two marches ahead of the enemy ...

* * *

It was to this setting of clouded departure that Mrs Foulkes and Sue rejoined the regiment – Harriet haunted incessantly by the bloodstained coverings of Tony's face. What horror lay behind that bandage? Every aspect of the overnight adventure lingered like a nightmare. Ought she to inform her husband of the pass in which they had found themselves? Recalling his attitude at Salamanca, she decided not. Again, he might suspect collusion. Better let sleeping dogs lie.

Before leaving the town she had called at the convent hospital and with mingled feelings of relief and disappointment learned that Captain Harte, accompanied by his servant, had already left for Benevente en route for the coast. Thus she was assured of his relative safety. But what of the grievous sabre stroke? The surgeon whom she interviewed, considered that with time and patience, one eye might be saved – more he would not venture. And with this information Harriet came away.

Then – though this was quite a separate problem – she had discovered the loss of her rings. Ordinarily she did not dwell upon her possessions, but recalling her lengthy absence from the house, coupled with a profound distrust of the old woman its owner, she decided to check her valuables. Two rings had certainly disappeared. "I recall perfectly," she said to Sue, "taking the diamond in my hand yesterday. I considered whether or no to put it on."

"Perhaps it fell to the floor?" suggested Sue artlessly.

"As if one wouldn't have noticed," snapped Harriet scornfully. She turned on her maid with an impulsive, "You haven't seen it?"

Sue answered sharply, "You may be quite sure that I have not!"

The marked indignation in the girl's voice checked that line of inquiry; and immediately both women began a thorough search of the room, moving furniture, running fingers along the cracks of floor-boards, and making such a commotion that the old lady herself appeared blinking and mumbling in the doorway. When Harriet pointed to a ring on her own finger, and with much dumb-show opened her jewel case indicating loss, she would have done well not to involve the old woman in her miming. The immediate effect was startling. The old crone, her gap-toothed mouth working convulsively, literally danced with rage. Extending her claws, her black eyes darting venom, she launched into a torrent of invective. She had no English, but the meaning was clear enough. Fixing Harriet with a basilisk stare, she made a movement with her arms as though she would fling her guests baggage and all, into the square. Drawing herself to her full height, she spat, and bounced out slamming the door behind her. Her shrill voice trailed away to the distant kitchen, where she could be heard banging pots and pans and chattering incessantly. Harriet, somewhat shaken by the old woman's frenzy, sank upon the bed. "What do you make of that?" she asked weakly.

"I think she knows nothing of the matter."

"If she be not play-acting," said Harriet significantly. "What other explanation is there?"

"I don't think the girl of the house would interfere with our baggage," said Sue, "she seems such a frightened little thing."

"Then in the name of heaven?"

Sue stood pensively for a moment or two; then she said quite deliberately, "The Colonel's servant brought a note."

"What of that?" asked Harriet impatiently. "We have no reason to suspect Raddock."

Sue did not answer.

"Well – have we?" persisted Harriet.

The girl eyed her mistress gravely. Ought she to speak straightly and reveal all that she knew of Harker and his past? She said reluctantly, "'T'is well, Ma'm, that you think so."

Harriet snapped to the lid of the case. "What do you infer by that? The Colonel thinks highly of him, and he has given me no cause for complaint – indeed, the reverse."

"That is, Ma'm, because you know so little of him. He is a wicked man."

"Pooh!" said Harriet scornfully. "I suppose he has attempted to kiss you!"

Sue made no reply. She began to replace the contents of the large valise.

"Really," continued Harriet reproachfully, "you lay charge without substantiating anything. What have you against Raddock?"

This, the girl felt, must be the moment of revelation. She faced her mistress squarely. "I had not intended speaking of him, Ma'm, it being my own private affair, but now I feel I must. His true name is not Raddock, but Harker, and I believe him to be a scoundrel."

"Well?"

So Sue braced herself to relate in outline all she knew of Harker's character, including his share in her brother's downfall. "You see now, Ma'm, why I suspect that he has it in him to have taken the rings, and I trust that what I have related will make no difference in your regard for me."

Harriet considered her servant thoughtfully. "Why should it? I shall always remember how faithful you were yesterday. I shall certainly speak to the Colonel about this fellow ..."

* * *

When Harriet persisted. "This, Colonel Foulkes, is a matter concerning the credit of the regiment. In a word, I have been robbed."

"Robbed? Robbed?" he repeated in a puzzled tone.

She related the loss of her rings.

"We will go inside," he said, and took snuff testily as he walked, at the same time wondering how much the loss had been due to her own carelessness. "You should be more watchful at your billet," he grumbled. "You know how light-fingered some of these Spaniards are."

"I don't lay this loss to the natives," she said.

"To whom then?"

"Raddock came to my lodgings yesterday."

"Certainly, at my orders."

"I suspect he has taken the rings. Thompson apparently knows the man by past reputation. She informs me that not only is Raddock an assumed name, but there are other matters such to his discredit."

"I have found him satisfactory."

"None the less I insist that he be searched."

Foulkes' brow wrinkled. "Horse, foot and guns," he thought, "a whole army in motion, and she dwells upon her finger rings!" Realising however he would have no peace unless he consented," I am heavily engaged," he growled, "but – very well …" And he ordered Harker to be brought in.

A model of formal behaviour, his servant stood to attention and saluted. "Trouble!" he thought, as he scanned the faces of the two women, and a tremor ran down his spine for their presence presupposed an accusation. Like many another of this kind to whom "luck" was a prime element in life, Harker had a certain strain of superstition in his make-up. That morning the scar on this hand had turned from blue to black. This may have been due to the icy weather, but it was queer all the same. Worst of all the ring was still in his possession. More than once he had considered discarding the bauble – a clod of upturned earth, a jab with his boot heel, and the thing would have disappeared forever; but after returning from Sahagun he had been tied up with this and that, always under the Colonel's eye so that disposal of his booty became difficult.

Besides the ring represented cash, and for this reason alone he was unwilling to part. He had gambled on Mrs Foulkes' negligence; now the trick he had contrived in the heat of wine would have to be faced in sober earnest. At present, the accursed ring, wrapped in wadding, was tucked in a corner of his cartouche box. If search were made – what then? His mind darted from one plausible explanation to another. Had the second ring been found in the girl's hold-all?

Colonel Foulkes cleared his throat. "Private Raddock," he said quietly, "Mrs Foulkes, has lost a couple of valuable rings. Do you know anything about them?"

"No, sir." The private's voice rang with assurance. So the ring in Sue Thompson's carrier had not been discovered.

"Not at all?"

"Never seen anything I know, sir, belonging to Mrs Foulkes, a lady who has my greatest respect."

"We can dispense with compliments. You were in her lodgings yesterday?"

"Only because you sent me, sir."

"I know. But you went – alone?"

"Yes, sir. Left the letter, sir – in and out, you might say. Mrs Foulkes being absent, I put the letter on the table."

"Two rings," continued Foulkes, " are missing from Mrs Foulkes' valise. The people of the house know nothing. You are the only other person involved."

Harker threw out his chest. "No, sir."

"What?"

"If I may make so bold, sir, there was another person in contact with your good lady."

"Explain yourself," said Foulkes wearily.

"It would be much against my inclination, sir."

"Don't read me riddles man! We haven't all day."

"I refer to the girl in Mrs Foulkes' employment, sir." Harker nodded in the direction of Sue, who gasped with indignation. "Though I have to say so, sir, she is not to be trusted. If you ask her – and let her but speak the truth – she will tell you that her family is of bad reputation her own brother a convict."

"Accusations! – counter accusations!" said Foulkes testily. Outside he could hear Serjeant Major Stubbs bellowing out orders, the steady tramping of feet, the creaking of wheels. "One thing at a time. Leave the girl aside for a moment, since you are the accused." He called for Stubbs, and Stubbs brought a corporal.

Harker flushed. God damn the women, and the younger one in particular, for the suggestion of his guilt could only have come from her. There was still a chance that the corporal of the guard, searching, would concentrate only on the knapsack. As this was unstrapped, Harker prayed that his luck would hold out.

"Spread the contents of the knapsack on the table," ordered Foulkes, the rest of an infantryman's equipment. Obligingly, the prisoner stepped forward to assist, but when Foulkes sternly waved him back, the accused with a resigned, injured look obeyed. The corporal brought to light the last item, a *New Testament*.

"My Bible, sir," explained Harker unctuously. He had picked up the little volume on the camping ground at Paco d'Arcos, and retained it. You never knew when such a work might come in handy, perhaps for swearing oaths.

The corporal shook the pages of the *Testament*. "Nothing here, sir."

"May I suggest, humbly, that it is the maid's turn now, sir?" intervened Harker.

"Don't be impertinent, Raddock, "rapped Foulkes. "Examine his shako, corporal, and then turn out his pockets."

But the shako was empty, and the pockets produced only a clasp knife, some small change, and oddly enough a combined silver fork and spoon, a curiously valuable article for a private to possess. There was no ring.

"That's all, sir," said the Corporal.

"You see." The Colonel turned to his wife reproachfully, and Harker heaved a profound sigh of relief, feeling that perhaps the worst was over. His heart still pounded heavily.

"The cartridge pouch, sir?"

"You may as well," muttered Foulkes tiredly. So much to be done outside, and little time in which to do it!

Harker swallowed hard against his leathern stock. His temples throbbed. He saw the Corporal slip a hand into the pouch and run his fingers loosely through the contents. "Bring everything out," said Foulkes.

One handful of cartridges after another spilled on the table – still no ring.

Was it possible that he would tide over; that the ring snug in a pinched corner would elude the question fingers of the Corporal? Harker reached out towards the pouch to retrieve it. "Keep your place!" said Foulkes.

"That's all, sir," said the Corporal, taking out the last cartridge. He allowed it to drop from his fingers and stood awaiting further orders; but the Colonel was occupied with the little heap of ammunition before him. "There cannot be anything like sixty cartridges here," he growled, making a rough count. "Are there no more?" The Corporal ran his hand carefully around the inside of the pouch again, and this time, produced a piece of wadding, "Only this, sir. I didn't think it of importance."

With a swift movement Harriet took it from the man's fingers, and produced the ring. "We were not mistaken," she cried triumphantly. "Here is my property!" She held it aloft. The diamond flashed in the grey morning light.

Foulkes turned grimly to Harker. "Altogether red-handed! What have you to say?"

"Only that I found it, sir."

"Found it?" Foulkes repeated incredulously.

"Yes, sir," continued Harker glibly. "I picked it up just outside the lodgings in question after I had tied up my mule – thought it had been dropped by some passer-by. If you tell me, sir, that the said ring belongs to Mrs Foulkes, you could knock me down with a feather."

Foulkes was silent. If the man lied, his effrontery was amazing. "Why," he asked, "with the knowledge that you held this ring, did you not mention the matter at the outset?"

"I was fearful lest I might seem guilty, sir."

The Colonel gave Harker a prolonged stare, while Harriet slipped the ring on her finger. "It is just possible that the ring may have been dropped," said Foulkes sternly, "but that is not the question uppermost in my mind." He turned to the Corporal. "Count this man's cartridges carefully."

The Corporal obeyed. "Only forty two, sir," he said at length.

"Forty two!" repeated Foulkes darkly, "when there should have been sixty."

"Forty two is the count, sir."

"Sergeant Major," said Foulkes, indicating the culprit, "this man carries deficient ammunition. Take him away, and book him. I will pass sentence at a more convenient time."

"But, sir—" pleaded Harker, about to point out how faithfully he had served the Colonel, but he was cut short by a flash of cold anger on the part of the commanding officer. Deficient ammunition in the face of the enemy! Away with him, and please find me another servant, one trustworthy in domestic matters, and above all, a competent soldier."

"Hi will do my best, sir," said Stubbs.

Harriet stifled an impatient exclamation. It would seem that cartridge deficiency counted a good deal more than the stolen ring.

Harker was marched away, and Foulkes rose to his feet. "So much for that," he said hooking up his cloak. "You say you lost two rings, Mrs Foulkes, and there was some reference to the girl. Hadn't we better examine Thompson's baggage?"

Sue flushed, looking down at her holdall, silently.

"Of course," said Harriet smoothly. "I will do it myself."

She took the bag from Sue and began turning over the contents. Presently she looked up. "Nothing there," she remarked.

"Then we can do no more," said Foulkes, "we have spent enough time over this business already."

"The man was lying," said Harriet.

"I agree, but his punishment must wait. You have probably made a mistake about the second ring, or possibly lost it yourself. Now we are about to march, and I must remind you that you should be ready too." He joined the adjutant who hovered in the doorway, and the two women went off to join the Baggage Master.

When they were quite alone, Harriet pointed to Sue's holdall. "Feel," she said, "in the right hand bottom corner, and tell me what you find."

Somewhat puzzled Sue obeyed. At last her groping fingers encountered a ring. She brought it out into the light staring at her mistress uncomprehendingly. "Oh, Mrs Foulkes, Ma'm" – was all she was able to stammer. Harriet, unperturbed, took the ring and slipped it on her finger. "Don't vex yourself unnecessarily," she said with a faint smile, "'tis as plain as a pike-staff that everything in this little drama was Raddock's doing. As I searched now my fingers touched the ring, but while (I reflected) you could not have placed the diamond in his knapsack, he had ample opportunity of concealing the ruby in your bag. I kept silence before the Colonel because we have embarrassments enough."

"I am much obliged to you, Ma'm," said Sue gratefully.

"And I am under great obligation to you," rejoined Harriet. "It is not necessary for the men to know everything."

CHAPTER XV

Thoroughly disgruntled with the routine baking and packing of biscuit, Assistant Deputy Commissary Harry Simms dreed his weird in Zamora.

The golden-brown bread of the region was of good quality, and the monastery in which it was collected stacked almost to the roof, but (Simms reflected) man did not live by bread alone. He hated the constriction of the town – above all, continued to nourish a sense of the injustice by which he had been relegated to this backwater. It was the thorn in the flesh, the worm in the bud, of his daily existence. A whipping boy for a domestic imbroglio! How tragically absurd!

Yet what could one do? In his own mind he had no doubt at all that Harker had been involved in the loss of the Colonel's pistols, and that the affair had touched off all Foulkes' latent animosity. As, after the day's work Simms sat in the café off the main square listening to the twanging of strings and the clicking of castanets, he tried to dismiss from his mind the whole sorry business, but the more he tried to forget, the more he remembered. He wished that he had never cast eyes on Mrs Foulkes and listened to her blandishments. She was little better than a courtesan, using others heartlessly for her own ends. Up to a point Foulkes was to be pitied, but Simms' compassion on that score soon evaporated. To every man his cross, and Mrs Foulkes was that of the Colonel.

By contrast it was pleasant to ruminate upon Susan Thompson. He liked to remember that she had thought him worthy of sharing her troubles. There were moments when he could see himself united with her, but the mood dissolved as he considered his present situation. They had still to face the worst hazards of the campaign, when a hundred misadventures might bring the fond relationship to a close. One might end up in a French prison, a possibility brought sharply to Simms' notice on seeing his first enemy captive, a Frenchman of early middle age clad in a blue uniform faced with red, and worsted epaulettes of the same colour. In the absence of boots – which had evidentially been taken from him – the prisoner's feet were bare and bleeding. A warrior of Jena, of Austerlitz, he was lucky to be alive at all, as surrounded by a hedge of British bayonets he was hurried through a crowd of cursing Spaniards to the town jail for interrogation ... No (Simms concluded) the hazards of war were too exacting to consider marriage ...

In Zamora, café gossip fed by rumour, was far from reassuring. The French were now across the Salamanca road, and communications with

Lisbon cut. Simms therefore was not surprised when orders came that the British were to evacuate the town and retire on Benevente, taking all possible biscuit with them; but on no account were they to leave until the enemy appeared within a mile of the walls.

When the Commissaries received this order they swore roundly. "One would assume," cried MaTavish, Simms' colleague, "that headquarters had never seen a bullock train in their lives. What do they take us for – steeplechasers? Both agreed that they must give themselves a more reasonable margin of time, and without delay brought together the bakers for immediate payment of three piastres each. "It shall not be said that we bilked our friends," commented McTavish, "however hurriedly we say farewell."

The Commissaries were wise. The last carts had just been loaded when a member of the Junta rushed in announcing that French patrols were within three miles of the town, and that they (the Spaniards) in order to allow more time for the British to escape intended to close the gate and parley with the enemy as long as possible. McTavish clapped the Spaniard on the shoulder. "Dinna look so dejected, man," he said, "we shall be back one day!" The representative of the Junta frowned. The French, he knew, would fall on the town like locusts, taking all things without payment. It was a bitter moment.

The Train, comprising a dozen carts set out, escorted by a detachment of the King's German Legion under the command of a certain Lieutenant Bruckner, a young moonfaced officer Simms had often noticed ogling Zamora senoritas. "More brawn than brain," thought Simms at the outset, but one had to admit that he was active enough constantly riding up and down the line urging drivers and animals forward. On the other hand the German looked back over his shoulder so often that the dour MacTavish christened him "Lieutenant Lot," though Bruckner's attitude was due much more to excess of zeal than lack of courage.

Bruckner was cheerful in his own rumbustious fashion, assuring the three soldier's wives who were with the train, of hot soup in Ariego. "You shall be well looked after," he boasted. "We Germans know how to forage if you English do not. My valiant fellows will find a pig or a turkey – you'll see!" The two Commissaries overhearing exchanged glances. "I shall be more interested to see how he entertains the enemy," commented McTavish, but Simms was silent. It was common knowledge that the Hanoverians not only attended more to their horses than English cavalrymen, but were capable both of good foraging and good fighting ... At dusk, ten miles out of Zamora they halted at a posada for the night, drooping tiredly on the straw of the stable. Thus far there had been no trace of pursuit. The French perhaps had turned back before the closed gates of Zamora ... The train set off again before dawn ...

With daylight a thin powdery snow began to fall whitening the whole plain and throwing the bullock train and its outriders into sharp relief.

Though the terrain was quite new to Simms, he became strangely conscious that he had passed this way, and in similar circumstances, before. The low lying hills on the horizon were familiar; the road too skirting substantial groves of oak and pine. Then in a flash he remembered the séance at Don Taboada's deserted chateau, the contending horsemen and the prostrate figures in the snow. He began to examine his pistols, and set these more conveniently in his belt. "So soon?" queried McTavish. "Look to your own," Simms replied, "I have a notion we are in for trouble." When the other began to point out that as a non-combatant he was under no obligation to fight, Simms did not reply, for both men knew that at a pinch they would do their utmost to defend the train.

About an hour later they were riding steadily somewhat in the rear, when they saw Bruckner who was just ahead, check his horse, wheel and screen his eyes towards the direction from whence they had come. Simms and McTavish turned in their saddles also.

Tiny black dots began to move slowly in the distance, but as these vanished almost immediately behind a grove of pines, Simms began to wonder if he had not been the victim of an optical illusion. "Wolves or wild cats," he thought. A few minutes later he knew he had not been mistaken. The dark dots reappearing, resolved into outlines of horsemen, but whether British, French or Spanish, he could not well make out.

The young German officer, whose sight must have been keener than that of Simms had no doubt whatsoever. Drawing his sabre he dug in his spurs and galloped down the line of carts bellowing, "French chasseurs! Enemy chasseurs! On your lives forward!" He struck with the flat of his weapon drivers and bullocks, flailing impartially. Arriving at the tail of the train, and marshalling his men, ten in number as rearguard, he hurried back to the two Britishers, grinning savagely. "We shall entertain guests – no?" And off he went using his sabre with undiminished vigour. As McTavish examined the priming of his pistols Simms could not resist a sardonic, "Remember, you are not compelled to use them!" … Looking back, they saw that one of the French men dismounting, had thrown back his cloak, and carbine to shoulder was taking deliberate aim. The weapon cracked, and a bullet droned overhead. "A visiting card, na' doot," said McTavish, raising his hat.

The Frenchmen, who numbered a dozen or more came up at a brisk trot. In a matter of seconds now they would overtake the convoy, which with the squeaking of wheels, the frenzied shouting of the drivers, and the pounding of hooves abated nothing of its pace. Faintly Simms heard a cheer which might well have been, "*Vive le Empereur!*"

"Save your breath," he muttered. "You'll need it!" …

The shock of the charge fell upon the solid body of Germans at the rear of the train. Simms heard the confused pounding of hooves, the rasping of steel on steel, a bout of cursing, a groan, and from the tail of his eye glimpsed one green cloaked horseman topple to the ground. But like a stream cleft by a rock, some on one side of the train, some on the other, the main body of the chasseurs swept forward. They struck fiercely at drivers within reach, but these by no means helpless, retaliated with blows from their cruel rawhide whips. One chasseur with loosely dangling reins, his hands clapped to his face, swung off at a right angle, badly smitten. A Spaniard armed with a musket brought down another. One of the women began to scream, but her cries were quickly stifled by her companions. The remaining Frenchmen overshooting the mark, wheeled for the return.

Surprisingly the two commissaries remained unscathed. Simms wondered if this was due to the fact that they were in civilian attire, but he was to be speedily disillusioned. Startled by the musket and pistol shots, his horse had become almost unmanageable, swerving so that he had the utmost difficulty in retaining his seat. Bringing his mount under control, he awaited the coming impact more coolly than he would have imagined, his pistol cocked, his hand steady. As the Frenchmen came up he caught a glimpse, half obscured by the head of a piebald mare, of a helmet visor, a heavy black moustache, a set of bared yellow teeth, and a sabre swinging upwards. With extended arm he fired almost point blank at a row of tunic buttons. A white and green saddle saddlecloth heaved as his adversary passed out of sight. A second chasseur bore down, and Simms had just time to pluck out his second pistol as the man swung alongside. Powder and shot were swifter than steel. He saw the Frenchman topple, fall over, and with one foot fast in the stirrup, drag across the snow making a dark weal on the unblemished surface. Once again Simms' own horse took fright, wheeled and plunged madly. He tugged at the reins, furious, helpless. "Here we go round the mulberry bush!" he muttered savagely as he tried to assume control. Thus circumstanced it was impossible to reload his weapons, and he wondered if by quickly dismounting he might relieve the fallen Frenchman of his sabre. But his horse continued restive, and once out of the saddle it might not be easy to mount again ... In spite of the French onset, the train was still in movement. At all costs he must keep abreast. What was happening elsewhere?

The Germans heavier at all points than their opponents, had come off fairly well, killing or disabling at least three of the chasseurs, the two commissaries and the drover accounting for one or two others. The attack had now resolved into a number of fierce single combats, though Simms noticed that Bruckner had gathered one or two of his men to make a solid body of resistance. The Lieutenant brought these forward, and the result was that the chasseurs already shaken by losses, began to disengage. They did so reluctantly, but there was no commanding voice. Was their officer dead?

The carts lumbered on, and still the chasseurs hesitated. Their figures in that snowy background grew smaller, but a couple dismounting opened a ragged carbine fire. One of the drovers fell without a cry and was dragged into the rear cart. A bullet carried away McTavish's hat, but with a snort the Scotsman dropped form his horse and retrieved it. He thrust his finger rue-fully through the hole. "Civilian wear and tear," said Simms. He clapped on his own more tightly.

They were drawing out of range now. The Frenchmen, attending to their fallen, bent over the dark blots in the snow. A riderless horse trotted towards the scrub oak, perhaps to nibble at the leaves ... The Germans too, had suf-fered. Two of their dead had been brought along; there were wounds among those still mounted. Of the drivers – apart from the first carbine casualty – one had been killed outright by a sabre stroke, and another, badly stricken, lay in his own cart. Lieutenant Bruckner, the broken strap of his busby dan-gling, abated nothing of his energy. "Arrivo! Arrivo!" he shouted, "no sloth now you cockroaches!" One of the drivers cigar in mouth began nicking at a flint preparatory to lighting up, but the German dashed the tinderbox from the Spaniard's hand. "Is this a siesta?" he asked furiously. He drew abreast of the two Britishers. "So, Herren Simms and MacTarvish, you will agree that we have our own means of dealing with marauders!" Looking back in the direction of the rapidly receding Frenchmen, he shouted, "You may go to your Emperor for biscuit!" It was a childish exclamation, but the man was still wide-eyed with excitement. With a satisfied grunt he dropped behind, but they noticed that he was still uneasy. Others would follow on the heels of the defeated chasseurs.

Simms and McTavish rode for a little time in silence, the former for his part dwelling anxiously on the disordered condition of the supply train. The latter, however, pondered a problem peculiarly his own. At last the Scotsman spoke. "Mr Simms," he said, "I hae been thinking—"

Simms gazing askance, waited.

"I hae been thinking," said McTavish after another pause, "that what yon man needs maist—" and it was evident that he referred to the German – "Is not only a few mair years to his back, but what is mair important, a leetle pheelosophy!"

* * *

The long march to Corunna had begun. Column by column the army drew away from the swollen flow of the Carrion, their faces set towards Astorga, but there were no marching songs. A sullen drum-tap set the note.

Sir John kept his own counsel. "It is not my wish to fight a battle, " he had written to Brodrick, at Corunna. "That at present is not my game, which is rather to save this army, and give time to the Spaniards to rally if they can. I may be compelled to fight one if pressed. If I once enter the mountains I fear the want of subsistence will compel me to go to the coast..."

Along the retreating route Spaniards took a poor view of the situation. They cursed bitterly as the redcoats tramped through their villages; and the redcoats in reply inquired why their detractors were not in uniform themselves.

Harriet in the rear of the column had much to occupy her thoughts. Where now was Tony Harte? The horror of permanent blindness continued to appall her. Sometimes as she rode, she closed her own eyes temporarily in order, as it were, to comprehend his grave limitation. But she was not assisted thereby. She comforted herself with the thought that at any rate he would not be again vexed by enemy action. On the other hand an arduous journey lay before him. He would pass through barren tundra, cross deep ravines and windswept heights – she envisaged a hundred situations in which he might possibly founder, and cry for help in vain. She had, of course, said nothing to Percy about the farmhouse affair, and even if she had been so inclined, she knew that her husband had more pressing things to consider. Why add to his troubles? Living as they were from hand to mouth, from one brief bivouac to another, better let sleeping dogs lie.

There were times when in the grip of chill foreboding, she felt that her association with Tony had been ill-starred from the outset. Her thoughts wandered to the Classical conceit they had adopted, the Hector-Andromache relation. Was this a portent? What innate mystique lay in these names? She did not know. She wished she did. In this mood, and finding herself alongside Captain Suckley, she opened a conversation. "I believe, sir," she remarked, "that you are something of a scholar?"

He made a deprecating gesture. "If carrying Shakespeare in my pack—"

"None the less, you have read much?"

"Not deeply."

"I don't believe that for a moment," she rejoined. "You are familiar with Classical lore?"

He raised questioning eyebrows.

"Allow me to explain," she continued. "the subject may seem trivial to you, Captain, but since Salamanca I have used a new horse to which I have not yet affixed a name. This you will agree is most unsatisfactory."

Suckley laughed. "The horse – does he mind?"

"I cannot say. Now – I had considered Hector. Is that a good name for an animal, or a bad one?"

"A good name. I should think," said Suckley, "two syllabled, easy to remember."

"I am intrigued by its origin," she said, "was there really such a person?"

"In mythology – yes," said the Captain, "a Grecian lord, a warrior of high renown."

"A Grecian? Tell me more."

Suckley smiled. "I must charge my memory. He figures in a lengthy story, an epic so called – his fortunes bound up with the beautiful Helen and the siege of Troy. Hector's wife, I think, was Andromache."

"Andromache?"

"The two names are in their way, famous – like Heloise and Abelard."

"I see. How were they involved?"

"At Troy?"

"I mean in their fates."

"Ah," said Suckley sadly, "they were doomed to misfortune, for this Hector was lamentably slain by one Achilles – in single combat."

"Killed?" She gazed down anxiously.

"'Twas a famous fight, but the unfortunate Hector was vanquished, and worst of all, his body like that of a slaughtered bull at the *corrida*, was dragged three times around the city walls. I think I am right in recalling that they paid him signal honour afterwards."

"Thank you, Captain Suckley," she said quietly. "Now tell me, what became of Andromache?"

"Of that lady, I remember little, except that most naturally she was more anxious for her husband, charged with a fearful premonition. More I cannot say."

"It is a strange story," she murmured.

"And a tragic one. When we are clear of this business, I must look into Homer again." He slapped the horse's flank. "Hector is a good strong name. I commend your choice."

"You must consider me an ignoramus," she said.

"Not at all," he replied. "You, dear lady, have reserves of knowledge which I have not."

What did he mean by that? As she moved forward she tried to dismiss the matter from her mind ...

The grey remained unchristened ...

* * *

Sue's mule in spite of its cracked hoof was marching well. A shapeless outline muffled in a blanket, she jogged along shielding her face against the driving sleet. Her hands were numb and badly chapped, but even so, she was more fortunate than many of the regimental women, who without gloves or stockings trudged cheerfully beside their men. Because of their condition, Mrs Higgenson had been placed in an ammunition wagon; her two small children wedged in mule panniers.

A general officer, his cocked hat dripping water, drew abreast of Mrs Foulkes. It was General Frazer, who paused for no more than a minute, but as he wrenched at his horse's head, Sue heard his remark, "Well, Ma'm, in spite of much to the contrary, a merry Christmas to you!"

"And to you also, General," said Harriet.

"We will drink on it," he jerked.

"I will hold you, sir, to that," cried Harriet. It was a gallant observation on the General's part, but the chances of a toast in these conditions were exceedingly remote.

After he had gone Harriet called over her shoulder, "Thompson, know you that tonight will be Christmas eve?"

"Indeed, Ma'm," she muttered, as her mind reverted to the quiet chapel at home … "O come all ye faithful …" the brightly berried holly laid across the mantelpiece and festooning the pictures; to the pudding bubbling in the cauldron, and no less to the village "Waits" bearing lanterns and strumming fiddles – a world so remote from her present condition as to be completely unreal. Suddenly she became conscious that her mistress was speaking, "I said if you will but listen, that we must drink a celebration."

"I should like to," said Sue, drawing her blanket closer, "at this moment …"

The road mounted. They topped the rise, and made a long descent. "I don't want to anticipate difficulty," said Harriet when they were half way down, "but I have the feeling that awaiting at the bottom is a great deal of water."

And water there was! The River Esla which they now approached was so strongly in spate that crossing denoted a painfully slow progress. Only two ferry boats were in use; but being mounted, the two women were ordered to joint a cavalry detachment moving to a ford higher up the stream. When they arrived they saw that a few horsemen had already made the crossing. As it was it had been touch and go. The angry water carried on its surface much debris, broken branches rolling and plunging, and although Harriet was genuinely apprehensive as she watched the scene, she gave no outward sign of alarm. She relieved Sue of the valise and set this in front of her own saddle. At a signal from the officer in command she tightened her reins and accompanied by him plunged girth deep in to the torrent. He spoke a reassuring word as she managed to keep abreast, seized the cheek-strap of her horse, and with a steady hand drew her to the farther bank, where drenched and breathless she halted to watch how Sue fared in her turn.

Two dragoons, powerfully mounted, ranged themselves on either side of the mule, and yielding the reins to her escorts the girl clung tightly to her saddle. She had only the most confused recollection of what followed – the shock of the ice-cold water, the relentless drag of the stream, the hopeless sensation of sinking to the waist, and an immense relief when the beast began to swim strongly beneath her. One sensation crowded quickly upon another. "Steady does it, and we're over," said one of the dragoons. Hold tight to where you are. I known wuss in Ireland."

"Not much worse!" she gasped.

"Another twenty feet and you'll be laughing at the rest."

Scrambling up the bank however, she was in no mood for laugher; she was rather more drenched than Harriet, and shivering miserably. The attendant officer gave them a nip of rum, after which there was nothing for it but to find a crevice in the rocks to wring the water out of their clothes. Chilled as they were, the smallest fire would have been welcome. Instead they walked and stamped to restore circulation. Downstream the infantry had been ferried across, and when the two women rejoined the main body, Sue noticed Harker. She had not seen him since the inquiry concerning the rings, but his eyes grinned hate as he recognised her. He made a gesture in her direction, and a remark which brought a burst of horse-laughter from his companions. She turned away contemptuously, wondering what punishment the Colonel held in store for him. The incident had not gone unnoticed by Harriet , who observed, "One day that man will be hung by the neck until he is dead."

"I don't want him to be hung," said Sue.

"The devil will take his own," rejoined Harriet.

* * *

The army moved on. Outwardly cohesive, a unified force, it was difficult to detect where the rot of indiscipline began – the first slender crack in the dam, the first stone launching the avalanche.

Rations were always a problem. During the first period of the retreat, each man carried three days biscuit, but a feckless tendency to encroach on this, left many a man without a bite. Then there were breakdowns with supply of meat. The third evening groups of hungry soldiers were clamouring for food, banging camp kettles with their side-swords, and emitting cat calls. It appeared that there was no meat ration. Why, the Quartermaster could not say, except that wagons must have broken down in the rear.

Foulkes riding up, surveyed the scene with anger and amazement, the more so since his presence seemed to have no effect on the malcontents. At once he called upon the company commanders and the Serjeant Major to restore order, but individuals were scattered and it took some time for the order to be given effect. At last the shouting fell into muttered grumbling, but the Colonel, grim, obdurate, waited for complete attention before he began to speak. Silence had fallen when someone in a rear rank said quite audibly, "For what we are about to receive may the Lord make us truly thankful."

"Which man spoke?" rapped Foulkes.

There was no answer. A laugh came from another quarter.

"Let the man step forward."

Foulkes watched dourly for a movement of any kind. There was no response.

"Very well," he said, "let the craven coward skulk where he is". His eyes ranged coldly down the ranks singling out certain faces – Bates and Jenks, two of the pickets on the Carrion bank with whom he had conversed, the delinquent Raddock, blandly attentive, and Corrigan who carried on his back from Guardia the scars of the Drum Major's lash. In a wild moment Foulkes thought, "This is incipient mutiny. What next?" But he sat rigidly, and still his men waited. Beyond a strangled cough or two, the loudest sound was that of the droning wind which brought the smoke of bivouac fires freakishly across the scene.

With a nervous jerk of his arm, Foulkes broke free. He knew that Major Daiches had come up behind him together with another officer, but he did not turn. The men standing with eyes fronted awaited his pleasure, if it could be so termed! Let them wait. He cleared his throat staring impersonally above their heads at a tangle of scrub fringing the barren rocks of the background. "Now" – he began harshly, "now that you are soldiers once again, and not a gang of raving hooligans, I will speak. You think because you are in motion, in retreat, that you may do as you please, but I will teach you differently. Food or no food, drink or no drink, I will not have unsoldierly behaviour. Serjeant Major, bring out your book, make inquiry from officers both commissioned and non-commissioned, for the names of a dozen men most concerned, and they shall eat only when all the others have finished – indeed, three hours later. Then let me see them. That is all. You may take over."

He wheeled abruptly and rode away, Daiches following, Had he said enough? Some commanders would have fallen back on the lash, but he had no mind to do that, for the men had an undoubted grievance. What shocked Foulkes profoundly was the ineffective conduct of his own officers. that would be attended to later. A detachment was sent back in search of the missing supplies, with instructions not to return without them.

Half an hour later the carts came in bearing not only supplies, but a sorry story of foundered bullocks and broken axles. Foulkes listened to no more than the outline of mishap. Apparently no one was to blame ...

When the men were fed, he spent some little time with Harriet eating morosely in a shepherd's hut which he had made his headquarters. A fire had been started, but as the chimney was a mere hole in the roof, lingering smoke stung their eyes and lodged in their throats. Cold though it was, he called for Richard his new man, to put the fire out. The floor was filthy; the walls mildewed, so that when he suggested that his wife would be well advised to seek a campfire, she was glad to go. Really he wished to have the place empty in order to admonish the officers.

Summoned to this primitive council chamber, they gathered uneasily. A candle fixed on a keg threw their faces into sharp relief. Foulkes' own features, more pallid than usual, seemed a ghostly emanation of the shadowed background, but when he spoke there was nothing ethereal in the clipped minatory sentences. "Gentlemen," he said, "I shall not detain you long. You may have wondered why I have brought you here, but you need not. I have throughout the day noticed the most appalling conduct on the part of all ranks; slovenly irregular formation, weapons carelessly handled, disorderly dress and behaviour. Some part of this may be laid to the inclement weather, so too the rough condition of the road we have travelled – but by no means all."

He drew a long breath. "There has been grave dereliction of duty, not only on the part of non-commissioned officers, but by yourselves as well. I will say nothing of the late disagreeable incident in camp – ponder that at your leisure, and consider what it may lead to. As Colonel of this regiment, henceforward, I shall look to you for a stricter discharge of *all* your duties. Let your orders be few and simple, but see that beyond all question such are carried out. The habit of disobedience grows. Make men fear the penalty of disobedience. I know the feeling of this army – some here may not approve of our present movement. That is of no consequence. We are here to execute such orders as the high command gives. In recalling you to a sense of duty I wish to remind you of the commission each of you carries from His Majesty the King." Foulkes lowered his voice, but the tense tone remained. "While I am in command of this body of men, I will see that discipline is maintained, and woe betide he who does not conform!"

He finished in profound silence. "Here endeth the first lesson," muttered Harrod under his breath. "I didn't think the old boy had it in him!"

"That will be all," said Foulkes, rising to his feet. He did not invite comment, nor did he expect any. "Don't go, Daiches," he called, as the others filed out, so the senior major remained, seating himself on a dumped saddle. For a little time as they listened to the wind whistling through the broken pantiled roof neither spoke. Foulkes took out his snuff box, tapped it, raised the lid, helped himself, and extended the box to Daiches. "Had to be done," he jerked.

"Yes, sir," said Daiches reluctantly. He took the snuff, not really liking it. "The pity of it!"

"An army in retreat, sir—" began Daiches.

"I will have nothing of that. Men must obey. Why do they not?"

Daiches tilted his hat backwards and scratched his head. "Frankly, sir, we carry too many Irishmen, shilleghly lads, Donnybrook boys, always rooting for trouble."

"Other regiments absorb Irish."

"True, but in less proportion."

"My officers are not Irish – explain that."

"If you would have me speak frankly, sir, their faith in Sir John is shaken."

"Then they are boobies! What can they know of the Commander-in-chief's responsibility, the forces at his disposal, those at the disposal of the enemy – the odds on every hand – information he cannot impart? If you hear such stupid observations, Daiches, for God's sake stamp on them, at once."

"There are other factors too."

"Such as?"

"The presence of the women does not help."

"We have always had women."

"They tend to straggle, and their husbands straggle with them."

"In heaven's name let them not march with their husbands. Pack them on mules."

"The subtler animals have enough to do as it is," said Daiches gloomily.

"We must make do somehow," replied Foulkes. "If that is the bane of the army—"

He started. Harriet was standing in the doorway. As she came forward, Daiches rose to his feet taking up his hat. "Anything more, sir?" Foulkes shook his head slowly, and saluting, the senior major passed out into the night. When Harriet glanced at her husband apologetically, he wondered how much of the conversation she had overheard.

"I saw them leaving," she said. "I am sorry to trouble you, but my harness needs attention – an almost severed rein."

"It shall be mended. You have had a hard day?"

"Not more than most. The river was difficult." She took off her oilskin and shook it. "I have some earache."

"You should make yourself plugs against the wind, and wrap a shawl tightly about your head."

"I will do that. How do you fare?"

He shrugged. "A touch of ague in my right shoulder – may have pulled a muscle – I don't know. We must not complain. Were you much with the women?"

"On and off," she replied.

"Take them into your care as often as you can. Daiches speaks of straggling. We mustn't have that."

"They become footsore."

"In that case they shall ride. No stragglers!"

"But stragglers are brought in by the rearguard?"

"Don't believe that," he said firmly.

"I concluded it was so."

Foulkes shook his head vigorously. "The business of the rearguard is to grapple with the French. The straggler will be left to his own devices."

"A pleasant prospect," she said dryly. "What would happen if I were to straggle?"

He looked at her strangely; opened his mouth to speak, but closed it again. In a little while he said, "At all time bind yourself closely to the regiment."

"I will do my best," she answered.

"Your harness shall be attended to."

As he stared anxiously through the doorway, her heart was moved to see how pale and drawn his face had become. She wished she could find appropriate words of sympathy, of comfort. She said, "Take care of yourself – wrap up well."

"You also," he replied. His face softened in a smile. "We are a long way from home."

"Yes," she said simply, "and the season of Christmas too. Had you forgotten? However, I have brought you a present which I thought you might like to interchange with the other." And she produced the snuff box she had found in Toro. "The design is quite pleasant."

"A snuff box?"

She pointed to the classical figures on the lid. "The Three Graces," she said.

"I am very grateful," he murmured taking the little object. "The lid has a good spring. I am sorry I have nothing for you, but then—"

"I understand," she said softly.

But further conversation was interrupted by the appearance of the adjutant, and again Harriet withdrew to her fire ...

To compose his mind before sleeping, Foulkes decided to read a few pages from Plutarch. He had not opened the work since Salamanca; but although the oil in the bulb was low and the wick sooty, he managed to decipher a passage from the life of Caius Marius – an unpolished fellow from all accounts, yet a soldier of stern resolution who held the hearts of his men. "There is not (Foulkes read) a more agreeable spectacle to a Roman soldier, than that of his general eating the same dry bread which he eats, or lying in an ordinary bed, or assisting his men in drawing a trench or throwing up a bulwark. For the soldier does not so much admire those officers who let him share in their honour or money, as those who will partake with him in labour or danger ..."

Foulkes re-read the paragraph. Here, he felt, was a central truth, but as between honour, money, authority and personal complication, how did one bring it into operation? ...

CHAPTER XVI

Benevente walls loomed spectral in the December twilight. To flickering, uncertain torchlight, they marched through shuttered streets. Half dead with cold, they deployed to their various quarters, thankful for a few hours respite from the wind and sleet.

Foulkes was distinctly pleased when he found that part of his force was to be billeted in the castle itself where all ranks, he hoped, would pass a comfortable night. "The building," he informed Daiches, "Belongs to the Duchess of Casuna, the great family of these parts. I don't suppose the lady will be in residence to receive us – so many of the grandees are in Seville, but we should be amply served." Preceded by a guide, he led his men up a gentle ascent, crossed a trout stream, and passing through a twin-towered gatehouse, dismounted in the courtyard. Five companies followed, the rest being quartered in the town.

Harriet and Sue were ushered into a large, splendidly furnished apartment leading off a patio. Louis Seize panels of watered silk, paintings after Lancret and Chardin graced the walls; but tables of beaten brass, and suspended from the ceiling, a curious lamp of Moorish design imparted an oriental note. A burnished copper gong stood beside the fireplace, and with it a pair of bellows, which a maidservant was using to revive the fire. This servant hovered discreetly in the background, but after serving a meal she disappeared, and they saw her no more.

Supper over, Harriet moved about restlessly with no more than a cursory glance at the pictures and general furnishing. She stood for a time in the open watching the play of torchlight in the streets below, listening to the rumble of wheels and the shouting or orders. Both women were tired enough; but after resting an hour, Harriet, filled with a new lease of life, announced that she intended to explore a little. To Sue's surprise, for she assumed that her mistress merely intended to look round the adjacent rooms, Harriet asked for oilskin, donned it, and without a further word departed. Really, Harriet had decided to visit the town, where at the Quartermaster General's office she hoped to gather some news of Captain Harte. Her husband, she knew, had gone down to look up the remainder of his men, but as there was a chain of communication between the castle and the town, she felt she could join a messenger detached for this purpose. As it happened the gatehouse had been made a depot for stores, and Proctor the Assistant Commissary in charge, was already dispatching his clerk, Mills, with a message to the centre.

The two set out. Mills, who was a talkative fellow, setting the pace. Proctor (he told her) was in a blue funk over a shortage of stores. How this had come about no one knew, but it was the clerk's present purpose to ask for further supplies. There would be a row he knew; but that would not hinder him taking Mrs Foulkes where she wished to go, and having fulfilled his own mission, calling for her on his return.

The streets of Benevente were more difficult than either of them anticipated. Troops were still moving in, and it was only by use of Mills' stout arms and shoulders that they forced a way through.

Fortunately the Quartermaster's office was in the same building as that used by the local Junta, so that it was not difficult to find. Here the clerk left Harriet to her business, while he went about his.

The large ante-room was crowded, British red coats rubbing the sober Spanish black; the fresh ruddy faces of her own countrymen contrasting oddly with the olive brown of their allies. Harriet was held up by the broad back of an English officer who was disputing with a Spanish official. The Englishman had a little broken Spanish, and the Official a little broken English, but the purpose was plain. The Englishman wished for supplies and the Spaniard had none to offer. This was conveyed with so much feeling, that Harriet had little difficulty in sensing the resentment of the Junta official at the British retreat. At last the English officer, breathing, "God Almighty give me patience," turned and found Harriet at his elbow. He apologised, though there was no need to do so. By his assistance she found the Quartermaster, though here she was compelled to wait her turn until he had dealt with other suppliants. He was, of course, arranging quarters. "On paper," she overheard him say, "but only on paper, there are ten houses in the street I have allotted to you, all habitable. Each house will accommodate fifty men – that is on the count five hundred. The wine shop – though I doubt it will be empty – should take fifty more, with a stable underneath for the overlap. You may find the nest is full. In which case, sir, God help you, for I cannot. And I will thank you to remove your sodden hat from my papers! Good night to you!"

He ran his fingers round the inside of his stock. "Astley's circus isn't in it," he grumbled. "I'd rather be in charge of animals!"

Observing Harriet, he turned a flushed face towards her. "Don't Ma'm," he pleaded in tones of mock despair, "announce that you have a regiment too!"

She smiled sympathetically. "Indeed, no. My wants are much more simple." And she inquired after Tony Harte.

"I remember the poor fellow," sighed the Quartermaster, "as near blind as may be – accompanied by a servant, he was – thought it best in the circumstances to push on. Don't blame him either."

"In what direction?"

There is only one direction. To Astorga, of course, Later, at the junction of the main road, if maps are anything to go by, he may have a choice between

Vigo and Corunna. We have vessels in both ports. For a man in his condition the best thing is to clear out of this country as soon as possible. I can assure you that he was in good spirits."

"You mentioned – his sight?"

"Of that," replied the other, "I can say nothing except that was heavily bandaged, though this may be in part have been some protection against the snows. The glare," he explained, "may be awkward. It is wonderful," he continued, warming to his theme, "how a man deprived of vision makes do. He develops one sense in compensation for another. I knew a sergeant of marines who lost both eyes in Sicily, and incredibly – evidence at which I have never ceased to marvel – could hear a hound walking twenty paces distant, and a church clock striking four miles away."

"Most extraordinarily," she stammered, placing her hand to her brow.

"What ails you, Ma'm?"

"Nothing really."

"I am not so certain. These are hard days for all."

Faint, she watched without further demur as he produced a silver flask from which he unscrewed the cup and into this poured a tot of brandy. "We are all on edge. Drink this."

"Dutch courage," she murmured.

"Dutch or not, it will do you good."

She drank the liquor, choked, gasped and apologised, but the potent beverage restored her. As she moved towards the door another suppliant had taken her place, and she could hear as from a distance the Quartermaster reverting to his habitual gruffness. "Sir, I cannot build houses with my own hands. We must take what the good Lord sends us. Now, a posada by the Astorga gate …"

She withdrew, and outside awaited the return of Willis who seemed an unconscionable time absent …

Meanwhile, Harry Simms, who with the biscuit convoy had made Benevente safely, approached the castle from the direction of the town. Still without fixed duties, the commissary had been ordered by Kearney to look into a request for stores replacement from Proctor, the Assistant Deputy. "He is deficient," stormed Kearney, "let him not think that because we are hustled and harried through these outlandish parts, there is no proper accounting. See what the fool is up to. If there are rats in the granary you can inform the commanding officer up there that it is his duty to catch them – or words to that effect."

Simms, nothing loath to be the bearer of such a message, chuckled in anticipation of sweet revenge, and picking up a spare clerk, who had come in from Baird's division, set out.

The clerk in question, a young man in is late twenties, wore a bottle-green surtout belted, at the waist, grey pantaloons and half boots. A stranger to Simms, the newcomer's shock of auburn hair, high cheek bones, and rather full sensitive lips, seemed vaguely familiar. The Commissary screwed up his eyes as he searched his memory. "We have met before?" he remarked.

"Never!" replied the clerk emphatically.

"Not in Oporto?"

The man shook his head.

"At Lisbon then?"

"I am quite certain that we never met."

"In that case we shan't quarrel over past misdemeanours."

"Misdemeanours?" repeated the clerk hesitatingly.

Simms laughed. "Never mind. What is your name?"

"Jones – Thomas Jones."

"Jones?" mused Simms. "Yet you are not a Welshman?"

"Why do you say that?"

"From your speech alone; still you are the member of a large family?"

"What are we at, sir?" asked the clerk changing the subject.

"Well Mister Jones," said Simms, throwing on his cloak, "we are to look up a commissary and Colonel Foulkes' regiment in search of certain missing stores. Mr Kearney thinks they have been ravaged by rats – two legged ones I fancy. Follow me."

The two pushed their way through the crowded streets, turned a corner, entered a deserted alley, lost bearings, and finally found themselves back where they started. After inquiries, they were put right, and again began the climb to the castle. For a time they conversed only in monosyllables, but presently it was the clerk who said, "You made mention of a Colonel Foulkes – would he, think you, hail from Bellaby in South Yorkshire?"

Simms thought this likely, but was not certain.

"He held the rank of Major in England," said Jones.

"You are right there," rejoined Simms. "The gentleman was promoted at Salamanca."

"Accompanied by his wife?"

"No doubt about that," said Simms sourly. "I knew the regiment for a time." He was about to add, "To my cost!" but feeling this was no business of the other man, refrained.

"In that case," continued Jones diffidently, "you may have noticed her maid, Susan Thompson?"

Simms almost came to a halt. "I may. Why do you ask?"

"With no particular purpose." The man named Jones pulled down the brim of his hat.

"Oh, come now!" Simms persisted. "Don't be coy."

"We met," said Jones reluctantly, " – once."

"Only once?" bantered Simms. "In Spain?"

"Not in Spain."

"A distant relation, perhaps?"

"In a kind of fashion."

Simms laughed at the clerk's obvious hedging. "Fashions come, and fashions go," he commented, "but the true heart beats forever."

Jones fell silent and remained so, while Simms continued to pace along thoughtfully. Odd – demand odd! Was Jones' acquaintance with Sue Thompson as fugitive as all that? To this he could find no answer, until with a wild surmise, which the more he dwelt upon the more he felt in accord with probability, produced a solution. The conviction grew that the man now walking beside him in the guise of a commissary's clerk, was none other than Susan Thompson's brother, Robin. Had the *Primrose* touched upon the coast of Spain, or possibly been wrecked there? From the outset Jones' face had been strangely familiar; and the direct series of questions involving the girl herself, almost clinched the matter. It was quite possible to be wrong, but Simms decided to put the issue to a test.

They approached a gateway over which a lamp was suspended; through the windless air the oil flame shed a steady light. As they passed beneath Simms said quietly, "Wait a moment," and taking a firm grasp of his companion's sleeve drew him to a standstill. Peering closely beneath the rim of Jones' beaver hat, he gave a low whistle, an action which prompted the clerk to retreat a step or two. But Simms followed up. "Yes," said the Commissary firmly, "I think I do know you."

"I have already stated—" mumbled Jones.

"One and one," observed Simms tritely, "make two. If you had not mentioned Susan Thompson by name, I should still have wondered somewhat; but your having raised the matter I must press a question of my own. Are you by chance the same young lady's brother who shipped on the *Primrose?*"

The man who called himself Jones drew a long and quivering breath. "What do you know of the *Primrose?*"

"A little," replied Simms.

"From Susan Thompson?"

"She was good enough to confide in me."

Jones took a step forward. "What are you to my sister?" he said sternly.

"The truth is out," said Simms calmly, "by admission, you are Robin Thompson."

"I asked – what are you to my sister?"

"A friend, I hope, though it is only fair to say that I have neither seen her nor heard anything from her since leaving Toro."

"But that you, a stranger—"

"A trouble shared, friend," said Simms, "is a trouble halved. A girl must talk with someone. I underestimated her concern when I saw she was greatly anxious about you."

"I am a marked man," said Robin Thompson softly.

"That being so," said Simms linking his arm in that of the other," we must walk warily."

"Tell me about my sister – is she well and happy?"

"In the circumstances. She has a considerate mistress."

Robin heaved a sigh of relief. "Thank heaven for that. At the same time I implore you to tell no man of my condition."

"I do promise," said Simms. "At the same time I am naturally curious. How does it come to pass that you are now in Benevente with Baird's force?"

"Cutting out all details," said Robin, "our vessel foundered, and I was washed ashore within ten miles off Corunna. Fishermen took me in, and from them I learned that Baird's force had just landed at the port. In a few days time I was able to make my way to the commissariat where I offered my services as a muleteer. The Spaniards being awkward with the General – I mean in the sense of providing means of transport – our own people were glad to use me. I told a plausible story, and they asked no further questions. When they found I could write a good hand I was attached to the Commissary's department, registering as Jones. It is a common name, and I must hold to it. The thing I most desire is to see my sister."

Simms pursed his lips. "That may not be easy. She is not a free agent."

"I can wait."

"Depend upon it," said Simms, "your anonymity is safe with me, but there is in the regiment a second person of whom you have knowledge, and who certainly has knowledge of you."

"A second person?"

"To cut the story short, I must tell you that the ranks contain an enlisted man by the name of Harker."

"Not Jacob Harker?"

"Yes, he is here too."

"God in heaven!" breathed Thompson, "my cup only required that – Jacob Harker!"

Now the dark bulk of the castle, its crenellations starkly outlined above, loomed before them. They both paced more slowly. "Here we are at last," said Simms, "now listen well. I appreciate your deep feeling in the matter Mr Thompson – or as I should say, Mr Jones; but I must remind you that however exercised your emotions, we have certain work to do, and that first. Afterwards, if the situation warrants I will try to communicate to your sister your presence here in Benevente. My credit is of no account with Colonel Foulkes. That may prove a difficulty. We will see. In the meantime you are under orders. Follow me."

They were halted at the gate where Simms was informed that Colonel Foulkes had gone into town. Thereupon he asked to see the senior major, and a sour-faced corporal went off swinging a lantern. From the interior, they could hear as they waited a hubbub of voices, and frequent burst of laugher. "Must be carnival night," said Simms tersely. "They are indeed making merry."

Presently the corporal returned with Daiches, who after hearing the purpose of Simms' visit swore roundly that since the Commissary was not under his control he could do what he damned well pleased. Stores were at the gatehouse in charge of that "Cornish fellow", a description Simms thought derogatory in tone. Feeling that perhaps he had been too brusque, Daiches jerked, "Glad to see you again!" and went his way.

When Simms turned to the gatehouse, he found that Proctor had bolted the door, and it was only with much hammering with a pistol butt that the Assistant Commissary and his clerk were admitted. "Thought it might be one of their confounded tricks," growled Proctor as he fastened the door behind his visitors. "Hearken! All hell is let loose. If it hadn't been for that powder," and he pointed to a number of kegs piled in a corner, "into which I swore I'd fire my pistol, the devils would have looted everything I've got."

Yes, the stores were in a sorry state; casks of biscuit and salted fish had gone, and all but one keg of rum, through from the manner with which the men were roaring and rampaging, he thought they must have found additional drink in the cellars. He did not lay all the loss to the British. For brief periods during which Spanish servants were in charge, the gatehouse had been left unguarded. "Unguarded!" Simms exclaimed. He made a pencil note. Foulkes should be reminded of that.

When Simms, having made his check, suggested a thorough search of the building, Proctor demurred. The men (he insisted) were still out of hand; for his part he did not intend to compromise his own position further by leaving the gatehouse. He held to his point stubbornly. Simms might do as he pleased. "Very well," said the latter, "we shall achieve little by sitting on our bottoms here. We will go ourselves." He borrowed a lantern from Proctor, and twitching his clerk's sleeve set out.

Skirting the confusion of the hall, they took the lower regions first, descending gloomy constricted circular stairs, and finding certain doors barred. From hushed voices at the other side, Simms concluded that the sounds emanated from Spanish servants who had taken some sort of refuge. One door alone swung free, but what they saw was enough – spigots dribbling, and two infantrymen stretched out in a drunken stupor on the flags. But there was no sign of the missing kegs. "Nothing for us here," said Simms, "we must hunt elsewhere."

Returning to the hall they ascended the main staircase, checking rooms to right and left of the gallery. Soldiers whom they encountered were much too occupied in searching to pay attention to the Commissary. Here again, the shadowed vistas yielded nothing. "I have the feeling," observed Simms, "that we are completely wasting our time. Wait – what have we here?"

His hand resting on the enamelled handle of a massive double door, he

pushed the leaf open and they entered a *salle des glasse*, the mirrored walls
flashing back the lantern flame in a hundred segments of light, a setting so
completely at variance with the chambers into which they had peered, that
Simms gave a low whistle of astonishment. He had read of the mirrored hall
of Versailles, but that one such should have been inserted within these grim
medieval walls struck him as bizarre in the extreme. "Jones, my lad," he murmured, "bring the lamp forward."

When "Jones" advanced his lantern, they saw that few of the mirrors set
between the slender gilt pilasters remained intact. Vandals had been busy.
Beyond a few overturned chairs and a rumpled dust sheet or so, the room was
empty. "A pretty picture," remarked Simms sardonically, "the music dead, the
dancers all departed!"

They were standing well inside the room, somewhat to the left of the
main door, when they heard the trampling of feet and the confused sound of
voices. Pine torches flared in the doorway. "We spoke too soon," whispered
Simms, "here are the revellers."

The flambeaux were carried by three soldiers, the foremost of whom strid-
ing incautiously across the polished floor, landed flat on his back. His torch,
falling, dashed out. "Lousy hole," he gasped, "might have lamed me'self for
life!" His companions however, only jeered hilariously as he rose to his feet
and relit the torch from one of the others. After a cursory glance around, two
of the men departed leaving the third, who intrigued by the coruscating
effect of his light in the mirrors, began a slow perambulation of the walls. He
threw no more than a casual glance at Simms and the clerk, kicked loosely at
a litter of broken glass, dragged at a dust sheet and let it fall again. At last,
his eyes lighting on a brass-bound coffer in the corner, he went over.
Commissary and clerk watched curiously. As he lifted the lid off the coffer,
his torch, which had been flickering uncertainly, went out. "O drat it!" he
cried, and without even a "by your leave" shouted, "bring that glim over here
and set me goin'."

"Talk of the devil!" muttered Simms. Through the uncertain light they
had both recognised Harker.

Robin Thompson drew a deep hissing breath, but the Commissary wish-
ing for no face-to-face confrontation either for himself or for "Jones", grasped
his clerk's arm tightly. "No nonsense! Keep your lantern low, and your mouth
shut. Give him the light."

"What's all the confabulatin' about?" said Harker impatiently.

Robin pulled down his hat brim and walked across. Harker, intent upon the
coffer did not look up, but waited until the lamplight fell upon the contents of
the box, which upon examination revealed nothing more than a stock of candles for the sconces set around the walls. He took a handful only to toss them
away. "Pah!" he snorted, "not worth knapsack room. Open your lantern mate
and set me alight." His eyes coasted around the room for further pickings.

In the meantime Robin Thompson had remained perfectly still. "What ails ye, man? Light up!" said Harker impatiently. Slowly Robin lowered his head, opened the lantern flap and watched the other apply his torch to the steady oil flame. The pine caught, and without acknowledgement Harker brought the flame within a few inches of the nearest mirror, inspecting his own reflection closely. Mirrors did not often come his way. Held by a certain unfamiliar fascination he inspected his smoke begrimed face, screwed up his mouth and made sundry other grimaces. He advanced his face to within a few inches of the reflection, and drew it back again. It was during the course of this oafish byeplay, that the face of the man standing behind him attracted his attention. Revealed by the torchlight were the features of one he had last seen far away in Hoober Wood, and whom he now believed fast in a penal settlement. He gaped incredulously, let out a strangled cry, and dropping his torch covered his face with both hands. "No – no!" he cried, "it can't be!"

Simms jerked into action. At once he grasped what had happened. "Out – out!" he hissed to his companion. At the same time observing that Harker stood upon the edge of a dust sheet, he stooped and with a vigorous tug brought the bewildered infantryman crashing to the floor. Hurrying his reluctant clerk through the *salle* door, he did not speak until half-way down the main staircase the room was well behind. "Jones," he protested, "you almost deprive me of speech. Why did you not conceal your face? What the upshot will be I do not know. You vow you wish to remain incognito, yet you display yourself flagrantly to the very man you should avoid. What folly!"

"It was his confounded torch," said Robin sheepishly.

"No matter. The thing is done now," continued Simms. "All we can hope now is that he feels himself to be the victim of an optical illusion. We will go now. Get yourself into the gatehouse and stay there. That is an order, Mr Jones. I think however, I will leave a discreet note for your sister. The news had better come through me."

In the gatehouse Simms scrawled a few lines on his tablets – "Robin is alive and well, and near at hand. Not a word to a living soul. Watch and wait. H.S." This, folded tightly, he left in the hands of Proctor for delivery at the first opportunity ...

In the *salle des glasse* Harker, having at least regained his feet, was groping blindly hand by hand along the wall. Missing the door he had started on a second circuit of the walls when panic overtook him. the darkness seemed to clutch at his throat. What indeed if there were no door, if the secret mocking surface mirrored only despair? "I know you're there, Thompson," he stammered, "You're keepin' quiet, but I seen you! ..."

He still continued to grope for the walls..

Mr Simms and his clerk however, were already making their way down the dark slope into the town. "When do you think I can see my sister?" asked

Robin, but Simms answered that he did not know. An opening might come at any time. On the other hand—

A horseman passed them on the causeway. It was Colonel Foulkes returning, but he went unrecognised ...

* * *

Alone in the Louis Seize apartment, Sue sat staring into the flames. After so many hours of bitter cold, the still chamber, the warmth of the roaring fire, and the comfort by which they were surrounded, induced a sense of blissful ease. Slowly the bosky vistas, the marble fauns and silken courtiers of the tapestry dissolved in gloom. Her head drooped. She fell asleep in her chair ...

The voice of Richards the Colonel's servant brought her sharply awake. He was apparently denying entry to a semi-drunk private who contended with oaths that the castle being now "Liberty Hall", he had the right to go whithersoever he pleased. And Richards in his lilting Welsh voice was saying, "I tell you man, that this is the Colonel's apartment. Be off, or 'twill be the worse for you!"

A thick Irish brogue tailed away, footsteps shuffled, and an uneasy silence followed. From the outer courtyard, muffled by distance, she could hear howling, hooting and occasional outbursts of laughter – immoderate hilarity. What was happening? Had the men broken into the wine cellars? The overall racket was punctuated by heavy blows, the smashing of wood, by the sudden rushing of feet.

She opened the door to find Richards pacing restlessly in the anteroom. "What is all this?" she inquired.

"You may well ask," he returned fiercely, his eyes starting from his head. "The devils haff gone mad, look you – quite ma-a-ad! Petter you go back to your own place, and in Got's name stay there."

Alarmed by these wild words, and less by the Welshman's emphatic gestures, she returned to the room, but had no sooner settled in a corner when Foulkes entered followed by Major Daiches who was wiping perspiration from his brow. The Colonel, white with anger, stormed his colleague as though he (Daiches) was personally responsible for the disorder. "Outrageous! Infamous!" cried Foulkes. "It is not to be borne!"

"But, sir," said the perplexed Major, "what can we do?"

"Do?" reiterated Foulkes, "the thing is done! Valuable tables broken up for firewood, tapestry of value torn from the walls and consigned to the flames! Confront the scoundrels with their handiwork and they spring to attention - protest they had no part in it, and by God, so soon as your back is turned they are at it again. One has to be in twenty different places at the same time. I leave the castle for a couple of hours, and return to find – this!"

"They are quite, quite mad," said Daiches.

"With drink!" jerked Foulkes. The rogues must have stumbled across liquor, and the fault is wholly ours, Daiches. We should have made a thorough search before we entered, and sealed up every cellar."

He dropped to a chaise longue too agitated to notice Sue who had drawn into a recess. During the past few minutes, he had for the first time in his life, been threatened by a drunken rascal with a musket, and this much more than the damage wreaked upon the furnishings, rankled intensely. "I hope to heaven," he said, "that Sir John – as well he may – does not come this night. One would think we had taken the castle by storm. I would bring in a detachment up from the town, but what would it look like? And there they are ranging up and down."

"They have some stupid notion of booty," said Daiches.

"Booty!" Foulkes snorted. "In the house of a friend?"

There was a knock on the door and Richards admitted Lieutenant Bird. He saluted. "Ah, here you are, sir."

"Yes, I am here," rejoined Foulkes severely, "and why are you not with your colleagues restoring order?"

"I came to report, sir."

"Very well."

The Colonel took out his snuff box, his hand trembling with suppressed emotion. To be threatened impudently by one's own men! What was the world coming to?

"We are doing our best to marshal everyone in the courtyard, sir," said Baird, "but the place is like a rabbit warren. We can't prevent some slipping away to forage."

"Forage? For what?"

Bird might have answered, any object the men could lay their hands on. "They have the notion sir, that the owner has concealed valuables."

"The ingrates! Return to your duties and send me Sergeant Major Stubbs."

"Yes, sir," said Bird. (Stubbs that moment lay prostrate behind a massive pillar in the hall, where he had been struck down by an unseen hand.) "And ask the Adjutant to be good enough to attend me here."

"Yes, sir." Bird, who was glad enough to depart, prepared to close the door behind him.

"Leave the door open," snapped Foulkes. "Leave both doors open." He glanced around the room, and was annoyed to discover Sue in the background. "Where is your mistress?" he demanded.

"She went out, sir."

"Where?"

"To explore," she said.

"To explore – to explore? then it was your duty to have accompanied her. Go find her at once."

"Have you got a message, sir?"

"It will be quite sufficient if you discover where she is."

"I shall need a lantern, sir."

"Then take that of Richards, and tell him to make do with candles."

"Thank you, sir." She adjusted her shawl, by no means pleased by the assignment. Suddenly she remembered Mrs Foulkes pocket pistol which after Sahagun had been replaced in the valise. She decided to take it. One never knew …

Foulkes watched her impatiently as she bent over the valise.

"What are you fumbling there for?" he asked impatiently.

Sue's fingers had already closed on the butt. "I am quite ready to go," she said tucking the weapon in her belt.

"Then off with you!"

She found Richards in the anteroom. "You are to give me your lantern," she said. "Colonel's orders."

He stared in surprise. "Whateffer for?"

"I am to find Mrs Foulkes."

"If the big man says so," said Richards, "take the lantern, but keep your wits about you. The heathen rage and imagine a vain thing. Myself would go with you, but to leave this place I would not dare."

"The men know me too well to do me harm."

"They know the Colonel too – with what effect, tell me that."

The thud of a falling body, and a subdued groan came from the archway admitting to the hall.

"Ye hear?"

"A drunk," she said quickly. The more she considered her task, the less she liked it. She set her jaw. "All the same, I must find Mrs Foulkes."

"Then look no farther than the courtyard itself, and let the rest to pot. And Got go with you. It is mad that she should be sent so."

Sue left him, and descended a flight of steps leading to the great hall, hoping fervently that Mrs Foulkes would not be far away – it was just possible that her mistress had wandered into a maze of darkened corridors and stairways. Apart from the hall, the girl did not know where to turn.

A blast of heat from a fire which was being fed by broken furniture of every description, met her in the archway. Oaken settees, carved and gilded chairs, tables, picture frames were piled up to feed the flames. She watched one infantryman fold a length of tapestry to make for himself a palliasse. Another, after putting his foot through a canvas of Virgin and Child, threw the whole, picture and frame into the fire.

It was an orgy of senseless destruction. An officer whose face she could not see – Bird perhaps – challenged one group, but all the acknowledgement he received was a mocking salute. One man brandished a musket, whereat the officer shrugged helplessly and vanished in the shadows. Where, she wondered, was that paladin of order, the valiant Major Stubbs, before whose eye the toughest ranker trembled?

A tipsy voice behind her proclaimed, "Look mates what I found?" A pair of strong hands fastened on her waist and propelled her protesting vigorously towards the fire. It was the first time during these months that she had been so manhandled, and the energy with which she hacked at her captor's shins was only a small measure of her resentment. The man hopping and cursing released her, but she had by no means finished with him. She swung her lantern at his leering face, missing it only by inches. "Square up, you miserable hound!" she said between her clenched teeth, drawing the lantern back for another lunge. As her assailant edged away in mock terror, she turned her back on his contemptuously, only to find that the lantern had gone out.

She elbowed her way to a point where unaffected it would seem by the prevailing racket, women were chatting around a smaller fire. Here she restored her light. When she inquired if any present had seen Mrs Foulkes, a Mrs Mayhew opined that she had. "A lady went a bit ago on up them steps at yonder end." And she pointed towards the encircling gallery.

"Are you certain?" asked Sue sceptically.

"Sartin as you can be in this madhouse."

Alas, if Sue had been better acquainted with Mrs Mayhew, she would have known that her informant was "tolerably sartin" about the most doubtful situations. The female figure this woman had noticed ascending the stairs was none other than that of Private Corrigan masquerading in a gown filched from the Duchess's wardrobe.

Following this tenuous clue, Sue mounted the steps of the staircase leading to the gallery. At the head she paused. She could turn as she pleased either to right or left, but activity from a room the door of which was half open drew her in that direction. A few steps further, and she looked upon a scene of complete disorder. It had been a study, or writing room of some kind. A bruhl cabinet had been broken open, and the contents including a number of sealed documents, scattered over the floor. Two infantrymen were tumbling books from the shelves, cursing with disappointment as they found only bare boards behind. A third, attempting to shed light on these proceedings fed a fire with sheets from a portfolio of engravings. A cloud of smoke enveloped the man on the hearth, so that he doubled over coughing and gasping. The spasm over, he looked up and observing the girl in the doorway dismissed her with peevish sweep of his arm. "Aawy wid ye, wumman," he cried, "back to ye donkey!"

"You needn't bother," she replied scornfully, meaning that she had use neither for him nor the work upon which he and his companions were engaged. She moved to the room beyond which was if anything in a greater state of confusion. The floor here was littered with dresses of many colours and textures dragged from cabinets and chests. The men trod indifferently on gowns of rumpled silk and satin; dresses stiff with lace and brocade. One of the intruders flaunted a ceremonial robe of black and yellow-barred velvet, a plumed cap balanced on his head. "Het Betsy!" cried this masquerader, "take your pick – nay, damme, you can have mine." And wrenching off the robe he threw it towards her. "Let's go forward mates," he said, "there's nothing but rubbish here." Riotously good-humoured, they pushed her and clattered down the corridor.

Sue sank on one of the chests thoroughly sick and tired. The air had become oppressive, tortured; the feckless cries and stupid laughter too much to be borne. Where would it all end? Mrs Foulkes was certainly not here, nor could the girl imagine her mistress tolerating such conduct for a moment ... A habit of neatness and order impelled her to gather up the scattered garments.

She was doing this when a man lurched through the doorway. It was Harker.

She suspected that he had been drinking, and had the way been clear she would have slipped out. As it was she remained perfectly still, although bearing a lantern as she did it was too much to expect that he would not perceive her. When at last he gathered himself, his gaze was one of recognition. He pointed a quivering finger.

"You!" he said harshly.

She did not reply.

"This," he said with concentrated venom, "is all your doing."

She stared dumbly. It was as though he accused her of the tumult and disorder which was taking place about them. "What do you mean?" she said scornfully.

"You know damned well!" he responded violently, "up and down, in and out with your green cat's eyes – always slinking!"

"Slinking indeed!" she said. "I am here in search of Mrs Foulkes."

Again he pointed a quivering finger. "That's what you say, but you'll not shelter behind her skirts. This is the end."

He lurched forward, naked hatred in his eyes. As he advanced, step by step she retreated.

"What on earth is the matter?" she challenged. "Try man, to control yourself." She cast a swift glance at the door which was wide open, but he effectively barred the way.

"Time's past for argument," he breathed. "If we can't stop it one way we'll have to do it another." He thrust his hand inside his tunic, and produced the stiletto which she had last seen in Salamanca. His eyes narrowed cunningly. "Remember – my present?"

"A fine present!" she said.

"But I kept it, didn't I?"

"Then don't fool with the thing." She took another step backwards, watching the slender blade of the stiletto.

"You can still have it."

"Not now, nor at any other time."

She retreated behind one of the disordered chests, her feet caught in the scattered finery; at the same time she tightened her grip on the lantern ring. As a last resort she would fling it at his head.

"I shall scream for help," she warned.

"Who do you think will hear you?"

"Stay where you are." She swung the lantern threateningly.

"Not till you've paid."

"Paid?" she repeated, playing for time. "You shouldn't have touched the rings."

"To hell with rings – where is your brother?"

The question, though completely unexpected, stiffened her. She dismissed her fear. "You of all men may well ask," she retorted with bitter scorn, "he is dead."

"You lie!"

"Dead – dead!" she repeated, biting off her words, "drowned in the ocean six weeks ago."

"Drowned?" Harker stared incredulously. "He's no more drowned than I am, for I've seen him."

"It's your own soul that torments you!"

"He stood right beside me, I tell you."

"And I hope he does to your dying day."

"If it was a ghost, then you worked the spell." He slipped the stiletto from left hand to right. The movement was charged with menace.

"In God's name," she protested, "come to your senses."

As he raised his arm she remembered the pocket pistol, and plucked it from her belt. Holding the lantern ring and barrel with one hand she managed to cock the weapon. "Take note of this," she said, "it's loaded." His eyes narrowed darting from the weapon to her face.

"T'wouldn't kill a cat!"

"Just try me."

Quite motionless he watched her finger curving round the trigger. She swung the lamp gently, deciding in the event of the pistol failing to swing the whole weight in his face. The seconds pulsed like heart throbs. She spoke again, "Now Harker, come to your senses. You are not yourself – not well."

"I am alright," he muttered.

"You are not well," she repeated, pity in her voice. "I wouldn't shoot a sick man." Her changed tone; the fact that she lowered her weapon an inch or two reduced the tension between them. He shook his head like a swimmer breaking surface. The hand grasping the stiletto also dropped. The man's body sagged. He passed his hand over his eyes. "You swear that your brother is dead?"

"It's true enough," she said slowly. A wave of sickness overwhelmed her.

"Then why is he in this place, walking on his own two legs?"

"I don't believe it."

Harker shook his head. "Nay – nay, he was in the room of mirrors."

"I repeat, my brother was lost at sea in a terrible storm."

"Then I must be going mad!"

The steel shook in his hand. She too was trembling. "No," she said, "only tired overwrought. There is no spell, no apparition. Go back to the hall and lie down – you will feel better in the morning."

"How do I know he won't appear again?" Harker's voice assumed an almost pathetic note.

She bit her lip, bewildered by his insistence. What more could she do, or say? With an effort he braced himself, and muttered a few words she did not catch. Then came the blessed relief of footsteps in the corridor, torchlight flickered, and a voice she recognised as that of Private Jenks impelled her to cry out loudly, "Jenks man, you are wanted in here at once."

"Who's a'callin?" asked Jenks. Through a swirl of smoke and flame, a homely familiar voice appeared.

"It's me – Susan Thompson."

"What are ye wantin', lass?"

Jenks came in, glancing curiously from Harker to the girl. "What's up with' thee, Raddock?" he asked.

"Mind your own business!" Harker thrust the other contemptuously aside and hastened through the door. They could hear his feet shuffling down the corridor.

"Nice fellow!" observed Jones sarcastically, holding up his torch and inspecting the scattered finery. He took up one of the gowns and held it to his waist. He shook his head sadly. "Won't do – not for me." He dropped the garment. "Now what was it you'd be wantin'?"

"I – I don't feel safe," said Sue. "I wonder if you would see me into the great hall?"

"Honoured, miss." Jenks offered his arm.

She forced a smile. "Always the gentleman," she said, a remark, which pleased him immensely, for compliments seldom, came his way.

"That article been molestin' you?"

"Nothing to speak of," she replied, disinclined to discuss the matter further.

They descended the stone staircase together, and without hindrance she regained the large room off the patio. The encounter had left her shaken. Harker's strange hallucination had opened the old wound, the unappeasable ache … She was glad that the room was empty. Mrs Foulkes had not returned, and the Colonel had disappeared … "Gone to headquarters," Richards said. Proctor, by the way, had left a note for her …

* * *

Foulkes returned to the castle in a black mood of frustration and self-reproach – frustration due to a lengthy delay at headquarters, the upshot of which was that they were to march out in the morning; and self-contempt at his own lack of resolution in dealing with the men. He had intended restoring order in the castle by bringing in a detachment from companies quartered in the town, but at the last moment decided not to. Such action would make the matter public, and that he wished least of all. Better wait for morning, although he would be lucky if come daylight some of his men were on their legs at all. The old fortress had brought no good, but the mess had fallen and must be cleaned up as best one could.

As he rode in he braced himself for an act of consummate discipline by which he would overwhelm the rogues. He felt for his pistols. "By God, I'll shoot the first man that answers back!" he muttered, but as he voiced the thought he knew how futile such an action would be. No, he must command by permissible means. The lash possibly? He winced. To be driven to that? At all costs he must find the Sergeant Major. Where was Stubbs? For the first time in memory, that indispensable arm had failed him.

Thus keyed up, Foulkes was almost disappointed to find that the tumult had died down, and that the men having outrun their exuberance were disposed quietly around the fires. He felt he had been subtly cheated. When Proctor came up with an account of Simms' visit, Foulkes listened indifferently. "That's your affair," he said curtly. "I have other things to think about."

Dismissing the Commissary, he halted at the foot of the staircase surveying the scene. No one took the slightest notice. A nerve in his face twitched, and he placed his finger upon it. What next? Let sleeping dogs lie? The ungovernable, the unspeakable beast, he thought. Oddly, he was reminded in this moment of a Carpathian bear, which tethered to a long, but slender chain, he had seen shuffling through the streets of London. When its keeper cried, "Oom boom pahlow," the beast halted, and in response to a similar cry, lumbered to its hind legs and balanced a pole. He had wondered if "Oom boom pahlow" would have been effective in the event of the chain snapping. He smiled mirthlessly. Somehow the chain needed strengthening. But where was Stubbs? The regiment seemed crippled without him.

With a sigh Foulkes shrugged, and through empty corridors and nocturnal silence, climbed the stairs. In the room off the patio he saw that Harriet and her maid were asleep. Not troubling to undress, he reclined in the patio wrapped in his cloak …

CHAPTER XVII

An early morning fog enveloped the castle, and the smoke of rekindled fires hung heavy in the courtyard. Men coughed and sneezed as they tackled their rations. A cold fit had succeeded the fever of the preceding night. Sergeant Major Stubbs carrying a bandaged head and the foulest of tempers was roaring like the Bull of Bashan. He had a score to settle with someone, and from time to time hinted that he knew the rogues who had so misused him. In due course he would nail them. He had his own means of detection.

During the night Foulkes had decided upon a definite course of action. The damage that had been perpetrated in the castle could not now be made good, but he would at least order a general knapsack inspection. Not a single object belong to the castle was to be carried away. He had the men paraded. The order was given – the yield substantial and curious in the extreme. A pile including candlesticks, plate bent and buckled, crystal glass, embroidered clothes, spoons, strips of tapestry, and wine bottles, steadily mounted. Foulkes watched grimly until company officer reported all complete. He then gave orders for the goods to be handed over to a responsible servant, and when the ranks had dressed, said his say.

The nerve in his cheek began to throb, as hardly looking at their dumb sullen faces, he spoke to the rank and file. He reminded them of their military duties, and the price he would exact before they rehabilitated themselves. Suddenly he could think of nothing more to say, and with jerked rein and tightly compressed lips rode through the gateway. He would, he felt, never forget Benevente, but there was a long day's marching ahead ... The columns followed, shadows melting in the haze. Through the deep recesses of the fog, an occasional musket shot reminded them that Craufurd's men still grappled with the French ...

In a monastery on the western side of the town, Harry Simms had been up before dawn. He hoped that a stand would be made at Benevente where magazines had been built up, but he was shocked to find a great bulk was to be abandoned. What a mockery it made of anxious accounting. He had been ordered to display at the monastery gate, barrels of meat, fish and biscuit, blankets and articles of clothing, so that passing soldiers could take what they pleased. Nothing must be left to bring comfort to the French.

Sir John, with General Craufurd was the last to leave. Simms looked up as the cream and black charger of the Commander reined beside him. "Are you well mounted?" Moore asked. Simms answered that he was. "Good," remarked Sir John. "See that you distribute to our people until the last moment, but before you go turn the remainder of this material over to the Spaniards." He pointed to a sizeable crowd which had gathered to watch the march-out. "It is the least that we can do."

Moore shook his reins and rode away followed by his staff, while Simms watched the town anxiously. Thank God the mist was lifting. Time and again armed formations passed through, baggage trains, and certain Spaniards, who at the last moment decided to place as many leagues as possible between themselves and the French. Neither Simms nor his clerk even glimpsed Mrs Foulkes and her maid for, constantly in and out of the gate, they had enough to do. When the first Rifle Men appear, thought Simms, it will be time to say goodbye. The mist thinned …

He had waited for something like two hours, when at the turn of the street he saw the first files of the rearguard. Firing had died away, and an unearthly silence reigned. Benevente, it seemed, now held its breath. Simms sprang into action. He beckoned to the crowd of watching Spaniards, men, women and children, waving a free hand to the remainder of the stores. "Take what you will!" he shouted.

There was a frenzied rush upon the casks and clothing, while Simms and his assistant ran through the buildings into the garden where brushwood had been piled around the rest of the stores. The two men all fingers and thumbs, nicked at flint and steel until they were able to ignite the oily rags which served for kindling. The twigs were by no means dry but at last the whole was safely ablaze, and as the French hammered at the gates of the town a pillar of smoke rose high in the air and drifted lazily towards the mountains. It was no time for loitering. Simms and his clerk mounting, set their faces towards Bembibre …

They pushed forward steadily uniting with others. Rumour was rife. The French they heard intended an outflanking movement, their cavalry already probing ahead; but though Simms scoffed loudly at the notion of horsemen ranging the hills, Robin noticed that more than once the Commissary cast an anxious eye towards every turn of the road ahead.

At La Beneza, bare poplars shivered in the mountain wind. Here all houses were crammed with the military; those who could not find indoor billets had to be content with cattle compounds and vineyard walls. Simms had hoped to overtake Kearney, but his superior officer having pushed forward, the Deputy Assistant found himself at a loose end. He was not however, greatly concerned. The whole force would be away again in a few hours.

At La Beneza Robin and his sister met. Sue had pondered long over the few lines which Simms had written in Benevene, but the categorical nature of the message and her implicit trust in Simms relieved her of all doubt. Thus she was prepared for the moment at the Alcalde's, as Harriet Foulkes had finished supper and she was drying blankets, when a young English civilian halting diffidently in the doorway inquired for Miss Thompson, and bowing to Mrs Foulkes, "craved (as he put it) a peculiar indulgence." Sue rose from her feet with a stifled cry. "First," said Harriet, "I must know you are."

"Oh, Ma'm," breathed Sue, "'tis he!"

"Have I permission to speak with my sister?"

But Sue came forward. "This is my bother Robin, Ma'm, of whom I have told you."

Harriet permitted herself a long and curious gaze. Though the room was shadowed she could detect the family resemblance. "What are you doing here?" she inquired, "in this place, and with the armed forces? I thought—" Sue kept silent since she had not communicated the bearing of Harry Simms' message even to Mrs Foulkes.

"It is a long and complicated story, Ma'm." Robin hesitated.

"So I should presume," said Harriet significantly. "But I don't in the least wish to stand between you. You must have a great deal to say to each other."

"That you, Ma'm."

With an indulgent nod Harriet retired to a recess of the fireplace, where the flames throwing more light than that shed by the little lamp on the table induced her to open *Tom Jones*. She had to confess herself intrigued. How much more exciting real life was in comparison with fiction! How Mr Fielding and of course Mrs Dadcliffe, would have revelled in the fortunes of brother and sister, who having been cruelly separated, at last united in the Galician wilds! With what high drama they would have infused every word! She stirred pleasurably. Her interest aroused, she could not help casting an occasional glance towards the shadows where brother and sister sat somewhat self-consciously, though only odd words came Harriet's way.

Throughout, Sue and Robin displayed commendable restraint. They had not embraced, but were none the less deeply moved. As Robin tried to relate the events of the preceding six months, he glanced only occasionally. Firstly he assured her that he had been able to send a guarded message to their parents from Corunna assuring the old people of his safety. "I am convinced," he said, "that they will read between the lines and keep their own counsel." He made little of his weeks of imprisonment at York and later in the hulks, reverting rather to conditions on the *Primrose*. the crew had been insubordinate, the Captain and Mate invariably drunk, so much indeed that when a great storm blew up, the vessel ineptly handled, had been dismasted and drifted towards the Spanish cost. The prisoners below imagined that they were nearer to France than Spain, and wondered if they were fated to exchange one kind of restraint for another. The hold, waist deep in water reduced them to the last point of desperation; but at last a friendly sailor struck off their irons. "Thus," continued Robin, "we were thrown upon our own resources. When we climbed out the deck was awash, but I managed to seize a floating hen-coop, and before you could say Jack Robinson, I was overboard with half a dozen drowned chickens for company. I lashed my arm to the coop, and after that have no clear recollection of what happened until I found myself on a pile of dry nets with a couple of fishermen bending over me. I had been washed ashore at a point just south of Corunna."

"How came you to be with the army?" asked Sue.

"All in good time," he said patiently. "These poor people gave me a shirt and a pair of old leathern breeches, and in a day or two sailed me into the port itself. General Baird had just landed. Our people had acquired mules, but few men to drive them. I gave out that I was a shipwrecked purser not realising that I might have been pressed for any of the King's ships then lying in harbour. However, the army swallowed me, and no further questions were asked. One day a commissaries clerk went down with fever, and the department finding that I could write a good hand, I got his place. And so ends my story."

Sue was glad to note that her brother spoke in a tone singularly free from bitterness or self-pity. "I heard also from Mr Simms," he said, "that the wretch Harker has found a refuge in the regiment."

"He is known here as Raddock," said Sue.

Robin locked his hands tightly. "I have already glimpsed him, and in a fashion I reckon that he glimpsed me. What to do henceforward I cannot say – time will tell. But you may be assured—"

Harriet Foulkes, unable to restrain herself longer, now came forward. "You are a very fortunate man, Mr Thompson," she said a little severely. "I don't know how this came to pass, but I am pleased that you are alive and well if only for your sister's sake. You will have to fend for yourself – I mean that we can do little or nothing for you."

Robin rose to his feet. "Be assured that I shall not impose upon your kindness, Ma'm. I only ask that you preserve my secret. If in future you have occasion to address, or in any way refer to me, please remember that my name is Thomas Jones."

"I shall have little difficulty in recalling that," said Harriet glancing at the book she held in her hand.

"And now I beg leave to depart," he said. "Good night to you, Sue, and to you Ma'm, with thanks again for your kindness."

The Colonel's wife smiled graciously, as bowing stiffly, Robin Thompson withdrew.

"He seems of good address, well-spoken," observed Harriet.

"My brother is often taken for a schoolmaster," said Sue, not without a certain pride.

* * *

Private Raddock dragged his feet on the Astorga highway hugging his firelock to keep warm. His head ached badly, and his tongue furred as a rabbit's skin, seemed too large for his mouth. Though he moved in broad daylight, the mirrored face of Thompson continued to vex his mind. Was it possible for the dead to return? He had never laid much account to ghosts, but he recalled now certain traditions of the mine – strange stories of dead colliers howling through deserted galleries, spectres that flittered in and out of the workings, sometimes walking beside men as they left the "face", sometimes watching as they hewed the coal, but never except as a portent of mischief to follow. Was the advent of Thompson's face a warning? If so – of what? In the cold light of day, Harker snorted angrily. "Aw, away and to hell with it," he muttered, "I'll worrit when the times comes."

His thoughts turned to the concrete problem of his own shoes; the sole of the left now parting from the uppers. He threw a sly glance at the feet of Henderson who marched beside him. Henderson's shoes were in good trim, and just about the right size for a swop, but odd rot, the man never took them off but once in a while. Now if on the previous evening, instead of roaming aimlessly for useless trifles he had concentrated on acquiring a good pair of shoes there would have been more sense in it.

The retreat as such meant little to Harker. His honour was not involved, let the conflict move one way or another. The campaign had produced nothing tangible, not a single beefsteak. He thought enviously of Jenks who now carried in his knapsack a jewelled watch, which he must certainly have picked up in travels. Jenks knew what was what! Some fools collected plate, candlesticks and such lumber, but the wise cove turned to the nicely portable: watches, trinkets and the like. He recalled Old Crabtree, a gardener at Wentworth relating how in his day they had rifled Colonial mansions, but devil a chance you had in this poverty stricken country! To hell with Spain!

He rubbed his numbed hands together – nothing to look forward to. Sentence for the slip at Sahagun still hung like a cloud. Altogether a dog's life! Enough to make a man take French leave. Come to think of it, there were far worse things than that. The "Johnny Crapaws" were jolly free-living fellows, never without a marching song, a fire to warm themselves, and a chicken in the pot. It would be an easy matter to fall out – a sprained ankle would do the trick. If (he concluded) Astorga brought nothing more to the kitty than other places had done in the past, he would have to give the matter serious thought ...

* * *

They filed in through the Astorga gate which had been blocked to allow the passage of only one vehicle at a time. The chimes of the cathedral clock intermingled with the tramping of feet and the shouting of orders. All shops had closed. Citizens had barricaded themselves in less from fear of the British incursion than that of Romana's raged Spanish legions who roaring for wine and bread were hurrying in. Certain units of Moore's forces had marched straight through the town, but for Foulkes and his men Astorga became a halting place for the night.

After eating at his billet, Harker whose predatory instinct had been stirred by the sight of substantial houses and shops at close quarters, drew together four of his boon companions – Henderson, Jameson, Crookes and Harmon – indicating with expressive nods and winks that it was time to look around. The possibility of "profit" was not excluded, though no plan of action had been formulated by their leader. Harker they knew was nothing if not enterprising. Thus they followed, two carrying muskets and all armed with side swords.

The party halted to take bearings in a deeply shadowed arcade, until with a whispered word or two they turned from the square into an empty side street, where overhanging signs of various shapes and sizes indicated the merchants quarter. It was difficult in the darkness to make out what these symbols represented; some were placed too high, though a number were conveniently close. Henderson thought he recognised a gilded tooth, Crookes a bale of wool, but neither of these objects gave Harker a moment's pause. He was looking for something quite different.

They strolled on, pausing from time to time to gaze upwards. Occasionally Harker tried a door, but all were locked and barred, all windows shuttered. About half way down the street he halted, pointing upwards. "Hey," he whispered, "ain't that a kind of clock?" He stepped back a pace or two. "A clock to the very life, with blow me, fingers set at half past three. Hang on! Spread yourselves out along the wall."

"What do we want wi' clocks?" asked Henderson.

"Nowt," said Harker, "but where there's clocks there's watches, and other trinkets maybe – a few lockets and bracelets."

A passing Spaniard swerved, giving the loiterers a wide berth. They waited until his footsteps had died away. "Now – quick's the word," said Harker, setting his eye to a chink of the shuttered window … At first he detected nothing but a misty glow which might have been an half-open door; then a light which varied in strength as if someone was moving around with a lamp. Pressing his ear to the shutter he heard voices wholly he judged, female. Drawing back he motioned the others in. "This is the place," he said. Intuitively he felt that male opposition would not be strong.

"Right," said Jameson lifting his musket butt to hammer on the door.

"Not that way, brainless!" hissed Harker, "leave it to me. And keep your mouths shut."

With a swift glance to right and left assuring himself now that the street was quite empty he knocked, not too forcibly, on the door panel. The five hovered with bated breath. They started, gazing apprehensively at each other when a musket shot and a burst of shouting came form the direction of the plaza. Harker, beneath his breath cursed the fool who pressed the trigger. But as no complication followed, after a short interval he knocked again, this time more loudly. He waited, wondering if the clockmaker, responsive to the first summons had crept down the passage and was listening at the other side of the door. Perhaps he employed a peep-hole?

In this however, he was mistaken; a voice from the interior sounded remotely, and footsteps approached. Asthmatic breathing accompanied the sound of a drawn bolt, and a key turned in the lock. There was a slight pause before the door opened an inch revealing a lighted candle. A wheezy voice in Spanish inquired their business.

"Amigo!" said Harker softly, airing what little of the language he knew, at which the door opened a fraction further revealing a pistol muzzle, a shock of white hair surmounting a wrinkled brown face, and eyes narrowed in the half-light, peering uncertainly. They were acutely suspicious eyes, but their owner being a businessman, seemed inclined to make allowance for the lateness of the hour.

"Amigo," repeated Harker clinging to his talismanic word, but in the most unfriendly fashion he thrust his foot in the gap of the doorway, and with his inserted musket barrel struck up the weapon in the clockmaker's grasp. The pistol discharged. A woman from the inner room screamed out, "Manuel! Manuel!" Harker following up his advantage thrust vigorously and brought the Spaniard flat on his back, the hapless fellow groaning and wheezing as the intruders scrambled over his body. "Shut the damned door!" hissed Harker, hoping that in a town so full of movement the report of the pistol would have passed unnoticed.

Having closed and rebolted the door, the soldiers lifted the dazed clockmaker to his feet, and hustled him towards a room where silhouetted in the doorway, a woman, presumably the Spaniard's wife, and three girls were grouped. At once the females moved backwards to the hearth, the elder woman placing herself protectively before the younger ones. Harker's enforced grin did nothing to reassure them, though for the time being they were much too frightened to be awkward. Pale, alert, the woman watched Harker's every movement, and once she glanced towards an iron pot suspended over the fire as though dwelling upon the possibility of flinging the contents over him. When she did find her tongue it was to unloose a flow of invective, the purport of which was only too plain. "Pipe down, Missus," Harker rejoined, "and you'll come to no harm. Now – now, that's quite enough!"

Meanwhile, the clockmaker, a stout fellow in a sleeved waistcoat, had recovered somewhat from his fall, and between violent fits of coughing was making his own contribution to the hubbub. He invoked a string of saints, together with the names of Generals Moore and La Romana for assistance, and was still doing this as they bound him tightly to a chair. Leaving Henderson and Crookes on guard, Harker seized a candle and hurried back to the shop.

Here he was surrounded by clocks of varied sizes and value; painted dials, faces of fine filigree, gilded fingers and cases of rare woods. A few ticked with impartial motion, but he was not interested in the larger specimens. His eyes fastened upon a large glass-fronted case immediately behind the clock-maker's working bench, containing watches. Here was the treasure trove. "Keep your fingers off," he warned Crookes and Harmon who had followed, "and stand back for splinters." Then with a slight grunt of satisfaction, he drove his musket butt through the glass and helping himself freely to the contents, dropped the plunder in his cartridge pouch.

The Spanish females were still bitterly reproaching Henderson and Crookes. He could hear Henderson saying, "If you don't carry on! That's right – keep your temper!" This was followed by the sound of a slap, but by whom administered it was difficult to say. Brisk footsteps sounded in the street. Someone paused outside the shop door, and a heavy knock resounded. Motioning the others to keep silent, Harker tiptoed down the passage and closed the inner door. The knocking sounded more vigorously, and the person in the street called out a name. Above the quiet breathing of the three men, the assembled clocks ticked against each other with supreme indifference. After a final knock the unknown visitor walked slowly away.

At once Harker sprang into action. It was time to go. He re-entered the living apartment. "Thumbs up!" he said, addressing his fellows at the same time jerking his head in the direction of the street. "Block the door. Sharp does it!" After dragging a heavy settee across the passage, and adding to this the clockmaker's bench, they let themselves out. In the quiet thoroughfare they could hear the muffled outraged voices of their victims as the barrier checked them. Somewhere beyond the plaza a house was burning fiercely, but the flames only accentuated the darkness of the street.

For a couple of hundred yards the five men ran lightly, until approaching the main square they fell into a brisk walk. As luck would have it, another detachment of Romana's tattered army had reached the centre of the town hunting for bake houses and wine shops, and to the background of this confusion, the five regained their billet. They did not for a moment doubt that the clockmaker once released from bondage would lay a complaint with the first British officer he could find; but with so many thousands of men widely distributed and on the point of moving out, the chances of detection were small indeed.

Harker, gathering his companions about him, distributed the spoil, "Loot," he reminded them, "is but part of our pay. It is no more than the soldier's right." After serving the others, he kept for himself – since he alone had furnished the brains of the enterprise – four of the most valuable watches, including one set with seed pearls, the lid adorned with an exquisite miniature of a lady. He purred with pleasure as he weighed the timepiece in his hand. It was worth a hundred guineas any day. A neatly finished job …

Feeling that the coup ought to be rounded off with a celebration, the five fought their way into a wine-shop where they all drank deeply. Harker, who carried his liquor well, became at midnight one of a detachment detailed to round up regimental absentees. This duty he performed with exemplary zeal, his animadversions on the evils of intemperance and theft, edifying to all who listened ...

* * *

"Taking all else into consideration," began Foulkes, addressing his wife – he broke off as a bullet from a carelessly handled Spanish weapon in the street below, slapped the stonework of the window beside which they were standing, flaking splinters. "Move back a little, will you?" he said quietly. "As I was saying, wherever possible, it would be well for you to push ahead. At any time we may be detained, but there is no reason why you should not steal a march on your own account. Make your way to Villa Franca, where we will overtake. If Sir John decides to make a stand, you will be well out of it."

"Do you think the General will stand?"

"We all hope so, but one cannot read his mind. I thought he looked exceptionally anxious yesterday. He is probably afraid of being outflanked. Be that as it may, I am quite certain that a passage of arms would put new heart into the men. Pass on however, to Villa Franca. I will arrange for Richards to attend you. We may follow in a matter of hours."

"Take every care, Percy," she said.

The use of his Christian name touched him. He threw an appealing glance, but that was all he revealed of his inner feelings. She knew that there were few in whom he could confide, and self-reproach overwhelmed her as she realised how meagre her own contribution to his happiness had been. Since Benevente she had sensed the profound disappointment he felt in his command, but there was no time to discuss the subject now. He passed a hand wearily over his eyes; with an effort stiffened himself and adjusted his sash. His balding head added to an ageing look. He took out his snuff box, and she was glad to note that her little present was in use. He dropped powder into the palm of his hand and sniffed vigorously. "All in a day's work," he murmured, As he replaced the box in his pocket, she thought of the many stories she had heard of bullets stopped and lives saved by such a simple accessory as this. Perhaps in his case her gift held a peculiar significance.

"Until Villa Franca then?"

He nodded.

"Good luck to you," she smiled.

"We shall need it."

With an enigmatic glance he left the room. He seemed so restless, always hot-foot on a mission which brooked no delay ...

* * *

Again, as in Benevente, baggage and ammunition wagons, blankets, trenching tools and other equipment went up in flames. The French were to inherit nothing – only the hundred or more sick including women, who could not be moved.

Again Harry Simms tackled the work of destruction, chafing and cursing at the abject waste of it all; but orders were orders and must be obeyed. "Who would be a commissary?" he grumbled, "first into a town and last out!" But there were none to listen, none to sympathise.

As the day wore on the sporadic musketry of the rearguard grew louder and louder. The handsome flint-faced Craufurd, iron handed with his own men, gave blow for blow to the French. Some of the British cavalry still remained in Astorga. In addition to other duties the commissary had the responsibility of providing fodder for the horses, an almost hopeless task.

At eight o'clock that evening when the quartermasters came in for forage, Simms, who had run out of wheat and barley, could only offer rye. The quartermasters objected strongly, for this tended to purge the animals, but rye was better than nothing at all. The local Junta gave no assistance. The English should find their own.

Find his own Simms did. Scouting up and down the thoroughfares, he detected at last in the lower rooms of a building, immense mounds of rye. The doors were locked, but Hussars soon broke through. Standing knee-deep in grain, with lengths of board for shovels, they filled the sacks. In addition, Simms considered himself lucky to find wine in an adjacent cellar, but they had no sooner begun to draw this, when a horde of Spanish infantry poured in crowding the place to suffocation. A fracas ensued, knives were drawn, and Simms and his men were thankful to get away spattered only with blood from chickens, which the famished Spaniards had hacked to pieces alive.

As the commissary moulded his hat into a recognisable shape, he realised that it was quite useless to look for wine elsewhere. so having satisfied the quartermasters with grain, he hurried back to his billet where to his consternation he found an aide-de-camp from Paget waiting. The general wished to see the Deputy Assistant Commissary immediately. "At this stage?" protested Simms.

The aide shot a single look. "At any stage," he said sharply, "and I should recommend you, sir, to hurry."

Almost breathless, Simms reported to Paget, who received him at once. "Commissary," said the General coolly, as though he were offering a steak at Whites, "the officers of the rearguard are dining with me tonight, and I have everything but bread and wine. See to it, will you?" The bread offered no difficulty, but when Simms expressed some doubt concerning the supply of wine, Paget crimsoned. "Damme!" he cried, "the gentlemen of the Junta have plenty on their tables – go to the fountain head."

Paget's complete assurance in the face of danger staggered Simms. "One would think," he groused, "that the French were on the other side instead of kicking at the front door of Astorga." None the less, off to the Junta headquarters Simms hurried, where he confronted a circle of gloomy Spaniards, some of whom booted and spurred were ready for the road. No, they were quite out of supplies; their own troops were in want.

"But it is for my general."

"Go with God," they responded indifferently.

Simms, reporting to Paget, was ordered to keep on trying, but the quest was a hopeless one. He scoured the streets of Astorga until he could do no more. Cold rain began to fall. Now the last of the rearguard was beginning to leave the town. Paget or no Paget, he decided, there was nothing more that a single commissary could do. No doubt the General had already dined – if not, the more fool he. Simms ran back to his quarters and was collecting his things when a trooper clattered beneath the window "Saddle up!" the horseman shouted, "all away!"

It was high time to go. Simms dashed out to his tethered horse, strapped on his valise, but as he mounted a loose girth brought everything over, and in a darkness complete save for the glow of burning wagons, tried to readjust the saddle. The buckle tongues would not find the eyeholes, the animal was restive, and the rain thrashed down with added force. Hoof beats receded in the distance – were these from the last of the cavalry? – a crash from the direction of the crown gate and a sputter of firing, nerved his fumbling fingers. At last, the saddle fixed, he mounted and spurred away, but taking a wrong turn, lost his bearings and far from riding in the direction of Villa Franca, found himself approaching the affray at the gate.

Wrenching round his horse's head, he returned to the billet, and started again. This time he was more fortunate. Other horsemen overtook him, and to his immense relief he found that these were white-coated English servants who were leaving with the General's spare mounts. Uniting with them, he gained the high road, along which they all cantered briskly. Quickly the rain turned into sleet, and the sleet to snow, driving so fiercely that all Simms could do was to follow the outline of the man immediately ahead. About a mile out of town, two horsemen drew abreast; when one of these spoke Simms recognised the voice of Paget. Discreetly, the Commissary dropped behind. He had no mind to be recognised by the choleric general he had been unable to supply with wine …

* * *

Harriet and Sue rode steadily towards Villa Franca. Tortuous, knee-deep in slush, the thread of life lay with the road. They passed abandoned vehicles and foundered animals; hapless stragglers plodding on foot. They had not covered many miles before they overtook an ornately decorated coach, lavish in crimson and gilt, impressive even in that land of coaches. The mules by which it had been drawn were standing hind-quarters to the wind, shivering forlornly. Inside, muffled in furs, four grandees sat imperturbably while a coachman and a footman struggled with a sagging axle. The Spaniards bowed gravely to the passing travellers, but Harriet insisted that there was no point in stopping. "What can we do?" she protested, "we are not wheel-wrights and they have the assistance of their own people. If the worst comes to the worst let them take to the mules." She rode forward uneasily, suspecting that such splendid persons had never ridden bareback in their lives.

Every vehicle bearing sick and wounded she examined closely. Pacing slowly on her grey, she looked down on bodies huddled in blankets, into pinched resigned faces. But none conformed to the figure of Tony Harte. She felt she would recognise him if only from the heavy bandages about his head. Where was he now? She scanned the road ahead unceasingly, watched columns winding across the mountain breast, and the slopes beyond where the tenuous thread dissolved in mist ... For a little distance they were accompanied by an officer carrying despatches for England, but as their pace was much too slow, he soon left them behind ...

The long descent brought them to a valley where they halted at a cottage of mud and sandstone, presumably that of a shepherd. The woman who opened the door to them peered suspiciously through a tangle of greasy black hair, a gilt crucifix gleaming dully against the brown Moorish skin of her neck. After snatching at the dollar, which Harriet offered, she permitted them to enter, but once inside they discovered that they had exchanged one level of discomfort for another. Smoke eddying from a fire of heath moss in the middle of the floor, almost choked them; half a dozen dirty, ill-fed, half-naked children, whispered and tittered in the background. Harriet shrank as one of these attempted to finger the fine cloth of her habit. They were in a den of fleas ...

The two Englishwomen began to eat their own rations, every mouthful watched by a circle of hungry eyes. Finally she handed over the greater part of their own sausage and biscuit to the children who snatched at it fiercely, cramming what they captured into their mouths. The patient Richards waited outside the hut, with not only the animals, but the fodder as well. After a brief respite, all three were glad to get away ...

They continued to follow the valley road which ran alongside willows and a swollen stream. Three hours later, a large village of mud and slate houses flanked by terraced vineyards loomed in the distance. They were in the country of wine, and this was Bembibre ...

Colonel Foulkes rode slightly ahead of the drummer and the leading files, his head down to the wind, melted snow trickling down his stock and soaking his tunic. His bay, beginning to lather, was stepping out well. He wished that in Astorga it had been possible to sharpen the animal's shoes – heavy Spanish nails would have served the purpose – but that would have to wait until they reached Villa Franca. All that one could do now was to watch for icy patches half-concealed by slush …

He worked his way around a stranded coach, and as the road for some distance ran straight ahead, fell back upon his own thoughts. Of what use were coaches in this country – nothing like a horse. He wondered how the Romans had managed, burdened as they were with armour upon these mountain tracks … Thank God the cuirass had gone, but much top-hamper remained …

He heard the clink of metal, creaking saddle, and the sodden mane of the adjutant's mount drew almost abreast of his own. Foulkes did not turn his head. "How are the men?" he asked.

The adjutant grunted, easing his cloak forward to keep the holsters dry. "Getting their heads down to it," he replied, "but I am sorry to say that many are not securing arms."

The Colonel frowned; instead of muzzles pointing to the ground so that water would not trickle into the firing pan, weapons were being sloped. "I will take up the matter at the next halting place," he said. "Are we dropping any?" This time he referred not to muskets, but men.

"A dozen or so," said the Adjutant. "Bad footgear. They may pick up again. It's quite surprising how some chaps manage to buck up and overtake. A hard thing to say, sir, but we'd be better off without some of the rascals."

"The muster rolls wouldn't," said Foulkes tartly. The bay, stumbling, came to its knees, and the rider held his seat with difficulty. "Now boy!" he cried, as the animal recovered, "steady!".

"All well, sir?"

"I hope so – ought to see if his knees are broken," said Foulkes as they continued the ascent. A few hundred yards father on, he said, "Pull aside. We'll watch 'em pass."

The two officers backed into a wide cleft of rock, and partly withdrawn watched the men go by, Foulkes, his keen eyes darting from weapons to boots, from boots to faces, made disapproving noises. Too many of the rank and file were lumpish, carrying odds and ends they had picked up in Astorga. "Sailors—" he began.

"What was that, sir?" inquired the adjutant.

"I was thinking," said the Colonel, "how much better placed the Royal Navy is compared with ourselves. At sea each man has his allotted share of prize money; but with us it is grab and get as you can, and the general effect is as bad as bad can be."

His voice tailed off as they watched more files go by. After a time the first of the baggage carts appeared, women peering out from beneath a canopy of canvas and blankets. They eyed the commanding officer incuriously, while he

for his part glared after them. A Tartar horde, he thought, must have presented a similar appearance – nomadic tribes trailing their women and children behind them. Aloud he asked savagely, "Why are they here? What
useful purpose do they serve?" It was as though he had noticed their presence
for the first time.

The adjutant made no reply, and falling behind the cart, Foulkes reflected
moodily that in all these five months of marching and countermarching, his
men had not fired a single shot. What kind of campaign was it? …

* * *

The greater part of the army marched on with dogged persistence. When
shoes fell apart they bound them together with twine, rubbed snow on their
frost-bitten hands and faces, responded by habit to peal of fife and tuck of
drum.

At Bembibre, never had the British seen such rotund casks or drunk such
ample wine. The liquor brought comfort, blissful oblivion from aching limbs,
chapped hands and faces, the looming, inhospitable mountains. The men jostled into wine cellars, splashed wine into their camp kettles, guzzled with
wine streaming down their tunics, and if they were able, staggered to their
allotted quarters, or fell where they tippled on cellar floors or in the open air.
One semi-drunk planted himself in the middle of the main thoroughfare,
and brandishing a musket proclaimed himself commander in chief, until a
passing dragoon with scant respect for this new-found authority, released one
foot from the stirrup and kicked the fellow flat on his back.

Harker and his pards, among the first to fill up their bottles, found a corner in a large stable, where to a flickering candle-stub, they toasted the King,
the Prince of Wales, the Duke of York, the Archbishop of Canterbury, and
lastly "The Colonel, damn his eyes!" Other men entered until the stable was
crowded, but unaffected by the prevailing hubbub, Harker announced that he
intended to oblige with a song, and at once broke into the strains of "The
Lincolnshire Poacher"—

O, 'tis my delight of a shiny night,
In the season of the year—

At the end of the first verse he paused to refresh himself, at the same time
inviting his fellows to join in the ballade. The only response was Henderson's
"Thou'll set all the dogs a howlin'".

"That remark," rejoined Harker thickly, "is from a chap that has no more
tune than a corn crake!"

He struck up again, and having with some difficulty negotiated the second verse, was stumbling into a third when a man who had paused a few seconds in the doorway, moved forward, and picking his way across recumbent
bodies, came to a halt just behind the soloist. Here he remained, half con-

cealed by a stout shaft of timber which supported the roof. It was Robin Thompson. He had no clear idea of what he intended to do – no more perhaps than to observe his enemy in secret and slip quietly away …

Harker, still intent on singing, began all over again, though by this time he had lost some of his initial fervour. The newcomer listened in silence until the last strain had died away, and then in a voice low but clear, said, "You did better than that in the *Miner's Rest*, Jacob." With that he withdrew behind the pillar.

"The *Miner's Rest*," said Harker loosely, "were nothing but an owd rat trap." It took a few moments for the full significance of Robin's remark to sink into his befuddled brain.

"Still blowing your own trumpet, Jacob!" said Robin from his place of concealment.

"Jacob?" remarked Henderson curiously, "whose callin' thee Jacob?"

"It's somebody," mumbled Harker confusedly, endeavouring to struggle to his feet, but his companions held him down. "Keep ye place, ye fool!" they warned, "or ye'll loose it for good."

"You haven't got a place," came the voice – "have you Jacob?"

"He doesn't mean thee," said Henderson.

"Hide and seek, is it?" cried Harker, "well, we'll soon see about that. Unhand me!" He flung Henderson violently aside. "Man or devil – I'll put a mark on him!"

This was the end. The cloaked figure of Robin edged towards the door, stepping carefully. Harker lurched after, but his lagging feet landed first on an infantryman's hand, and off balance he trod on another's shoulder. In the hubbub that followed he lost sight of his mysterious tormentor. When finally he did make the door and burst into the night the road was dark and empty. "I can see ye," he shouted stupidly as a shadow slid between the houses. He swung the bottle which he still carried to his lips, drained it, flung it away, and staggered forward in pursuit of the shadow. But for once he had drunk too deeply. His legs crumpled beneath him, and he fell face downward in the ruts. He did not see the flickering torch, which approached, nor hear the wheels of the wagon to which it was fastened. A second or two later all he felt, was an intense burden of pain in his body, and after that nothing at all …

* * *

When he regained his senses, he was laid flat on his back starring from beneath the fold of a heavy blanket at the low grey ceiling of the sky. It was fully day, and across his field of vision, a few snowflakes drifted. His limbs were numb, and his teeth chattered with cold. What had happened? When he tried to raise himself, he ached so badly that he groaned, and fell back into his former position, watching the play of snow.

Slowly he began to recapture the incident of the previous evening: the uncertain light of the stable, the voice from the shadows, certainly a voice from the past, the pointed allusion to the *Miner's Rest*, the pursuit of the shadowy demon into the road.. But this effort at recollection tired him – his head was bruised and aching. Sighing deeply, he reflected no more. The effort was too much. And yet? ...

Nothing could be more certain, however, than that he was laid in a wagon, that the vehicle jolted along a most uneven road, and that when he drew a breath a stroke of pain ensued. Yet, how had all this come about?.. He realised now that he was not alone. Wedged between a number of kegs and the wagon side, were three other unfortunates, who except for the jolting of the wagon, lay inert. Their faces were covered. Was this the death cart, and its destination the pit? ...

He fell to watching the snow as it flickered overhead. The flakes were real enough; he could feel the gentle fall of each one on his face ... A wagon presupposed a Waggoner. Where, and who, was he? From his present position Harker could see the outline of a shoulder and a hooded head. At that moment the driver sneezed – an uncomplicated human sound which somehow brought the injured man a scrap of comfort.

"Hey – you?" said Harker.

When the driver turned his head, it was Robin Thompson who looked down. "So you've decided to come round," he observed calmly.

Harker stared – and stared – turned his head away a moment, and closed his eyes. He opened them and stared again.

"You may well look," said Robin.

"How came you here? asked Harker in a low voice.

"Wouldn't you like to know?"

Harker pondered the rejoinder in silence. By what quirk of fortune had this man, sentenced in the courts, transported overseas, believed by his sister to be as dead as mutton, contrived to appear hale and hearty in the mountains of Spain? To these questions he could find no answer, nor did the tone of Robin's voice invite further inquiry. One thing at least was certain – that the features viewed in the mirrored room at Benevente had been no figment of the imagination. He found his tongue again. "Where are we goin'?"

"Some place."

"We're bound mate, for Villa Franca." It was the muffled voice of one of his fellow unfortunates. "And by Christ, don't we wish we was there! Rattle 'is bones over the stones, 'E's nobbut a pauper that nobody owns!"

Harker dwelt on this interjection for a while. At last, he ventured, "Thompson – what is my condition?"

"That of a complete rogue."

"You know well what I mean," said the other ignoring the thrust, "how do I come to be here?"

"Dead drunk and run over – lucky for you I picked you up."

"I must see a surgeon," said Harker sullenly.

"*Must* will have to wait."

"Have you no fellow feeling?"

"Not much."

Silence fell for a time. A general officer eyed them curiously as he passed, but said nothing.

"How did you come to be here, Thompson?"

"The mules brought me."

"About your level!" In spite of his aching ribs Harker sniffed sardonically.

"Now you are coming to," said Robin.

"You only copped me because I was helpless."

"Others would have left you!"

"The good Samaritan – hey?" jeered Harker.

"Yes – the Devil knows his Bible too."

Colonel Foulkes drew alongside. He looked down with hard grey eyes. "Any of ours?" he asked.

"One of 'em might be, sir."

"M-m-m—" It was not an approving sound for he recognised his former servant. "Flotsam and jetsam," he jerked, and pricked on.

"You heard that?" inquired Robin.

"No."

But Harker had. "Helpless on your back," he thought bitterly, "and insulted into the bargain!" Aloud he said, "That Foulkes is lucky to be astride a horse. I want a nip o' rum."

"You'll get your ration in Villa Franca."

"If I last that long."

"You're not dead yet."

"I must have a surgeon," groaned Harker.

"There are grand surgeons in the hulks," said Robin

The wagon tilted, and bounced level again. Harker winced. "You did that o' purpose!" he shouted.

Robin did not answer …

CHAPTER XVIII

It was a full day's ride to Villa Franca. The snow, wind-driven, funnelled through crags towering on either side of the road, grim walls which reminded Sue of a picture which hung on the parlour wall at home, of rugged chasms through which hapless thousands fled from the wrath to come. At times the gorge narrowed until only a feeble light filtered through from above. In this dismal half-world creatures of shadow hailed them as they passed. A few crouched over ineffectual fires; in one of the groups Sue noticed women.

Presently the sweating walls receded, and they emerged in full daylight, once again holding to the river bank ... They heard the distant barking of dogs – that was Cacabelos – but if they were to make Villa Franca before darkness fell, there was no point halting by the wayside ... Dark came early in an afternoon so murky, that they were almost at the walls of the town before they saw the gleaming windows of the palace fortress. They had been in the saddle ten hours ...

Villa Franca, its white walls and irregular roofs dominated by a massive place of brown stone, was as large, if not larger, than Astorga. A chill wind blew from the mountains so that the two women were vastly relieved to enter the house of a well-to-do merchant to whom they had been assigned. Rooms of size, furniture of brocade and leather albeit redolent of camphor, were an uncovenanted blessing after the open, harassed road. It was pure bliss to bask in the warmth of a fire, to wash in clean earthenware bowls, to dry oneself on towels of fine linen. Harriet was shocked as she studied her own reflection in the looking glass; she announced she would not proceed a step further without a mask to protect her skin ... They drank coffee from Sevres china cups, and slept in velvet fringed, canopied beds.

Yet within these walls a profound disquiet prevailed. The surge of war ran too close for comfort. In the great kitchen the youngest son of the family – two others were with La Romana – was oiling a musket, while his mother hovered anxiously in the background. The young Spaniard's eyes glowed as he sang a song in praise of "the noble, the valiant, the victorious Romana." When he had completed the task he threw the rag aside and ceremoniously presented arms to the English girl. The musket was an exciting toy. Sue, recalling his compatriots, hungry, half naked and demoralised, rampaging through the streets of Astorga, summoned only the faintest of smiles. The boy did not – could not – be aware of these things. She turned away.

When the following day Foulkes joined them, Harriet was startled to note how drawn her husband's face had become; how swift and darting his eyes. With an impulsive gesture she stretched out her hand towards him, and his face relaxed in a smile. Over wine he became talkative. "We shall probably stay here another day,." he said, "make the most of it. From Villa Franca, you will of course, stay with us."

Harriet looked inquiringly. She had hoped, once again, to push ahead.

"Make no bones about it, the worst lies before us. We shall be marching into barren heights, with no shelter to speak of, no creature comforts. Going will be especially difficult for the animals. How is the grey?"

He stirred angrily when she informed him that the beast had contracted a sore from a creased saddlecloth. "I trusted Richards – if one does not see to everything oneself!"

"But was it Richard's fault? The cloth may have worked so."

"Not if one saddles with care."

He took snuff brooding over his servant's neglect.

She changed the subject, asking if he had spoken with Sir John.

"A brief exchange in passing," he said. "I can tell you one thing – he will not stand."

"Does that please you?"

"It does not."

He did not pursue the matter, but sat watching the flames reflectively. The back of the fireplace had been completed by the insertion of a cast-iron plate adorned by a moulded equestrian figure from a bygone age. A horseman in a feathered hat, cuirass, baldrick and bucket riding boots, caracolled imperturbably through the smoke and flame. As though prompted by a glimpse of this debonair figure, Foulkes remarked, "Are you aware that Captain Harte is lodged at the Franciscan convent of this place?"

She looked up startled. "Indeed, no."

"That is the case. I heard General Frazer, to whom he is some sort of relation, mention the matter. He is apparently, badly wounded." Her husband's tone, though casual, was not unkindly. "The Franciscans have a large building beside the river," he explained.

Harriet sat very still. Such information from her husband's mouth was all the more surprising. He could easily have held his tongue. In a low voice she said, "Poor fellow – it were an act of grace to see him."

Foulkes drew his hand across his eyes with a resigned gesture. "I don't know – why not? He is in bad shape. I am told that he cannot see, poor devil! The hour is late now; perhaps you could manage to go first thing in the morning."

His equable attitude moved, yet at the same time perplexed her. Was it possible that he had more knowledge than that which he conveyed? – that the terribly injured Tony might now be completely written off? The thought shocked her, but she displayed no outward sign of emotion. She began to discuss the idea of cutting out, and wearing a mask, the better to withstand the hard weather which lay before them. Conversation then turned to Bellaby. Her sojourn in Spain had filled her with new ideas about furnishing: the wretched oak panelling at home ought to be replaced by tapestry; a filigree screen would add attractively to the drawing room; she was not sure that scroll work balconies would not add to the exterior of the Hall. In Vigo or Corunna they might acquired a Moorish table? He shook his head doubtfully, at the same time pleased that her thoughts had concentrated on home.

Before she went to rest that night, Harriet slipped through the outer door and gazed across the open square towards the austere outline of the Franciscan house in which Tony lay. Of lights that showed in the many windows, she wondered which one it was which threw a feeble ray upon his darkness, and by whom he was attended. But the wind from the mountains cut to the bone. She shivered, and was glad to return to her own room …

* * *

Harker had been dropped at the same Franciscan hospital, where he lay in doubtful comfort dwelling upon the future. Had it not been for the deeply rutted road at Bembibre his condition would have been much more serious. The ruts had saved him. No bones had been broken, though under the surgeon's probing fingers he had found it expedient to cry with pain. He had no wish to leave these quarters, which though bleak to distraction, offered fare much better than that to which he had been accustomed. His ribs bandaged, Harker sat upon the pallet edge and struck up a conversation with his neighbour in misfortune, an artilleryman from Hope's division, whose leg had been injured by a fall from his horse. Despite this handicap, the gunner exuded optimism. "I shall get me out tomorrow," he said confidently.

"Yes," said Harker, "wi' a thumpin' pair o' crutches!"

"Why not?" rejoined the man. "You can do anything when you try. I once walked wi' crutches from Uxbridge to Bow."

"Downhill?" asked Harker sarcastically.

"Never you mind," said the gunner.

"How chaps," said Harker contemptuously, "can live in a hoppit like this staggers me, but it's better than nothing. I think I'll stop put for a day or two."

The lame gunner twisted on his elbow. "You what?" he cried incredulously. Harker repeated the remark, and the other shook with silent laughter.

"What's so funny about that?"

"You wait till Johnny comes!"

"He's not here yet."

"No, but he will be within the next twenty four hours. Let me tell you, cully, 'at I heard an officer tipping the surgeon that wounded as can't fend for theirselves is to be left behind as there ain't no more transport to carry 'em. And God help, says he, them that is left behind. So I collared a pair o' crutches."

"Where are they?" asked Harker.

"Where I can find 'em," said the gunner artfully.

"Holy Moses!" breathed Harker. He did not doubt for a moment that the man was right; and bruised and aching though he was, he too decided to leave. He still retained the full use of his legs; at a pinch he could march with the best, and with a little soft sawder persuade a comrade to shoulder his musket. Yes, he would rejoin his company.

Assisted by the gunner he dragged on tunic, knapsack and pouches, furtively checking his little store of watches as he did so. All were safe. Really, he didn't feel so bad. With a hasty farewell to the lame one, and a swift glance around, he sauntered into the hall. No one took the slightest notice. A few more steps and he was in the open. He had no idea where his regiment had been quartered, but it would not be difficult to find out. he would report and pick up where he left.

Threading his way through a huddle of carts and animals, he met a man he knew, and was directed down a narrow side street where (he was told) he should look for the sign of the Golden Lamb, now headquarters. He walked stiffly along perhaps for two hundred yards craning his neck, but still no sign of the Lamb. He halted where a trooper had been posted beside an open door. "Hi mate—" he began, but before he could complete the sentence, the other turned his back and slipped into the house. Puzzled by this unfriendly behaviour but still questing, Harker followed into a short passage only to find his way blocked by the man he had questioned. "Push off!" snarled that individual, "and mind your own bloody business!"

The latter's business was all too obvious. Harker peering over that unfriendly shoulder saw in the room beyond another trooper covering a Spaniard with his carbine, while a comrade standing tiptoe on a bench was unhooking a ham from the ceiling. The soldier to whom Harker had spoken thrust his body forward with a savage, "Get out – we don't want no strangers here!"

It would have been well if Harker had followed this advice immediately, but a fatal curiosity held him as he watched the trooper step down with the ham and make for the door, while the man with the carbine backed away still menacing the Spaniard. Up to this point the raid had gone unhindered, but the intruders had still to disengage, for in spite of the carbine barrel pressed into his chest, the irate householder followed in turn by the women of the house pressed into the passage. The women, who had recovered from the first stage of fright, began to scream at an amazing pitch calling upon the Mother of God to blast and confound the English brigands. There was a scuffle in which the Spaniard was thrust aside, and his place taken by an old woman with fleecy white hair who contemptuous of powder and shot seized the carbine barrel with both hands forcing it upwards. The trooper unable, and certainly disinclined to discharge the piece, cursed roundly as he continued backing towards the outer door. Now, two girls, encouraged by the resistance of their elders wriggled through and fastened upon the cross-belts of the troopers. A third girl who seemed to rise from nowhere flung her arms tightly around Harker, who in his present condition could do little or nothing to restrain her. He protested that he was a mere onlooker, but his words were lost on the girl, who reacted by releasing the grip of one hand and scoring her nails down his cheek.

They were now all on the pavement, and in the midst of this fracas when a number of horsemen rode up and a stern voice rapped, "Attention! What have we here?" It was a general officer who spoke with such authority that the tumult at once died away, but only for a few seconds. By this time a sizeable crowd had gathered. The hubbub increased. The Spanish family grouped before the General voiced their grievance, holding the ham, which they had recovered, aloft, indicating Harker's bloody face, and the dishevelled uniforms of the troopers as sufficient evidence of assault. Harker heard the general officer call for someone to translate. Whereupon, phrase by phrase, the Spaniard made good his complaint.

The general officer was Moore himself. "Take away the ruffians," he ordered, when the householder had finished. "A disgrace to the whole force. Make a record – there shall be an example."

In vain Harker protested his innocence. The General's escort dismounted, and the four prisoners hustled across the square and thrust into the town jail, were left to meditate upon the ill-fortune which had brought along the Commander in Chief precisely at that moment. "Ruffians! … Example … Disgrace to the whole force," were words which continued to ring through Harker's confused mind. He reflected bitterly upon the impulse which had prompted him to pause when and where he did. Since Sahagun he had been the victim of one mishap after another, and to crown everything – this! Innocent as a newborn babe, he was awaiting court martial, the verdict of which might well be death. Who would believe his story? He touched the smarting weals on his face angrily. Scars! More scars! The weal on his hand he noted, had turned dark again. His head dropped to his chest and he groaned.

* * *

Day dawned on Villa Franca. During the night a magazine had been looted, and three fires started; but it was now generally known that Sir John had caught certain culprits red-handed. There was to be an execution parade.

Throughout the morning clouds of acrid smoke drifted across the town.

Wagons were burning beside the river bank; powder barrels rolled into the water. Two hundred worn out horses were slaughtered, and stolid troopers hissed between their teeth as they carried out the grievous task. Hour by hour the intermittent cracking of their pistols was echoed by the musketry around Casabelos where Craufurd's men bickered with the French. Ovens in the town were baking to capacity; the hot bread being loaded up immediately and carted away. Prudently, Harry Simms filled his saddlebag with sausage and biscuit ...

Harriet Foulkes donned her cloak, and through the drifting smoke went on to the convent. She had spent a restless, sleepless night, the square a bedlam of clattering wheels and shouting ... Sue served her with a cup of steaming chocolate, and a dish of small sweet cakes, but she ate mechanically. She told herself that in view of the impending journey she must indeed eat well. She would attend to that later. Before going out she ordered everything to be ready for immediate departure.

Flurries of snow stung her cheeks, but her hands were buried deep in her muff as she picked her way to the Franciscan house. Her head ached abominably, and her mouth was dry; most of all she trembled with apprehension at what she might encounter. The calm acquiescence of her husband to the visit implied the worst.

A spasm of terror filled her as she observed a string of vehicles winding slowly towards the Corunna gate. Was it possible that Tony occupied a place in one of these? Feeling that this would be the last straw, she hurried on breathlessly ... The Surgeon's orderly in the great hall reassured her. Captain Harte was still with them, but he would be leaving soon. "Thank God!" she muttered. How cold and cheerless the building was! – everywhere stone flags, stone pillars, stone steps, stone balustrades. She followed the orderly, their footsteps sounding leadenly.

Tony occupied a sparely furnished cell, containing the usual crucifix, while around the walls carved panels depicted the stations of the Cross. The air was slightly tempered by a brazier, and a large candle helped out the little light which filtered through a window high up the wall. Fully dressed, covered with a blanket, Tony half-reclined, half sat upon the bed. The orderly advanced announcing a lady visitor. The injured man raised his hand slightly in acknowledgement. The orderly withdrew.

"I can imagine only one lady in Spain who would wish to see me now," said Tony, " – Andromache."

The classical conceit fell strangely in the austere quiet of the Franciscan house. Swiftly she remembered her conversation with Suckley and trembled. "Not Andromache," she disclaimed, "simply Harriet."

"As you wish."

His voice was level, composed. He might have smiled faintly beneath the bandages. Certainly he made no attempt to deplore his condition, but she was not surprised, for such was not in his nature. She dropped to her knees beside the bed, and took one of his hands in both of hers. How cold it was. She said, "I wish I knew of some means by which I could assist you." At all costs, she felt, she must not yield to emotion.

"The surgeon is most attentive. He has done what he could."

Tony went on to assure her that by displacing the bandage slightly he could at least discern the candlelight. He did not add that the sabre stroke had somewhat fractured his skull and that at times he suffered from an appalling head. She braced herself to imitate his composure, and listened patiently while he explained how meeting with one breakdown after another, he had come to be delayed. "When I arrive in England," he said whimsically, "I shall assume a black patch. They are quite the fashion."

"Ever *a la mode,*" she rejoined. What else could one say? But after that he refused to discuss himself. "I must know," he said, "how you have fared." She related something of her journey from Sahagun, but what were snow and discomfort, mountain roads and river crossings, compared to the tragic condition of the man now before her? He asked when she intended to leave, and she replied sometime during the morning.

"I am due within the hour," he said. "They have found for me a kind of gig – or as near a gig as the region provides; in effect a light cart – very gay, I'm told, with red and yellow wheels. Should be easy to recognise if we meet on the way. Of course, my man Johnson will be with me. He has seen to everything, including the usual dainties."

"Dainties?"

"Biscuit, salt fish, pork." She felt he would have grimaced if he could.

"It is possible that we may overtake you."

"In that case you will have to march fast. If Sir John makes a stand in the mountains you are bound to lag. As it is, he won't need my services. I shall push on to Corunna."

They were silent for a little while. From a distance, muffled by the walls, came the faint sound of cracking pistols as the last of the horses were dispatched. An odour of woodsmoke crept into the cell.

"Given a reasonable road to the coast, and after that a favourable wind," he mused, "we should see England within a fortnight. Thus farewell to onions, garlic, fleas and Frenchmen. We shall no more—"

He was toying with words, and both knew it. "Promise you will do nothing rash," said Harriet.

"My dear – what? Handling the ribbons myself?"

"I mean – attempt nothing beyond your powers."

"My powers!"

She wished she had not spoken …

Time was passing. A cough from the corridor indicated that Johnson the man was waiting, perhaps to deliver a message – or was this a discreet hint that it was time for the visitor to go?...

"Goodbye."

The last word had to be spoken. She bent over and kissed his half-concealed lips. He pressed her hand gently. "Until we meet again," he said.

"Assuredly we shall."

"Of course."

"You will be improved out of all recognition."

"But absolutely I trust!"

The irony of the words were too much for her composure. She wrenched away her eyes blurred with tears, the last impression that of a faceless head turned towards her. Outside the door she encountered Johnson, took from her purse a couple of guineas, and pressed these into his hand. "Look after the Captain well," she said.

The man eyed the money, frowning. "That I will Ma'm," he said, "but I didn't need this."

"Money is always useful." The implied reproach touched her.

"It is a privilege to serve Captain Harte."

"A good journey then to you both."

"And to you, Ma'm as well."

She searched his stolid earnest face. He seemed a good reliable man. The fact that he would be in charge reassured her.

She dragged out across the cold flagstones. At the foot of the stairs hung a massive crucifix in alabaster, thorns pressed into the stricken Lord, the body crimson with wounds. A monk passed, his face concealed, but as he paused momentarily crossing himself Harriet too was impelled to halt and to murmur a fleeting prayer. A craving for some omniscient force, transcending heat and cold, darkness and light, the arid mountains and the lonely sea, overwhelmed her. If there were guardian saints and angels, she would invoke them now...

She regained the open air hardly conscious of the biting wind. One could not leave Villa Franca too soon ...

* * *

Through the last stage of his protracted nightmare, Harker paced between two huzzars. Wrists pinioned, he ached with pain. Even now he did not know the names of his companions in misfortune, nor did he care. In a short time it would be as though such names had never existed. "Ashes to ashes, dust to dust" Already he could hear the Chaplain's sonorous plaint.

The court martial had occupied no more than a few minutes. Throughout the trial his stomach had griped, and his knees turned to water. There were moments when he watched and listened numbly, as though he had been a mere spectator, until the harsh reality rushed in and struck him with the force of a blow. No voice had been raised on his behalf – certainly not that of his own Colonel. The tell-tale weals on his cheek, the imprint of a stupid girl and a complete stranger at that, were altogether damning. As he studied the flinty eyes and grim weather-beaten faces of the officers who constitute the court, and to whom the affair was no more than a temporary nuisance, he knew that his doom was sealed. He heard as from a great distance the sentence of death ...

Even now he could not believe that this was the end, though beside him one of his fellow victims was reciting the Lord's Prayer – "Our Father which art in Heaven—" A second mumbled, "my poor Betty! – my poor mother!" The third in the grip of sullen resignation, was silent.

Troops had been drawn up in a hollow square, the ranks enclosing a chestnut tree, its branches naked except for a few withered leaves. It was towards this tree that the little group was making. The chestnut branch was the gallows, the rigid lines of shakoes, cross-belts and palisaded muskets, formed the last prison walls. A company of horsemen had jingled in, wheeled in a half circle, and halted about twenty-five to thirty feet from the tree. No need to inquire the identity of these ...

The condemned men halted beneath the giant outstretched branches. Sir John, leaving his staff rode forward alone, reined to a standstill and addressed the square. He spoke in a clear parade ground voice, and although the wind carried away much of what he said, Harker heard fragments, sometimes single words such as "determined" ... "shameful" and "disgrace"; once "the discipline of this force is my concern, and—" The last words he could not hear at all.

It was over. The Commander in chief then wheeled his horse into a position just ahead of the others. He sat like one carved in marble, facing the spot where the Provost Marshal and his assistant were waiting. "Ye hear what he said?" breathed one of the escorts in Harker's ear. "O'ny one is to die. Ye are to draw lots."

Sir John had so far relented ...

A flood of hope surged in Harker's breast, but almost immediately this ebbed, leaving him chilled and limp as before. He could see an orderly handing to the Provost Marshal a handful of straws which the latter at once began to arrange between his fingers. "The death gamble," thought Harker dully, "and this poor beggar's in it!" One straw caught by the wind was whirled away. "There goes a life," he thought, but there were other straws left.

All ranks stood in perfect silence, tense, watchful. Harker, his heart thumping against his ribs groaned, "for god's sake don't fumble – get the thing over!" Suddenly every scrap of hope forsook him. He felt that he was marked for the grave, and oddly began to speculate on the fate of the watches he had purloined in Astorga. He could see his goods passing into the capacious hands of the Serjeant Major, who would doubtless slip the best into his own fob.

With incredible speed and intensity, his mind ranged over the past: the pillared hall at Wentworth; lines of horses nuzzling food in their boxes; candlelight flickering in the subterranean galleries of the mine, the singing of larks as one rose to the surface ... The accusing eyes of Susan Thompson fixed him, the gaunt features of her brother reflected in the wall of mirrors – rare news this would be for the pair of them – and at the *Miner's Rest* the wiseacres and toss-pots nodding at each other over their ale, "Aye – aye, I allus thowt 'e'd come to a sticky end!" ...

The horror was that he was innocent! He emitted an inarticulate cry, but was at once admonished to "shut his mouth!" and "die like man!" The irony of this observation made Harker give a strangled laugh. That was all they wanted – no trouble, no inconvenience, choke a fellow's life away, and thank you, sir, very kindly!

The Provost Marshal was now ready. The straws, three long and one short, had been arranged between the fingers and thumb of his right fist, the unequal ends hidden. "He that take the short straw," said the officer in a flat businesslike tone, "stands condemned."

The fist extended to the trooper on Harker's right. With trembling fingers the man drew a somewhat lengthy straw staring at this talismanic wisp of the cornfield like one bemused. "Hold to it man!" barked the Provost Marshal. At the moment there was no measure of comparison with the other straws; you had to wait – to wait. "Oh Lord God," breathed Harker, "I've been a wicked wretch in my time, but save me this once, and I'll reform!"

He was next. The fist extended. He noticed the coast black hairs with which the back of the hand was covered, and drew a hissing breath between his teeth as his own fingers hovered. "Come on," rasped the Marshal, "we can't wait all day." Slowly Harker took the centre wisp. It was a fairly long slip, similar in length to that drawn by the first trooper. He drew a shuddering breath of relief, but his heart quaked as he reflected that the difference between the long and the short straws might be of an inch only.

The officer's fist moved on, and the third prisoner drew. His straw being so much shorter than the others, the Marshal clinched the matter by exclaiming, "Your's it is man!" The trooper stared at the straw almost derisively, until opening is hand he allowed it to drift away. He was ordered to step three paces forward. As he did so, Harker swayed. "I'm feeling badly," he mumbled. "I—"

Words failed him. He turned his eyes to the snow-capped mountain peaks, remote, austere in the thin winter sunshine; but these began to revolve in the most surprising fashion. The earth rose up to meet him. He remembered no more ...

CHAPTER XIX

As the last regiments marched out and French bullets began chipping fragments from the roof tiles, a sapper officer cantered through the streets shouting, "Listen all you British – everyone across the bridge by six o'clock! We blow up the bridge at six!"

The last surge began ...

Harry Simms, who had been ordered to cart away all the flour he could lay hands on, and to follow with the rearguard, stuck to his job at the last moment. He had lost sight of Robin Thompson who had been sent off with some form of transport. Simms was now alone. Already the Spanish drivers were slipping away on their own account, and as he had no means of binding them to their duty, he left the few who remained to their own devices, and set his horses head in the direction of the bridge. Here barrels of salt fish had been broken open for all who passed to help themselves, but this food had been largely ignored. "You little know how soon you will need it," thought Simms grimly ...

The bridge when he came to it was jammed with troops and fugitives, but joining the press he jostled through to the other side. About half an hour later when he was well down the road, he heard a heavy detonation in the rear; a vivid flash of light threw the walls of the defile through which he was riding into savage relief. Craufurd's sappers had done their work, but there was only passing comfort in that. The French were not far behind, and they too were not without skilful engineers ...

* * *

By an irony of circumstances a half dazed Harker found himself once again in the wagon driven by Robin Thompson. How this had come about he did not know, and for the time being did not much care; but as he recovered himself, heard the familiar voice, and saw the unwelcome profile, he grinned ruefully. The ordeal of the preceding day was still heavy upon him. At times he was seized with fits of trembling which were certainly not the effect of cold. He had known many tight corners in the past, but none where he had peered so closely into the eyes of death. The imprint of Moore's stern features, the gaunt arms of the chestnut tree, the line of straws in the Provost Marshal's fist, would be felt, remain with him until his dying day. He would never have the heart to chew a straw again ...

His mind clearing, he scanned the distant scene. Clouds of fleecy white streamed out like wool across the sky; he never could have believed that mountain slopes were so attractive. All in all, it seemed, the hand of the Lord had been stretched out to save him. He had always regarded religion with profound distaste, the deity he considered a figment of the imagination, the parson a privileged spoil sport hand in glove with the squire. Now, recalling the fervent appeal that he had made in the moment of extremity and the unexpected response, he felt that there might be something in religion after all. The difficulty was that observance meant giving up so much of what you enjoyed, and other things too. There were the watches for example still in the knapsack which untouched, had been returned to him. He could not, even if he would, return these to their rightful owner; to confess to theft implied further punishment.

Perhaps God would not mind if for the time being he retained the watches?

Further – how could he hope to appease the man, who now huddled over in front of the vehicle, had every intention of bringing him to justice? If God in His mercy had seen fit to snatch a fellow from the gallows tree, was it fair now to mark him for a second death in the hulks and chains? The good Lord, he felt, would do nothing of the kind ...

Harker abandoned these philosophic reflections to note that the aching around his ribs had lessened, so that he could now bend without involuntary groaning. Better say nothing about that. In the meantime nothing would be lost by making a friendly approach to Thompson. He wetted his lips, hesitated, and finally called out, "Hey, lad!"

A pause ...

"Did you speak?" said Robin at last.

"Aye," said Harker, "when do we stop to eat"

"When the mules are hungry."

"I'm faint."

"You're lucky to be alive at all."

"I was innocent as a new born babe."

"No doubt! Always the others – never Jacob Harker."

"God's truth! I was a harmless spectator."

"The Spanish girl didn't think so."

Harker fingered his scarred cheek. "I've been through something I can tell you. It's made me think—"

"What?"

The hard, sceptical rejoinder checked Harker. He had no words with which to express his recent reflection. He altered his position slightly, and watched the winding road as he considered his next move. Deeds after all spoke louder than words. He took from his pouch the best of the Astorga watches, and opened the case, the diamonds encircling the miniature flash-

ing palely in the grey mountain light. It was so exquisite a piece of workmanship that it cut him to part with it. He snapped the lid to and sighed.
The sacrifice would have to be made. "You got a timepiece?" he asked.

Robin glanced over his shoulder. "What was that about time?"

"I asked – ha' you got a watch?"

"I had one, but the turnkey took it in York – and forgot to hand it back."

"Well, here's one that will make up," said Harker extending the watch.

Robin took the timepiece and eyed it appraisingly. "A beauty," he said.

"Never seen a finer. Keep it."

"No thank you." Robin handed back the watch.

"But you have no watch?"

"I can do well without."

"Please yourself."

Rebuffed, but at the same time relieved, Harker returned the watch to his
pouch. The way of reconciliation apparently, would be hard.

"Where did you buy that?" asked Robin.

"I had it given."

"You have generous friends."

Harker lapsed into brooding silence. After a time – "Rob?" he resumed,
more intimately, lowering his voice.

"What now?"

"I have been thinking about us."

"And not before time."

"I am in a position to let thee have fifty guineas – when we make
Corunna. A farewell gift. With that tha' can set off for America, begin afresh
– let bygones be bygones."

"Fifty guineas?" asked Robin incredulously.

"I have means."

"For two pins I'd throw you out."

Climbing steadily, they have reached a spot where the road hacked out of
the mountain side, revealed a sweating wall of rock to their immediate left,
and a sheer drop of some hundreds of feet to the right. In the gulf, unseen, a
stream chattered among the crags. Harker eyed the narrow verge. "You
wouldn't," he said coolly.

"Why not?"

"Because it ain't in your nature."

"What do you know of my nature?" inquired the other bitterly, "all you
appreciate is craft, deceit, lying."

Harker shook his head half admiringly. "Now that's quite a little sermon.
I've heard many a wuss in church, but tell me Thompson—"

"What now?"

"Strikes me as peculiar I'm in this wagon again. How come?"

"Because I hadn't forgotten you."

"Meaning what?"

"You're pretty stupid if you can't guess."

"I'm not good at guessing," drawled Harker tantalisingly, feeling less and less contrite as the conversation continued.

"Well, because I had much rather you were safe in England than a prisoner in France. Ever hear of justice?"

"I see. Like a beast to the slaughter, eh?"

But Harker said no more. The wheels creaked; hooves beat into the slush. From time to time, leafless scrub snatched at the wagon sides. And still they climbed ...

* * *

The Colonel rode ahead; Harriet and Sue a good length behind. When they looked back it was to see muffled faces, bowed shoulders, sloping muskets – a human chain bending pliantly to the road. Far down the mountain slope, trees clung tenaciously, their roots knotted in deep crevices of rock. An occasional rumble above their heads, and at times in the gulf below, alarmed them. Sue, to whom the sound represented no more than distant thunder gazed askance at Harriet. But her mistress knew better. She had read of great Alpine avalanches, terrific movements of earth, ice and snow, obliterating all human life in its path. Pray God they would be relieved of that! She watched a solitary eagle break free from its eerie and flap into the haze. If only one had been equipped with similar wings!

An imperative voice cried, "No dropping out there! Fall in! Keep the road."

It was so easy to fall out, to sink on the wayside boulder-dripping wet though it was; to chafe one's numbed feet, to discard the intolerable musket ...

"You there! – does it take three to tie up a shoe. Fall in!"

You could walk on bare bones for all the officers cared!

"No shirking now! Best foot forward!"

But not where recesses invite; where beneath the shelter of a blanket one could listen to the soughing wind, indulge in a little blissful sleep ...

"On no account fall out – keep marching!"

"I can't bear to see their eyes," said Harriet, as they passed a wretched pair of stragglers.

"Then don't look," replied her husband.

"One feels so helpless."

"Your own horse," said Foulkes, "bears a sufficient burden. Hold on to that thought. They must pick up and follow as best they can. He knew, even as he spoke, that not one in ten would ever rejoin their units. There was a limit to human endurance.

"What will become of those who are left?"

He took off his cocked hat and slapped it free of ice. "I don't know," he said bleakly. "One hopes for the best." He would have indulged in a pinch of snuff, but the track was treacherous. "Careful here!" he warned as they crossed a difficult patch.

The road levelled somewhat, but he still gazed anxiously ahead. Foulkes was not a suspicious man, but he looked with a jaundiced eye upon the serried peaks and shadowed valleys which ringed the horizon. Was nature itself resentful of their presence, jealous of its secret places, conspiring subtly to enslave the will? He had read of trolls and gnomes, mystic guardians of lonely places, nonsense of course, but an eerie feeling that nature deliberately conspired to hinder the army's progress …

He was glad when the adjutant came, if only to report the defection of three more exhausted men. Had they rations, he inquired, blankets, a measure of rum. Then there was nothing more than one could do. A woman had decided to stay behind with her husband. "Utter madness!" Foulkes protested. "Keep everyone in movement."

He looked back at the intermittent line drawn out across the slope. "There is a solid core," he thought, "but how long will it hold?" Even as he watched, an infantryman with a furtive glance around dropped his musket in the gulf below. Foulkes snarled, furious that Lieutenant Carworth and the stupid ensign close at hand, should not have noticed. They should be brought to account! Already he could hear the ingenuous excuse of the infantryman, "I stumbled, sir, and the weapon flew out of me 'ands," and Carworth's bumbling, "I cannot say it came within the range of my observation, sir."

Bricks without straw! Water poured into the sand. He chewed over his grievance as he waited for the men to come up …

* * *

A crack like a pistol shot. Spokes and felloes gave as the wheel collapsed. The cart tilted and all three occupants were tumbled in the snow. Dazed, shaken, two scrambled to their feet, Johnson at once darting to the assistance of Tony Harte. The third member of the little party, a sapper with an alleged frost bitten foot, whom they had picked up when about five miles out of Villa Franca, swayed uncertainly. He did not meet Johnson's accusing eyes, for he was conscious that his extra weight might had had something to do with the breakdown.

But this was not time for recrimination. Ruefully they regarded the disabled vehicle, its traces twisted over the flanks of the horse which fortunately had not been overthrown. The iron tyre and the woodwork having parted, the damaged wheel was quite beyond repair. In the vain hope of splicing the spokes, Johnson produced a coil of rope which with foresight he had brought along, but he might well have spared himself the trouble. The wood had snapped cleanly. The plain fact was that the cart, which at the outset had seemed substantial, had not been built for use on mountain roads.

"Well, what do you make of it?" inquired the Captain who was propped in a sitting position at the roadside, nursing his crutch.

"I reckon, sir," said Johnson, "that what we want is a new wheel, and with it a wheelwright."

"As well cry for the moon," said Tony. "What do we do next?"

Johnson scratched his head. "Wait till others come along – failing their assistance, there's always the horse for you, sir. I can walk."

"We shall have to think about that," said Harte. "Meanwhile, let us make a virtue of necessity and wait. I'm peckish, and I'm sure you must be too. The gig, I take it, is on its side – with a blanket or so- improvise a pavilion."

"A pavilion?" thought Johnson. "Where does he think we are – at Kew." He looked up and down the deserted road. "A rabbit hutch, more like!" Aloud he said, "Very good, sir. A pavilion it is. If you will be good enough to take a few steps with me." He drew Tony aside, and with some help from the sapper heaved the cart more on its side. Using a spade, which at the last moment he had remembered to throw in, he flattened the surrounding snow, threw up two flanking mounds as some protection against the wind, and with a blanket hitched by two corners to the body of the cart, made a passable shelter. "I think that will serve, sir."

"For the time being."

"Indeed," said Johnson, "we must collar the next division that comes up. I don't doubt but what we shall find friends."

They ate together, swallowed a little brandy, and Johnson having tethered the horse securely, fed it rye. By the time this was over the short winter's day was drawing to a close.

With darkness came snow …

By turns Johnson and the sapper kept watch. They had not calculated upon the thickly driving snow which brought visibility down to only a few feet. Shadowy figures tramped towards them, drew abreast, and vanished as quickly as they had come. More than once Johnson marched step by step for fifty to a hundred yards with dim outlines from whom he implored assistance, but always in vain. He was thrust aside by men much too preoccupied by cold and the flurried darkness to bother about the fate of strangers. Frustrated, angry, he rejoined his companions, whose shelter now covered with snow, was easy to rediscover. When during long intervals none passed at all, they heard only the restless shifting of the horse, and the wind teasing branches in the crevices overhead. It was by now unsafe to leave the shelter for more than a step or two. The road, less than a dozen feet in width had thoroughly whitened over, and still the snow fell. Sleep being out of question, each man sat occupied by his own thoughts. Presently the Captain nudged Johnson. "What was that?" he asked.

"Don't hear nothing," said his servant.

"A cart or wagon for a ducat," said Tony, who had caught the sound clearly. "It may offer something." He spoke in a level tone, but that did not surprise Johnson; during the past few days his master had become oddly resigned to his lot, never complaining, requiring only a minimum of attention.

Now Johnson heard wheels. A vehicle was crawling at some risk, driven perhaps by an experienced Galician who relied more upon the instinct of his animals than that of his own perception. Tony's servant scrambled to his feet, crept from the shelter and waited anxiously. The wagon came up and as it wheeled slowly by, Johnson could see that it was piled with baggage and carried passengers. As he fastened on the side, one of these inquired testily who the devil he was. "I have Captain, the Honourable Anthony Harte here," said Johnson, making the lost of his master's title, "he is in great distress and you must take him with you."

"What's that you say?"

Johnson repeated the statement.

"We're all in distress," came the voice. "We couldn't pack another in not if it was the Archbishop of Canterbury. There's no more than a pint to a pint pot! Get forrard!" The wheels squeaked, and the dark shape disappeared in the blizzard.

"God damn you to hell!" shouted Johnson. "I hope you tumble in the pit!"

"Compose yourself," said the Captain when his servant reported his none-success. "Don't go out again. The main thing is to keep warm."

But Johnson was not to be appeased. He gestured fiercely at the darkness, and fumbled with the priming of his pistol. "The next that comes I'll stop wi' this."

"Ah, if we were on Bagshot Heath!" observed the Captain tolerantly, "but we are not, and must shape accordingly."

"Very well, sir," grunted Johnson, "I'll reserve action."

"That's better. We can do nothing until daylight. Lets sit more closely together. We hold one ace at any rate."

"An ace, sir?"

"The horse."

"Sir?" said Johnson. "Promise not to stir a handsbreath wi'out I'm with you."

"I will if that comforts you. Draw closer."

Throughout this and other exchanges, the sapper had said nothing really because he had nothing to say, but in response to the Captain's invitation, sat shoulder to shoulder with Johnson. His name was Miggs, but apart from the remark that his legs were killing him, he remained silent. There seemed no point in enforcing a conversation; so all three disposed themselves to sleep …

Several hours passed. Snow seeped steadily between the blanket's edge and the cart. Once, when Tony awoke, he had grown so numb that he could not feel his feet. He tried to knead with his hands the sodden leather of his boots, but without much success, and he dozed off again. He was dreaming in a confused fashion, when he was awakened by Johnson shaking his shoulder vigorously. "Wake up, sir, wake up!"

"What is it?" inquired the Captain dully.

"The sapper's gone, sir, and the horse as well."

"No doubt he's riding for help."

"Helping himself!" flamed Johnson, "that's the size of it!"

"Well, rejoined Tony philosophically, "there are two less mouths to feed."

"I didn't like his phiz from the beginning. Feed a cur, and he bites your hand. I blame myself for not keeping awake."

"None of that now," said Tony. "You have done what you could. Come into the shelter – its damned cold, man."

"You ought to move about a bit, sir, to keep up circulation."

"I would," returned the Captain, "but my feet refuse their office. Besides, we might well be blown over the edge. What time do you make it?"

Johnson nicked at the flint, and produced a light. He consulted Tony's watch. "Near two o'clock," he reported, "early morning." He squatted, drawing up his knees.

"Come closer," said his master. "We'll have a shot to liquor to liven us."

When Johnson felt for the bottle, it had gone. "It was here last," he said. "I can't understand –" Then with a baffled cry, "That sapper hound has prigged it – of all the devils in hell!"

"Well, we must do without. I am more than sorry, Johnson, to have drawn you into this pickle."

"No need to apologise, sir."

To ward off sleep, the servant began talking of his native Manchester, the spinning mills, the rows of houses which were being built, so much better than the mouldy hovels to which the labourers had been accustomed. The Captain listened attentively, from time to time, asking a question. It was a world of which he had no knowledge. At length he said, "Are your parents alive?"

"Both."

"And you, a married man?"

"Indeed, no."

"Ah –" breathed Tony with a long-drawn sigh. "Johnson," he said, "are you listening?"

"Yes, sir."

"I have been reflecting on the situation. You had best move out, make your way down the mountainside until you meet a responsible officer and march back with him. It is too much to expect that the sudden accosting we make here will be taken much notice of. Acquaint the officer of the pass we are in. You will do that."

Johnson did not reply.

"You heard what I said?"

"Yes, sir." Johnson forced the words between his clenched teeth.

"Very well. That is an order Private Johnson."

The servant did not move.

"Must I repeat myself?"

"I promised I would not leave you, sir, and that I shall not."

"Private Johnson!"

"Yes, sir."

"You will set aside all previous commitments, and assume contact with the nearest British officer."

"I am sorry, sir."

"You are a damned stubborn fool I shall remember this."

"I don't mind that, sir. Let me point out that it isn't yet daylight – a man can do little in the dark."

"How right you are." Captain Harte's chin sank to his chest. His interest in Johnson slackened. "Yes, the wild Galician night," he murmured, "gaunt rocks, driving snow, a yawning precipice , a blanket flapping in the wind, and two lonely travellers cowering for shelter – pure Salvator Rosa! ..."

"What was that you said, sir?"

"Thoughts ...random thoughts."

The Captain's meditation was not such that the rough, untutored Johnson could share. In the sealed chamber of the former's mind, outlines, colours, sounds ... half remembered scenes and faces.. voices whispering in shadowy pavilions ... feet tripping down lengthy corridors ... drifted in and out. The pain across his brow had gone, though the intolerable weight of his head remained. But that would pass ... all things passed ...

He came to himself, trying to reach out with his hand. "Are you there, Johnson?"

But Johnson was soundly asleep, and presently the Captain too drifted into a world relieved of time and space. A warm and ineffably soothing wind swept through the darkness, and once again came voices: that of his father presenting him, as a boy, with his first pony – "Equitation first, you young devil!" ... admonition from his mother which had something to do with rock climbing, or was it a last emphatic warning not to scramble across the roofs? Then silence, and the gentle sound of wavelets lapping as it might be in the heart of a cavern...

After a time a familiar voice curiously muffled, cried, "Captain Harte ... Tony ... Hector!" But try as he would he found it impossible to reply. He could only make a courteous gesture, the slightest bow, but even that was difficult ...

"Hector!"

He was inclined to respond, "You should not have ventured into the bar-

barous country – for your life and reputation, go!" But he could not, and more than ever his limbs refused their office. Presently the voice faded and was gone. He drifted in complete darkness.

Steadily the snow formed a long and sloping drift across the overturned gig. Within the improvised shelter both men were still. The wind howled and whistled, the rocks cracked with cold, the blanket sagged, and snow sweeping through the exposed gaps mounted around the half recumbent figures. As time passed, the drift deepened, until all that projected from the flawless mantle concealing the cart, was a yellow segment of wheel, the one stroke of colour laid upon the crystal surface …

* * *

Tired, sodden, famished, the regiment passed the first night out of Villa Franca at a small village in the mountains.

Following Simms' advice, Harriet and Sue had two blankets each, one folded around the other, so that when at the day's end they halted, the inner was dry. Oblivious of the snores and groans about them, they slept deeply, but with the first glimmer of dawn, heavy eyed and aching, they were in movement again. Fortunately the animals were in good condition.

All the league stones had been snowed under, but debris human and otherwise left by the advance divisions marked all too clearly the course they were to follow. For some hours the snow stopped, and a fierce wind swept the sky free from cloud, revealing a stark panorama of mountain heights, awe-inspiring vistas of slopes and valleys. Sue, recalling a Biblical phrase, thought it the abomination of desolation; but Harriet in spite of discomfort, found herself sketching with an imaginary pencil the streamers of dry snow, which, caught by the wind, swept towards the sky.

About midday, snow fell again in thin feathery flakes. With lowered heads they made several more miles, trusting wholly to their sure-footed beasts for safety. The snow brought with it isolation. They saw their companions dimly through driving curtains of white. At times they lost sight of each other completely.

After a long and arduous climb Sue suddenly found herself confronted by the Colonel. Looking down with anxious bloodshot eyes, he shook his cloak free of snow as he inquired, "Where is your mistress?"

The girl stared back in surprise, assuming that husband and wife had been riding together. He rapped again, "Where is she?"

"Sir, I cannot say."

"But you were with Mrs Foulkes?"

"I was for a time. I thought—"

"You thought – you thought!" he interrupted impatiently. "God in heaven, don't you know?"

The snow drove fiercely between them, but there was no mistaking the anger in his eyes. He was venting on her (Sue felt) his own anxiety, his own resentment. "She is not here," he continued, "nor am I able to find her, though I have been up and down the column twice. I will look again. She cannot have gone forward alone. Follow me."

He wrenched his horse round, and Sue turning her mule, the two began retracing their steps, halting at times for files to pass. They had proceeded steadily rearwards for about a quarter of a mile without any sign of Mrs Foulkes, when he pulled up with an impatient gesture. "This," he said bitterly, "in spite of all my warnings—"

"Perhaps, after all, she has gone ahead."

"She has not gone ahead," he answered firmly. "I was in the advance, and I swear that no one passed me. I haven't been asleep."

The implied reproach stung the girl for whom the blizzard had made every step difficult; but she realised that he was not in the mood to listen to explanations. A baggage train went by and he turned with it. "Have you seen a lady on horseback?" he shouted to the baggage master, "I am in search of my wife."

"She passed us a while back, sir."

"How long ago?"

"About half an hour, sir, I fancy."

"So long? Did she speak to you? Did she appear indisposed?"

"Not that I noticed, sir. I asked if there was anything I could do, but she said 'no' – she was looking for something."

"Did she say what?"

"No, sir."

"Very well."

The baggage train moved on, and Foulkes halting, cursed beneath his breath as the carts disappeared. Had Harriet's grey gone lame? But no, she appeared to be in no difficulty. Had she lost some valued possession – her satchel, the valise? To these and other questions he could provide no answer. He chewed his lip angrily, torn between two possible lines of action – first, in duty bound to accompany his own men; alternatively to push back still further in search of his wife. He decided on the later course, and for about half an hour rode in silence, his heart heavy with foreboding. At last he stopped, addressing Sue. "Did she say anything – even by a single word to indicate why she should go back?"

"Nothing at all, sir."

He glowered in response. With every step that they had taken his men had marched two in the opposite direction; with every passing second, the gulf widened. It was an intolerable situation. What could one say if a general officer – the Commander in chief perhaps – were to ride up and inquire, "Why, sir, are you not with your command?" What answer to that? He stared with unseeing eyes at the tousled mane before him.

Sue remarked, "I will continue to look for her, sir."

He came to – glanced at the road they had traversed, and at the downward track. In a steely tone he said, "You will do nothing of the kind. We shall both return. Follow me."

He jerked his rein, and taking Sue's obedience for granted, set off so quickly that in a moment or two the driving snow had hidden him from sight. For a few hundred yards the girl followed reluctantly, her head set to the storm. She overtook the baggage train of which they had spoken previously, and it was now that she made her own decision. "I am not one of his men," she concluded, "he cannot and shall not, control my actions. My first duty is to Mrs Foulkes."

She checked the mule, brought it round, and once again took the downward track. She was still perplexed. What object of value had Mrs Foulkes lost? Sue passed her hand over the valises. These beyond all question were safe. What then had prompted her to leave the column? Though she could not provide the answer, the girl held to her course ...

* * *

As Harriet Foulkes went forward the plight of Tony Harte oppressed her. Since leaving Villa Franca, she had passed so many disabled vehicles and stranded travellers that she was filled with increasing anxiety concerning his welfare, and the staying power of the light cart, or gig, in which he intended to cross the mountains.

About midday she had passed, almost completely covered with snow, a collapsed vehicle showing only part of a wheel, but it was not until she had gone miles forward that she remembered Tony's casual reference to a conveyance painted bright red and yellow. The wheel in question had struck bright yellow through the snow.

At first she told herself that she must have been the victim of hallucination, the effect of constant riding, of a certain eye-strain, of snow dazzle. Yellow was a colour universally adopted in Spain; there must be hundreds of vehicles so decorated throughout Galicia. The clue, she felt, was too elusive for serious consideration, and yet – and yet—

She hesitated. Assuming that the gig had broken down, its occupants might well have secured other means of transport. They were by no means helpless, and an officer had prior claim. From another angle she remembered the emphatic warning that on no account must any person leave the column. It was her bounded duty to do this. Duty ... duty ... duty ... she repeated to herself ... one must conform, obey ...

Yet – the submerged wheel in her mind – it seemed that every step forward might be a betrayal of Tony Harte. In all that frozen wilderness, she alone had knowledge of his poignant need. Supposing the man Johnson had been stunned, or worse still, fallen into the abyss, what of Tony then? He would be utterly helpless. She envisaged his bandaged face, sightless, without hope, without comfort, and this speculation plunged her deeper into torment. If following no initiative action on her part, the worst happened, she would never forgive herself. Life would remain a burden, a misery. She could not, of course, consult her husband, now riding ahead. His answer, stern, categorical, could be presupposed. She must act alone – alone—

Waiting until she was well ahead of Sue, she pulled out of line, the driving snow effectually screening her movements. From a shallow bay in the rock face she watched Sue's outline pass. Men followed, their heads bent to the blizzard. None noticed. She pulled the grey's head round and started the long descent. She passed more lines of marching men, and paused only to answer an observation of the baggage master. No-one seemed in the least interested in her except where the line had thinned and broken, a straggler with every intention of hanging on to her stirrup leather, or possibly to unseat her, seized the reins and ordered her to turn about. His unkempt hair, stubble-bearded chin, and wildly starting eyes, appalled. He tried to wrench the horse around. "Yond is the road," he shouted, pointing in the direction from which she had come, "that's where we're again, you and me, to the inn in the mountains!"

She struck out with her switch, but he snatched it from her hand and flung it aside. His feet were almost bare, the rags which had served as a foot covering, dragged about his ankles. As the horse wheeled sharply, the man trod on these wrappings, and crashing to the ground he released the reins. She trotted away, but although the poor wretch scrambled to his feet immediately, and cursed her roundly, he did not attempt to follow. Harriet hunched her shoulders half expecting a parting shot, but none came. She did not look back.

More men passed, but her eyes were fastened upon every successive snow-drift, every outline which might denote the object of her search. Once the grey came to his knees, and though she managed to retain her seat, for he was up at once, the mishap left her faint and sick. Without the horse, she would be helpless … She had lost count of time and distance. Was she in quest of a phantom, a figment of the imagination? Her doubts increased. She could not now be certain that she had seen the segment of wheel at all. She stopped, and sat quite motionless … then moved on. More mounts appeared, and then a clean wind-swept stretch of road with no vestige of life at all. The wind had played tricks with the snow at every turn …

Ah, there it was! She knew that she had not been mistaken. The bright yellow woodwork was almost hidden, but an exposed inch or two remained. With a cry of intermingled fear and hope, she slid from the saddle and stood uncertainly at the shallow edge of the drift. Then she stepped forward and was almost immediately knee-deep in snow. A little further, and she would be waist high, and still some feet from the vehicle. Having no tool with which to dig, she tried to scoop a passage with her hands, but this proved more difficult than she expected; the surface covered by an icy crust so that her gloves were quickly sodden and torn. The unwonted exertion in the mountain air brought a band of pain across her chest. Panting heavily, she was compelled to stop. Yet she could not, dare not, desist. Wildly she glanced down the empty road, until she remembered the horse. she seized the reins, and backing the grey into the drift, by the sheer weight of his legs and haunches managed to clear a rough path to the gig. She fell to scooping again with her hands, until she touched the blanket, which formed an improvised wall. Stiff as a board, held firmly in place by the weight of snow, it gave scarcely an inch. She tore at the edges, until quite breathless, she was compelled to give up. Through all this time no sign of life had come from the interior. As she dropped to her knees helpless and panting, she prayed fervently that she might find the shelter empty.

Again she made use of the horse. Unbuckling one of the reins and slipping the strap through a loop of rope attached to the blanket, she led the animal away. The rope gave, but at the same time the covering was partly displaced, dislodging snow. By now, working in and out of the drift, she was sodden to the waist. Unconscious even of this, she turned to the gig and peered inside.

It *was* occupied. The two men were sitting perfectly still, one with his arm around the shoulder of the other. The bandage on Tony's head had frosted over. Both men appeared to be asleep, and involuntarily she cried, "Wake up! Wake up!" Neither stirred. She called upon Tony by name, but a frigid and faintly ironical smile remained fixed upon his exposed lips. She tried to shake him by the shoulder, but the two linked figures were solid as rock. Their continued silence mocked her.

With a despairing cry she wrenched at her sodden gloves, but these clung to her fingers like things bewitched. When she had freed herself of them, she began to chafe Tony's rigid hands. After half a minute, feeling such action quite futile, she rose to feet and staggered into the middle of the road crying loudly for help. But no-one broke through the vistas of snow. She wondered when the next retreating column would pass, for there were intervals (though not lengthy) between each division. Perhaps all had gone, and the next force to appear would be the French. Everything now depended upon her own exertions. "Whatever happens," she told herself, "I must not panic, and I must never give up!" She refused to believe the worst.

She returned to the disabled gig with the notion of lighting a fire – but how? It did not occur to her that Johnson might have flint and steel in his pocket, or that if wood were available that it would be hopelessly wet. She remembered a remark by someone that the application of snow was an excellent remedy for frostbite. At once she applied herself vigorously to this task working on the exposed hands of the two men. It was labour in vain. At times she sank breathless, exhausted, but still she persevered. Johnson's mouth, partly open, gave the impression of impending speech.

She took the saddlecloth from the grey and carried it to the shelter. The fabric was dry, and something of its immediate warmth might be transmitted to the helpless ones. She would wrap it around them, nestle closely herself, and hope for the best, for patience was in the end bound to be rewarded. She bitterly regretted that she carried no cordial. So, with the single advantage of the saddlecloth, she huddled up to Tony. Once she fancied he murmured, "Who is there?", and she breathed, "Andromache," as though a whisper alone would penetrate the frigid wall of isolation. She began to utter commonplaces with a desperate tenderness of feeling, but it was so completely one-sided that she stopped.

After a time she remembered that she had forgotten to tether the grey. She rose to her feet, staggered out, and to her horror found that he had gone. Sliding, floundering, she hurried down the track, but the animal had vanished completely. This was not strange. He had not baited since morning, and had probably wandered off in search of forage. There was nothing left but to return to the point of vigil. Though the loss of the horse was serious her first duty was to attend to the men in the shelter, to see that they were revived and picked up ... It began to snow again ...

As she pressed close to the strangely quiescent figures she wondered if her absence had been noted by Percy. There was no doubt that he would make a search. Perhaps the riderless horse would return, but what clue was that to her present position? She could still hear Percy's categorical statement about straggling, and although she had no doubt of his righteous indignation in the matter, she did not believe that she would be written off heartlessly, abandoned like so many others.

Though she retained her grip on Tony Harte's icy fingers, the time for soft endearments had gone. When she did speak she heard her own voice as a croaking in the silence. "Hector dead – and his body dragged around the walls of Troy." Why did she remember that? Inactive for so long, her clothing icy, her legs had grown numb. Once a considerable body of men approached. She heard the tramping of feet, the clink of metal, the rumbling of wheels. Unable to stand she contrived to raise an arm, speaking desperately. But the passers by had seen many such hands, heard similar voices. They went forward without halting ...

The drift of snow across the shelter increased, smoothing out the track she had made. She tried to fix the blanket to provide more shelter, holding it in place for a time with one hand. When she began to chafe her numbed fingers she found that accumulated snow now held the frozen cloth in place ... Light began to fade, and oddly, darkness brought with it a measure of peace, ineffably soothing. In this condition her thoughts drifted ... She was in the drawing room at Bellaby with an open work box drawing silken threads through canvas ... soon the candles would be lit, the shutters closed ... the fire, so bright and warm, made one too sleepy for anything ... she was tired too ... much too weary to concentrate upon a pattern ... "Don't trouble me now," she murmured, a propos of nothing, "later – much later ..."

Outside the drift mounted. The wind had eased, but the flakes whirled and drifted until even the broken arc of the wheel disappeared. All movement inside the shelter had ceased. The three were as one. And still the snow descended, soft as lawn, white as a shroud ...

CHAPTER XX

At the next halting place three wounded Rifle Men were transferred to the wagon driven by Robin Thompson, adding to the heavy load already drawn by the patient mules. Other men attempting to board were unceremoniously thrust off. Once an officer claiming to be sick of fever climbed up. His shrift was short. Lord Paget who happened to be passing ordered him down again. "Set an example by walking with your men," he said sternly, "let us have no more nonsense about fever!"

As they began to climb once more, closely hugging a perpendicular wall of rock, Robin's scalp crept as he peered into the gulf. Far below from an unseen ledge, a bird detached itself and fluttered to another lodgement. The full depth remained unplumbed but it was not reduced by imagination. Robin, particularly allergic to height, profoundly wished himself elsewhere. The Rifle Men who had been arguing about the respective drum beats of the French and British armies, became silent. Harker peering out of his blanket folds, liked the lay of the land no more than the others. He would be glad when they descended to a lower level.

After half an hour of this precarious climbing they drew near to a coach abandoned by its owners. The vehicle which had been drawn aside into a shallow bay of rock, still made a sizeable obstruction. In such a place and at such a time it ought have been toppled into the abyss, but no one had considered this to be his business. The prudent course for the present travellers would have been to await assistance in moving the obstacle; but Robin feeling that with due care he would manage to pass, decided to go forward. So he moved on, but drawing alongside the coach he found that there was less than two feet of freeway between his outer wheels and the verge. He was poised on the very edge of the precipice.

He brought the mules to a halt, his eyes fastened on the vital stretch which lay immediately ahead, for not only did the coach present a problem, but a fall of rock beyond offered another impediment the second, more serious than the first. Impossible to turn, it was in view of the wounded men unthinkable to abandon the wagon. The situation called for a clear head, and infinite nicety of action. "Don't stop here, for God's sake!" said one of the Rifle Men in a voice strangely hushed and tense. "No – no!" interposed Harker, "drop back." "Be quite, all of you," hissed Robin, as he listened to these divided counsels. He gathered the reins in his hands, but made no attempt to urge the animals forward.

The dilemma increased as the ledge upon which they were standing cracked ominously, and a tiny dribble of stone issued from a fissure beneath and fell into the gulf; frost, and the recent heavy traffic had obviously weakened the foundation. Robin saw that the mules were trembling. "Why in hell didn't they shift the coach," cried Harker – an observation which did nothing to help. "Keep very still, everyone," Robin ordered, hardly conscious of the tremor in his voice, "we must go forward. The Rifle Men are out of action but you Harker, aren't so bad. Climb out gently, and attach yourself to the rear wheel. Sprag it with a stone- we're on a slight incline. We must keep the wagon perfectly still."

"What then?" asked Harker.

"Never mind 'what then?', do as you're told. I will myself unhitch the beasts and lead them forward. That will release some weight. After then we must move the wagon by brute force ourselves. It will be safer so." He turned to the Rifle Men. "You chaps, don't stir."

Harker, quick witted enough in an emergency, rose cautiously, slid one leg over the wagon side, and lowered himself to the ground. As though impelled by this gentle movement, another cascade of rubble started from beneath their feet, but Harker finding a sizeable stone blocked the wheel, and stood his hand gripping the spokes.

Now Robin stepped down. Deftly he unlinked one set of traces and then the other. He had drawn the first two animals into safety, and was returning for the others, when the rock cracked again. The whole ledge seemed to shudder in its foundations. For a moment he stood rooted to the spot listening; then without further hesitation hurried off the third and fourth mules. "Hold fast!" he warned Harker, who pale and grim, was still attached to the wheel.

The mules safely disposed of, Robin, stepping lightly, hurried back to Harker's side. "Now," he ordered, "you go frontwards, fasten on to the pole, bear inwards with it, and if you can pull when I shout, do so. I shall try to turn this wheel."

Silently the other, who realised that this was neither the time nor place for argument, obeyed; and as soon as his companion was in position, Robin summoned all his strength to move the wheel. At first, the wagon, a dead weight, shifted only an inch or two. With cracking muscles Robin tried again, but in spite of the additional power exerted by Harker in front, the wheel turned once and stuck, though by easing the stone into place the advantage was held. But the wagon had not moved anything like its own length.

Robin gave a savage groan. "Put your back into it!" gasped Harker, his face contorted with pain, and once again the wheel advanced another foot or two. For the two men straining on the road, as indeed for the disabled occupants of the wagon, time throbbed in heartbeats.

"I said, 'put your back into it'", repeated Harker desperately, and with this advice which was less a figure of speech than a reminder of pit practice, Robin edged to the rear. He stood with his back to the vehicle, and after the manner of shifting corves in the galleries, planted his feet firmly and thrust with his whole body. The wagon moved. "Bend the pole towards the wall," he gasped to Harker, as he paused for a second attempt. Again he exerted all his strength; a bolt head bit into his back, but he did not dare relax. The wheels had found a surface which was reasonably smooth. "Another lap," he panted, "and we shall make it."

They were a little beyond the coach when Harker gave a despairing cry. In his rearward position, Robin could see nothing of the other's difficulty. What had happened? Cry or no cry, this was not the moment for hesitation. He thrust with all his might, and maintaining pressure rolled the wagon into safety. His first action after wedging the wheel with a stone, was to drag inwards the prostrate Harker, who had collapsed on the lip of the gorge itself. Robin, his own lungs tight to bursting in the thin mountain, had difficulty in moving at all. However, he managed to prop the other in a sitting position, before he sank limply to his own knees. The Rifle Men, ashen faced looked down without a word. They had made the crucial passage not a moment too soon. There was a rumbling in the heart of the rock followed by a terrific crack, and five or six feet of the road upon which they had lately stood, fell clean into the abyss. "Christ almighty!" breathed one of the Rifle Men.

Harker began to show signs of recovery. He staggered to his feet. "Let's get away from here," he gasped, "we should ha' let the damned wagon go!"

"You don't know when you're lucky," rasped Robin. He too wished to see the last of the place, but it would have been utter folly to have abandoned their vital means of transport. Trembling with exhaustion, he began to hitch up the mules, deciding to lead them for a while. As the vehicle once again lurched and rumbled on its way, the Rifle Men found their voices. "When I heard that crack," said one, "by God I thought it wor the day o' judgment!"

"Ah'd as leave face fifty French," said another, "wi' me hand tied behind me back."

"Stop blatin'," growled Harker, pressing his hands to his ribs, "You did nothin'."

"What did you expect us to do?"

"If it hadn't been for me, you'd all ha' been at the bottom."

"What do you want for that – promotion?" With heightening spirits the Rifle Men laughed.

But Harker, hugging his sides, was in no accommodating mood. "I was a fool to attempt anything in my condition."

Robin turned in the driver's seat. "You'd no option," he said.

"I should ha' kept off the pole."

"Why didn't you?"

"I didn't want to cheat the assizes," said Harker savagely.

"Tek no notice," said one of the Rifle Men, "he's all talk."

* * *

When Colonel Foulkes tried to rejoin his command, time and time again he was held up. He had not succeeded in finding Harriet, but he was not without hope that she would be waiting for him when he did arrive. It was not so and he continued to ride with a gnawing fear in his heart.

"How many miles to Lugo, sir?" inquired Lieutenant Bird. Looking down on the dogged face beside him, reflecting how crusty he had been with this same young man in the past, Foulkes became almost indulgent. "He is giving of his best," he thought, "and what can man do more?" Aloud he said, "Plenty perhaps. If we could see the league stones it would help—" He had the feeling that he had underestimated. "Remember," he continued, "that it is just as hard for the French as it is for us. The snow falls on the just and unjust alike."

He had not attempted to quip, but Bird laughed as though the observation had been so intended. Foulkes smiled slightly and pricked on.

He came across Stubbs, who in spite of the upward pull, marched sturdily along. "How is the head?" he inquired, for the Sergeant Major had not completely recovered from the blow he had received at Benevente. "Still singing?"

"Hat times, sir. Not a tune hi like."

"It will wear away. Pass the word to all and sundry that we shall find ample magazines in Lugo – all the bread and meat we need."

"Yes, sir," said Stubbs, "hif the Spaniards don't get in before us."

"Well, they will have to be quick now."

"A private minus the sole of one shoe came up limping painfully. Foulkes beckoned. "You , my man – what is your name?"

"Private Henderson, sir."

Foulkes dismounted. "Well, Private Henderson, up you get on my horse."

"Yor horse, sir?" said Henderson surprised. "I couldn't do that, sir. What will you do?"

"That's my business. Obey orders and mount."

"If you say so, sir."

"Hand me your musket."

The private, unused to riding was hoisted into the saddle. Once seated, he looked down. "My musket, sir."

"I'll hold to that," said Foulkes sharply. "The stirrups – what do you think they are made for?"

"The feet, sir," said Henderson sheepishly.

"Shape, and put them in."

Foulkes shouldered the weapon, slapped the flank of his horse, and the two set off together. Snow whipped across, and although he was sheltered somewhat from the full fury of the gale by the animal's body, the Colonel bent his head. He would walk for a couple of hours, perhaps unto nightfall; match himself with those who were marching behind. Except for Harriet's disappearance he would have been relatively content. Despite losses his force remained intact. What more could one ask?

* * *

Sue Thompson continued her movement rearwards. Of the officers whom she questioned, none had seen a lady mounted on a raw boned grey. Mr Foulkes had completely disappeared. Was it possible that she had fallen over the precipice? But the grey was remarkably surefooted, and Harriet an experienced horsewoman. Perhaps by some mischance she had been compelled to abandon her horse, but it was inconceivable that a lady of her standing would not have found alternative transport. This thought sustained the girl, but not for long.

A general officer accompanied by aides approached, and noting Sue, stopped. At once the girl recognised the pale face, the brilliant eyes of Sir John. He smiled. "On picket duty, madam?"

"I am looking for someone, sir," she said. But when she outlined her problem, he shook his head. They had met one lady so muffled to the eyes that it was impossible to tell if she were Spanish or English. An aide thought the lady might well have been Mrs Kennedy, the Assistant Commissary General's wife. "I am sorry," said the Commander-in-Chief that we can do so little for you. My advice is that you should not stay here a moment longer. You are too much in the rear. Rejoin your regiment; you will probably find that the lady has by now returned."

He touched his hat and rode on followed by his companions. Sue could see that he was shaking his head doubtfully. But she was determined not to give up. They had mentioned a mounted lady, and grasping at this straw she decided to venture at least another half mile. In spite of Moore's warning she did not appreciate how close she had drawn to the rearguard. More infantry passed. They ignored her and were very soon out of sight.

The mule, its pace slackening, began to hobble slightly. At first Sue laid this condition to tiredness, but soon the animal trod with difficulty, and to her consternation she realised that it had gone lame. Dismounting, she lifted the right foreleg. The shoe had been cast, and the crack in the hoof held together since the first day of purchase by an iron clip, had widened. Here was a pretty pass! She scraped the hoof clean, but that only exposed its utter weakness. She bit her lip angrily. The beast, now unrideable, would have to be led ...

Return was now the only course open, so reins in hand she turned about and trudged along making very little progress. After a time the mule refused to move at all. She tugged, implored, threatened, all to no purpose. She unfastened the valises, and slinging these about her own shoulders, tried again; but laden or unladen, the mule had definitely given up. "If I'm not just about sick!" she exclaimed, though words did nothing to ease the dilemma. She stood arms akimbo, staring at the mule, while the poor creature remained dumbly inactive, its right hoof slightly touching the ground.

All this trouble had eaten into time. Dusk deepened in the valley below. She could hear the distant beating of drums – the last warning of withdrawal. Thoroughly tired, she had grown not much to care. She saw that she was almost abreast of an abandoned wagon. Leaving the mule, which in its present condition was not likely to wander, she clambered over the rear boards of the vehicle, and almost collapsed upon rotund sacks of which there were about half a dozen. That these were cold, unyielding, and a lightly covered with snow, made little difference. She cleared a rough place to sit, intending to rest for only a few minutes. Foolishly, she closed her eyes ...

* * *

She awoke in complete darkness to the sound of furtive voices. the snow had stopped, and overhead she saw the faint glimmer of stars. A profound silence reigned; at first she felt that the whispering she had overheard might have been a figment of imagination. But no – the sound broke out again. She head someone say, "Come on 'Arris, roll 'er out of the way," and a pitying voice in response, "I ain't a touchin;' the dead. Let 'er rest, poor soul!" A third voice intervened, "If she's dead, what's the odds? It's the stuff we're after."

She sat up. "You are not the French?"

"Holy Mike!" One of the men bent over so that she could feel his breath on her cheek. "She's alive!"

"Who are you?" she asked.

"The Ninety Fifth," said the man addressed as Harris, "the finest regiment in the army."

"What are you up to?"

"What are we after?" said Harris, "well if you must know, this wagon carries new shoes, and we've neddied back to get some. Now no more talk, Missus, time's precious. Hob, slit this sack, and keep the blade off my fingers."

"Instanter," said Hob, "but let Bill help the lady off first."

The lady, grateful for the assistance, scrambled to her feet and slid down. As she stamped around and thrashed her arms to restore circulation she counted two outlines dark against the snow, and two in the wagon handling the sacks. She heard a knife blade rip into canvas, and a low murmur of triumph as the men discovered the shoes. They threw out a number, which immediately they slung around their necks with lengths of twine. "We've to guess sizes," said Hob, but it was the third man, Bill, who prodded Sue asking if she would like a pair. "They're on the big side," he said, "But they may come in handy."

"If you can spare them," she said, and they laughed softly. Although she had been riding most of the campaign, she was in dire need of footwear.

"We can spare them," said Harris, looping a pair together. "Here ye are with the compliments of the Ninety Fifth!"

She took the shoes with a word of thanks, but as she did so he turned from her abruptly, stiffened, stood listening, and stared intently down the road.

"What is it?" asked Hob. Sue saw that Harris was gazing fixedly towards a pale streak of sky which lay beyond the shoulder of the mountain. They heard a long drawn cry.

"Nothink but wolves," said Bill.

"Wolves wi' little tin sabres," retorted Harris, spitting emphatically. Hurry up, you lot. Get ready to move, Missus, if you want to go." The men of the Ninety Fifth had drawn together; the French were too near for comfort.

"How far must we make?"

"A couple o' miles back," said the fourth man. "We risked a bit doin' this, an' now 'tis come."

"My poor mule is lame," she explained, but they were not listening. Harris stabbed the air with his finger. "Yonder – I think I spot 'em!"

Wisps of shadow detached from the mountain side. The watchers caught a faint clink of metal, of a scabbard on a stirrup iron. "We'll not hear the hoof beats for snow," said Harris, "but if them ain't French chassoor, I'm a Dutchman!"

"They may be some of ours," said Hob.

"If they were," snorted Harriet, "would they hang around foolin' there?"

The four men continued to watch the advancing shadows. Now they could hear the steady beat of hooves. Surely it was time to go. A faint, long-drawn, "Ha-a-a-lt!" broke the silence. For what were the horsemen waiting?

"It'll have to be lead pills," said Hob calmly. "Let's slew the wagon across the road. Good job it's 'ere."

At once the four men fastened on the vehicle, and with a subdued, "yo heave ho!" ran it to a defensive position.

"Get behind," ordered Harris, and turning to Sue, "You Missus too, an' keep yer 'ead under yer arm!"

He fell on one knee at the wagon corner, advanced his rifle, and called on one of his comrades to join him, while the two others took up positions at the second end. Cool, intent, they might have been practising at the butts. Their supreme self-confidence in the face of danger was impressive.

"All set?" Harris inquired, "wait a minute though." And darting to the spot where the wagon had rested, he returned with an additional musket. "Thrown away, but it seems in condition," he announced, and propping his own rifle against the wagon wheel, began to load the newly acquired weapon.

With a final thump of the ramrod, he addressed Sue. "You like to earn your keep?" he asked. "Do you think you could fire this piece off?"

"I'll try." Her teeth chattered, partly from cold partly from excitement.

"Good girl!" he said with a hearty pat. "Look, kneel down, put the weapon through the wagon wheel, and when I say 'fire', pull the trigger hard, though look out – it'll bump back on you. Understand?"

"I think so."

"For God's sake, don't fire afore the time. All ready?" he said, addressing the others. "We'll hit 'em when they begin to shift."

The shadows were in movement again. Sue thought she could hear the creaking of saddles. Now the horsemen were in clearer outline.

"One – two – three," intoned Harris. "Fire!"

As she had been instructed, Sue pulled hard on the trigger, and the five weapons shattered the dawn silence. Sue's musket gave an upward jerk, and would perhaps have left her hands had it not been thrust through the wheel spokes ... When the smoke had drifted away, they could see a horse floundering in the snow and a second plunging wildly as though it had been hit, but Sue alone continued to watch. The Rifle Men were busy reloading. Thump – thump – thump, went the ramrods. Hob gave two extra thumps for good measure. "They don't know how many we are," he chuckled. "We might be a whole company."

As Harris began to reload Sue's musket, two orange flashes flicked the darkness. One bullet droned overhead; another smacked into the rocks. "Pooh, carbines!" commented Harris. "Not bad for amatoors. Now aim from where they fired."

The five weapons spoke again, this time raggedly. They heard a single cry, but that was all. The stricken animal down the road continued to kick spasmodically. "Do you want this again?" asked Sue, extending her weapon. Her shoulder ached from the recoil, but this was not the time to complain.

"I'll keep it," said Harris. "No listen to me, mates – push off. I'll delay 'em a bit with two last shots. As parson says, "Go ye, and tarry not in the order of yer goin'.""

"Wait a minute," said Sue. She dashed to the patient mule, stripped from its back the valises and slung these across her shoulders. How to cope with so heavy a weight she did not know; but it was unthinkable to leave this property behind. With a final regretful word to the beast which had carried her so faithfully, she joined the others. It pained her to abandon Sancho, but there was nothing more that she could do.

At a jog trot four took the upward road, leaving Harris still beside the Wagon. When they were perhaps a hundred and fifty yards away, his rifle spoke followed a few seconds later by the report of the musket. He soon overtook them, running at full speed. In the rear the French had again opened carbine fire. "Chatter away!" he panted, "and the devil go with you!"

"They'll overtake us?" said Sue anxiously.

"Not that fast," he replied confidently, "they've had one taste to be going on with, and we could make a stand. All the same, hurry up."

The Rifle Men were in high spirits. Hob took over Sue's valises so that she managed to keep pace. When half an hour later they were challenged by a picket of their own regiment, the girl listened with astonishment to the lies they told – how cut off from the main body they had fought their way through a whole French battalion. The young officer eyed them sardonically. "And I suppose you robbed them of their shoes too!"

"What shoes, sir?"

"Go on! Get out of my sight, and take your booty with you."

At daybreak, refreshed by a tot of rum and a ration of meat and biscuit, Sue still burdened by her valises, resumed her journey. For a time she threw these over the back of a sumpter mule, but the animal being required for some special purpose, she was compelled to carry the baggage herself. She plodded along glumly. The thought of the abandoned mule depressed her ... and she had failed miserably in her search for Mrs Foulkes ...

* * *

She was still hobbling along painfully, her eyes heavy from lack of sleep, when she was overtaken by a horseman, and a familiar voice hailed her.

She looked up into the face of Harry Simms, who releasing his foot from the stirrup would have her mount behind him. It was not a comfortable seat, but it was at least preferable to slogging along the road. When she told him her story, he frowned. "What a mad tangle it all is," he remarked, "but don't be downcast. Mrs Foulkes, as we know, is a woman of some resource. Somehow I can't see her at a loss. We will keep our eyes skinned, and make inquiries as we go along."

He explained that having lost touch with his own headquarters he was at a loose end. As for Robin, Simms had not seen him since Villa Franca where he had been put in charge of a stores wagon. "He should be well ahead by now – possibly arrived at Lugo."

Joining a stream of men and vehicles, the bedraggled tail-end of a division, they began a long ascent. Now the bleak panorama of the world's roof lay before their eyes. As they climbed, the wind tore across fiercely, snatching at their cloaks and blankets, cutting to the bone. Wind whipped the powdered snow in clouds; the horses tails streamed out, wagon covers bellied like sails. Across the summit men linked arms leaning against the wind's pressure, shouting fiercely to make themselves heard. Booming at sudden turns of the road, whistling through unexpected crevices, the wind raged without ceasing ... There were scenes of distress from which Sue could only avert her eyes – a man half buried from a fall of stone; two exhausted wretches trying to erect a tent; a trooper, head in hands sitting on the fallen body of his horse; anonymous mounds of snow from which an arm of a leg protruded ...

The shorter winter's day drew to a close, and still through the darkness, impelled more by instinct than reason, the half dazed army stumbled forward...

Dawn broke a second time on the mountains. They knew that after Nogales lay a reasonable stretch to Lugo where the back of the long march would be broken. Most men had forgotten which day of the week it was. No matter, they must keep on movement ...

On the verge beside a fallen mule, an infantryman hugging a bundle in a large shawl waited for Simms and Sue to come up. As they drew near they saw that the bundle contained a child. "For heaven's sake," the man croaked as they stopped. It was Higgenson of the regiment.

Sue dropped to the ground, while Simms remained mounted. "Why are you here?" she asked.

"I'm left with him," said the man simply. He motioned to the child and fixed them with despairing eyes.

"Where is your wife?"

"Gone," said Higgenson with quivering lips. He turned away overcome. Blithe, bonny Mrs Higgenson had they gathered, died of exposure. The hapless husband in a few broken sentences tried to explain how, falling away in the night, his wife had tried to protect the child from the cold with her own body. Returning in search of her he found that only young Tom displayed any signs of life. She had had her baby in one of the villages. That too was sad. "She never spoke to me, not a single word more, so what was I to do except cover her up with stones?" He shook his head hopelessly.

"Give me the boy," said Sue gently, conscious that the horse would now have to bear the additional load. "Rest assured he shall be taken care of—" Her voice broke. So she mounted, and young Tom was handed up. They moved on.

For a few paces Higgenson stumbled behind them, his arm extended as though to bring his son back. "Be a good lad, Tom," he cried, "don't give trouble. I'll have you again." Then with shouldered musket, head bent to the wind, he plodded on ...

* * *

At Nogales the Spaniards had bolted all doors against the British. "A fine welcome from the nation we came to save!" said Simms caustically. The men of the Twenty Eighth however, who had just marched in had ideas of their own. Fastening a stone in a sergeant's sash, they banged with such effect upon the door of the largest house, that the Spanish occupant decided it would be safer to let them in, and it was in these premises that Simms first tying up his mount with those of the officers, managed to insert his two charges. In a very short time the place was full. Wedged together, all ranks dozed fitfully. In an hour or two they were on the road again.

Just beyond Nogales, Simms to his immense relief contrived to find a place for Sue and the boy in an ammunition wagon. By some magic which he did to attempt to explain, he produced a couple of Spanish cloaks which were as worn by the local shepherds, each having a vent for the head. "Not a word as to where these came from," he grinned, "but I don't doubt they'll do." Reasonably warm with the additional clothing, Sue and Tom held to it for the rest of the journey ...

Steadily they descended the foothills. Villages appeared more frequently. Peasants, aloof, suspicious, watched as the grim unkempt strangers streamed past their doors. At last, Lugo, a compact town of dark grey stone, showed on the horizon. In the shadow of the great cathedral, Sue and her charge found shelter in the house of a substantial merchant. The bulk of the army did not follow, but took up a position three miles outside the walls. The British were not now in full strength, three brigades having been dispatched for embarkation at Vigo.

Substantial though their quarters were, Sue and Tom were sparely fed. Their host who had no English, seemed sedately unconscious of their presence. Smoking one slender cigar after another, he bent his bony head over a volume containing curious diagrams as though to distil from the printed page the secret of existence. His servants kept to their own quarters. At intervals the iron tolling of the cathedral bell resounded overhead. Had it not been for the company of the child, and the little games she devised, Sue would have found the house intolerable. To this sombre background, the English travellers found comfort in sleep.

Nest morning, carrying the boy, Sue set out in search of news. Firing sounded in the distance, but when she inquired of a passing orderly if the battle had begun, he told her offhand not to "worriet herself" as the French were "o'ny making faces!" Another whom she questioned was more forthcoming. He had heard that Soult intended to attack the British centre, and would do so when the rest of his men came up ...

Throughout the morning guns jarred and musket cracked, but there were long intervals when the only sound was that of the melancholy bell in the cathedral tower. Still feeling that she might meet some person of her acquaintance, perhaps Mrs Foulkes herself, she wandered in and out of the arcades; but sleet beginning to fall she picked her way across the slush of the square, glad in spite of its sombre atmosphere to regain the shelter of the house ...

The hours dragged. When towards evening, Simms called to inform her that they were to make a night march towards Corunna, she was more than ready to leave. His instructions were simple. She was to met him at a precise spot in the market square at nine, where she would be picked up by cart or wagon. The march would be difficult – trusses of hay were to be dropped at intervals to help guide the columns through the darkness. He assured her that Robin had gone forward. When she saw him to the door the sky was lit with flame from burning stores; but turning his back upon the darkened town, he pointed to a chain of campfires ringing the eastern slopes. "Those will be kept alight until morning; but by that time we shall be well away."

"There will be no battle?"

"Sir John would have obliged I am told, but alas! there is every indication that Soult is holding back."

Conversation lapsed, but Simms still lingered. Her wistful face in the lamplight held a strange appeal. "I must away," he said reluctantly. She was silent …

"We have the satisfaction of knowing," he continued, "that we are very nearly out of the wood. The ships will be waiting."

"You are sure?"

"Of course, and don't forget your Spanish blankets. You will need them at sea."

There was a pause …

"Mr Simms," she began impulsively, and stopped.

He looked up. "You wished to say—?"

"Mr Simms," she blurted a second time, the words crowding on her lips, "you have been kind to me on so very many occasions – in fact I do not know what I should have done without you, that in the event of not seeing you again—"

"Don't say that," he interrupted. "God forbid!"

"Mischances do come," she insisted, "we have seen too many in the past not to take warning. You and I may sail separately, and once aboard ship who knows where we may land?"

"You will rejoin your regiment, and there I shall find you."

"That is by no means certain." Sue's voice trembled anxiously. "Mrs Foulkes may not reappear, so that my occupation will have gone. That being so I feel I must speak now. I cannot find words enough to thank you."

"As if one required thanks!" he said indignantly – "thanks for what? An odd service now and then—"

"I should be an ungrateful creature not to try. With all my heart Mr Simms, I shall remember you to my dying day—" And she burst into tears.

Simms, for once, seemed bereft of words. He stammered something, then said more coherently, "You really mustn't – don't distress yourself."

"I am not distressed," she said in a strangled little voice, "quite the reverse."

"Then all is well. Dry those tears."

"I am sorry I am making such a fool of myself," she said, dabbing her eyes.

Simms drew nearer and placed his arm about her. "Not anyone's fool," he said gently, "least of all, mine! Remember that you are in my care, and I will see that it remains so."

For a moment or two they stood quite motionless, until a series of shouted orders came from the plaza. With this reminder in his ears, Simms released her. "In you go," he said, suddenly brusque and businesslike. "And remember – nine without fail!"

"Yes, sir," she said smiling.

With a swirl of his cloak he was gone ...

* * *

Simms had not exaggerated the difficulty of the night march from Lugo. The wind carried with it hail which slashed into their faces like pebbles. The road was knee-deep in mud and slush, and the bales dropped at intervals to guide the uncertain columns, were torn apart and soon scattered over the country-side. Their guide having wandered from the track was stubborn in his error, refusing to concede that he was lost. Wagons began to lurch among the rocks, and it was only by the remote, wind-borne shouting of others, that they were able to regain the main road ...

At Bentanzos Sue dragged the boy and herself into a stable where they dropped on a bed of evil smelling straw, but she was beyond caring. When she awoke in broad daylight, the odour of wood smoke invaded her nostrils; men were already boiling their camp kettles. As she rose to her feet a jubilant voice announced that they were only ten miles form Corunna, and a ragged, almost derisive cheer followed.

The wind had dropped almost completely ...

* * *

The wagon driven by Robin Thompson made Bentanzos without further mishap, though at times the track presented appalling difficulties. Descending the slopes, wheels had to be chain-locked. At times even this proved insufficient, and the two able-bodied men had to strain also on the spokes. Harker grumbled as he took his share, though Robin noticed that the nearer he drew to Corunna the more he complained of his disability. On the other hand he could be most accommodating, so much indeed that Robin stared suspiciously. Once Harker intercepted his gaze. "What are you look-ing at?" he asked slyly.

"At you."

"So what?"

"You puzzle me."

Harker grinned. "I shan't be round your neck much longer."

"Won't you?"

"Here today and gone tomorrow – that's me!" And he began to sing with a tantalising lilt—

Catch a fox and put him in a box,
And never let him go!

"But first," he remarked, "you must catch the little bleeder."

"He'll be caught," aid Robin.

"Ah, the hunt's up again is it? You'll all agin me – but what's the odds? I don't care." And he turned his back, whistling.

But even in repose he was watchful, dozing with one eye open. Unwashed, unshaved, there were times when he bore an uncanny resemblance to his father; then with a word or two, and a brazen grin he could dispel the illusion by imitating in a manner which the elder Harker could never have achieved, a cultured voice repeating some phrase of Mrs Foulkes or the Colonel's as though it were his own. Yet despite fooling, mimicry, and implied good fellowship, the shadow of the assize court, the hulks and the convict ship, still lingered in the background.

Breaking bread daily with Harker, it was difficult for Robin to harbour resentment. He was not a good hater, and after a conversation in which they discussed familiar scenes and characters around Tollgate, the vagaries of pit life, the doings of the great house in the park, about which Harker had a fund of amusing if somewhat scandalous anecdote, resentment became more difficult still. Yet though for the time being Robin thrust the problem into the background of his mind, he was conscious that sooner or later the nettle would have to be grasped …

At Bentanzaos where the three wounded men had been left in charge of a surgeon, Robin and his companion were lucky to find a posada where they could stable the mules. A detachment had just marched out, so that when they called for supper the innkeeper threw up his hands, shook his head vigorously, pointed to the empty pot on the hearth, and brusquely left them.

"And so the poor dog had none!" said Robin ironically.

"Not this poor dog," rejoined Harker, laughing scornfully. "Mine host is a liar. Think ye he's dished up every chicken he's got? Not likely. You see!"

What Robin was about to see was not at the moment clear. A hearty meal seemed as far off as ever. But Harker grimaced knowingly. Lightly as a cat, he prowled around the room, stopping at times to listen intently. Presently he halted beside a small padlocked door fixed in a stout timber partition which formed part of the outer wall. Placing his ear to the crack he gave a low murmur of satisfaction, and to Robin's surprise between cupped hands crowed faintly in imitation of a cock. Then he stopped and listened. Robin approaching, was waved away impatiently, as a responsive cluck, and a rustling of straw sounded at the other side of the barrier. "No chickens!" commented Harker scathingly, "Well, we will soon find one he knew nothing of. Wait a minute."

He drew from his pocket a strip of iron which might well have been a fish hook, and with this began probing the padlock. With a quick twist of his wrist the tongue gave. "Go you outside the door," he directed Robin, "and keep the Don busy if he comes back. Double up – pretend you've the belly-ache. I'll polish this off."

He disappeared through the wicket, while Robin moved uneasily to the archway through which the Spaniard had disappeared. It was dark and empty, but he could hear the innkeeper upbraiding some person, possibly his wife, from the shrill feminine response. Harker behind the partition, was still clucking softly, endearingly. The seconds dragged. Wings fluttered … followed another spell of waiting, until Harker appeared grasping a limp, but still twitching, bird by the neck.

"Quick's the word!" he hissed. Deftly he readjusted the padlock.

"You wait here," he whispered, "I'll be back directly." Tucking the bird under his coat he slid out into the night.

He was absent a few minutes only, but as his return from the street coincided with the Spaniard's entry bearing logs for the fire, he disarmed possible comment by holding the bird aloft. The Spaniard eyed both Harker and the bird suspiciously. His next action was to walk over to the little door and test the lock. Finding this secure, he stood for a moment or two looking at the flags of the floor. He scratched his head dubiously. When Harker indicated by sign language that he would like to roast the bird on the spit, the Spaniard nodded, but before he left the room once again he tested the padlock. "Safe bind, safe find!" said Harker blandly, Robin looked away. He heard his companion say, "Mucha gracias for everything." The Spaniard withdrew reluctantly, and stood in the shadow of the doorway, watching. "Let him stare," said Harker softly, "he can't reckon it up!"

Deftly he began to pluck the bird, while Robin roamed around uneasily. "He has only to count up to find one missing," he said.

"Use the brains you were born with," returned Harker. "When he does we shall be far, far away."

The chicken smelt good as it hissed and sizzled over the fire. "Hungry?" inquired Harker.

"What a question to ask," said Robin.

"Of course, you'll take none."

"Why not?"

"Because you never did hold with poaching – it's wicked."

"If I did eat, I should certainly leave something for the innkeeper," said Robin lamely.

"Don't make me laugh," said Harker.

"What's wrong with that?"

"Conscience money, that's what."

"I'll go without."

"You do! More for me!" Harker chuckled.

But gnawing hunger prevailed. Reluctantly, Robin accepted a leg. "Remember," grinned Harker, "'at you're an accessory after the fact." But it made no difference; the chicken was too tasty to ignore.

For a time they ate without speaking, until Harker observed, sadly, "You know Spain ain't all that it's cracked up to be. Sunlight and dancin', my foot! It's brought to us poor devils nothing but starvation and scrambling up and down bloody mountains. I was better off i' the pit, but let 'em wait – just let 'em wait!"

"Let who wait?"

Harker wagged a knowing head, and flung his knuckle end into the fire. "You'll see," he answered enigmatically. He leaned back against the wall and closed his eyes. A minute later his repose was interrupted by half a dozen infantryman who charged in roaring for wine. "Less noise there, "he growled, "I'm a sick and wounded man. Can't you let a fellow sleep?"

"We're all sick men," said one of the newcomers.

"Sick of doing you're whack, I'll be bound," said Harker, "all bounce and rattle. If it weren't for my broken rib—" He rolled his eyes fiercely, and the infantrymen lowered their voices.

A few hours later as the wagon lumbered along the Corunna chausee, he said, "Thompson, you've no more sense than a new-born babe."

"You may think so."

"I tell you, you've no need to worrit."

"What – with the convict ship waiting?"

"That needn't be," continued Harker, "you're in the army now, and such being so are safe."

"I don't want army service."

"Then use your cards. It's your job to play for a pardon. Listen, I'll tell you what – you will land in England by and by. Get yourself of home; but lie low until you're able to see the Earl when he rides round the parkland in the morning. You wait for him, take off your hat, and you say pathetic like, "My Lord, I am come from the Army of Spain of which I bear record. Let my service for the brave Sir John Moore – bless his soul! – speak for me." Tell him how you was washed ashore, but was minded to serve old England in spite of all, and after a hard campaign you throw yourself on his mercy. And what does the good Earl do – he being Lord Lieutenant of the county – he lifts his little finger and your troubles are at an end. Back you go to the loving arms of your parents, and all is as before."

"Quite the barrack-room lawyer, aren't you?" said Robin scornfully.

"Never you mind."

"The scheme won't work."

"Why not?"

"Because Senor Wickedshifts I will not admit to a crime I never committed. My name is befouled, and only you can cleanse it."

"And land myself in gaol?"

"Put it as you like. What is to prevent you from interviewing his lordship in a like manner? He has but to lift his little finger and you can join your old man again."

Harker laughed outright. "Very good, my lad, but not this time. No boy, I've finished with touching my cap to superiors. 'Please may I lick your boots, sir?' … 'Please kick me hard if it will give you pleasure, sir!' … No more of that. The slate's wiped clean."

"You mean you'll desert?"

"I should resign my commission."

"Not until you've paid."

"Nothing doing, mate!"

As the wagon wheels ate up the remaining miles to Corunna, Harker's spirits rose. He whistled, sang, exchanged aimless pleasantries with peasants. At times he complained of acute aches and pains, but these did not prevent him being active when he wished. He kept a close eye upon his knapsack.

For his part Robin plunged deeper into gloom. The conditioned freedom, which in spite of the hazards of the retreat, he had enjoyed, would soon end. He felt he would be compelled to embark with the rest – unthinkable to look for shelter in Corunna – but as the wind blew in from the sea he could smell not only the fresh salt air but also the bilge, the malodorous background of the hulks. He had brought Harker to the final stage of the journey – with what effect? Rehabilitation seemed as far off as ever. More than once he had dwelt upon the possibility of taking refuge with the fishermen by whom he had been befriended, and from their obscure village making his way to Vigo, possibly to Lisbon; but two considerations checked him – first, he knew next to nothing of Spanish or Portuguese; and second, it was likely now the French would soon engulf the whole of the Peninsular, a condition in which every stranger would be suspect.

On the other hand what had England to offer – a hide-out possibly under an assumed name in a region far removed from home; a life of shifts and evasions, in perpetual fear of arrest, of fatal recognition. The prospect appalled him … Then other problems pressed. Where was Susan? He tried to comfort himself with the thought that in close association with Mrs Foulkes she would be safe, but there was no guarantee of that. What of the old people in Tollgate? His heart yearned towards them, but so much now lay between …

Morosely he eyed the port, which they were now rapidly approaching – the outline of the harbour, the lay of wharves and quays. Both men studied with interest the stretch of grey Atlantic water which flecked with sails, lay beyond the rocky spit and the lighthouse; the thoughts of one man in striking contrast with those of the other …

CHAPTER XXI

Colonel Foulkes riding down to the sea gazed sombrely ahead. It seemed as though through curtains of fog and snow they had suddenly burst into Spring. Across surrounding fields rye was showing, orange and lemon groves budding and wild flowers spangling the grass. But what he saw brought no uplifting of spirit. If only he could forget the bitter words of Moore: "Rather than command," the General had said, "men who behaved in such an infamous manner, he prayed God that the first bullet sent by the enemy might enter his own heart." Foulkes felt the words would forever be written into his own mind. True the force behind him was more in shape than at Benevente and Astorga, but the men had still to redeem themselves, by some unusual act of courage and endurance to purge their indiscipline.

He crossed a bridge guarded by a detachment of the Sixtieth Regiment quartered in Corunna. How smart and soldierly the men were; how trim their uniforms, and in what good order their weapons. He saluted, pursing his mouth self-consciously, at the same time fixing his eyes upon the neck of land covered by the town, and beyond that the misty reaches of the Atlantic. Despite the orderly appearance of his own uniform, the carefully adjusted cloak, the gleaming metal of his harness, he felt inconceivably shabby, a poor mendicant of honour. He, who had hoped so much from this campaign, had garnered only chaff. It did not occur to Foulkes riding in gloomy isolation, that Moore too was similarly oppressed. The Commander in Chief had looked upon the bubble reputation, accounting of which lay over yonder at the Horse Guards, the Commons House at Westminster, and the Cabinet Room in Downing Street. Thirty thousand men marched in and out of the Peninsular – to what end? Moore could hear his name bandied by members of the Opposition who would be more than ever prejudiced against Continental expeditions; and by Ministers more conscious of their own place and power than the reputation of serving officers. The scapegoat was already marked for the slaughter ...

So far Foulkes had gleaned nothing from any quarter concerning the vanished Harriet. He had questioned all who might possibly have seen her; had urged his officers to do the same, but without result. His nights had been haunted, his days bedevilled, by fruitless speculation. Sometimes he fancied he saw her riding in the distance, and would prick forward hoping to overtake her, only to discover that he had been trailing a mounted officer or a baggage woman huddled on a mule. Thompson the maid, had disappeared too, a circumstance which nourished the belief that somewhere the two had united. But in what place? A French prison? All, he continued to reassure himself, would be made clear in Corunna. He profoundly hoped so ...

He rehearsed their next meeting. He would be patient, speak only with forbearance, listen sympathetically to her story. As from this distance he scrutinised the russet roofs of the port, there he felt, in some comfortable hotel she would be drinking coffee with the ladies who had come over with Baird. She had always been self-reliant, and there was no reason to believe that this essential quality had been denied her ... Yes, he could see her advancing across the floor of the hotel lobby with that characteristically surprised, and amused, lifting of eyebrows ...

In the meantime Moore was placing his army along the mile and a half long ridge of Monte Mero, something less than three miles from the town. Towards the western end, on a low ridge, stood the village of Elvina, a key position where he most expected attack. On this crest he established two of his four divisions; in reserve stood Paget at Eirio, and Frazer in the suburbs of Santa Lucia. Should Soult try to outflank the main force, Frazer's division would be brought forward from the Corunna suburbs, and used if need be. This strategy suited Foulkes very well. He would be able to enter the town, make inquiries concerning Harriet, and rejoin his men without delay ...

* * *

Susan Thompson walked in the citadel quarter of Corunna, alone. Since clothes had to be renewed, she had brought from her little stock of dollars a black Spanish dress, the full skirt trimmed with crimson braid, and a brightly coloured kerchief for her head. Also a cap and a smock for Tom. On the whole she was pleased with her shopping.

Descending from the upper to the lower town, she lingered for a while scanning faces around her in the frail hope of meeting Mrs Foulkes; but though there were ladies of quality about, she saw no sign of her mistress. She considered approaching one such person, a befeathered lady who might conceivably be English, but reflecting that she might be a newcomer to the port, refrained ...

Hailed by a familiar voice, she was startled to confront Colonel Foulkes himself. His face at once registered surprise, delight, relief, "Ah," he cried with upraised arm, "the lost found – at last!" He looked her up and down quickly. "Where do you spring from, and in heaven's name, where is your mistress?"

"Mrs Foulkes?" she inquired blankly.

"Of course."

Their voices clashed; her eyes alone told him she had no news of Harriet. "I had thought –" she muttered.

"I was hoping—" he said. But it was no use.

He had searched every hotel in Corunna, beginning with the Fontana d'Oro. Here the dining room, for months past a rendezvous for English civilians and officers, was almost empty. When he inquired after Mrs Foulkes waiters gazed at him blankly. Other hotels were no better. He had interviewed the Town Major without success. Sue Thompson was the last resort.

"I thought that you of all people, would have known –" In his tragic disappointment he seemed incapable of competing a sentence.

"I had no news for you, sir," she said. "I wish with all my heart I had."

"But you continued your search?"

Of what use were words? "I went a long way to the rear, sir – almost to the French army, but never found her." It seemed irrelevant to mention her own narrow escape.

He sighed heavily and bit into his lip, until noting how distressed she was, and feeling that the conversation might best be continued in quieter surroundings, he said, "You must take a cup of coffee with me."

They entered a café and took a seat at one of the tables. The place almost empty, they were served immediately, the young waiter glancing curiously at a senior ranking British officer, who in this hour of crisis, could find time to entertain a female companion. These strange Ingleses!

"I know you were devoted to my wife," said Foulkes in a low voice. "Charge your mind, Susan – tell me, did she at any stage of the journey drop a hint of anything which might lead her to fall out? Is it possible that she had lost something?"

Sue shook her head. "Not that I can remember."

"Any object of value – her jewel case for example?"

"Nor, sir. That is in the valise, which I still have."

"I will see that it is collected," he said quickly. "So you remember nothing?"

"That is so."

He sat, his hands clasped tightly between his knees, in his eyes a fixed, haunted expression.

"Do you think she returned to assist foundered regimental women? A number fell away – she had spoken of that."

"Your wife had been much concerned about them, sir, but felt that they were all safely placed."

Foulkes frowned. "Then this is of all problems the most inexplicable. I see no way out. But you are not drinking your coffee." She might have pointed out that he was neglecting his. She sipped to please him.

"Could she have been taken by the French, sir?"

He looked through the doorway at the winter sunlight. He had dwelt upon that possibility, but dismissed the idea. "Apart from her concern about the women, did she in the course of that afternoon mention anything at all?"

Sue racked her brain trying desperately to recapture the slightest clue. "I am certain the stragglers troubled her," she said at last. "Mrs Foulkes seemed to notice every one of them. I remember her saying that she had seen an overturned gig which she thought she recognised. She said she wished she had stopped."

"For what purpose?"

"To examine it I should think."

"Did she mention a name – that of a person to whom the gig might have belonged?"

"She said something about Captain Harte."

Foulkes stiffened. "What exactly?"

"She was anxious for his welfare."

"What more?"

Sue shook her head. "Nothing."

"You are quite certain?"

"Yes."

Foulkes sat still, a faraway look in his eyes. So that was it! Harte and his man had set out in a light cart from Villa Franca. What more likely than that a breakdown of this had attracted Harriet's attention? – and in some way or another had become involved in the mishap? The more Foulkes considered the matter, the more he became convinced that here lay the true explanation; but he was much too withdrawn to impart his thoughts to Sue. It was not her business now. He must meet the loss alone.

He continued to sit so still and silent that the girl wondered if ever he meant to speak again. His coffee went cold, and was not renewed. At last, raising his head, he inquired abruptly how she had fared. When she told him she had picked up Higgenson's child in distressful circumstances, he started. "Higgenson? Higgenson?" he questioned, and his mind reverted to the favour this man had made on the Carrion bank. "Draw rations for the two of you." He consulted his notebook, and scribbled a line. "You will find the women quartered in this street, though you will have to hunt them out. When the time comes, you will of course, embark with us."

She lingered holding the slip of paper in her hands. "I hope, sir, that before we meet again you will have better news."

"Thank you," he said quietly. "I hope so too – profoundly."

He took up his hat and hurried away, leaving her in the café …

* * *

The regimental women whom Sue discovered later, hailed her with delight. "We had writ you off for stone dead," said Mrs Jenks bluntly. "Ah, dearie, the miseries and wonders of army life!"

"We're not out of the wood yet." gloomed Mrs Rayner.

"God be thanked that we can smell the seaweed," said Mrs Fenoughty, "for the weed is of the sea, and 'tis on the sea that the great ships of war will bear us all away."

"It's them as we left behind that I can't forget," said Mrs Jenks. Sue noticed that her plump cheeks sagged, though two reluctant patches of colour remained. "The Mother of God herself would have wept to see what I have seen, to hear them that expired in these arms. It robs me of my sleep."

"Honour the brave," murmured Mrs Fenoughty, wiping her eyes with the corner of her shawl, "the high and the low alike. Poor Mrs Foulkes that was so tall and proud on her fine grey horse – she went with the rest."

"What do you know of Mrs Foulkes? " asked Sue sharply.

"I seed her in a dream," said the woman simply, "like a ghost i' the night, and so it came to pass. We heared next day that she had gone, lost in the dreary snows."

"But I've returned," said Sue, "why not she?"

Mrs Fenoughty smiled secretly. "Ah, but I didn't dream about you, dearie. Handsome and brave Mrs Foulkes was, like one o' the mighty O'Neills – and now she's gone to the land of shadows." And the Irishwoman, swaying her body to and fro began to croon, "Hil-lallaboo-och-one-ochone-"

"The sights I've seen," resumed Mrs Jenks, "barrels of silver dollars poured down the mountain side like torrents of shining water, a-rollin' and a-jinglin' amongst the flinty rocks. There'll be fine pickings in the Spring for the Spanish boyoes with their big black eyes and monkey teeth."

"We'll s'll all be laughing about it then," said Mrs Rayner, cheerfully.

"I don't so easy forget," said the other …

* * *

On the morning of the 16th the French guns went into action. Their troops poured down the valley, and up they moved to the Elvina position. A desperate struggle, followed – in and out of the village, first the British gave and then the French. Cannon smoke hung thickly in the valley, and still through the drifting haze more troops were sent in. To check outflanking, Frazer's division marched from the suburbs to the ridge of Santa Margarita, where they were threatened by Fransechi's cavalry.

"So," thought Colonel Foulkes setting a field glass to his eye, and noting the enemy action, "we come to grips – at last!" As yet out of range, he watched detachments of French horsemen who were moving steadily up a winding track towards more level ground on his right where they could manoeuvre with comparative ease. Well it was all one. Foulkes felt assured in his own position. Dry-built stone walls patterned his front; it was upon one of these walls that the Colonel now stood.

As the dragoons climbed upwards, their helmets flashing back the thin rays of the January sun, Foulkes smiled confidently. No need in this country to "form square", the stone walls were defensive enough. And, of course, the fire-power of his men, many of whom had been served with new muskets from the stores in Corunna ... He noted that the Frenchmen were beginning to dismount and to unsling their carbines. Let them. This would reduce their effectiveness, since every one man in three would be required to hold horses. It was quite possible that with most of the British secreted behind the walls the enemy imagined the ridge to be held lightly at this point. At the appropriate time Foulkes' men would reveal themselves – but not now.

Soon bullets would fly, and he signalled with his hand to one or two incautious fellows who were showing their shakoes. In this moment of acute tension it did not strike him to doubt the morale of his men. All the indecision, the anxiety, the frustration of the past few weeks, had blown away like mist before a wind. Their swift response to orders, the expectation on every weather-beaten face, told its own story. The officers too were tense, alert, a few perhaps a little too much so, and Foulkes bent his mind to that. He wanted no over-run charging. He must hold the hounds in.

He heard the quick clatter of hooves in the rear; and it was Moore himself who came galloping up on his familiar cream and black horse. The recent frigid aloofness had gone. Now the eyes of the Commander-in-Chief were brilliant, darting, receptive. Scanning the position swiftly from one wing to the other, he nodded greeting to Foulkes and said crisply, "Anchor yourself here – you know what to do!" With no more than that he clattered away, taking the successive stone which impeded his path as neatly as in the hunting field ... The Colonel knew well enough. He stepped down for a word with Daiches. As he did so a slight wind arose, and the colours which had been drooping in the grip of the ensign began to flutter animatedly. A good omen, thought Foulkes ...

The dragoons had dismounted and taking cover behind a transverse wall, edged nearer. A ragged fusillade broke out; bullets slapped the stones behind which Foulkes and Daiches were standing. His head exposed, the Colonel refused to duck. One had not merely to retain coolness, but display it to others. He exchanged a tight little smile with Daiches. A man who had been hit began a piercing scream. "No more of that!" he shouted, as though by the imperative order he would check the soldier's distress. He made a signal for the wounded man to be carried to the rear.

As the dragoons advanced with scrambling little rushes, foot by foot, Foulkes gauged the intervening ground. He drew an imaginary line between an empty gate far to his right and an isolated silver birch on his left. Breaking cover, the advancing French came forward, but so raggedly that he allowed a few of the foremost to cross the line before he gave the order to fire. "Ready – present—" His own muskets crashed out, but the result was disappointing. Three dragoons fell – the remainder ran back to their original positions.

There was a pause of no more than half a minute, then the second rush came. "Aim low!" Foulkes shouted, "fire at their legs and you've got 'em!" It was comforting to hear the steady thump of ramrods as his men reloaded. Stubbs, almost purple in the face with excitement, repeated the words of his superior officer, "Aim low, you beggars – aim low!"

"If they were in column," said Foulkes to Daiches, "we should mow them down – it's this plaguey scattered formation."

After a second volley, the French with belated wisdom began to filter round the position, seizing what cover they could to direct an infilading fire. Two redcoats crumpled up and lay twitching spasmodically; from the tail of his eye Foulkes could see that others were dropping. Lieutenant Bird seemed to be in difficulty having a neckerchief bound around his head. He was pale, but decidedly energetic. Glancing towards the foot of the hill, Foulkes could see that the French were being strongly reinforced. Their weapons bristled formidably. There was still time to clear the approach. "We have dallied too long," he thought as he watched a young French lieutenant drop his helmet on a sabre and raise it high overhead. For what purpose – encouragement to his own men, or a signal to oncoming reinforcement? When a pot-shot from the British line by sheer luck struck the helmet and sent it flying, there was a derisive cheer from the redcoats. "We will do better than that," said Foulkes motioning to Suckley, "Clear the slope will you, but do no more than that. Be off with you!"

He saw the side swords fastened, and the red line move forward. He was confident that his men would not falter nor fail. The ridge would be held …

* * *

Watchers in the port saw cannon smoke drift lazily across the pastel buff and green of the hillsides. A burning house in the village of Elvina threw a dark scroll across the valley. The women who could do nothing to help, moved restlessly from billet to street and back to billet again. They did not doubt for a moment that their husbands would hammer the French, but each dwelt upon the personal safety of her own man, the probability of wounds, of death.

Leaving the boy in charge of the other women, Sue made her way to the quay level where ship's boats were moored. There were boats everywhere, while in massive guardian strength, oaken hearts at the centre, rode the battleships *Victory, Implacable, Audacious* and *Barfleur*. As the vessel to which the women had been assigned was the *Canopus*, Sue inquired of a duty midshipman if he would kindly point out where the vessel was anchored. He obliged, but when she inquired if it would be possible to embark when they wished, he answered sharply that she must obey orders, adding that the Royal Navy had been maid-of-all-work to the army too long; that there was no glory in it, and that for his part he had had more than enough. But he was an ageing midshipman, soured probably by promotion long deferred. She thanked him and strolled on.

The day was cold but fine. There were many Spanish ships in the harbour, coastal schooners, luggers and the like whose masters not intending to be caught by the French, were preparing to sail. She watched personal belongings – cases, brass-bound trunks – of Spanish families being carried aboard and wondered who they might be and what their destination. A year ago, six months even, she would have been shocked at the sight; but within that limited time she had seen so much of crisis and disruption that the movement seemed normal. These refugees would linger until the last moment, their eyes fixed upon the mountains in the frail hope perhaps that by some miracle the French would be driven away.

As she turned to leave the quays, a Spaniard with hat drawn over his eyes, and cloak wrapped up to his chin approached, walking briskly. Had he not halted almost when he came within a few yards of her, it is likely she would not have given a second glance. As he lowered his head drawing the cloak an inch or two higher than his chin, she caught a glimpse of the flittering eyes of Harker. He passed however without any sign of recognition, and standing between a mooring post and a pile of creels, she watched as he scrutinised successive vessels tied up at the wharf. Not once did he look behind.

His appearance on the wharf puzzled and disturbed her. Why was he not with his company in the hills, and why indeed, in Spanish garb? She saw him cross a gangplank, parley for a short time with a seaman in the vessel's deck, and then with an abrupt gesture leave immediately ... He resumed progress along the quayside, noting the name of each ship and its port of register. She lost him for a moment or two, and when he reappeared, followed slowly. He boarded another vessel, this time a schooner, and glanced around inquiringly. A seaman in a red cap accosted him; followed a bout of shrugging and gesticulating. At last Harker nodded and extended his hand, though what it contained she could not see; whereupon the seaman touched his cap and the cloaked figure disappeared down the companion way. There could be no doubt now in Sue's mind that he was deserting.

With a rapidly beating heart she drew nearer. As she came up to the stern she noted a name, that of the *Esmeralda* of Lisbon. She watched three seamen, each carrying a kit bag go on board, but there was no further sign of Harker. Was it possible – indeed probable – that the captain intended to cast off immediately? If so, there would be the end of Robin's rehabilitation. In a wild moment she dwelt upon the possibility of stowing away on board, and denouncing Harker to the authorities at Lisbon, but who would listen respectfully to the accusation of a serving maid? What, if once aboard, she were discovered and flung to feed the fishes, or sold into slavery? In that moment she remembered the boy in her charge – a direct obligation; and her place in Mrs Foulkes' service. Thus she hovered in a torment of indecision.

Where in this extremity could a poor girl turn? Simms and her brother were not accessible; Colonel Foulkes was, of course, with his regiment, already engaged in the hills. There were people on the wharves, but not a British uniform in sight. She must find someone.

As she returned to the harbour front, sporadic drumming on the hills continued. All Corunna was in the streets, some citizens confused and questioning, some making gestures of defiance, others hinting at a "French fury" of arson, murder and rapine. Spanish civilians shouldered new muskets drawn from the British stores, but of what avail were these against the seasoned columns of Marshal Soult? She saw a gang of boys brandishing British cavalry sabres, filched no doubt from the general magazine. How in such circumstances did one set about arresting a deserter?

An infantryman limping badly, turned the corner. He had been in action. His eyes were red-rimmed, his face begrimed with powder, but when she plucked at his sleeve, he stopped. "You must help me," she said.

"In what way, missus?"

"I want a man arresting."

"No doubt," he replied, narrowing his eyes. "Would it be your fancy man?"

"No – no!" she protested. "Nothing like that."

"Then why so?"

"A deserter, who must be stopped at once."

"Madam," said the infantryman wearily, "I've all on to look after myself. You need an officer."

"But where shall I find one?"

The man shrugged, twitched at his stock, and walked on grumbling at the importunity of some women. A deserter! – and with French fists hammering on the door!

Desperately she sought among the black and brown coats around her for a glimpse of red. Suddenly a pair of broad blue shoulders appeared, and thrusting through a press of indignant Spaniards, she almost flung herself upon the chest of a burly huzzar lieutenant, who seizing her by both arms held her off. "Steady lass," he grunted, "What's the hurry?"

"I have to report an infantryman deserting," she gasped.

"Let the poltroon go!" said the officer contemptuously.

"That won't do – he must be stopped."

The huzzar drew a long breath. A worried officer, he had been ordered to shoot all horses not fit to be embarked, and the assignment was as ashes in his mouth. Releasing her arms he said, "I am sorry, but I can do nothing for you. Better see the Town Major for advice – yond's his office." He pointed to a large house fronted by iron balconies. "Go there, and good luck to you."

She thanked him an darted across to the building he indicated. As the main door was open, she entered.

After the sunlight and hubbub of the street, the hall of the Town Major's quarters was shadowy and still. She paused indecisively, not knowing which way to turn, but hearing muffled voices to the left knocked on a door from which these sounds had emerged. Someone cried, "Enter!" and opening, she faced an officer busy cramming papers into a valise. At the same time an orderly and a clerk were heaping documents in the fireplace. The orderly held a lighted candle about to apply it to the papers.

"Office now closed!" said the officer curtly. He had already packed, made his farewells, and was clearing all records.

"You, sir, are the Town Major?"

"I was – for a season." He rubbed his nose doubtfully with his forefinger. "What is your business? I warn you, the hour is late."

"I bring you information, sir, that Private Raddock of Colonel Foulkes regiment is in the act of desertion."

"A deserter?" said the Town Major in a puzzled tone. "What the devil has that to do with you?" he eyed her suspiciously, but in a not unfriendly tone added, "You had better get your breather. Sit down."

"No time for that," she jerked. "I am Mrs Foulkes maid, of the same regiment, and I am come from the quays where I recognised this man boarding a vessel."

"What of that?" said the officer, "we shall all board vessels ere long."

"But this man, whom I know well was dressed in plain Spanish clothing, and the vessel he boarded was Spanish too."

"Oh, dammit," said the Town Major impatiently, "one can't work on hearsay. Where is your written authority?"

"Authority?" she repeated, quite bewildered, "Were Colonel Foulkes in town I should have approached him, but he is in the hills. Don't you see? Please hurry!"

"I don't know about that," said the officer.

"The quay is not distant."

"I know where the quay is," he rejoined scathingly, "this request my girl is most irregular – most irregular, but I'll come to humour you. I want no mare's nest, mark you! Give me his name." He turned to the orderly. "Omerod, accompany me – armed." And as the man stared doubtfully from the girl to his superior, "Your musket, fellow. Jump to it!"

The three set out at a pace, which to Sue was exasperatingly slow. The officer did not speak at all until they reached the quayside. "How was this man dressed?"

"In a broad brimmed hat and cloak."

"The ship's name – you said?"

"Esmeralda."

"A brig – a sloop – a lugger – what?"

"I cannot say."

"Well, lead the way and point out the vessel."

Almost three quarters of an hour had passed since she had seen Harker disappearing into the hold of the Spanish vessel, but Sue advanced hopefully for the lines of shipping had the same appearance as before. They worked their way along, noting one name after another – *Juanita, Catalonia, Gitana*.

"I see no Esmeralda," said the Town Major darkly.

"You will," she replied confidently. At the same time a tight knot fastened in the pit of her stomach – they were approaching the end of the quay, and only two vessels remained. They examined both, and standing at the end looked down on the emptily washing waves. There was no *Esmeralda*. Sue evaded the Town Major's accusing eyes.

"Your ship seems to have been a figment of the imagination," he said severely.

"There was such a vessel," she protested, looking back vainly at the length they had traversed.

"Yes, a dream ship," he said in a resigned voice. "If it were not that you were a woman, and I a creature of incredible patience, you would discover – but no matter, no matter!"

The *Esmeralda* must have moved out," she wailed. "Look!" and she pointed to a schooner, which with mainsail set, bore out to sea. "There it is, with green and gold at the back – I mean the stern."

The Town Major grunted sceptically, but he was sufficiently interested to bring out a small field telescope, which he adjusted to his eye, and trained on the craft in question. She waited breathlessly for him to speak. "By gad," the officer murmured at last, "I believe you are right. I can read the lettering plainly. I see beside the helmsman a fellow in black hat and brown cloak. Is that your man?"

He handed Sue the glass, but she fumbled at the instrument with shaking fingers. "Adjust the focus," said the Town Major patiently, "steady does it, bit by bit."

She could see more clearly now. The man in the cloak had pushed back his hat, and with his face turned towards Corunna, was standing with both hands on the rail. She focused on the brown face she knew so well. Presently, in a matter of moments, the features blurred, and though she continued there was no more point in watching. Slowly she handed the telescope back to its owner. "The man in the cloak was he whom I had in mind," she said.

The officer snapped the glass to. "So we can write finis to that," he observed. He motioned his orderly away, and with a dry smile turned to the girl. "Your patriotism, interest, or whatever else you had in mind, has come to nought. We are, no doubt, well rid of the man, though I wish we had copped him. However, there it is. I must go."

With a glance slightly amused and quizzical as though he believed only part of her story, he left her, and began to thread his way along the wharf.

Sue stood rooted to the spot. A dead weight of failure overwhelmed her.

She stood staring after the *Esmeralda*, until round the lighthouse, the vessel became a speck on the surface of the heaving water. There was nothing left now but to return into the town …

CHAPTER XXII

When Sue found her lodgings once again artillery fire was so continuous that infrequent spells of silence became unnatural. She entered to find the Spanish landlady telling beads. As the girl watched the ivory pieces slip one by one through the old woman's fingers, each bead she thought counted out the final hours in Corunna.

About four, Mrs Fenoughty rushed in wailing, "Ochone! We are intoirely undone!" She gazed around distractedly, and became so incoherent that Sue led her to a chair. "Take your breath," she said gently, "and speak when you are able to." For the moment Sue felt that the worst had happened to Fenoughty himself, but the news was of wider import.

"Gineral Moore," the Irishwoman sobbed, "our hope and joy, is cruelly struck down in the battle, and brought to a house on the quayside. Sure, he is dead already. Pray – pray on your bended knees for his soul!"

The words struck a chill in Sue's heart. Moore the indispensable, the heart and brain of the army – gone! It was unthinkable. Now they were leaderless. No wonder Mrs Fenoughty cried that all was lost. It did not strike them that another general officer would immediately have stepped into Moore's place. "The best go," lamented Mr Fenoughty, "always the least is spared." Quickly, however, she changed the subject. "I have to tell you also, that in two hours we move to the quay and take to the boats. Don't forget dearie."

Sue was not likely to. Ready to go, she packed what little there was, and at the appointed time joined the others.

As they waited, their few possessions beside them on the bare stones of the wharf, darkness fell. Lights glimmered in the town, and ship's lanterns were hoisted … At six o'clock, the French, badly mauled had withdrawn to their former positions on the heights. Gradually firing died away, though an occasional shot broke the silence. Meanwhile a small procession climbed to the ramparts where Lieutenant General Sir Jon Moore, all military and political problems resolved, was laid in his grave.

Steadily the British withdrew, although a skeleton force remained in position tending the campfires and moving busily to and fro to convey the impression that the ground was still held. Hollow-eyed, unshaven, powder grimed, bloodstained but grimly triumphant, men marched into the town. During recent months many soldiers had passed through Corunna, but none so eathern-worn or battle scarred as these. They crowded in the boats, oars at once dipping rhythmically towards the towering bulk of the battleships and transports.

The women with their compact bundles still waited patiently for the regiment to march in. What could be holding their men? A mist fell on the harbour, through which they could see the feeble gleam of the lighthouse, but
little else. They peered anxiously through the darkness as each fresh formation arrived. "What Foot are ye?" they cried, moaning with disappointment
when they were informed that Colonel Foulkes' men were of the brigade
which would be last in ... Time dragged leadenly; it became so cold that Sue
ran back to her lodgings to make the boy a jug of hot chocolate. While she
was busy with this, the Spanish woman presented her with a parting gift of
a small wooden box containing a flask of wine, some coffee, sugar and sweet
cakes – a gracious gesture, all the more touching in view of the state to which
the town would be reduced when the French arrived.

She had rejoined the group with Tom's drink when she heard Harry
Simms calling through the darkness, "Whose people are you?" She thrust her
way to his side. "Thank God you are here," he said in tones of profound relief.
"I was afraid with all this coming and going you would be misplaced – that
is flung into the wrong ship." Yes, Robin was at hand, unharmed, and the regiment, he gathered, would be in shortly. For his part, he would take pot-luck
and embark with them. "Things will sort themselves out later," she said
cheerfully, "the main thing is to embark."

And still they waited. Other regiments marched in, took to the boats, and
disappeared over the dark water ... time dragged ...

Grey dawn broke. A dull boom came from the height of St Lucia; a few
seconds later a round shot whistled over their heads, and striking the water
sent up a fountain of spray. "Our French friends are up early this morning, "
remarked Simms coolly, but he was far from feeling comfortable; he knew
that the gunners were trying the range. They would certainly hot it up, but
there was nothing that one could do save to exercise restraint and patience.
"Arrah, and would they eat us up for breakfast?" cried Mrs Fenoughty ... a
little later a second shot glanced from the masonry of the quay showering
splinters, but beyond that doing no harm. A third shot crashing into the
midst of the fleet, brought down a frigate's mainmast like a slashed thistle,
upon which three of the seventy fours began to return the French fire, but the
trajectory hopeless, desisted. "The ships are sitting birds," said Simms tensely.
"I can't see this lasting."

Almost immediately, ships of the line and other vessels, aided now by a
rising wind, began to move out, but with great difficulty, cutting cables, some
colliding, breaking bowsprits and yards. One ran aground, and was blown up.
Three drifted ashore, but most got away without further mishap, and cruised
outside the range of the French artillery. One or two of the larger vessels
remained comparatively close in to pick up their quota.

At last the foremost files of Colonel Foulkes' men appeared, but as they
mustered at the quayside there was no breaking of ranks no intermingling

with their womenfolk. When Mrs Jenks with a joyful cry ran forward, a brawny tattooed arm interposed between herself and the object of her affections. "Pipe down Matilda," grinned a sailor, "ye are meant for yer own boat."

"But I want my husband."

"And I want my Nancy," rejoined the sailor, "we'll both have to wait, won't we? Orders – soldiers only."

"We shall all be killed dead," she waylaid.

"Not all" said the sailor coolly, shooting a jet of tobacco juice into the harbour," only a few."

"Strong i' the arm, and weak i' the head!" she jeered.

"None o' your flattery," said the seaman unwilling to be silenced.

His body formed an unyielding barrier.

The French opened out again. A round shot, striking through the floor boards of a long boat, killed two of its crew and hurled the rest into the water. Half a minute later another shot fell within a few yards of the first, so that the remaining boats began to back oars. Whereupon there was an indignant outcry from the quay. "The spalpeens," cried Mrs Fenoughty, "is deserting us! Call yourselves men? Shame on ye, and on the mothers that bore ye!" But she might just as well have saved her breath. An officer standing in the stern of the nearest boat, shouted, "Too hot in this quarter! Turn all of you – march through the town to the shore at the lighthouse; we'll lay to, and take you off there." He repeated the instruction, this time interlarding his message with a few salty oaths. At last (for some felt that they were exchanging the frying pan for the fire) the company obeyed. "The lighthouse," said Simms, "is out of range, but it won't be an easy place from which to embark. At any rate we can take our time there."

They hurried past the house where Sir John had died, and straggled towards a rocky spit of land, for them the last few yards of Spain. Soon they were clambering across the slimy, weed-covered, shell encrusted boulders; Harry Simms, young Higgenson riding pick-a-back, leading the way. They halted where waves washed among the rocks looking for reasonable foothold, and at last found a broad ledge, not completely dry but sufficient for their purpose. Shivering in the morning breeze they watched with eager eyes for the boats which were to take them off. The massive black and buff hull of the *Canopus* loomed like an island in the middle distance.

Pulling with what seemed to the refugees lazy deliberation, the seamen drew in. "Jump as you can," bawled a midshipman in charge of the foremost boat, "But bide your time. If you don't make it altogether, grab one o' the oars and we'll haul you in. Cast aside your baggage, you'll need both hands. I repeat throw aside your belongings."

A cry of consternation arose; the packages that the women carried contained not only spare clothing, but souvenirs collected in the course of the campaign and other personal effects. If they were to follow the advice thrust upon them they would all leave Spain much poorer than when they entered. But the midshipman was firm. "I said, drop your baggage, or by God you'll drown. It's that or your lives."

One by one the bundles were discarded. Sue dropped her holdall containing as it did the little box of provisions provided by the thoughtful Spanish lady. She could do no other.

"Now Missis, who's the first?" called a seaman poised with a boathook in the foremost craft. "We're coming as near as we can, when I shouts – jump!"

As the boat swept along the shelf where she was standing, and the seaman found a brief lodging place for his hook, Sue sprang lightly, dropping with more luck than judgment between the seats. Meanwhile, the seaman having relinquished his hold was groping for another. Again he managed to fix his iron, and Simms lowered the boy in her outstretched arms. She would have collapsed completely if sturdy hands had not seized and upheld her. The child yelled, as well he might, but his cries soon fell into a whimper.

Throughout this operation the seamen were cheerful and incredibly active. Mrs Jenks was one of the few who suffered immersion, but with a "Yo heave ho!" she was hauled aboard, a dripping bundle of petticoats, until in relative safety, she could regain her breath. With varying fortunes the rest of the women were gathered in Simms and Robin were the last to leave.

At length the rocks were cleared, and as the little flotilla crept towards the towering bulk of the parent vessel, the women looked back. Corunna lay strangely peaceful in the morning light. Soult's guns were silent. Beyond the walls columns of marching men, and a faint ripple of steel showed where the French were moving down to the port. Soon the narrow streets would resound to the tap of drum, the hotels and cafes throng with unwelcome patrons; but for those who, wet and bedraggled, swung beneath the protective bulk of the *Canopus*, the last chapter of the Spanish venture had closed.

* * *

It was difficult to find a comfortable corner in the overcrowded ship. The wounded, the infirm, and those who bodies were intact, were wedged together almost anyhow. Each deck held its quota. Moreover, men were ordered not to roam. There was no place on deck for any but the crew. Already, the foam-flecked Biscay sea leapt from a dark tempestuous horizon.

Many hours passed before Simms and Robin (to whom victualling gave a certain liberty of action) were able to encounter Sue. At last on the main deck they squeezed into a corner beside a gun carriage. Tom Higgenson having been left in charge of Mrs Rayner, Sue was free.

They had much to ponder, much to discuss together. As the *Canopus* rolled and pitched, the girl listened to the unceasing wind, the rattle of blocks, the creaking of yards, the strumming of backstays, she drew her shawl more tightly around her shoulders and shivered, but not altogether from the exacting cold. Neither on the quays, not thus far in the *Canopus*, had she said anything about Harker's bid for freedom – the prospect of adding to Robin's despondency alone impelled her to silence – but soon, very soon, the truth would out. What then? In a few days time the English coast would loom ahead, and the dilemma of her brother's future confront them. At first, by implied consent, Harker's name was not mentioned, or even hinted at. The three discussed their last hours in Corunna, the tragic death of Sir John, the wretched condition of those round about them. "What England will say when this batch of scarecrows tumbles ashore," said Simms, "is anybody's guess, except that they will not be surfeited with bells and bonfires."

An orderly threaded his way towards them, peering into the faces of such women as impeded his line of progress. He stopped to ask a question, and a finger was pointed in the direction of the three in the corner. It was Sue he was after. She knew the man well by sight, and smiled recognition. He handed her a letter. "From Colonel Foulkes," he said, "directed to you."

She took the missive from him, and read the superscription slowly. "To Mr T. Jones, in the care of Miss S. Thompson." The number of the regiment was written below.

"The Colonel wished me to inquire if you knew this man, and if so I was to leave the letter with you."

"Mr T. Jones," Sue repeated. "Indeed, yes," she said hurriedly, "he is known to me. I will see that he receives it."

"It remains in your charge then." The orderly still hovered, a little curious perhaps concerning the identity of Mr Jones.

"Certainly." Sue dropped the letter in her lap with a show of indifference. "And please thank the Colonel from me."

"Your order, Ma'm, shall be obeyed." The man grinned, saluted holding on to the gun carriage with his free hand, and was about to go when with a swift afterthought she asked, "You say this is from Colonel Foulkes. How did it come into his possession?"

"He just give me the letter," said the other, blankly.

"So I gather," she persisted, "but from whom did the Colonel receive it?" A sudden panic seized her. The conjunction of her own name with that of Jones suggested inner knowledge on the part of the sender.

The orderly's brow furrowed as he charged his memory. "It comes back to me now – I heard him say to his clerk, 'The letter the priest handed in.'"

"A priest? What priest?"

"I'm almost certain," said the orderly, "a priest was mentioned. That's all I know."

"Not that it matters," said Sue, placing the letter in the folds of her shawl. "Thank you again. I will see that Mr Jones receives it."

So the orderly went, while the three gazed after him.

When he had quite disappeared in the throng of the main deck, Robin spoke. "What have we to do with priests? I can't imagine—"

"Better read the letter," suggested Simms, "and the mystery will be solved."

Sue handed it over. When her brother paused to examine the seal on the flap, she cried impatiently, "Oh, do open it – please!". Robin broke the seal, his companions eyeing his every movement closely. He turned his head to ensure more light from the port, and as he read a look of pure amazement spread over his features. He gave a low whistle.

"What is it?" asked Sue.

"The most unexpected, the most extraordinary thing in the world," Robin replied. He looked from one to the other.

"What," inquired Simms dryly, "is the most unexpected, the most extraordinary thing in the world?"

"You'll never believe it."

"No doubt. Can it be that Soult has surrendered?"

"It has to do with Harker. Read it for yourself." And Robin handed over the paper.

Simms took the letter. "I think it would be better if you read it aloud," said Sue, "but keep down your voice."

"Very well," said Simms. "The script is a little strange, but the language is certainly English. Here we go—"

"To the Right Honourable Earl Fitzwilliam: My Lord, of my own free will and facing danger unto death, I must relieve my soul of a crime which has long weighed with me. I beg to state that I and I alone, am responsible for an unfortunate lapse into poaching on your estate in the year which is past, and for which Robin Thompson was at the time wrongfully accused, he being tried at York and sentenced to transportation across the seas. Having regard to this open confession of my misdemeanour, I trust that the aforesaid Robin Thompson will be exonerated in the eyes of the law, of which you are so great an ornament, and given sufficient recompense according to Your Lordship's will and pleasure.

Signed: Jacob Harker (x) his mark, sometime stable hand in Your Lordship's service. Witness: Rodriguez Morla, Priest. Patrick O'Donnell, Priest.

Corunna, January 1809

Sue drew a long and quivering breath. Simms tapped the letter with his finger. "Harker never had the art to compose this."

"Let me see it again," said Robin. He scrutinised the writing closely. "The hand is undoubtedly that of the priest inscribing himself O'Donnell. What do you make of that?"

"An Irishman, evidently," said Simms, "with a knowledge of English. There are many such in Spain. I recall an Irish college in Salamanca."

"But the letter and its content," said Robin. "I brought the fellow into Corunna where he reported as an injured soldier of the Line. I was requisitioned immediately, and so lost sight of him, but I was not greatly perturbed. I felt I should trace him through the regiment."

"Which he must have rejoined," said Simms. "He speaks here of facing danger unto death. Is it possible that he expected to be struck down in action? The letter may have been an act of premonition."

"I can't think of Harker dead," said Robin uneasily, "removed forever."

Sue stirred guiltily, feeling that she had been silent too long. "Removed – yes," she said, "but not in the manner you think. I can assure you that he is very far from dead, and that he played no part in the battle."

Both men stared at her in amazement, though even now she hesitated to tender information, which at its best could do nothing to improve the situation. "Before we proceed further," she continued, "I must tell you that he is at this moment on this way to Lisbon, masquerading as a Spanish traveller. I saw him board ship, although I did everything in my power to stop him."

"Yet you said not a word," cried her brother reproachfully.

"I intended to –" she began.

"Never mind," he interposed, "that being so it's all one now." And after listening to her account, he made a resigned gesture. "Disguised as a Spanish traveller, how do we explain that?"

Simms turned to Robin. "In what condition did you leave him?"

"That's the amazing part of it," said the other. "He was a sorry spectacle – dirty, torn uniform, etc."

"There must be some rhyme and reason in all this – let me think." Simms closed his eyes and leaned back against the gun carriage. He made no movement until he addressed Robin again, then – "You say that he had a sorry appearance?"

"Very much so."

"There you have it. We may be quite certain that being what he is, he would at once play upon the sympathy of the people at his billet – lament his injured condition, look misery. After inveigling the maidservant, or it may be the good woman of the house into mending his tattered tunic, he would meantime borrow civilian clothes, and pleading the necessity for a breath of fresh air, sally out alone. You follow me?"

"Up to a point," said Robin doubtfully.

"In his new outfit," resumed Simms, "he would make his way to the nearest convent. Oh, I can see him now, halting before the gate, an unfortunate traveller or some such, certainly a devout Catholic in need of assistance. Heaven knows the tale he would tell. He might present himself as a valet, in the confusion of the times separated from his master, stranded in Corunna, but determined to scour the danger area until he found him. Of course he would ask for an Irish priest who could speak English. He might even pose as an Irishman."

"That would be difficult," said Sue.

"Not for Harker. It comes to my mind also that this same Fitzwilliam the grandee he invokes had a great name in Ireland."

Robin nodded. "The Earl was in 1795 Lord Lieutenant; he has also estates in Mayo."

"Ah!" exclaimed Simms triumphantly, "there's the link."

"Ireland was much the subject of talk at Wentworth. Some of the servants had been over."

"In that case Harker would contrive a plausible story."

"But the content of the letter?"

"All else follows," continued the Commissary with an assurance that Sue and her bother by no means shared. "You forget that conversion and repentance play a great part in Catholic devotions."

"Repentance!" scoffed Robin.

"Confession then. And having deluded these worthy Spanish priests to the top of his bent, he would leave probably with funds."

"For Lisbon," said Sue.

"Yes, because there, more than at any other part of the Peninsular, vessels put out for the Americas. My own feeling is that he will make for one of the sugar islands, and that if, in the fullness of time he does not round off his career by decorating the gallows, he will finish as a landed proprietor, sitting on his own veranda, surrounded by a bevy of female slaves." Simms turned to Robin. "This makes your own course clear."

"I wish I could think so."

"Of that I have no doubt at all. Grasp the nettle boldly. There is, I agree, a characteristic impertinence in the last paragraph of the letter, a suggestion of recompense which is no part of the Earl's duty, though his feelings might well be moved; but let that pass. My advice is that you secure a corroborative statement of service in Spain from my own department, and an addendum possibly from Colonel Foulkes, who I am sure, would be indulgent for your sister's sake. Do this, and your troubles are at an end. Of what character is the Earl?"

"A worthy, generous man."

"And Harker groomed his horses?"

"He might remember."

"All the better. Here is an affidavit, a solemn sworn statement, backed by servants of the Church. Your nobleman, if he is so minded, can work wonders. This letter is your passport to freedom. Seek Fitzwilliam out boldly – frankness serves best with men of consequence. Is the Earl a cloistered person?"

"Far from it. He rides out daily."

"Then take your chance. Wait for him and present your petition."

Robin at last contrived a smile. "I still can't understand why Harker brought himself to do this."

Simms said nothing, and drew from his pocket a crumpled cigar which had survived the hazards of the past twenty-four hours. He wetted the outside and rolled it between is palms; then lit up. "Harker," he said gravely, "is the chameleon type, elusive by nature, but not completely inhuman. In one way or another he was badly shaken. Apart from anything that happened at Benevente and Bembibre at Villa Franca he escaped hanging only by an hair's breadth. Consider the effect of that. Then for miles, Robin, you and he shared much difficulty together. It may be that during the course of the journey he revised his opinion of you – indeed, though you may find this difficult to accept, grew a little fond of you."

Robin grunted sceptically. "The only person Harker considered was himself."

"You may be mistaken."

"Does the leopard change its spots?"

"Leave the animal kingdom be." Simms blew a thin jet of smoke across the rotundity of the cannon. "Let me put it this way – there is no man however base who does not pride himself upon one redeeming virtue; the thief who scorns to murder, the sot who scorns to thieve, and so on. Our man, I fancy is no different from the rest. The letter propounds not only Robin Thompson's innocence, but Harker's solitary streak of virtue."

"Virtue indeed!"

"I am trying," said Simms patiently," to find a reasonable explanation of his conduct."

Sue, listening to the conversation retained her own thoughts. She remembered the rain-swept arcade at Guardia when to her half-despairing suggestion, Harker had cried bitterly, "I can't write – can't write!" Had the seed been planted there? How far had his approach at Salamanca been sincere? Foolish perhaps to imagine, she felt somehow that intermingled with his undoubted vanity was a tender feeling for herself … She gazed with unseeing eyes at the rim of the gun beside which she was sitting. Aloud she said, "I think he was a creature much to be pitied."

Her companions seemed not to hear. Simms remarked, "Whatever the impulse, the rogue had a sense of the dramatic." He waved the letter, "With which he bows himself off the stage."

Really, Simms' essay in conjecture had not been far wrong. Harker had in fact presented himself at the monastery, but in full uniform announcing that as he was about to rejoin his regiment, and unable to face the prospect of death with so great a burden on his conscience, wished to make both private and public confession. He had not – as Simms suggested – invoked monetary assistance; disposing of the Astorga watches to a Jewish dealer, he had ample means at his disposal. Later, buying civilian clothes, he discarded his uniform, and as we have seen, made good his escape. The informing motive had been rather more complex than either Simms or Robin suspected, for Harker had arrived in Corunna with no greater affection for the man he had wronged than before. But the girl was a different case. He had tried his best to impress her favourably, and in the hard rebound had tried to put her in the wrong; both courses had failed. Now, in the most unexpected fashion, he would heap coals of fire on her head, or in his own words, "Make her sit up and stare!" She would ponder his action all her life. Others might scoff when his name was mentioned, but whoever looked down their noses at Jacob Harker, among these would not be numbered Susan Thompson!

Having planned this course, he little guessed that his last walk in Corunna would coincide with her appearance on the quays. Thus, as the *Esmeralda* moved across the harbour mouth, he fixed enigmatical eyes upon the diminishing figure in the flowered shawl and fluttering black skirt. He had played the joker in the pack. What the deal would bring forth next he did not know, and because it was in his nature to take things as they came, did not much care. He would find a corner somewhere. He continued to watch until the outline of Sue's form became no more than a fleck of black and brown among the dark gulls and interlacing masts of the harbour ...

* * *

Aboard the *Canopus*, the regimental women also dwelt upon the future. What kind of reception would they meet on landing – to what quarters would they be dispatched? Some, all too familiar with the bleak, rat-infested barracks of Ireland, and others with the mouldy, dripping casemates of around Rochester in mind, expected little by way of luxury; but all agreed that any accommodation in the Old Country would be preferable to the verminous, malodorous posadas of Spain. At least you would not be expected to sleep with animals.

Huddled together on the draughty, heaving desk of the battleship, they coughed and sneezed and gossiped the hours away. Sometimes they sang artlessly songs with which they were most familiar: "Sweet Lavender", "Drink Away Dull Care", "Dog Tray", and "Sally", nostalgic tunes of the English countryside, or its urban streets and alleys. They spoke wistfully of open fires and good kitchen fare: barons of beef, apple pies, bowls of steaming broth. Often they would fall into long spells of silence, brooding on the terror they had left behind, and faces they would never see, voices they would never hear again.

Much to Sue's relief, Tom Higgenson, sadly alone since his father had not reunited with the army, was adopted by Private and Mrs Rayner. A whip around in the boy's favour produced a respectable sum, Mr Jenks contributing the not inconsiderable amount of five shillings. Later, Colonel Foulkes would be approached on Tom's behalf for a levy on the regimental charity fund.

For the next twenty four hours Sue saw next to nothing of Harry Simms, who was assisting in the distribution of rations drawn from the limited reserves of the *Canopus* – biscuits riddled with weevil, and water the hue of muddied ale. The gale showed no sign of abating, the sails boomed, the wind tore through the rigging, and the great ship shouldered into seas which swept the decks and wrenched away everything which was not securely lashed down. Sickness intensified the ordeal. Sue yearned for a stable foothold, a blessed release from the perpetual creaking and groaning of timbers, the sepulchral half-light of the deck. But on the evening of the following day, Simms discovered her pretty much in the same place as before. He settled down awkwardly on a coil of rope. Exchanging commonplaces for a time, he appeared a little nervous, clearing his throat at times before speaking. Even in the lantern light, he looked tired, but she reflected, all were under strain, and the discomfort of the crowded decks was beginning to tell.

At last he regarded her with a slightly quizzical air. Once again he cleared his throat. "I don't wish to appear impertinent," he began, "but have you considered what you intend to do when you land?"

Sue pursed her lips doubtfully. She had considered the problem often, but with no satisfactory result. It was fairly certain that Colonel Foulkes would remain on the active list – Mrs Foulkes having vanished, the girl could see no renewal of her place at all, not even at Bellaby. She might possibly return home with her brother, to await his rehabilitation.

"It all depends," she said. "If Mrs Foulkes is to be counted as lost I must look for other service."

"Where?"

Sue hesitated. "I cannot say. I shall have to make inquiries round about home."

"But you have no positive idea at the moment?"

She shook her head.

"Good!" he ejaculated with an air of satisfaction which startled her.

"I shall be lucky to improve on Bellaby," she said.

He smiled disarmingly. "I wonder," he said slowly, "if for my own part I might make a proposal?"

She was frankly puzzled. "A place in service?"

"Of a kind." The smile that trembled on her lips faded when he said, "I speak seriously."

"What have you in mind," she asked doubtfully.

"The place – or service – I suggest," continued Simms, "will offer little comfort, perhaps at times, danger. You may be required to live a wandering life, moving from camp to camp, from one lodging place to another, although as time went I do not doubt that your position would improve."

"Has it to do with the army?"

She trembled slightly as she spoke, conscious that he was regarding her with tender interest. She adjusted her shawl, fingered the ribbons at her neck; but when he spoke again he was gazing sternly into the darkened perspective of the deck, as though he would still with a glance the hubbub of voices lifting there. With what seemed a painful effort he turned to her and blurted, "I will put all my cards on the table, not dear Sue, that they are of any great value. You must bear with me also if I am extremely mater-of-fact – it is in my habit."

Pausing, as it might be for breath, perhaps the better to collect himself, he continued, "I am twenty five years of age, and bachelor with no encumbrances. I have one hundred and seventeen pounds, ten shillings with Mr Coutts, the banker; such, except for the things that I stand up in, are my material assets. As an Assistant Deputy Commissary I draw a modest seven and sixpence a day – not, you will agree, a fortune – but when the war is over I hope to return to my old position in the wine trade, where I shall be in much better shape."

"Why do you tell me all this?" she inquired. Her hands were now still in her lap, but her colour had heightened. The premonition of what he was about to say, deepened.

"For the simple reason," he said, "that I invite you to unite your fortunes with mine." He leaned forward. "I may prove thoughtless and difficult at times, Sue, but over and above everything else I offer my sincere devotion."

She returned his gaze for a moment or two at a complete loss for words. Observing that her eyes clouded, he hastened to speak again. "My dear friend I cannot expect you to give me an immediate answer. Take time to consider the matter, and I will approach you again as we draw near to Portsmouth." When he placed his hand over hers, she did not attempt to withdraw, but remained silent. "Take time," he repeated, "that is all I ask."

She took her hand from his as though to imply some measure of reserve. "I will speak now," she said softly. "Mr Simms, you have always been very kind to me, so understanding, so attentive, that I fear –"

He shook his head. "I can assure you that I have considered the matter for some time."

She swept a lock back from her forehead. "I was about to say that I cannot make an inventory of my possessions as you have done, for apart from myself, I have nothing."

Confused, she paused, on the verge of tears, conscious of other deficiencies – her humble origin, her lack of social graces. "Quite nothing," she murmured.

"In that case, "he said cheerfully, "there can be no quarrel over settlements. Once again, I ask you to marry me."

Her eyes spoke before her lips. She said simply, "I should be very happy to do so, Mr Simms."

"Mr Simms?" he questioned reproachfully.

"Harry," she replied.

It did not need the *Canopus* taking a green sea and lurching in the trough of the wave to bring them more closely together …

* * *

Foulkes sat in the stern cabin, but not alone. The Captain, his Clerk and the First Lieutenant occupied one corner; Foulkes and his Adjutant, the other. From time to time the interior was shadowed when curtains of spray streamed down the windows. The cabin, though chilly was compact and dry.

Beneath the Colonel's hand lay the last general order issued by Sir John Moore. He was familiar enough with the text, but he read through it once again—

"Head Quarters, Corunna, 16th January, 1809.

The Commander of the Forces directs that Commanding officers of the regiments will, as soon as possible after they embark, make themselves acquainted with the names of the ships in which the men of their regiments are embarked, both sick and convalescent; and that they make out the correct states of their respective corps; that they will state the number of sick present, also those left at different places ..."

A voice indeed, from the grave ...

Foulkes swallowed a tot of rum. Cold and tired, he needed a stimulant, for now he was to grapple with a task he thoroughly disliked – a report to the High Command. From the welter of harassed days, and complex situations, he must compose a document truthful enough to withstand official eyes. At best it would be a sorry tale, redeemed only in the final stages by the exemplary conduct of his men outside Corunna ...

He cast his eyes around the cabin walls, noting the heavily gilded frame encircling a portrait of the Captain's wife; a chart of the English Channel; the nautical almanacs, the quadrant and other mathematical instruments adorning the place; but finding no inspiration there, began to pencil introductory sentences. Corunna was freshly in his mind, but what of the preceding months?

He set down a few figures. Of the eight hundred men with whom he had landed in Portugal, he was taking back between five to six hundred. Roughly, one man in four had been lost, but not in action – casualties in the Corunna engagement had been slight; sickness, intemperance, straggling and possibly desertion, accounted for the rest. How many had fallen into French hands he could not say, though certain of the sick had been abandoned at Villa Franca. Equipment was not really in question; they had drawn liberally upon the Corunna depot. Lost weapons had been replaced – not the men.

"Won't bear looking at," he breathed, as he tried on his thumbnail one of the new steel pens with which he had been provided by the Captain. He was still showing signs of acute strain; the nervous movement of his hands, the twitching of his left eye, were constant. By night he had been sleeping badly, falling into dreams so confused and horrible that he was glad to wake again. The Adjutant watched his Colonel covertly. Foulkes, who could feel the eyes of the other man upon him, shifted uneasily. "The rot began," he said, "when we turned about at Sahagun."

"Oh, Lord," thought the Adjutant, "he's off again!" Aloud, he said, "I think we carried too many Irishmen."

"Irishmen? Irish?" rejoined the Colonel testily, "from Deventer to the Boyne, from the Boyne to Fontenoy – always the Irish!" It was an old complaint, the rebel, the intractable, the unpredictable element, discussion of which led nowhere.

Foulkes eyed the portion of liquor left in his cup as though the drops winked back the regrettable orgies of Bembibre and Villa Franca. To Captain Harrod's astonishment he poured the remainder of the drink into a scuttle. There could be no doubt that the Colonel was a little "Touched". Most of all, he needed a long rest.

"I find some element missing," said Foulkes, "some measure of contact between us, which marred disciplinary behaviour."

"I am certain, sir, that you have nothing with which to reproach yourself."

"How do you know?"

The Adjutant evaded the smouldering eyes that probed his own by turning to the muster rolls and running an assiduous finger down the columns. When he came to the additional name of Mrs Foulkes, he held his peace. Foulkes never mentioned his wife; Harrod felt it would be an immense relief if he did, but the Captain had no intention of reopening the matter now ... After they had discussed the condition of the rank and file in general, Foulkes asked quietly, "How do the families stand?"

"All told, sir, forty five. We lost fifteen women and children between Villa Franca and Lugo. We carry one boy, an orphan."

"His name?"

On receiving this information the Colonel sighed. Where now was Percy Foulkes Higgenson, the child intended to bear the Colonel's name – a stark little morsel in the icy snow? He did not pursue the subject, but watched for a moment the stern window and the thrashing spray. "Back into the ocean it falls," he thought, "lost in the greater whole ..."

"Take an abstract I can use," he said suddenly. "I wish all casualties in the late action to be held separately from those of the retreat. Be exact in your particulars. Omit nothing." Already in his mind he was framing the bleak official opening – "As Commanding Officer ... I have the honour to report ..." And after that? "Considerable losses ... unusually difficult circumstances ... regret a measure of indiscipline ..." generalised statements all, which conveyed everything – and nothing! He held a feeling that on perusing these words the High Command would not much care, except to hunt for a scapegoat, and it was pretty certain who that would be ...

As the Adjutant made notes, Foulkes listened to the droning wind, the tumult of the waves, the incessant creaking of the ship's timbers, and his mind reverted to Harriet. What had really happened to her? Even now he could not believe that she was dead. At this very moment (he fancied, clinging to the inch) she might be safely lodged in Villa Franca, or captured and released by the chivalrous French, making her way back to Lisbon. Somehow he could not see her at a disadvantage. The ultimate horror – isolation in the frozen waste, her body torn to pieces by wolves ... he thrust the thought into the background of his mind ...

It was all so very strange. She had declared once that he had espoused two brides – the Forces and herself – and both marriages had failed. He had been neglected by the first, and savaged in turn. How long he would retain his present commission he did not know. As for the second allegiance – Harriet had drifted like a wraith away.

Her face outlined as in a delicately painted miniature hovered before him as he had first seen her at York in an Empire gown of shell satin, her hair dressed *à la Greque*. Attempting one of the new waltzes he had been most awkward, clumsy even. "You have much to teach me," he had observed, and with a laughing glance at the scarlet and gold of his uniform, she replied, "I have much to learn." With a casual gesture she had fingered the gold bullion of his epaulette, inquiring, "What can be the earthly meaning of these?"

What indeed? ...

He recovered himself, sat stiffly upright, pulled down his tunic and readjusted his sash. Now in trim order, he took the summary from the adjutant and began to write in his elongated, carefully spaced hand – "To Lieutenant General Sir John Hope, Commander-in-Chief of the Army lately operating in Spain, I have the honour to report ..."

www.ingramcontent.com/pod-product-compliance
Lightning Source LLC
Chambersburg PA
CBHW032242010726
47494CB00002B/598